The Day
is a
White Tablet

Jill Fletcher Pelaez

Wendy Pelaez Morgan

WiDō Publishing • Salt Lake City

WiDō Publishing
Salt Lake City, Utah
www.widopublishing.com

This book is a work of historical fiction. Names, characters, places, organizations and and incidents are either products of the author's imagination or are used fictitiously. Any resemblance to actual persons, living or dead, events or organizations is entirely coincidental.

Cover Design by Amie McCracken
Book Design by Marny K. Parkin

Print ISBN: 978-1-937178-24-6
Printed in the United States of America

To
Claire Hamner Matturro

Contents

Foreword

WHILE LOOKING FOR SOMETHING ELSE IN MY FILES, A LET-
ter I had long forgotten fell into my lap. Dated 1966, this letter was
handwritten by my grandmother to my mother. It read:

Dear little one,

*Jill, I had one of my wild "book dreams" last night…It was in the huge
private library with so many books you had to pole and hook those on the
top shelves from a runner ladder on a track…*

*All of a sudden a myriad of voices seemed to encircle me. For a minute
I was bewildered. I tried to sharpen my auditory nerves in order to make
sense out of all the confusion of their voices…*

*I realized their agitation was centered on a new book that lay half-
opened and looked invitingly intriguing in its white and gold encasement
and its strikingly simple modern print…*

*Then suddenly a wildly curious interest drove me to the book's open
pages. I glanced quickly at a few of its revealing sentences and in my excitement read, "Only by rebuffs, frustrations and death with renewals of self
can the change and attainment of true selfhood be realized," or words to
that effect. I wanted immediately to know the author. As I closed the volume, flipped it over and opened the fly leaf my eyes were blinded with
tears, for there was your name…*

*I think my arteries and veins were bursting with the thrill of these
books and their talk, and their assessment of Jill Pelaez's great book when
I was impelled by my own bursting emotions back into the world of reality.*

As readers will discover, a recurring theme throughout *The Day
is a White Tablet* was first articulated in my grandmother's letter:
"only by rebuffs, frustrations and death with renewals of self can

the change and attainment of true selfhood be realized." My grandmother's words to my mother were, I believe, a direct inspiration for some of the most profound passages in *Day*. To me, the words had a deeper meaning because my mother had been working on her manuscript off and on for fifteen years, with many "rebuffs and frustrations," and was offered a contract on her book two weeks after she was diagnosed with pancreatic cancer.

When I read those words that found their way from the letter to the novel, I felt the past, present and future all at once. My grandmother's words from the past, the brutal beauty in sharing my mother's dying experience with her and my closest friends and family, and the future publication of her book all seemed captured together in that moment.

Four months before I found the letter and the doctors found her tumor, Mom expressed two wishes: to publish her manuscript and to be interviewed by a newspaper. At 88, my mother still had dreams and her dreams were still coming true.

My friend, Claire Hamner Matturro, also an author and book doctor, agreed to edit the manuscript and found WiDō, a small literary press, that soon offered my mother a contract to publish *The Day is a White Tablet*. Her dream was accomplished.

On a whim, I emailed *The Tallahassee Democrat,* and told them about the book contract and my mother's fifteen-year quest to finish and publish this manuscript. *Democrat* Reporter Tamaryn Waters immediately picked up the story about my vibrant 88-year-old mother. The newspaper made my mother's book publication and impending death front page news. Mom died ten days later.

During the last few days of my mother's life, one of the hospice nurses told my mother that she, too, used to write. My mother asked her why she stopped writing. The nurse said that *life* was the reason she stopped writing. Mom replied, "Life is what should make you write."

Wendy Pelaez Morgan
August 2012

April 2, 1865

I MUST BE CAREFUL.

Yankee soldiers are everywhere. Rebels, too. Any of them would kill for a horse and I have Lance's horse. He's not easy to handle. When he backs and rears and tries to shake me, I hang tight. But he's better than he was. He's beginning to get used to me, the feel of my body, my hold on the reins. He sure misses Lance. Like I do.

My cousin Lance kept me from a lot of trouble. Sometimes I have a temper that goes off like a spark in an August cornfield.

That quick anger near cost me this morning, when I was poking around by White Oak, feeling lost and sad, but still with the sense to keep out of sight of the main roads. I forgot for a bit to be careful. A house in a clearing jumped out at me. An old woman was sitting on the steps. She called, "Get out of here, Nigra. Your kind has caused enough trouble. Get out." She looked like an old scarecrow in the wind when she waved her arms and shook her rag-mop hair. "Get out."

"Shut your mouth, old woman," I yelled and took a stone from my pocket and flung it at her. When I saw her pick up a rifle by her side, I dug in my heels and gave Night, Lance's horse, free rein. We galloped into a thicket away from the shots popping behind us.

I was too riled and full of grief to be ashamed of smart-mouthing the old scarecrow. I had just buried Lance. When the end came, I had been off cooking fish for the generals. Not even near enough to hear the shooting.

How it started was yesterday about noon, Lance had settled me near the creek behind White Oak Road where General Pickett and the other generals had set up their troops in a long line. We'd had rainy weather for most a week. The wet was down to a drizzle, but the ground was soggy, so I had climbed to the high branches of an old spreading oak when I saw General Fitz Lee and General Rosser come up on horseback and talk to General Pickett just below me. When I saw the three of them together, I had figured that something was about to happen. I had dropped down lower where I could hear. Though I was remembering it, the whole scene was like I was right there, because this was the last time I was with Lance.

"How does it look?" Fitz Lee asked.

Then General Pickett's strong voice, "All's quiet. A welcome lull between storms." General Fitz Lee drew up his reins.

General Rosser leaned forward in his saddle. "How about taking time out for a little refreshment?" He lowered his voice. "I have some brandy and a mess of shad the men caught down on the Nottaway this morning."

General Pickett laughed and I saw his curly head nod. "Our scouts think the Feds are too scattered to pull a strike today."

Rosser spoke, "There's a perfect hideaway near Hatcher's Run. We need a cook who can keep a secret."

"Let me get my cousin's cook." General Pickett sent for Lance and I lowered myself down. I swung to the ground just as Lance rode up on Night.

While the general spoke to him, Lance glanced at me and dismounted. He came to my side, saying, "The generals need help, Tench. Go with them. Show them what a good cook can do. Take Night. He's a good horse and he'll get used to you. They're going to the other side of the pine woods."

Ordinarily, I'd do most anything Lance asked. Most times I was proud to please him. Maybe not all the time, but he knew me well. I'd give him a message of how I felt. It might be by a look in my eye, or a slump of my shoulder, or a twist of my mouth. I looked at him and he knew I didn't want to go.

He put his hand on my arm. "These gentlemen need rest, Tench. Do your best."

I pushed my cheek out with my tongue and looked away and jumped on Night. He reared like he always did when I got on him. With him fighting me all the way, I followed the officers until they reached a heavy stand of pines at Hatcher's Run. We entered a clearing where I saw a circle of wagons. A fire was burning and two soldiers were cleaning fish. I tethered Night and right away set to work and helped by salting and flouring the fish. I did as Lance had bid.

I feel bad because I didn't say goodbye to him. I wasn't anywhere near him at the end. Maybe if he'd kept Night with him, he'd still be alive. Or, if the generals had stayed their line, he might be talking to me right now. Over at Hatcher's Run, we didn't even know the Feds were attacking. We couldn't hear the gunfire behind the thick pines. The generals hadn't told anyone they were going. No one knew where to find them.

Near about four o'clock, we headed back towards White Oak Road. As we got out of the pinewoods, we heard explosions. Shortly after, some horses galloped by with empty saddles.

General Pickett shouted, "Back to the line, men!"

"Our line is lost!" Fitz Lee called.

Many times Lance had warned me, "When firing begins, save your own neck, Tench. I can't save you. Do everything to stay alive."

I think the generals headed towards the sounds of battle. I raced towards the shadows of the woods. I led Night into the wildwood and tied him to a tree inside the brush. For myself, I found an old ghost oak. Limbs grew on one side of its hollow trunk and made a screen of new leaves. I stepped inside and it fit around me like the arms of a coat.

When I looked in the direction of White Oak Road where the officers were headed and where I had left Lance, clouds of smoke rose as cannons exploded and gunfire flashed. A blur of soldiers passed, running and struggling. I shivered at the sounds of yelling, screaming, and groaning. Night whinnied and I saw him thrashing in the thicket. Cannon wagons creaked and ambulances rumbled through the thick mud. I sank into a heap at the spongy bottom of the tree, covered my ears with my hands, and shut my eyes tight.

A rifle crashed down near my hiding place, making me jump. Reb soldiers were throwing their muskets to the ground as they ran into the woods. A bunch of them were herded together guarded by a single Fed soldier. What a sad looking bunch with their raggedy clothing and muddy bare feet. Now my own belly is full, but their stomachs weren't. In the past days most of the soldiers only had parched corn, sifted from the horse's feed, to eat. These Rebs didn't look strong enough to carry a musket. I didn't have to go into battle, but I hunted and begged and plundered wherever I could for Lance and me. We'd been lucky.

Somewhere in the mud and screams and smoke, Lance was fighting to stay alive. I was only hiding. If he died, he was supposed to. If I died, it'd be an accident. Still, my hiding shamed me some.

Once, early on after I joined Lance, I remembered him grinning at me when I woke up and a battle had exploded around us. He had known I was scared. Cannons had been booming and smoke had filled the air just like now. We had marched most of the night and he had bedded me behind a big boulder where I had fallen asleep.

"Tench." He had been shaking me. "You're not going to let me go out there again without something in my belly, are you? We have to give those Yankees something to shoot at, don't we? Time I eat your hoecake, they'll know I'm there."

I had rummaged in our sacks for the skillet and corn meal and used a dying campfire nearby to cook. By rooting beneath the leaves for some dry kindling, I had managed to keep a steady flame going. I'd fried a piece of fatback and made a hoecake. By putting a portion of roasted grain and sugar and water in his tin cup, I'd made what passed for coffee and set it to boil. I had shivered with each shell burst. I'd been so scared my knees 'most buckled under me.

Lance had sat on a fallen tree emptying a box of cartridges into his pockets. He hadn't paid any attention to the shells scudding through the woods or the shrill whistle of minis before they slapped the trees or whatever was in their path.

"Lance, one of those shells hit you, it'll blow you clear up to Heaven," I had warned him.

"Is that a promise?" Lance had laughed. "Long as I don't get blown in the other direction."

That memory of Lance laughing was a while back. Now I was hiding again and worrying about him. I don't know how long I waited in my cramped hiding place in the tree, but even with the sounds around me, I was so wore out, I dozed off.

When I woke, I was stiff and numb. It was dark as a cave now and all around, slush lamps and lanterns twinkled like fireflies. The gunfire and explosions had stopped. In the strange quiet I was aware of every sound. I heard soldiers trampling and ambulances slushing through the mud. The cries and moans didn't sound human.

In the direction of White Oak Road I heard, "Over here. Bring the wagon. Here's four of them—all alive."

I moved stiffly in the direction of the trees where Lance had hidden me this afternoon. Or was it yesterday?

"Over here," then a pause, "No, God Almighty. They're three deep n' not a living soul among them. Daylight, we'll fetch the dead. Let's get the live ones to surgery."

Lance might be one of them. That's what I thought when I saw the great number of bodies and among them, the leaden movement of the injured, voices, faint and dying. I moved towards a circle of lanterns surrounding the ambulances where the wounded were being loaded. No matter how many times I see sights like this, I won't ever get used to it.

In the pit of my stomach I felt their hurt; it burst through me and I felt holes in myself wherever I saw holes in them. I gritted my teeth and clenched my fists and prayed, "Please, God, take the pain away."

Still hoping to find Lance, I wandered around until shadowy dawn broke. Clouds hung low and a thin mist hovered over the shambles of bodies scattered and piled up around me. I called Lance's name, hoping for an answer, and searched the faces. All that remained of one of them was two very brown eyes. The rest of the features were like a bloody mash of clay.

One was sitting up, his arms hanging loose like a marionette, and eyes, wide and empty, like he couldn't see. Nor could he hear the soldier who sat at his side shouting over and over, "Berry. Gawd, Berry. Can't you hear me? You all right?"

Another screamed, "God help me. Help." Then, "Please," his voice trailing away. I could see his insides pouring out while one of his buddies yanked off his own shirt and tried to stuff it into the big gap.

I shivered when I saw the stretcher men load five of the injured onto the shelves of the four-wheel ambulance. Once, I had ridden on one of those shelves. After awhile, my bones ached and I couldn't breathe. Just riding in one when nothing is wrong is enough to send you to the hospital.

The two-wheel ambulance is worse. They call them hop-step-n-jumps. They're like wild teeter-totters loosening every bone, muscle, and nerve in you. They can shake your brains out along with your eyes and teeth. I heard of a soldier who got his legs and his head busted riding in one of them. When the wagon tilts forward, the feet hit the backboard and push the body backward, then the head bangs against the front board. Feet, bang. Head, bang. Back 'n' forth. Bang. Bang.

In either of the wagons—the two-wheeler with two horses, or the four-wheeler pulled by four or more horses—both the driver and the stretcher men have to hop out and take the wounded off every time they get stuck in the mud. There they have to stay in rain, snow, or shine until they got the wheels loose and turning again. In rainy weather with the soggy ground we'd had these past days, you can be sure they didn't get far without plenty of drop-offs and reloads. The Yankee wagons weren't any better than ours.

I ran from one ambulance to another and was still searching as the sun finally broke up the fog. I was surrounded by Yankees, but they paid me no mind while I searched among the Reb soldiers. I was only looking at them, while others were taking things from them—both the living and the dead.

Some Rebels huddled together on the damp ground and guards were marching others off to a new location. I knew they were tired and hungry, that most hadn't had food or even water for several days. They wore a patchwork of tattered clothes and worn-out uniforms and had no shoes or boots. Many wore clothes taken from dead Union soldiers during some other battle when their own gray uniforms had been worn to rotting. (And, dear Miss Lottie and Mama Zulma, rotting they were. With only one shirt and a pair of pants, most wouldn't risk taking them off to wash because they had to wait naked for them to dry. Don't worry. Not Lance. He had three sets and I managed to keep them clean. I'd wait for them to dry and catch up with him later. I can tell you it was one smelly Army.)

I heard one Yankee soldier say they had taken five thousand Reb wounded, dead, and alive. How could I search through all of them? Well, I'd try. In the fields there were no shelters except for the large tent set up for surgery. The wounded who could sit up were settled on a large tarp near the tent. The clearing was filled with row after row of injured, lying on stretchers on the wet ground. Their moans sounded like hornets swarming, their cries, like wild birds screeching.

Over the air and through memory came the smell of the old butchering shed at Avalon. Then I saw a bloody leg fly through the door of the surgeon's tent. It had fallen on a mound of body parts—arms, hands, feet, and legs. I had to get away from it. I felt the strength in my arms and legs give way and I began to keck.

I fled behind the nearest bushes at the edge of the field and vomited until I could only retch, trying to bring up the lead knot in the pit of my stomach. Finally, I leaned against a pine and closed my eyes. The thump of my heart drowned out all other sound except that of Lance's voice that kept sounding in my mind and I swear I could hear him say, "Keep your guts in your head, Tench. That's where real guts are."

I pulled out my shirttail and wiped my face and began to walk up and down among the soldiers, pausing to look into their faces. I kept calling his name. After searching the field of wounded, I turned and shouted, "Lance Matthews. Are you here? Answer me." For a moment, there was a hush. I shouted again. Still, no answer.

My search among the living was over. I turned back to White Oak Road where I last saw Lance. Dead were everywhere. Bodies had begun to bloat; the smell of death mixed with that of the earth and gunpowder and sap bleeding from battered trees.

The quiet of the fields made the small sounds of day ring louder. Flies sawed the air. A woodpecker drilled in a hollowed tree. Grackles fussed and all about I heard doves mourning. Never had their call sounded so sad. I wondered if they cried because they had lost their mates, or had exploding shells shaken their babies from their nests? Wagons creaked as men moved through the fields. They spoke in hushed, low voices as if they were afraid they'd disturb the sleeping.

Most of the morning I searched among the bodies. Sometimes turning one over to wipe off the mud covering a face, I would open a closed eye to see its color. I felt whipped. There were so many. But not the one I searched for.

While the troops were gathering yesterday, I had hidden across the road on the far end of this field in one of the big oaks. I had crossed here to follow the ambulances in the dark of early morning. I walked now beside bodies I had passed in the lantern light, to three, fallen together.

I could not be mistaken. Before I reached their side, somehow I knew—one of them would be Lance. His face was turned upward, his Traymore-green eyes were open, his arms reached out. At that moment, a man in an empty wagon approached. He was collecting muskets and other arms that had fallen during battle. I had gotten there before the clothes scavengers. Lance still wore his uniform and boots.

"This is Lance Matthews," I said. "His folks are my people. I was raised with him. I am his cook. Been looking for him all night."

"How'd I know you tellin' me the truth?" he asked, coming to my side. "Can you prove he's who you say he is?"

"He has a journal strapped on under his shirt," I answered quickly. I lifted his shirt so he could see. "His name is Lance Traymore Matthews from Thomson, Georgia. It's written in the journal, if you want to look. His eyes are green like mine. He's more than a foot taller than I am—"

He nodded, "Alright, it's alright, I reckon. Go ahead and do what you need to do."

I gently shut his eyes and unstrapped the bag that held his journal and took off his boots. Then I strapped the journal across my chest just as he had and put on his boots.

He had faced up to his foe. Two enemy soldiers had fallen backwards before him. Yes, his guts were where they were supposed to be to the very last. It was plain to see that many others had died running from the battle.

A Yankee sergeant and a corporal were working nearby with a crew of gravediggers and a death wagon in tow. I soon found out they were identifying and burying the dead. The sergeant held a large record book and after searching each body, made notes. That'd be one of the worse jobs I could think of ever doing.

They had to search each one. Some had scratched their names on their belts, or inside their hats, or wrote them on a slip of paper and pinned them on their clothes, their jackets, their shirts, or put them inside their shoes. Most of the Yankees wore metal disks around their necks with their name, company, and regiment. When they found a soldier without a name, they somehow guessed the age, recorded it along with the color of hair, eyes, and any unusual marks on the body. After they had made their identification, they loaded the body onto the death wagon.

When they reached Lance, I told them everything they needed to know. Then I asked if I could bury him. They agreed. I didn't want him to be buried without me watching. Nor did I want him in a big open field of graves. I would put him under the oak where we had parted yesterday. Who knows? Maybe someday I might bring some of the family to the spot where he died and was buried. To set the place in my mind, from the creek I counted off fifteen oaks to the largest one where I had waited for him the day before.

The gravediggers helped me. Lance was a big man. They hauled his body in the wagon over to the big oak. While they were digging, I knelt beside him and in the quiet of my mind I talked to him. I felt he would hear.

"I've always been with you. What should I do now? You should've hidden from those shells the way you hid me from them. You dug holes for me to hide in, pushed me behind boulders and trees and caves, and shoved me into scrub thick as jungle. Yet because I washed your clothes and blackened your boots, scrounged for food and cooked for you, you said I took care of you. But you took care of me. You were like a brother to me. You tried to teach me everything you knew. I can read and write because you taught me. But I never learned to be brave like you. Not your fault. You tried, but you couldn't teach me that. I'm sorry about yesterday. I'm sorry I didn't say goodbye."

The corporal and sergeant returned just as the men finished digging the grave. They helped me lower him to the bottom. I told them I'd do the rest, that I had promised Lance that if this happened, I'd see that he'd be buried Christian.

Just as if I weren't there, the sergeant said to the others, "Here is something I like to see—a loyal nigger."

His words hit like hammers in my mind, but I turned to the grave and they went on with their work. I said the Twenty-third Psalm. Like Lance and I used to say together.

As I filled the grave with spade after spade of damp earth, I thought about Lance in Paradise. God will wipe all his tears away for him. Up there, there's no sorrow, no pain, no death. For him, God's glory will be so bright, there's no night. Maybe at this moment, God is showing him around His city with its streets of gold and walls of precious stones and Lance is wearing shoes with golden wings and he is moving like a bird among the angels.

How lucky he is. He has left his family and everyone behind and feels no pain. I wish I didn't hurt the way I do. I hate to say it, but I felt forsaken and in a strange way, for the first time, I felt that Lance didn't care about me. He was with the angels, so why'd he study on me? We always worked out all our problems together. Now, they're all mine—everything is up to me. I wish you had taken me with you, Lance.

When we had left Avalon, I was thirteen. My mother had said, "Tench, you're just a slip ready for planting and Lance is a young sapling. Time we see you again, you'll be a young sapling and Lance will be a man, strong and big like an oak."

Mama, I hate having to tell you, you were wrong. I'm going on fifteen and thin as a reed in a wet ditch. Lance came seventeen and now he's dead.

April 10, 1865

I'M HEADING SOUTH, TRAVELING THROUGH THICKET AND underbrush. I can't take chances with either Night or myself. I have to be careful and go slow, and very quiet.

That quiet's all different. Last two years, my life has been troubled by cannons and echoes of musketry and cries and moans of the dying. Now finally, I'm most disturbed by life that could spring suddenly from out of the living ghosts plodding these dusty roads.

Some mean people been traveling on these Virginia and Carolina roads. I'm afraid of them—those living ghosts. I never felt this way before. I don't think I'll be able to trust anyone till I reach Thomson.

To keep out of the way of the men that would steal Lance's horse and rightly kill me, I had been traveling all night. Early this morning, I found thick brush where I thought I could hide Night and spread a blanket to catch some sleep. I was moving through the thicket when I came upon two men just ahead.

"Look!" The man shouting was short and scruffy. His beard and long hair were patched with gray.

The other was big-eyed and skinny like a long-legged bird. In a flash his sharp eyes raked over me and Night and he said, "Look at that horse. Now where you think the little Nigra got that pretty horse? Jes' what we need." He reached for a rifle at his feet.

I pulled the reins tight and turned Night around in a space no bigger than a fry pan. We skittered out of the brush with gunshot whizzing by my ears. I didn't look back, just kept to the main road south as fast as Night would go.

For sure, I'm learning to dodge gunshot. Night and I did all right. We're beginning to understand each other.

Down the road, I pulled way off to rest Night and wipe him down. As I dismounted, I heard sounds sweeter than birdsong—the voices and laughter of women and children. Peeking around in the brush, I saw two dusky women playing with two small children. Another sat against a tree nursing a baby. They spooked some when I came up on them.

Out on the road, everyone's too scared of each other to be nice. No one knows what it'll cost. Nobody can tell what a stranger might do—rob or kill you or take your horse. So, soft like, I told them who I was, where I came from, where I was going. They watched me closely as I talked. They spoke quiet-like, too, and didn't tell me much about themselves, least in the beginning. After some time passed, we all felt easier, especially when they understood it was just me and I saw they were alone, too.

At first, they kept mentioning William and Thomas, two men I thought must be with them. When I asked who William and Thomas were and where they were, the pretty one nursing the baby answered, "They's our protec'ors."

"Yeah, they's always out huntin'. You can look for 'em all the way to Richmond and clear down to Savannah, but you ain't gonna find 'em nowheres." The plump girl began to giggle.

The third girl raised her hand to her mouth and shook her head, "Shush, now, Rose. We only talks 'bout William and Thomas when we need some hep." She turned and pointed at me. "Can't you see? He jes' a boy. He ain't gonna harm us no more than if'n there was a William or Thomas to hep us."

I think we all had the same thought at the same time. Since we were traveling in the same direction, maybe we could help each other. I knew I could help them and it might be safer for all of us. They'd made up the story of Thomas and William so people wouldn't bother them. It didn't take long before they were smiling and talking like they'd known me always.

The plump one eyed me sharply and asked, "How's come yuh din't jes' start runnin' til you got up nawth? If'n I didn't have no one to worry about, that's what I'd done. I'd jine up with the 'bolitionists jes' like our pa done."

"I had no reason to do that," I replied. "I'm part of a white family, like—same blood, my mama and me. Family cares about us. We care about them."

She continued studying me and said, "Reckon that 'splains them green eyes."

That's how I set out with the three sisters, Daisy, Rose, and Lily, and Daisy's two children, Hyacinth and Snapper (short for Snapdragon), and Lily's baby, Marigold. I call them the Flower family—a regular Virginia garden. We've decided to stay together as far as Augusta, where they'll go down to Savannah when I go to Thomson. Now that we got the little folks, we set out to travel in daylight because night travel would be too hard on them.

The peace of their company crowds out the fields of the dead that keep living in my mind—and the awful missing feeling I have for Lance.

April 12, 1865

It's good to hear those women chattering and laughing. I let one, then the other, ride behind me on the saddle. Night doesn't seem to mind. He was used to me riding behind Lance. He's not ready for Snapper or Hyacinth yet. He's got to get used to their squeals and cries.

I keep the saddle on him all the time and leave him saddled at night, ready to go if I need to. In the evening, before we make camp, I leave him to graze, then I whistle the way Lance called him. When Lance spoke or whistled, Night understood. Now he understands me.

The sisters are different. Lily is little and about my age. Light-skinned, her face is small like a squirrel's with huge, shiny eyes and a smile so wide it cuts her face in two. Her baby girl looks just like her. I haven't been around babies, but the girls tell me that she's an example of everything that's best in a baby. They said neither Hyacinth nor Snapper had been precious-sweet like her. I toss blossoms in the air just to hear that baby laughter and see her tiny hands reach up for them.

Rose is right when she says, "This one merry and she pure gold. Merry Gold, she jes that."

Rose's face and body are as round as a full moon rising. She's younger than Lily and has never been with child. She's not like the other two because she doesn't smile much and is always complaining, but she loves Marigold and hangs on to her like she's her baby.

Daisy must be seventeen or eighteen. Not little or big, she always has one of the children straddling her hip and chatters like a jaybird giving flying lessons to its babies. On and on, she goes. She told me they came off a big plantation on the James River. Long time back there were two hundred slaves, but they took off and scattered like wild seeds in the wind after they heard news they could join with the Yankees and fight for their freedom.

"When the war start," Daisy explained, "our folk, name of Loyal Smith, was lef' without as much as a field hand n' they beat the road to freedom and not long afta, the women took their chillun and snuck off in the night and head nawth to fine their men. Miss Cynthy, she good woman, t'weren't hers nor Mistah Loyal's fault. They los' everthin'. She suffer jes like he did and they 'cided to move to her kinfolk in Savannah."

That was months ago, I learn. Their mother had moved to Savannah with Miss Cynthy and Mr. Loyal, too.

"It wasn't like we was young'uns—we growed women," Daisy said. "At first, we lived alone in the big house jes' fine, but raiders and looters come and tore the house down. For a spell we live in the barn. We's glad for the cow they left and we rake the barn and field for grain and beg off people so much that no one wanna see us comin' no more. So our time come to take off."

Daisy went on, "For couple days, we walk, tryin' to drag the cow along. Hard goin' with the little un's, but dat cow done wore us plum down. Some folk with a shed, say we could live there. After two day, we get on our way. The war come right up to dat shed. We hear cannon 'splodin' n' we took off agin. Ol' man 'long the road had a pig. We trade our cow for his pig and a supply of cornmeal and grits 'sides. We eat that pig nex' day. Whole thing. We took it off the road good way and roast it over a pit. Folks down the road smell it cookin' and they follow the smell right to our camp."

Daisy stopped talking and looked at me. "You can't turn hungry folks 'way if'n you got somethin' and they ain't got nothin'. Specially chillun. Lots of us done ate off that pig." She glanced at her sisters. "Din't they?"

Lily answered, "Sure did. No prettier sight in the world than to watch hungry folks eat."

Then Rose spoke, "I can think of somethin' prettier. Its folks what ain't got no place to live come to fin'in' a place to rest they head, what's they own place."

"That's what we doin', Rose. We gonna fine us a place. We headin' for Savannah. Miss Cynthy hep us fine a place. Mama'll hep," Daisy said.

"If Miss Cynthy or Mister Loyal care, they'd took us with Mama," Rose said. "If Mama care, she not leave us in the first place."

Daisy's eyes flashed. "Ain't no such way she could take us wit' her. They had ter run off in a hurry. Din't even know if her mama had a place for them an' our mama knew I'd take care of yawl."

"She care more for them white Smith chillun than for us. Left Lily to birth by hersef." Rose's voice crackled with anger.

Daisy shook her head. "Everthin' we done ever have come from Mister Loyal and Miss Cynthy. Things jes' ain't how they seems to you. That's what Mama and I know and Lily know and you jes' can't get into your head. Mister Loyal had no place to go. They had to fine somethin' for themsef first. So, now we got people there to go to."

Rose clutched Marigold tight and trudged along, the corners of her mouth turned down, her eyes flashing. When we put down to camp, she gave Marigold up long enough for Lily to nurse her. In the night when Marigold began to cry, she passed her back to Lily. The baby couldn't get satisfied. Just kept crying. Rose held her again and walked back and forth in front of the campfire. She crooned while she rocked her. Once she caught me watching and said, "We need somebody to hep."

I took my turn. I rocked and jiggled her and made bird noises. I mocked a mockingbird, fussed like a grackle, cawed and hoo-hooed. No use. She sobbed and her body stiffened like a wood doll. I handed her again to Rose.

I heard Lily say, "Milk mus' be dryin' up."

"'N' we don' have a cow no more. What we gon do?" Rose asked.

"She be all right in the mornin'. Just watch. You see," Lily answered.

"I reckon there a settlement some kind 'round here. I hear dogs howlin' and barkin' not far. Someone sure have a cow or goat. Maybe a fresh mama have some extra titty," Rose kept on.

"Might could. We see in the mornin' light, I reckon."

Most the night the baby fussed. She got tired and her crying faded off. Then she'd wake with a sudden sob and start again. When Lily tried to nurse her, Marigold drew her legs up and screamed.

"She sick!" Rose cried.

"Colic," Daisy said. "Hyacinth and Snapper used to get it."

"She sound so sick. Awful sick."

"All babies git it. You gotta wait for it to pass."

"She git sick enough to die." Rose wouldn't let up.

"No sich thin, Rose. Ain't gonna die. Stop it now. Don' say such as that." Lily sounded scared.

"No one doin' nothin'. I'm gonna take her someplace and fine someone to hep. I'm gonna." Rose folded her apron and tied it into a sling around her neck and put Marigold inside. Before we realized what was happening, she climbed on Night. Hanging onto the saddle with one hand, she pulled herself up with the other, with the baby swinging in the apron.

Night shied and raised up on his hind quarters trying to shed her. She tottered in the saddle and he streaked like a meteor-flash through the woods. After all my warnings to the sisters about Night, I couldn't believe Rose would try to ride him in the half light, with a baby, and I was too slow to stop them.

There were no paths through these woods. I had slashed our way into this thicket counting on the thickness of growth to hide Night. I didn't have to go far to find Rose fallen in a heap under the low branches. Night, prancing and circling, was blocked in every direction.

It was dead quiet. The apron hung limp at her shoulders. I had started searching the underbrush when I saw the baby still and silent on the leaves. I stopped to pick her up.

Lily and Daisy followed. Lily took the small body from my arms and cried, "Marigold. My Gold." She clutched the baby to her breast and sobbed, "She dead. Dead!"

April 13, 1865

I WAS WRITING BY CAMPFIRE. THE DAY HAD BEEN LONG. The sisters and their children were bunched around Daisy like grapes on a stem. We had buried little Marigold. I dug her grave and buried her with my own hands.

Scarcely a sound came from Lily—only something soft as wind threading through the pines. Her face was still and full of pain. When she held the baby for the last time, she sang the lullaby I'd heard her sing every time she put her to rest. She wrapped her in a cocoon of moss and laid her in the small grave.

As I began to cover her with the earth piled at the side, Daisy reached over to help. Rose had been sobbing, but after watching for a while, she suddenly reached for a handful of soil, held it to her lips and dropped it lightly into the hollow beneath.

At first Snapper and Hyacinth had cried because Rose was sobbing and carrying on. When she stopped, they began to play. Got big sticks and pretended the sticks were horses and went galloping in and about the woods. It was hard to listen to their happy voices.

Now we were silent in grief. Daisy said things had to go on. She cooked and washed and comforted and kept patting and hugging her sisters. I heard her say, "Marigold is Lord Jesus' own little breast pin now."

They are asleep. I'm alone at last. I've been browsing in Lance's journal, trying to hear his voice. He believed all the hard times you went through made you strong—said they made character and muscle. When it's happening, it's hard to realize this.

While I read, I try to hear Lance talking. Just as if he were sitting beside me by the campfire. I've read this page over and over trying to make his words come alive. This is what he wrote:

July 3, 1865

This was another day in Hell. General Pickett might have promised my mother that I'd be his aide-de-camp, but with all the other men fighting and dying for Georgia and Virginia and the whole Confederacy, sometimes I go off with the cavalry or the infantry. The fighting men are always glad to see me. But I'm afraid it has become the usual thing and I'm sick of the killing. I wanted to kill Yankees because they killed my brothers and crippled my father. My driving motive: I wanted to get even. The family hasn't owned slaves for a generation. Poor Tench, a leftover from that generation. Tench—whose great-grandmother lives on in his black skin and whose great-grandfather (who is also my great-grandfather) still looks out of his green eyes.

How much I owe Tench. He provides the only touch of normalcy on this God-forsaken horizon. He creates an oasis for me. When I'm hungry, he bags a rabbit, dove, or crow and cooks for me. He keeps my canteen filled and brings cauldrons from the quartermasters' wagons to boil my clothes to keep the vermin down. He pours water over me when I bathe. Without him I would be thirsty and hungry and covered with filth and vermin.

This morning I took him to a hideaway burrowed in the side of a steep bank beside a stream in these woods. "Be careful," he said. "I'm scared one of the shells will get you. Next time you come face to face with a Yankee, he might shoot you for sure."

I told him then what had happened out on patrol. Musket ready, I was rounding a corner of a deserted farmhouse when I met the steel barrel of another musket head-on and looked into the clear green eyes of my enemy. His face was apple-fresh without a sign of a whisker. It was like looking into a mirror.

He was as surprised as I and backed off as I advanced. I paused. I could not press the trigger. A moment of recognition passed between us. In that moment, he was not my enemy. We were the same and I believe we saw our own self—in each other. I think he had the same thought.

April 18, 1865

THE PAST FEW DAYS WERE HARD. FIRST, WE DIDN'T GO VERY far. Everything suddenly changed. It had rained every day and we were wet and cold and hungry and Snapper and Hyacinth cried most of the time. No one felt good. We had camped under a bridge and Daisy was sitting out in the drizzle beside the fire while she cooked hoecake with the last of the flour. I'm remembering now how it was.

Rose spoke up, "I worry about these young-uns cryin' so much."

Daisy looked at her hard and said, "Time to worry if they stop cryin."

"This's no way to live," Rose harped.

"It's not gonna be forever." Lily leaned over.

I tried to soothe her. "From now along, it won't be so far."

"Maybe for you," she snapped. "You know what you goin' to. When we gets to Savannah, we mightn't got no place to live."

"Something will work out," I said, but it was now that I was worrying about. We'd reached the end of our food.

Daisy divvied up the hoecake. I put mine back in the skillet. "Give mine to Snapper and Hyacinth," I said. "I'm going hunting."

"Maybe you goin' and won't come back," Rose grumbled.

"Don't, Rose. Tench's been good to us," Lily said.

"I don't know why he stay," Daisy said. "Us eatin' all his food and him takin' care of us 'sides and you fussin' the way you do. He could've took off long time ago."

I was thinking if Rose were the only one, I wouldn't be here. Lily and Daisy and the young ones made up for all of Rose's contrariness. It was like we had become a family.

I turned around and looked at Rose and said, "We have all helped each other. After living close to battlefields for two years, it's good to hear women's voices laughing and singing and seeing children play-ing. If you'd been scared as I've been, with soldiers dying all around you and not knowing if Lance would get killed, or if it would be me to stop a shell, then you'd know what I mean." Then I exploded, "But I'll tell you this, Rose, you are one troublesome woman and if you were the only one, I would have been long gone."

The children stopped whimpering and were watching me. I said, "Don't worry, Hyacinth and Snapper. You're real good." I took a feed sack from our pile of belongings, threw it over my shoulder, and said, "Everyone's lucky to have you to look after them, Daisy." I squatted beside Lily and touched her arm, "And you, Lily, are sweet as fresh pressed cane." I rose to leave.

"I guess you sayin' goodbye." Rose shouted after me, "I hope you take your horse and go fast."

The only reason I left Night behind was because I wanted to show her she was wrong. If I had taken my horse, I would have gone by the trail. I wouldn't have gone frog hunting. Now I was following the stream on foot. There was a slight drizzle in the air. I strapped Lance's Record in its leather case under my shirt.

Hunting would be good on a night like this. Already the night throbbed with many voices—frogs and night birds were singing. I hadn't gone far when I heard a flutter behind me. I stopped and look-ing back, I saw a light twinkling through the shadows.

"Tench. Tench." It was Lily. I walked back towards her. "I thought you might need a lantern."

"Might." Pleased she had thought of it, I reached for the long wire handle.

"I hope you din't pay no mind to Rose. I don't know why she say such a thing. When she fret thataway, me and Daisy don't pay her no mind."

"Well, I don't either," I said.

"When she hurtin' inside, that way she do." Her eyes glistened.

"I know," I said. "Go back, Lily, before you get all wet and it gets real dark."

She looked up and leaned towards me. Without another word, she walked back into the shadows. I continued downstream toward the voices of the night. Ahead, the frog chorus peaked, suddenly hushing while another chorus answered off a ways.

I hung the lamp from a branch leaning over the bank. Some of the shadows faded in the blinking light as I moved quietly at the water's edge. Without a gigging pole, I had to be quick. Ahead were two frogs nestled in the water grass. I scooped them up, catching one by its collar and snatching the other in the middle of a high jump. I threw them into the sack.

I filled the bag quickly, but before I realized, I had wandered beyond the circle of light. I was hunting by a certain knowing of sound and shadows and I had left the slush lamp behind. I was sorry Daisy's cooking-fat was wasting. We'd need it later to cook the frog legs. I decided then to go back. They needed me.

I tied a knot in the sack and climbed to the top of the bank thinking the soft ground next to the stream would slow me. I was aware of the smell of food cooking before I looked through the brush at a group of ragged men huddled under a giant oak before a bright campfire. They had stretched a tarp over some lower branches for shelter. Behind them were horses tethered and a supply wagon.

At that moment I got an idea. I would circle the campsite to the supply wagon and maybe find some real surprises for the girls. I had no doubt that we could use whatever I found.

All but one seemed to be dozing and he reached for a tin cup and dipped it into a big pot hanging from a rod over the fire. He took a spoon from his pocket and dipped it into the cup, blowing on each spoonful before he ate.

I held my breath and listened to the sound of fire crackling and the calls of a chuck-wills-widow, the hum of cicadas and crickets chirping and frogs tuning up in the stream below. With my every move, the ground and brush around me rustled. I only hoped the night sounds would drown out any noise I made.

The rain had stopped, but the wind stirred the branches of the tall trees, shaking a fresh shower over me. I was thoroughly soaked. I reached the other side of the oak when one of the men stretched and yawned and moved over to the fire and began to talk.

"We ain't got much time, Sam. Gotta stay ahead of the Feds as much as we can. They'll be all over Georgia in a couple of days. Guess we better split up and meet down in Florida."

"I aim to look up some of my kinfolk near Madison. We could meet there, Jake."

"I got some people down short ways. I wanna look them up. Madison suits me good, Sam. But now, let's get some sleep."

I could see in the wagon from where I stood. On one side were bowie knives next to a stack of muskets. An open barrel lay on its side and I could see potatoes and dried corn inside. Scattered around the wagon were hams and smoked turkeys, some wine jugs and cartridge boxes. It looked like loot from a bummer's wagon. Whether these people had done their own looting, or whether they'd stolen from Federal bummers, who knew? Them wanting to keep ahead of the crowds that'd soon fill the roads was answer enough.

I dropped the bag of frogs on the side of the wagon. A piece of carpet hung over the back. I spread it on the ground, then reached into the wagon for a bowie knife and stuck it under my belt. I fished out some turkeys and hams and lay them on the carpet then I took some sacks of potatoes and meal and put them on top, and scooped salt from an open bag and filled my pocket. I joined the corners of the rug and after tying them, dragged the new carpet-sack into the brush.

Why I went back for the bag of frogs, I don't know. Now I surely didn't need them. I guess I just couldn't waste good food from a hard hunt. When I picked up the bag, I heaved it against the half empty barrel. The barrel began to roll and set off a noisy alarm as the jugs and tins rolled about the wagon floor. Jake and Sam sprang to their feet, waking up the others. I dropped the bag and grabbed the branch overhead, scurrying, hand over hand, up the tree. When I put my weight on one of the branches, the tarp, spread across the tree, collapsed and fell on top of the men. They began hollering and cursing.

All except Jake. Below me, he was yanking my leg and shouted, "Hey you. Wha'cha doing? Wha'cha after?"

I fell and he grabbed me by the neck, just like I had captured the frogs. I looked up into a rough pirate-face with one piercing yellow eye and a hole as big as a walnut where the other should've been.

Immediately I was surrounded. Dirty and heavy-bearded, they seemed to be dressed in layers of ragged clothes. I knew now that they were a foraging gang and I was scared.

"Frog-hunting, sir." I squealed. "Been huntin'. My folks are hungry. Smelled food and saw the light. I was just snoopin'."

Jake turned me loose. "Whatcha mean—family? Where's the family?"

"Upstream from here."

Sam picked up the frog sack and peered in. "Boy ain't jes' lyin', Jake. Sack's full of frogs."

"Might could use a frog-hunter," Jake said. "We need a hunt-boy."

"Please sir, I can't leave my family. They can't do nothin' for themselves. They'd all starve without me."

"Let him go," Sam said.

"Boy who hunts up frogs like that might come in handy," Jake argued. Samuel shrugged.

Someone shouted, "Lookit that Nigra's green eyes. Green-eyed Nigra bring bad luck."

"Well I ain't 'cided to let him go," Jake said, ladling soup from the pot into a waiting cup. While a couple of them began to fold the tarp, the others sat down to eat by the campfire. Nothing more was said and they mostly ignored me.

As I watched, they gulped down their portions and returned again and again for more. Watching them made me aware of my own hunger. After they had all eaten, Sam handed me a spoon and a dipper and poured what was left into it. He took some hardtack from his pocket and broke off a piece for me.

Jake snarled, "You're damned soft, Sam."

Everyone began to take notice again and I was uneasy with their eyes on me, but I scraped the bottom of the dipper and wished for more. I was warm now and no longer hungry. My thoughts were on the girls. What had they thought when I hadn't returned? I didn't have to guess Rose's thoughts, but I hated letting all of them down. Even Rose. They needed me. The roads were getting crowded. Lately, each day, more than ever, I feared for them. I thought about Night. I wondered what these men were going to do about me. For a long time I stared into the fire before I finally dozed off.

The sun was high when I woke. For a moment, confused, I sat up and looked about. The campsite was deserted. A few coals were smoldering and the ground was criss-crossed with boot and wagon tracks. I had been covered with an old blanket and someone had hidden some hardtack under the blanket beside me—Sam, probably. They had taken my sack of frogs.

I thanked God for my green eyes. I believe they might have taken me with them if it hadn't been for them. I jumped up and hurried to the brush near the oak. My cache of food hadn't been discovered. It was where I had hidden it. I had lost an entire night, but I had some fine new provisions for the family.

They had taken the pot and forgot the metal rod. I wiped the soot away and fastened it through the bundle, flung it over my shoulder and made my way back to the stream. Although it was heavy, I didn't have to worry about rain or that gang of pirates anymore. I couldn't wait to show the girls what I had bagged on my hunt.

Retracing my steps along the stream, I didn't find the lamp where I thought I had hung it. I hurried until I reached the path leading to our shelter under the bridge.

For the second time today, I found everything gone—the campsite was deserted. There wasn't a sign of Night in the brush where I'd left him tethered.

Bewildered, I started down the road we all had hoped to journey to reach Augusta. Angry thoughts flashed. This was Rose's fault. If it weren't for Rose, I wouldn't have left on foot last night. I wouldn't have been stopped by the gang in the woods. Rose had caused nothing but trouble.

Almost at once, my anger turned on myself. I am the one who had wanted to prove something to Rose—that I wasn't the kind of person who'd desert them. I'd left the horse behind just to show her she was wrong about me. It didn't make any sense. I was afraid to be myself and do what I really wanted to just to keep her from being angry. In one way, I'm being just as much a coward as when I hid from shells exploding on the battlefield.

I can't write anymore. Awful tired.

April 20, 1865

FOR TWO DAYS, I'D BEEN WALKING THE ROAD ALONE. I thought sure I'd catch up with the girls by now. I had looked for their small footprints, but it was useless to look on this road scarred by hooves and wagon wheels and boot tracks. I'd looked under bridges, searched out little coves and heavy brush, hoping to find their camp. I knew their ways—some of the ways they learned as we traveled together.

I can't help but worry. How will they find enough to eat? Will they be safe? What about Night?

Alone. It was hard to be alone. I'd always lived close to somebody, caring for somebody, and they caring for me. Now I had only myself to think about. Not even a horse.

After I cross the Savannah River and reach Augusta, Thomson won't be far. Lord, how glad I would be to see my mother and Miss Lottie and Mister Carson and the young ones. How would I tell them about Lance? It would be so hard.

I was tired tonight. I'd bedded in a quiet wood circled by the hum of crickets and whip-poor-wills and owl calls.

Would I ever see Daisy and Lily again and—Rose? Poor Rose. I realized now it really wasn't her fault. What was it Mama Zulma used to say? "To know all is to forgive all." I shouldn't have been so hard on her. I wish I could take back my last words to her.

April 21, 1865

THIS MORNING WHILE CROSSING A ROCKY CREEK, I PITCHED
my bundle onto the bank and stumbled forward into the stone-filled
stream. I didn't know I had cut myself until I saw a red trail in the
water after I'd waded out. I noticed then my torn pants and the big
cut on my knee—it didn't hurt but it was bleeding bad.

I took off my soggy boots and stumbled up the bank. I reached
over my head and cut a loop of vine with my bowie knife and tied it
above my knee in a tight knot.

The air was still night-cool and I rested in a warm spot of sunlight.
Discouraged, but there was no use fussing. Done is done. Whenever
I used to get myself in a jam, Mama would tell me to sit still and think
it out. It's not like me to do so, but that's all I can do now.

As I sat, the sun flickered through the leaves of new green covering the heavy branches of the trees. This old oak had dropped a lot of
dead wood in the winter storms and, next to me, a spider had woven
a huge web and waited for something to drop in. I flicked her off with
my thumb. I had a use for her web. I loosened the tourniquet and
looked at the wound. If I had Daisy's needle and thread I could have
stitched it shut. It was wide and deep. I spread the cobweb over it to
keep it from bleeding and for the rest of the day I stayed off my feet.
After that, the next day, I slept off and on, waking long enough to
move with the sun and eat a little ham or raw potato. My leg swelled
up clear down to my ankle. The whole leg hurt and I was tired. I just
couldn't seem to get enough sleep.

April 22, 1865

WHEN DARK CAME, I FELT COLD AND SCRATCHED A BED IN the leaves. I hid my supplies under some of them and nested among them, then pulled the carpet over me and fell asleep.

Sometime in the night, I heard something stirring about in the leaves. It sniffed the length of my body. I held my breath and closed my eyes tight. When it moved away I drew a long breath of relief. In daylight I discovered the visitor had taken a ham. I had no quarrel with that. It had left me alone.

From part of a broken branch, I made a crutch to take some weight off my bad knee. It would be slow going, but I knew I wasn't too far from the river and that much closer to home.

This morning, I began to hobble beside the creek. I was sure it would lead me to the river. Since it suddenly had gotten warmer—or perhaps it was the result of the new effort I was making—I was grateful for the cooling mists. Moving was work and I was sweating. The creek got wider, and ahead I saw heavy fog rolling over the wider waters of what I now knew was the Savannah River. It was a mysterious sight, the river fog in the spooky light of a clouded sun.

Two years ago when Lance and I waited on the other side of this river for the ferry, he had said, "Tench, we're leaving behind everything we've ever known and everyone who loves us. We don't know what lies ahead of us on the other side of the river, but I do know we'll never have so much again. Do you understand?"

I understood. We had scarcely passed the long rows of cedars that edged both sides of the lane entering Avalon where we had left Mama and Miss Lottie and Mister Carson and the children, crying and waving to us on the verandah, when I saw Master Lance's eyes fill with tears and I started to cry and sob out loud.

Lance had said, "That's all right. That's all right."

Just before the ferry came, he spoke again, "If you want to turn back, you can. It's not too late. Tell the folks that I sent you home."

I answered quickly, "Oh no, sir. I'd never want to leave you."

Here I am at the river again. Like the first crossing, I don't know what's on the other side. The good feelings that I might have at coming home are mostly wiped away by the bad news I bring of Lance.

On both sides of the river, as far as I could see, people were camped and moving about like ants. Never had I seen so many. I found that some had been waiting as long as a day to get across. Some anxious ones had left behind, on this side of the river, prized possessions they had carried with them on long marches, or had hidden in thickets, or under sand through hot, warring summers, or on cannon-battered winter fields. All at once, impatient to wait any longer, they had dived into the shivery waters of the Savannah to reach the side they had longed for so long. How well I understood.

I started to join a long line of those waiting to buy space on the ferry when a hawker waving tickets in his hand shouted, "Wha'cha gimme? Wha'cha got?" I quickly traded him a ham and joined the other ticket-holders camped on the river bank.

At the landing and along the waterfront, there were skiffs and large empty cargo boats and a steamer, the *Savannah*, with long lines of passengers waiting to board. People were waiting their turns on five other lots. Over the hours they had worked their way from one lot to the next. I joined those on the last lot and was told it would be morning before our turn came, then we could cross because the operator had to get some sleep.

By noon, I settled among the crowds in a space where I had a view of the docks below and the people scattered over fields and on the banks. I was wondering about the girls as I studied the faces in the crowds. I saw so many Lilys, so many Daisys, so many Roses. Everywhere I looked, there were children who could have been Snapper and Hyacinth. If wishes made magic, I'd have the magic powers of an obi-man and I'd patter-dance in a circle until they appeared.

I took out my lunch and an old Negro man sitting nearby came to my side. He didn't say anything. His eyes spoke for him. I held out some ham and hardtack. He took it gratefully.

I told him where I came from and where I was headed. "Can you tell me about yourself?" I asked.

"Name's Luke. Been food scrounging best ah can. Ain't nothin' lef' nowhar. Nothin'. I'm with a bunch cross the river at Shelby's Hollow, close to Thomson. Shelbys done took off. They went south of Augusta. There's six of us hepin' each other to keep 'live."

The Shelby plantation was on the way to Avalon. I remembered when Lance used to visit Shelby's young folks, I'd go along and play in the woods or visit in the quarters.

"Been there," I said. "I used to go there with Mister Lance Matthews. Were the Shelbys your people?"

"I come there after Shelbys took off. Nothin's left 'cep' part of the smokehouse. That's whar we're livin'. Gen'l Sherman's men done burnt everythin' down. Us colored folk call that time them soldiers come the black days cause it so dark us couldn't see the sun for all the smoke from the fightin' and the burn'n. Heard Sherman and his soldiers come in the night and round' up the Shelby fam'ly. All in their nightclothes and barefeet. Sent all the colored folks out and were shootin' in the air to make 'em go fast. They round' up the wagons and took all their food and furnishments. Din't leave nothin'. The last anyone seen of 'em, they was walkin' down the road to Augusta in their night clothes. Miss Shelby jes' a-cryin' and hangin' onto her two girls. Massa Shelby, with his one arm gone in the wah, was carryin' the least one in his good arm. That's what they tell."

"I wonder about the three older Shelby boys, Lance's friends. What's happened to them?" I asked.

"No one say," he answered.

Something down on the bank near the shore caught my eye. I jumped up. "I'll be back," I said to Luke.

I thought I saw Night. There he was—shiny black, and head held high. I picked up my crutch and hurried fast as I could. The horse and rider stopped beside the ferry gate where the man got off and led the horse to the water.

I hadn't seen the man's face, but there was something about the way he moved—a kind of a strut, that reminded me of somebody. I knew I'd stand out with my limp and crutch, so I stayed among the crowd and worked my way down towards the water. I needed to be certain. When I got behind them, I put two fingers to my lips and whistled.

The horse stopped drinking. His ears quivered, then perked upright. He looked around and whinnied. No doubt. It was Night.

The man yanked on the bridle and shouted, "Shush, you demon."

Night rose up on his hind legs and tugged from one side to the other. The man kept yanking. When I was at their side, I saw his face. It was Jake from the camp where I had stayed four nights before.

When I saw his grizzly face, I doubled my fists and clenched my teeth, I was so angry. I had to rescue Night, but not under these circumstances. One thing I needed was a clear road for a fast escape. Jake was going on the ferry to get to the other side of the river. Chances were, we'd cross at the same time. I wouldn't easily lose sight of a man with a big black horse.

I climbed the bank to my spot to eat lunch. I wasn't surprised to find the old man going through my bundle. He didn't stop even when I sat down again. He asked me how I got the food. I explained. Soon I was telling him about Lance, Lily, Daisy, and Rose. I told him I was going to Avalon and how I dreaded taking the news about Lance. Luke watched and listened. I told him about Marigold and Night. I talked on and on.

I told him I wanted him to take some of my food back to Shelby Hollow. I wouldn't need it after I got to Avalon.

"Looka heah, Tench," he said. "Yuh don' know what's waitin' thar. Yuh ain't gon fine nothin' that's here is way it was befo' yuh lef'. Heah 'bouts, no one has nothin' to eat no mo'. It been five months since ole Sherman come through. What he din't take, he burnt. They all kilt this land, took 'way all its good. Ain't no'ne gone take care of us no mo'." He shook his head, and added, "But they tell us, we's free." His voice was a moan.

I shuddered, reached over, and picked out some food from the bundle. I gave him turkey and corn, saying, "This will feed you for a couple days." I shaved off more ham and gave him another piece of hardtack. Together, we sat enjoying our meal. He chewed quietly and seemed to be making each mouthful last as long as he could.

I was thinking about what he had said. "Luke, you're right," I said, "I don't know what I'll find at Avalon."

"Ever one say go to Savannah. That's whar we all gonna head. Say Sherman lef' Savannah clean and whole cuz he wanna giv it to Prez'dint Lincoln for a Christmas present. That's what they say."

The idea of Savannah being clean and whole was good. If it was true, it'd be better for the girls. But my heart sank when I realized I hadn't really faced up to what I might find at Avalon. It could be as painful for me as the message I carried to them. I thought of the Shelbys. I was afraid.

Before I settled for the night, I filled a canteen at the well and washed the cut on my knee. It felt better, but it wasn't strong as it should be. It almost could bear my weight. Another night's rest would really help.

In the night, I heard a wee voice bleating like a lamb and then I heard a soft crooning. I saw only a few flickering lights scattered through the campsite. I lay down remembering the sounds of Lily and Daisy with their children. Rose, too. She was good with the little ones.

Then I was remembering my own bedtime long ago, when Mama Zulma used to sing to Lance and me with, "In the valley, in the shadows, Lord, take my hand." Her voice, rich as molasses, was part of the night into which we so mysteriously disappeared.

Sometimes, Miss Lottie would come in and give us both a pat and ask God's blessing. But how I loved it when it was Mister Carson who put us to bed. He'd sit on the edge of Lance's bed while I lay on my pallet.

"I'm here to prime your dream pump," he said, and he'd tell marvelous stories of gods and goddesses, King Midas, Ulysses, and the Trojan War. I'm sure he knew every story ever told. I remember how sometimes I struggled to stay wide awake, for, with the first blink of an eye, the story would stop. So long ago.

After a restless night, I opened this Record. Since first peeking light, I've been writing. I used to watch Lance writing and never thought of keeping my own record. Now, knowing the joy of saving memories, I want to keep everything that happens alive and forever fresh in my mind to share with the family, later. At first, I wished to do it for Lance. Now, I do it for myself.

The sun is rising like a great barn on fire yonder at the rim of the world. Bodies are stirring and twisting like caterpillars under a mulberry tree. Down by the water I see Night tethered on a long rope to Jake, who is crouched on the slope above him.

Whistles are sounding as boats move on the river. Lines are already forming at the steamboat dock and ferry landing. I've got to wake up Luke. We have lots to do.

April 24, 1865

My birthday, now I was fifteen. What a day this had been.

Luke stayed by my side this morning hanging tight to his smaller bag as he helped me shoulder mine. The crowds parted when we came aboard. He was old and I was crippled and—like everybody else—poor and homeless. Most everyone acts kinder when they see someone with a burden heavier than their own.

I saw Jake lead Night aboard and head to the opposite side of the deck next to the exit gate. Night was loaded like a pack mule with feed sacks hanging from his neck and four saddle-bags slung over his back.

Nudging Luke, I said, "See the man with the horse? That's my horse, Night. I aim to get him back."

"If yuh ask me, man looks mean as fire. How you 'speck to do it?"

"You watch." I dug around in my food sack and filled my pocket with salt. "I don't know how he got my horse. I'm going to find out."

With bells clanging, the ferry pulled away from the dock. At the same time, the steamboat started its engines and blasted its whistles. I moved to the rail and leaned over to watch the people on its crowded deck.

At that moment, I heard a high-pitched cry, "Tench! Tench!" Then another, a child's voice, squealing, "Tench!"

"Dear God, there they are," I cried. On the deck of the steamboat opposite us was the Flower family—Daisy, Lily, Rose, Snapper, and Hyacinth. I looked right into their eyes and began to wave and shout. Rose leaned over the rail, waving and calling as they chugged away. They were going down the river as I crossed to Augusta—just as we first had planned when we'd arrived at Augusta.

"Them's the 'uns yuh tol' me about?"

"They're the ones. I wish I could've talked to them. I wonder how they got on the boat. They had no money. They only had the horse."

They had been somewhere in those crowds last night. If only we could have found each other and learned what had happened since that rainy night. If only they knew I hadn't deliberately deserted them. If—if—if.

"Jake knows the answer," I said, "and I'll find out. I wonder how he ever got my horse from them."

"I'll tell yuh how he come to get your horse," Luke cackled. "He jes' plain done took it."

"It's likely," I said. "I've got to know the real story. Luke, I've got a plan. I'm going over and talk to him. Come, stand next to me. Just watch and don't say anything. We'll be docking."

I went over by Jake and stood close enough to put my hand on Night's muzzle. In a flash, Jake turned his fierce yellow eye on me.

"This is a tetchy brute. Leave him be," he warned. He bent over and moved closer to me. "Them green eyes. Here's them green eyes ag'in. Where was it I done seen yuh before?"

"Down the road a good piece from here," I answered. "One night I was frog-hunting in the rain. Spent the night 'side your campfire. When I woke in the morning, you'd all left."

"Yeh," he nodded, "by Spider Creek. I pulled yuh outta the big tree. We et yer frog legs. Good eatin'. We should've done kep' you for our hunt-boy."

Night was restless. "Good horse," I said.

"Devil hoss'. Needs taming n' I aims to tame 'im right." He picked up the whip hanging over the saddle and passed it slowly through his fingers.

"Where'd you get him?"

"Real bargain, if yuh call a demon like this 'un a bargain."

"How's that?" I asked. " What'd you pay for him?"

Jake laughed, "Hell. I don't buy nothin'. I mean nothin." He hung the whip back over the saddle and took a bowie knife from a sheath hanging on his belt.

"How's that?" I leaned back against the rail and watched him. He lay the loop of tether loosely over his shoulder and, squatting down, began to dig out his nails.

"Short way up from Spider Creek I met a little ol' Nigra gal just a-screamin' and a-cryin' and hangin' onto the neck of this hoss'. It was jes' runnin' wild tryin' to shed 'er. Me and Samuel, we done lit out afta 'er and cornered the hoss' in the brush. We heped 'er fine 'er people back a ways near the bridge. Samuel give 'em some vittles and coins and I tole 'em I'd take the demon-hoss off their hands. It'd likely kill one of 'em, what with their little jigawoolies runnin' all round and road pirates raidin' the country. Guess I scared 'em real good. Don't know how they ever come to have a frisky spirit hoss' like this 'un. Takes a real man to ride 'im."

I was glad to know the girls had food and money and was grateful to Samuel for sparing the coins. I didn't think Jake would have done that. It had to be Rose who'd tried to ride Night again—taking off where she had no business. Daisy might have handled him. Lily was shy of him.

I reached up and stroked Night's neck. "Hold on, boy," I said, my voice low so Jake couldn't hear me. Night turned and, for a moment, I thought I saw a piercing light in his big eyes.

The whistles blasted again as the ferry pulled into the landing. Jake was now reaming out his ear with the point of his blade, then he wiped it on the knee of his pants. Just as the ferry bumped the dock, I threw my crutch on the ground and moved to Night's other side. I lifted the rod with my bundle to Luke's shoulder and put the sling of the smaller one over his arm.

"You and the folks back at Shelby's can use this," I said. Luke gave a little gasp.

The guard opened the gate. Just as I saw Jake return the knife to its sheath, I jerked the tether away and jumped up on Night. Jake lunged forward, reached for the rope, and pulled on my bad leg. I dipped my hand into my pocket and threw a handful of salt into his one yellow eye. I kicked, yanked the rope, and shouted, "Out of the way, old Cyclops. Let's go, Night."

Like a comet, Night struck out onto the dock and crossed over the busy embankment up to the road. On the Georgia side of the river, unlike the South Carolina side, no long lines of people waited, but the port was awake and lively. People parted with the flurry of our passing.

"Night, go," I urged. We stayed our course. I gave him free rein. He followed the practice of his past and raced down the roadway that led to Thomson and—Avalon.

Night left the main road and held to the hidden ways through the deep woods where Lance's hand once directed him. We stopped at a stream where we both drank. I dug into one of the saddlebags and found a flannel shirt and lightly rubbed him down. I was curious about what I'd find inside the bags, but didn't tarry. Time enough, later. No way of knowing if someone might be trailing.

Much later, as I sat among the bordering pinewoods, I saw the brick chimneys of Avalon. That was all that remained. They stood like giants hovering above the ashes. A new grief came over me—cold and heavy. My hope was shattered. After Lance was gone, I thought only of returning to Avalon where I would find my family. Now I felt as if I had lost them as well.

As I stared at the chimneys and despaired, old acquaintances came to my side. Kind, familiar faces. They were camping here in the woods, away from traveled roads. There was old Annie who lived nearby at Cedar Lane, a woman who used to be hard and straight as a ladder. She was all doubled up now. Her eyes were sunken and her bones protruded like a skeleton's under her thin, blotchy skin.

She said to me, "Miss Lottie tol' the Yankee soldiers Massa Carson was crazy in the head and the chillun couldn't walk far and this young Fed sojer let her take a mule and a haywagon. She took the reins and put the chillun and Massa Carson and Zulma in the back. Took a cow with 'em and it followed 'longside the wagon. Theys lef' goin' south. Some'un says they set out for the St. Johns River in Florida where Miss Lottie thought she'd build her another Avalon. My Cedarlane folks headed t'wards Savannah. Wisht I could of gone. Couldn't of walked—didn't have the stringth. When my stringth comes back, that's whar I'm gonna go."

Folks gathered around. Everyone had a story to tell about General Sherman. I told them some of my story. About some of the fighting. About Lance. A slight, slanty-eyed boy about my age kept coming close, like some hungry, bright-eyed animal. Finally, he spoke, "'Member me? I'm Cicero. I 'member Mister Lance's hoss'. I 'member when Mister Lance gentle 'im down in Three Mile Pasture. He a wild 'un."

I said, "Mister Lance used to say, 'The wilder the horse, smarter he is.' This one is smart."

The boy said, "Lucky the hoss' las' through all the fightin'. Lucky you las."

"Night and I are lucky," I said. "I'll spend tonight here in the woods. While we were on the road coming home, someone stole Night from me and I had a chance to get him back. We have to keep out of sight."

Cicero followed me as I moved into the deeper shadows of the woods. I tethered Night and threw off the saddlebags, and dumped them inside out on the ground around me. I found changes of clothes, some bowie knives and cooking pans, blankets and rain tarp and camp tools and grain. Two bags were stuffed with the same good food I had found on the supply wagon. In the bottom of one, I found writing tablets, some good Yankee pencils and a tobacco pouch, lumpy and full, its string knotted tight. I stuffed the small things into my pocket and kept a tablet out to put in my journal later.

The boy studied me and the things spread before me. One by one, others came up. For many reasons they were curious. They all had known Lance. They must have all probably thought that he would be the master of Avalon someday. Maybe my connection to him was all that remained of this thought. They seemed amazed that both Lance's horse and I had returned to the home that was no longer here. There was not a horse in the whole countryside that didn't belong either to outlaws or the Feds.

As Annie came to my side and leaned against me for support, I watched the faces quickly surrounding me. The last rays of sunlight strained through the shadows, grazing their bony faces and sparking their eyes. I saw they were hungry.

"This food is yours," I said to Annie and the boy and nodded to all the faces around me as I gave them the food in the largest bag. The little one would do for me.

By flickering firelight, I wrote in my journal as Annie made some pones, which I'll take with me. While we each did our tasks, some campers came from Augusta and said a column of Yankee Cavalry had set up a pontoon bridge and crossed the Savannah River north of Augusta that afternoon.

I felt I had to get on the road. My plans were to head for Florida and try to find Mama and the family. I planned to do as I did when I first started out, travel by night and keep to the woods and back roads. There was no time now for tears.

As I left, Annie said, "Even if yuh get pass raiders an' Yankees, it's likely yuh may not find yer people."

She may be right. But I've got to try.

April 30, 1865

MY KNEE IS MUCH BETTER, BUT IT'S BEEN SLOW GOING AS I push through the woods and shadows. I'm afraid of attracting attention with a campfire or by traveling the main road, and I'm afraid of losing Night and my supplies. I won't record here what I found in the tobacco pouch among Jake's things. More reason to be careful. I'm trying to restore Night's trust. Without a doubt, he was mistreated by Jake. I'm not riding him much now. I lead him as we move through the darkness. As long as he grazes during the day, he'll have grain to last a while.

My folks, if I can find them, are far away. I'm really alone now. I think of what Annie said—that I wouldn't know where to look for my folks. Florida's a big state. Miss Lottie had a sister who moved many years ago to Florida with her husband who was a purser on a steamboat on the St. Johns River. Maybe that's why she chose to go there.

Though I've been searching through Lance's pages in the journal, I never found anything about his aunt. I loved to read through our times together, even though it made me sad. Sometimes I thought I could almost hear him talking. There were—and are—many things I'd like to ask him. He always could answer any of my questions.

I was interested in this entry after the very first battle when he joined up with General Pickett:

July 14, 1863

I have before me a strange camp scene. Our men are exhausted and hungry, their bodies worn hollow. They've raked leaves into nests and have fallen into them, sabers and rifles beside them. Their clothes, stretched over broken branches, are drying in front of a row of campfires.

What a day. For a week we've been in retreat. I'm afraid our noble kin, my cousin, General George Pickett, brought us to this moment. We fought and fought and lost. I can say I am proud of how we fought. Some of us survived—for that, I thank God. Though as General Pickett's aide-de-camp, I might have avoided the battle, I couldn't watch the other men go and leave me behind to run errands. Like the rest of the men, I was honored and proud to be a part of his fresh division with eager hopes and dreams of glory. It wasn't to be.

I wanted Tench to stay back. He refused to listen. He wants to keep me in sight, or is it I who wants to keep him in sight? I settled him in an entrenchment behind Seminary Ridge and from there—I'm afraid he was witness to a nightmare that may haunt him forever. I know I can't shake the horror of it. The voices of my compatriots live with me. Again, I hear them, their voices lifted first in triumph, then in agony, and finally—silenced. (The sound of that silence is the hardest to bear.) I still see them as they charged and returned again and again, then fell—like broken statues covering the fields.

Badgered by stormy weather, we've clambered our way through underbrush, mud, and water, in battering rain and lightning. No, Tench sleeps sweetly, his cheek rests on the cold blade of his hatchet, cushioned with a pile of wet leaves, his face gaunt, and ribs embossing his small torso.

At one point on this march, the little beggar really glorified himself. He took the load of twenty-seven men on his scrawny shoulders. We're back on march again, thanks to him.

This morning we discovered, too late, we had hiked too long on the nearside of the stream. We should've crossed miles back, where the waters weren't so wide and the currents so strong.

The men, all twenty-seven in the ragged remnant of our regiment, whose humor has served them well throughout this grim business, suddenly were showing signs of dismay. They had fallen silent, matching the dreary day—faces clouded and bodies drooping. In just such a moment, it was easy to remember when our company had started out marching with a regiment of sixty-three men. With the rout, we lost over half our original number. We saw some buddies die, some fall wounded, and some—run from battle. The present dilemma was my fault. Had I been more alert and less caught up in my thoughts, this might not have happened.

I noted two slender ash trees on the bank by my side and turned to Tench "Your hatchet, boy. I'm going to fell this tree to bridge the stream."

"Then what?" someone asked. "It's a mighty skinny tree. It wouldn't hold all of us."

"One at a time, it might." I lined it up with where I hoped it'd fall. "Take a rest, men, while I put it down."

I chopped it clean, close to the ground. I thought I had a good set so it would fall on a promontory on the far side. I moved around to the back of the tree and with the last fall of the axe, several men grasped and held the trunk, but it slipped slowly from their hands. It poised and trembled, then crashed, and we watched its top fall just short of the opposite side, sliding down the slippery bank into the roaring currents. We watched it bob about, then swirl out of sight.

Tench nudged me. "Look over there, Mister Lance." He pointed to a tree on the other side. "Yonder's the perfect tree. Tall enough to fall across to this side. Wide enough around to hold the men."

"It's on the other side."

"I know, sir. Go ahead and cut down the skinny one here. It's much taller than the one we just lost. Has more top and a broader trunk. I could pigeon-walk across. Like I used to up in the branches of the big old trees in our woods."

"This is different, Tench. Really a man's job. With the wind, and rain, and rapids below and the height, it's dangerous."

I'd made him angry. He shouted, "Please, sir. I've done it before, I've cut down bigger trees than that. Corporal Berry's carrying rope. Fasten it to my waist." He paused, then leaned close and added quietly, "And you're not so good with heights."

The soldiers nearby cheered him on. I reconsidered. We'd anchor the rope and many of us would hold it fast. I felled the second tree and watched it land as we planned, on the far bank. With a shovel, our men dug a trench under the tree and jumped upon it, settling it into the earth. Then we wedged our sabers in the earth to the tree all the way to the edge of the bank. Its tall crown reached securely beyond the opposite bank.

Still, the tree trembled in the high wind and I worried when I saw Tench's small frame perched on it. Now, I confess to what Tench alone knew. I possess an unreasonable fear of heights. I could never stand as he *did on so frail a platform high above the rapids.*

He seemed no more concerned than when I saw him scaling the rafters of a barn or raiding a nest of eggs high in a tall tree. He claims I've taught him all he knows. Well, I certainly wasn't his model for such high jinks. He fastened the rope around his waist as a concession to me, but it seemed more a bother to him than a help, so I shouted to him that I'd let it go and he unfastened it while Berry pulled it back.

Halfway across, he changed from pigeon walking to side-sliding, his toes grasping like claws around the curve of the tree. During one awful moment, his foot slipped and he landed sitting upright on the tree. Twenty-seven of us gasped and held our breath. He only seemed amused, but from that position above stream, he dared not stand again, and we watched him rump-bump the rest of his way across. The fellows clapped and cheered when he set foot on the other side.

Tench turned and gave a deep bow. A smile circled his face as he waved. Over the rush of waters, we heard him shout, "Goodbye. I'll be on my way now." He turned away, pretending to take leave. What a chorus of shouts and catcalls echoed after him.

He halted and stood grinning, enjoying his moment of play. I pitched him the hatchet. The marked tree was a beauty. With slow even strokes in the late afternoon hour, Tench finally brought the tree toppling across the stream to our side. It was twilight when twenty-seven of us followed Tench's lead on our firmer, broader bridge and did as he bade as we pigeon walked, side-slid, and rump-bumped to the other side.

As a tree, it is forever lost. May Mother Earth forgive us for plundering her treasure. I'm certain those men never saw a more beautiful bridge.

Strange. However difficult it has been, I'm grateful for all that's happened during this short breath of time. With every obstacle overcome, I've uncovered a strength I hadn't known I possessed. Through it all, I feel I've become a new person.

I understand now that it is only through rebuffs, frustrations, and death, with constant renewals of one's life, can the change and attainment of one's real self be realized. Zulma said I would be a man when I return to Avalon. She was right and—Tench is not far behind. War speeds the process of growth.

May 2, 1865

ALONE WITH NIGHT, I EXPLORED THE BACK ROADS AND hidden paths through unfamiliar land and woods. At the same time I sorted through memories and I felt again every joy and pain of my life. Sometimes I saw with new eyes, as if for the first time. As I read through the journal, both Lance's pages and my own, I tried to understand things I never questioned, just accepted, about myself, Lance, and the Traymore family.

As my green eyes show, I am a Traymore. One generation gave my family their blood. The next gave us their name. They were kinder. They wanted to do the right thing. I am grateful for that. Although they freed all their slaves, my mother and her mother stayed in the family, perhaps because they were Traymore blood and felt they belonged.

I heard the story of our great-grandfather all around the countryside, when I was growing up. Mama Zulma says people always blame everything on those who came before. She said, "They say it the sin of the fathers." She said that I must remember that it was also those who came before, who kept us in the family because that's where we wanted to be. My parents and grandparents cleaned and cooked and nursed the Traymores, and they didn't want anyone else to take their place. But sometimes when I had to go away to the kitchen to be out of sight when the real cousins or fancy folks visited, I wondered why they really stayed—could it be maybe they were afraid of what the North or the West would have been like for them? Or had word gotten back to my family that the North was brutal cold and our kind had trouble getting work and finding places to live, and that the West was still wild and we might get killed out there easy as anything?

It didn't matter that my great-grandmother Joanna was the daughter of Gabriel Lerval or that my grandmother Satin married Lucius Pentor, or that my mother Zulma married Pleasant Waters. They all took the name of Traymore.

So layers of family names have been lost or hidden under the Traymore name. I do not know who my African family is, but I think they must have been warriors and very strong and brave. My mother is proud of our kinship—both the African blood and the Traymore blood. I am too. Only, sometimes—when I was lying on my pallet at the foot of Lance's bed—I longed to be a real cousin, one who slept on the real bed beside him. One who didn't have to disappear into the kitchen or quarters out back when the real cousins arrived. One who could always join in the fun and laughter and lives of all the family.

It wasn't that Lance and I didn't share plenty of laughter and good times together, but there were a lot of things we didn't share. His friends and kin weren't mine. At least they didn't claim me as such. Something inside me rankled when I heard their excited voices and shrieks of laughter muted by closed doors. Or when they chose up sides to play ball. I'd be watching from the thick branches of a nearby tree and secretly rejoiced when Lance's side lost. I'd be thinking that he would've won if he'd had me on his side. It was so easy for me to forget that I wasn't like them. Why couldn't they?

May 5, 1865

AT LEAST MY LEG SEEMS AS GOOD AS NEW NOW. BUT STILL, the dangers out there worried me.

Night or day, I didn't know which was worse to live and travel through.

The night is a black slate. Yet I had learned to read nearly every sound and smell. Everything I felt or touched was like a word shining in the dark.

The day is a white tablet. Its messages read clear and bold. If I saw, I could be seen. If I heard, I could be heard. I tried to stay out of sight. Day had no hiding place. Night and day, the enemies were the same. The sound of hoofs and boastful voices and the clack of wagons. Smoke and fire and meat cooking. Barking dogs. Georgia folk don't have horses anymore. Or wagons. They speak softly. They cooked potatoes or grits or mush. But they had no meat.

Now I hid from everyone—both black and white folks, as much as I hid from the Yankees. Unless they had known my family and me, like the folks back at Avalon, they couldn't possibly have understood how a Negro boy had a horse or wore boots or had saddlebags which they'd guess were stuffed with loot.

Maybe my dream last night had me thinking on these things so hard. I can't free myself of that dream. In it, I was camping on the road again with the three sisters. Daisy and Rose were asleep with the children nesting close. Lily was murmuring as she nursed Marigold. I closed my eyes and pretended to sleep. Even with my eyes shut, I saw her. I turned onto my side with my back towards her. Her image stayed with me.

Suddenly, I felt the soft of lily petals against my face. As I reached for them, I wakened and my hands folded on the emptiness. For a long time I lay thinking—of her small face and her voice that sounded like the whish of a wood stream. I remembered when joy filled her like all glory. Her tears.

Awake, as I thought of the three girls, I remembered how Rose aggravated me. Now I remembered that it was Rose's voice I last heard as she leaned over the boat railing and kept calling, "Tench! Tench!" I remembered how Daisy mothered. But Lily? What was this I felt about her? Something I could not wholly explain. I missed her. I think that was what my dream was about.

May 8, 1865

SOMETIMES I LED NIGHT INTO BRIAR AND BRUSH SO THICK I had to hack my way in and out. I don't know how many times we had strayed too far into the scrub and gotten lost.

This morning as I passed through thick woods, I came upon a Negro boy and girl collecting a basket of sticks for fire wood. We told each other our names. She told me she was Effie Wees and he was William Curtis. They came from a small settlement nearby. They told me the roads were filled with Feds and paroled soldiers. She showed me a handbill she had found on the road.

"Can you read this?" she asked.

I read, "Reward $100,000 in gold for the capture of Jefferson Davis, Traitor, President of the Confederate States."

Effie Wees' eyes opened wide. She squealed, "That be a lot of money. I wish we could fin' 'im n' capture 'im n' pen 'im up n' colleck all that money. We be rich."

"Don' wish nothin' sech," William Curtis responded. "Ain't nothin' you can buy, even if you had all that money."

"But I be rich." She smiled.

"Are there Yankees on the road?" I asked.

William Curtis thought for a moment and answered, "E'ryone look and ack the same. Can't tell none from the oder. How yuh tell?"

"Must be plenty Yankees," I said. "They don't look scruffy and poor as our soldiers. They're likely to have horses or wagons. Our folks have wagons, but they pull them themselves."

I didn't pass any more time with them. I'd been thinking I'd try the main road. If anyone came after me, I'd bear down on Night and head straight ahead. Night would outrun them. Mustn't look anyone in the eye. I'd be lots safer, I thought, once I reached Florida. Everyone was in such a hurry to get home—or wherever—most likely they'd pay no attention to me.

When I started out, I didn't think I'd get as far as Thomson with Night. I most didn't. I was lucky.

May 9, 1865

YESTERDAY, AFTER I LEFT EFFIE WEES AND WILLIAM CUR-tis, Night and I moved onto the main road. I eased along quietly. Everyone was bent on their own business and really took little notice of us. Night was dusty and so loaded down, he looked as scruffy as a mule. I'm such a scrawny slip, neither of us were worth an extra blink in passing.

We traveled a good piece among the other travelers. Once I did hear someone say as we passed, "Lookit who's on that horse. You reckon he stole it?" Most people either ignored us or were friendly.

Later, as I felt easier, I spoke to other travelers. I talked to a paroled soldier. I needed to know the road to Florida.

He answered, "The one with the most travelers. Everyone's headed there. Stay on the road to Irwinville, then follow through to Tifton, then it is straightaway to Valdosta. Then it's from there to Madison. There are back trails you can take. Likely you'd be on the road without even asking, if you go due South."

When the sun was directly overhead, I drew off the road to a large open field to rest and have lunch while Night grazed on a fresh growth of meadow grass. After I ate, I lay in the deep grass letting myself drift like a cloud in the blue above, free and rudderless. In their rolling forms, I saw David and a giant and there was God with a nightcap and a long beard sitting on a great cotton throne. David fluttered in the winds and he and the giant broke apart and scattered into flocks of sheep. God flattened out into a long island, His nightcap, a big smoking volcano among quickly multiplying small islands. I got very drowsy.

I dozed. When I heard a rough voice grate the quiet noon, I bolted upright.

"Lookit, a horse. Just what we need."

I sprang from the grass, raced to Night's side and mounted. I saw no one coming from the road. I turned and looked towards the scrub edging the far end of the field. Two burly men were fast approaching. One was leading a horse. Horse? A bony old plug who'd bring tears to the eyes of anyone who loved a horse. They wore ragged clothes and each carried a rifle. Although Night could race the wind, there were no trees to dodge behind. I recognized their advantage.

"Stop there, you."

I froze.

"Git off the horse. He's ours now. Git down."

At that instant, I hadn't a thought, only anger spreading like wildfire through my blood and bones. I leaned forward on Night and shouted, "Go!"

Night darted across the field. Looking over my shoulder, I saw them lift their rifles. Shells zipped around my head.

One of the men hollered, "This one's got your name."

Night reared. I feared for him. I knew what I must do. I reined him to a stop.

"Up yer hands!" one of them ordered and I obeyed. As they approached, I thought they were going to kill me. I closed my eyes tight and prayed, "Precious Lord, take my hand. Please." Mama Zulma's prayer. From first memory, it was the one with which she sent me off—whether it was into Augusta, or merely to bed, or when I woke at night, scared of the dark.

"Now, whar yuh think yuh goin'? I could squash yuh like a little black ant." He spoke gruffly as he shoved me off Night.

I fell in the grass with him holding the butt of his gun over me, ready to crack my head open. His burly carcass hovered above me. Circles of fat rose up from his middle, to his chest, and all the way to his short neck, and red, greasy face.

The other was on his horse now and came to my side. I noticed only his chin jutting out hard and sharp like a blacksmith's anvil.

"Wha'cha sayin', little black ant? Say it so I can hear," the fat brute yelled.

My voice was as thin as thread, "Precious Lord, take my hand."

"Hear that, Shears? Ain't that sweet?"

Shears had laid his rifle across the saddle and taking a knife and a plug of tobacco from his shirt pocket, peeled off a chunk and popped it into his mouth. His jaw began hammering away.

"Sweet," Shears laughed and spurted. Tobacco juice spilled down his chin.

"Lissen, little black ant," he lowered his voice, "we only want your horse. We're after big game. The big man, hisself. We gonna git 'im."

I felt less in danger and asked, "May I have my bags, sir?"

"What's in 'em?" Shears asked.

"Camping things. Bible. Clothes. Blankets. Cooking things. You may keep the saddle blanket—"

The fat one interrupted, "Yeah, yeah. Let 'im keep is stuff. We don' want 'is Nigra things."

He began to throw off the bags. They needed to know how to care for Night.

"Let the horse graze on soft land. The new grasses. Like here."

"Hey, how come yuh talk like some high-toned white?"

I stayed my point. "When he's heated, wipe him down with this old cotton cloth." Still on my knees, I tossed him a cloth on top of the bag and shouted, "Keep him off hard ground. He's got tender hoofs and a tender mouth, too. Don't yank his bit."

"Well, we'll just have to tough'n him up." The fat man laughed as he jumped onto the saddle. Night reared and whinnied when he drew back hard on the reins. Then he struck him with the butt of the gun and horse and rider streaked off like lightning across the field to the road. Shears leaned forward and spat. A shower of brown juice slavered across the horse's withers. "Beats all!" he shouted. "Gonna ketch them." He twisted around in the saddle, slapped his horse on the rump, and chased down the road after Night and the Fat One.

I was on my knees in the middle of a pile of bags. Anger burst inside of me and I let it go into a raging yell and beat my fists against the saddlebags.

Almost at once I realized I was wasting precious moments and over and over again, I gave the loud whistle that usually brought Night to my side. Too late. Now my effort brought only silence into which the sounds of hooves and even the birdsongs had vanished.

In the silence I rose and threw my bags over my shoulders and headed into the settling dust. At that moment I was unaware that the bags were heavy and awkward. I was thinking of those two devils and Night and what I should do next. Today, I had risked traveling the main roadway, but my enemies had come from the backwoods. There was no way of knowing who the enemies were and where they might be.

I told myself that Night was gone and I had nothing anyone would want. Then I paused and reached into my pocket. My fingers curled around the tobacco pouch I had found in Jake's bag. I moved its lumpy contents between my fingers. Only one person would suspect they'd find something like this on me. Jake.

I kept to the edge of thicket bordering the road so, if need be, I could quickly get out of sight. Some, passing along the road, carried knapsacks or bags over their shoulders or pulled wagons behind them. Like me, they were probably hoping for a reunion with their families or looking for a place to settle, but unlike me, they seemed to know where they were going.

Anger had numbed me. I was unable to think or feel. It took a long time to shake it, but it gradually fell away. My senses returned. I became aware of the weight across my shoulders, the bright sunlight and the light breezes touching my cheeks. My eyes stopped watering. I quit grinding my teeth and doubling my fists.

The memory of Lance's words again echoed through my mind. "These things, the hard things you face and overcome, will make you strong." I wasn't convinced now that this was so, anymore than before. I just couldn't appreciate any good in hardship.

After a while, my shoulders ached and my pace slowed. I was about to find a spot to rest when I caught a whiff of food cooking and followed its trail into the woods. I came upon a Negro man kneeling before a campfire with two young boys at his side. As I came closer I saw he was ladling hominy from a pot hanging from an elbow rod over the fire. After he served them, he rose and filled his own tin cup.

They began sing-songing together:

No chicken in the pot so hominy will do.
To fill your empties up
And make red blood fo' you
And make red blood fo' you
1—2—3—4—5—6—7—
Make red blood fo' you.

I had come from behind and when I made a noise, I surprised them. The man whirled around, his eyes popping. The children hid behind his long legs.

"Whatcha want, boy? You alone?" he asked.

"I'm alone," I replied. "I'd like to trade you some ham for a cup of hominy. I reckon I'm as hungry for something hot as you are for a piece of meat."

He studied me for a moment before answering, "Evens up. Ain't no cause to hide, boys. The strangah ain't gonna take nuffin' from us that we ain't gonna giv 'im anyhow." He ladled some hominy into my tin as I sliced some ham into their open hands.

Everything they owned must have been in the dirty cotton sack beside them. The man's and the boys' arms and legs were stringy-thin and the children's bellies bulged. The three of them had the hollow look of being hungry I'd seen before.

I told them where I was going and the father helped me get my bearings. He told me, "That stream yonda will take yuh towards Irwinville. Aft' that yuh go bit east 'til yuh reach the Withlacoochee and follow 'round to Valdosta. Then, yuh'll find your way to Florida. Folks are friendly-like down thataway."

"Here on the road, it's hard to tell who is friendly and who's not," I said.

"I heard nawth of heah, in Macon, Feds'r all ovah. Ain't no mistakin' 'em in thar fine clothes. They're lookin' fer Prez'dent Jefferson Davis. Givin' a passel of money to anyone who'll bring 'im in."

"Heard tell," I replied.

The hominy, hot and smooth, melted on my tongue and made me think of Mama Zulma's kitchen. I could see the embroidered roses on her apron, the sash tied into a big butterfly bow in back, and her, heaping piles of food on my plate. I most could smell the coffee and the pones baking and hear the pots bubbling on the great wood stove and see rows of jars of peach jelly, gold as sunlight on the table.

Still thinking of Mama Zulma, I saved a stub of ham and a couple of potatoes for myself and handed over the leather bag and its contents to him. "For you," I said.

He folded both his hands over mine and the children drew closer. "See, chillun," he said, "Yuh nevah know whose table yuh set. Fo' sharin' one cup a hominy wid a strangah, we be settin' the table many times fo' us's sef."

The children were reaching into the bag and stuffing food into theirs. "No, no. You can keep the bag. I don't need it anymore." I didn't take time to find the cook's name. No time to tarry.

May 9, 1865

LONELINESS MADE PICTURES IN MY MIND. I NEEDED TO BE on my way. I had a long way to go to make those pictures real again. I picked up the bag and threw it across my shoulders. It was mid-afternoon. The day soon would be over.

My steps were easier. My load was lighter and so was my mood. I was glad some good had come from my last encounter.

I came to a narrow wooden bridge and stood for a while watching the current below. Perhaps the stream would lead me to the Withlacoochee and I thought I'd cross to the west bank.

All of a sudden, squeals and clatter sounded behind me. I turned just in time to see a large sow with her litter rushing across the bridge. The sow brushed against me. I lost my footing and fell flat against the rough wood just as the sow and one of her piglets skidded off the bridge into the water below. The rest of the litter cried and circled, trying to figure out how to follow.

For a moment I listened to the ruckus of the sow and piglet grunting and squealing as they splashed and struggled below. At once, I shook off the bags, pulled off my shirt, and unstrapped this journal. I sprang to my feet and scampered over the bridge and down the bank and waded into the stream. The piglets had followed and were squealing on the shore. Just as I reached the sow's side, I stumbled into a hole. I was straining to get to the top of the water while the hog snorted and splashed beside me. Then I realized I could not work myself free—my boots were stuck in the muddy bottom.

Struggling, I eased one foot then the other from the boots. Now free, I nudged the sow and pushed her broad hams towards shore while she shook and sputtered and grunted, calling her family. I looked for the piglet and spotted its little head bobbing downstream.

Knowing I couldn't let the little one drown, I pulled off my pants, lay them on the bank, and waded after it. Every time I reached her, she slipped through my hands. There, midstream, she grounded on a narrow rise of sand and I picked up the gasping, twisting little creature and set her on the bank.

The sow began snorting and nudging the little ones. I watched as she herded them up the bank. As their squeals faded away, I began to laugh out loud and shouted, "Crazy pigs."

Just then I became aware of other voices—I wasn't laughing alone. A woman's laughter turned into a cry as she called, "No, Jess. Don't hurt the pigs. Please leave them be."

I saw then, a short, plump marksman taking aim in the direction of the pigs. He had set the barrel of his musket in the fork of a tree. Further back, half-hidden by the glossy leaves of a large magnolia, was a group of people. It was too late to hide. I was so embarrassed I couldn't look at them. In nothing more than my bare skin, I had put on quite a show.

Quickly, I waded into the stream, pulled my boots from the mud, stepped into my pants on the bank, and ran to the bridge. I strapped on my journal and put on my shirt. I felt inside my pockets to see if I had lost anything. I thought I'd move quietly out of sight. Glancing behind me, I could see the women had thoughtfully turned away. I couldn't help thinking that if I'd had Night, this never would have happened.

Just as I bent to pick up my load, a voice called, "Ho there." I looked up. A tall, bearded man was coming towards me. "Good job," he complimented. "Very good job."

I turned from my audience and, keeping my eyes on my boots, muttered, "Thank you, sir." I was embarrassed and wet and suddenly too tired to run. I couldn't escape. Three women, one was black, were in the group with several gentlemen.

"What a nice thing to do." One of the ladies approached me, speaking after I had dressed.

I looked up at her and replied, "Thank you, ma'am."

Her voice was strong but gentle, her eyes, large and brown. "You're very kind," she said. "Youngster, come. Don't be afraid. We'll dry your clothes by the fire." She put her hand on my shoulder and asked, "What are you doing here? Where are you going? Tell us about yourself, child. Are you by yourself?"

I was shivering. I didn't know if it was because I was cold or frightened. I've shivered plenty before—during battle when shells were exploding all around. Now the sun was nearing the horizon and the air was cooling and my clothes were wet. Likely it was both reasons. Quickly, as best I could, I told her about myself. About Lance and my return to Avalon and my mission now, to find my folks somewhere in Florida.

She said to me, "I'd like to help you. We'll start by finding something to wear." Then she turned to the black woman and said, "Please help the boy, Louella. Give him one of Mister Davis's nightshirts. The children's would be too small." Again, to me, "What is your name, child?"

Just as I answered, "Tench Traymore," the bearded man lifted the bags from my shoulders and we walked up the rise above the stream to a large encampment circled by wagons and horses. Four tents were set up in the center and bed rolls were scattered under the trees. A fire danced under some large cauldrons and a big spread of food had been set out over the tops of trunks.

Louella and I followed the gentlewoman to the large tent and watched as she took a white sleeping-shirt from a pile on the trunk. She handed it to Louella, saying, "Tend to him, Lou."

Remembering now the pleasure of all that attention, I especially mark how quickly and willingly I became a helpless child again, with people suddenly caring for me, dressing me, feeding me. How good it was to have them ask me questions, listen to me, and to exclaim and laugh over me.

"Ain'tcha the one," Louella said as she took my clothes after I took everything from my pockets. "Miz Varina giv yuh the prez'dent's own nightshirt and I'm about to take these clothes down the stream and wash 'em good fo' yuh. I'll put 'em at the fire to dry. Here, take this hankerchief to tie yuh things up."

What had she said? "What do you mean—the president?" I asked.

"Bless yuh, yuh don' know." Louella pulled back the tent flap. "Yuh be in the company of Mister Prez'dent Jefferson Davis and his wife, Varina, the lady who wanted to dry yuh off."

She left with my wet clothes. I was sitting on a cot when the flap opened and four children quickly surrounded me. I knew that three of them must have been Miss Varina's. They looked at me out of the same brown eyes. The fourth was a Negro boy, smaller and younger than I.

They were eager to talk and introduced themselves. "I'm Jim Linder," said the dark child. "I'm Mister President Davis's adopted boy. I'm eleven years old. They call me Young Jim. The President's own personal darky is Old Jim. He's twenty."

The young girl spoke, "My name's Margaret. Everyone calls me Maggie. I'm nine."

"I'm Little Jeff. I'm named for Papa and I'm seven. And—" Little Jeff put his hand on the smallest, sitting on Maggie's lap—"this's William. We call him Billy."

"Our baby sister is with Mama. She's nursing her now so she won't be fussin' when we eat," Maggie explained. "Her name is Varina Ann and we call her Winnie, but Papa calls her Piecake."

"And—who are you?" Little Jeff asked.

"Tench," I answered, "Tench Traymore."

"Tench?" he screwed up his face. "What kind of name's that?"

I finally answered, "Mine." They all laughed.

"You running away?" Maggie asked.

"You might say so."

She put a finger to her lips and lowered her voice. "We're running away too. The whole Federal Army's looking for Papa."

"I'm scared. Are you?" Little Jeff asked.

"Not right now," I answered. "But I've been scared plenty."

Jefferson touched my arm, "Uncle John's taking care of us.

"Papa says long as Uncle John's with us, we'll be all right. Uncle John is really Captain John Taylor Wood and he's from the Navy. It's funny because he's also a Colonel in the army," Maggie explained. "Papa's really his uncle and he's really our cousin, and because he's older than all our other cousins, we call him uncle."

"He's the best sailor and soldier in the whole South. Papa says so and General Lee said so too. Uncle John is Papa's number one man." Margaret set William down, leaned over and looked into my eyes.

"Why are your eyes green?" she asked. "I've never seen a colored person with green eyes."

"It just happened," I answered. "Like your eyes are brown."

"Like my mother's. Your mother's eyes are green?"

"Yes. My great-grandfather had green eyes. My grandfather had them and my mother has them, too."

That was settled. She began again, "Can you go with us? Where're you headed? Louella sleeps in the tent with us children. Papa and Mama sleep in the big tent. Where're you going to sleep tonight? Have you ever slept in a tent?"

"Many times," I answered. "When my clothes are dry, I'll be on my way. I'm going to Florida. Going to find my family."

"We're going to Florida, too. Papa's going to get a boat to take us clear across the ocean so the Yankees can't get us. You can go to Florida with us. Let me ask Uncle John if you can."

Jim Linder jumped up and clapped his hands. "Yes! Yes! Come with us."

Just at that moment, the tall bearded man pulled the flap aside and entered. Margaret sprang to his side and grabbed his hand. "Uncle John, can Tench go to Florida with us?"

He smiled, answering, "We'll see. Food's ready now. Let's eat. Join us, Tench." I looked down at my nightshirt.

"Don't worry. Everyone knows what happened to your clothes. You should be proud. Come, we'll get your bags."

I wasn't shivering anymore, but I was ashamed to be seen in a nightshirt that looked like a dress. I followed slowly. Captain Wood led me into the brush where he'd left my bags. He told me to take my utensils and follow the others. Then he picked up a musket and disappeared into the brush.

Miss Varina and the man I now knew was President Davis were serving themselves at the head of the line. He was fine looking with a slender body and stood straight and tall. The children, already eating, sat together with Louella on a blanket spread up on the rise overlooking the stream. They called me to join them just as Miss Varina called me to her side.

"Jefferson," she said, "this is Tench Traymore who saved the little piglet and sow."

Half-smiling, the president turned to me. His voice was soft. "And I know, dear Varina, you prevented them all from becoming victims of Jeff Medlock's musket." As they moved on, I heard him say, "I knew the Samuel Traymore family of Virginia."

He knew my people. I wanted to follow and tell him about Lance and Carson and Lottie Traymore Matthews. But that wouldn't be right. I could hear my mother warn, "It's not fittin' for folks of color to speak unless spoken to."

As they took their food, I watched them. Jess Medlock followed and spread a blanket on the stream bank where they sat with the other lady, the one the children said was their aunt. I knew someday I would be telling Miss Lottie and Mama about this meeting.

I wanted to remember the moment, how they looked, talked, all about them. How could I describe them? Let me see.

His was the face of a high-born gentleman with large, deep-set, gray eyes, like moonstones in a dark pool. His hair was silver-frosted and neatly trimmed and brushed off his wide forehead. He had a sharp-cut nose, a strong chin, and shadow hollows under high cheek-bones and a small mouth with thin lips. Everything about him was neat, his trim clothes looked so clean and fresh-pressed, and his boots polished shiny black.

Yet there were no words to describe the sadness in his face. Once I saw a man watch his brother die in battle. Jefferson Davis had that same look.

And Mrs. Jefferson? Though they were different sizes, she reminded me of Miss Lottie of Avalon. Maybe only in their kind ways, that's what seemed so alike because Miss Lottie was small, with olive skin and green eyes. Miss Varina was a larger woman with dark coloring. Miss Lottie's voice was so soft, I'd turn to watch the words her lips were forming, at the same time moving closer to hear her. Miss Varina's voice was nice, but strong and ringing. In a group with everyone else talking, hers was the only voice you'd hear and her voice keeps sounding in your mind long after she has spoken. She seems to take the whole world into her huge dark eyes and appears interested in everything and everybody. I believed Miss Lottie was just as interested in others, but she was more shy.

One other thing, Miss Varina's face was not at all sad like her husband's.

After I filled my plate, I sat down in the shadows along the edge of the campsite. The children called, but, still ashamed of my dress, I shied away until Louella came over and urged me to join them. I needn't have worried, the children were all kind and made no mention of my dress. Later, when she put the children to bed, she put blankets on the ground for Young Jim and me outside their tent.

For a long time, I lay still and listened with my back towards the campfire. The children giggled and laughed while Louella kept scolding, "Hush, children, sleep now." At last, she fell silent and their giggles faded away. Jim was fast asleep at my side.

I heard Miss Varina say, "Dear Sister, sleep well." I turned to see her give a hug and leave her at a nearby tent. She took her husband's hand as they walked towards theirs. Before she entered, she called quietly to Captain John, "I know it's futile to tell you, John, but I do hope you'll try to get some sleep."

How could anyone sleep? They all should be on the road, moving towards Florida fast as they could. It seemed as if these folks were merely vacationing in the woods and picnicking on the banks of a peaceful stream and, perhaps, hunting wild pigs, and strolling through the woods.

Down at the creek, I heard pans and dishes rattling as Old Jim and other servants washed up. They quietly chatted and laughed and occasionally hummed or sang. Some soldiers sprawled in front of the fire and at the wood's edge and encircling roadway, while others patrolled the camp's boundaries, on foot and horseback. Captain John and Jess Medlock were down on the bank, their voices a low drone. Behind them, down creek, a frog chorus sounded, and nearby I heard the mournful call of a chuck-will's-widow.

Finally, I took the blanket and moved towards the trees where Captain John had stashed my bags. When he saw me he rose and gathered up my clothes hanging from a pole balanced between two Y branches in front of the fire.

"You can take these now, Tench. Dry."

I thanked him and went into the brush to dress. I rolled up the nightshirt and stuck it in my haversack and removed my strap and journal.

"You're leaving?" He was waiting for me.

"Not right away, sir. I have something I must do before I leave." To show him, I held out my journal.

"What is that?"

I told him about my journal, that Lance had started and I continue keeping. Suddenly, he said, "Tell me about your people, Tench."

If Lance had only been here to tell him, I thought. But then I answered the man. "I heard the president say he knew the Samuel Traymores of Virginia. They were some of my people. Samuel Traymore II was my great-grandfather. Although Miss Alice Lovell was his wife and the mother of Samuel III, my own grandmother was Joanna. Their son Solomon was my grandfather."

Captain John, listening closely, said, "So Samuel III and your grandfather Solomon were half brothers?"

"Yes, sir. Born same year, same month, but—two different mothers. My grandfather Solomon was the beginning of the dark side of the Traymore family tree."

"And you're the last of that branch?"

I nodded, "I am. Samuel III and my grandfather Solomon were nineteen when their father died. That was when Samuel Traymore III moved all the family to Georgia. In the 1830s."

"Solomon was your mother's father?" he asked.

"Yes, sir. He was." People often get confused when I explain the family connections. To some, it seems strange how proud I am of the Traymore family—but they are the family I know, them and my own blood. I do not know and likely will never know who my African family was or what name they might have borne. It's the Traymore family I know, and I know more about them than most people know about their folks. Nothing was ever kept from me by any of the Traymore family.

The firelight reflected in Captain John's eyes. He nodded, repeating, "Samuel Traymore. I've heard of your family before."

"My mama and Miss Lottie Traymore were raised together. Miss Lottie married Mister Carson Matthews from Charleston, and they had a daughter and five sons. Their oldest, Traymore, ran off and joined Company F of the Tenth Georgia Infantry in October, '61. Mister Carson wouldn't let his son go off to war without him and caught up with him when Tray's regiment joined the Army of Northern Virginia." I paused. "To understand Carson Matthews, there are things you have to know about him first."

Captain John smiled and sat down opposite me on the trunk of a fallen tree. I continued, "Mister Carson wasn't a fighting man, but his son Traymore was. That's what Miss Lottie used to say. I have to agree."

When I saw Captain John lean into me, listening, I went on, "They spent '62 fighting in Virginia. At least, Tray was fighting. Halfway through '62, their next oldest son, Edelman, joined his papa and Tray. Miss Lottie used to read their letters to us, and I remember Mister Carson writing that he hadn't had a single experience in his lifetime to prepare him for war—the killing, the misery, the loneliness, the pain, the filth, the food. In all his life, he hadn't ever hunted wild game or shot an animal. When he was a young man, he had studied at the College of William and Mary. Miss Lottie said her husband knew everything she'd wanted to know about art, music—he played the harpsichord, studied literature and philosophy—"

"What we'd all like to know." Captain John nodded.

For a moment, I thought about what the captain said. "Miss Lottie said her husband gave a much needed quality to the family. Maybe so, but it was Miss Lottie who taught all of us to farm, ride and hunt and work. Miss Lottie had learned everything from her father, Samuel Traymore III. She was the youngest of five girls. Old Samuel had always wanted a boy. He'd chosen boys' names for each new child and had had to change them each time. Samuel became Samantha, Edward was Editha. Frederick, Fredericka—and Louis changed to Louise. Lottie was born last. By that time, her father knew there wasn't going to be a boy so he named her Charlotte. Everyone called her Lottie, but he called her Charlie."

I glanced at the captain, think I was talking too much. "Maybe you don't want to hear this?"

"But I do," he assured me. "Please, go on. I appreciate how deeply you are aware of your family history."

"The Tenth Georgia Infantry was in many battles—Yorktown, Seven Day Battle. Also, at Aliens Farm on Malvern Hill. But it was Antietam I'll never forget. After every battle, there had been letters from Tray and Edelman who were fighting and trying to keep their father safe and undercover. Imagine, in battle, they took care of their father just like my cousin Lance took care of me."

I sighed, sad with my memories. "After Antietam, last of September 1862, there were no more letters. An Army escort brought Mister Carson home. Both sons had been killed. He had no scars you could see, but Miss Lottie said his mind was lost and his heart shattered on the battlefields where his sons had fought."

Captain John picked up his musket and placed it across his knees. His voice was low. "Yes, of course, I see, I see."

"When Lance, the third son, turned fifteen and wanted to join the Army, Miss Lottie shouted, 'No, no no!' She already had lost two sons. You might also say a husband as well. But Lance wouldn't give up. He kept after her, telling her he'd run away, just like his brother had before him. She finally told Lance that if he went, he couldn't go alone. She had decided. He had to take me with him. She thought that might change his mind. I hoped so, too."

Captain John nodded. "How often our own wishes have to give in to those of others." He threw his head back and locked his fingers together behind his neck. "Did Lance join the Tenth Georgia Regiment, too?"

"Oh, no, sir. His mother was determined he was not to join up where his brothers got killed as she thought that regiment was a jinx for our people. She wrote letters to her kin in Virginia and to General George Pickett himself. See General Pickett is kinfolk. He and Lance were second or third cousins. But Miss Lottie knew enough of the right people in Virginia and in Richmond, and, next thing you know, General Pickett had a brand new aide-de-camp, and one with his own horse and his own cook. One time Lance showed me the letter Miss Lottie wrote to General Pickett, she sent it by way of Lance, and she asked the general to watch over us." I laughed, remembering how embarrassed Lance was about that letter. "But he had to give it to the general because he had promised his mother he would do so."

"Poor George." Captain John's laughter joined mine.

"General Pickett had all he could do without looking out for us. Even so, he was good to us. At first, he tried to keep Lance away from gunfire, but Lance wanted to be in the middle of things. He just followed any brigade headed for a battle. He was in a siege at Suffolk in Virginia—then, on Edenton Road in Suffolk. In each instance, I was burrowed in a ditch. At Gettysburg, he hid me in a bunker before he struck off, charging in the middle of the Confederate line, facing the devil's fire. Pickett sent another aide after him. He told Lance the general said to come back, that he didn't want a good horse like Night killed, that he was the only one who could ride him. But Lance wouldn't leave the soldiers and the aid went on back to the general. I waited a long time. I was too scared to come out of hiding. When I finally did, I watched bloodied soldiers limp by, groaning and crying. A wagon passed full of the dead and dying—boys who never would know anything after that moment. If I had been them and had a choice, I wouldn't be here. Why were they?"

Captain John answered, "They didn't feel they had a choice."

"I know you're right," I agreed. "Like Lance, most of them wanted to go to war, and I'll never understand why. We went through a lot, Lance and me. It was a miracle he stayed alive as long as he did. The shells couldn't find me. He hid me. He was killed on White Oak Road. In my heart I keep remembering. I hadn't said goodbye."

After I said that, I was quiet. For a long time, so was Captain John. Jim had finished his chores and was banking the campfire. Captain John rose, took a small tablet from his pocket. "I keep a journal also, Tench. I think of it as my voice in time. When it's all over, this will be all that's left." He started to leave then turned back. "Are you on your way home?"

"Been already, sir. The plantation was in Thomson, not far from Augusta. Sherman's men burned it. All that was left were the brick chimneys. Folks living around there said the family set off for Florida."

"Do you know where in Florida?"

"No, sir. Miss Lottie had a sister who lived somewhere around the St. Johns River. Thought they might be going there."

"It's a long river and a big state. You could go a ways with us. We're headed in that direction."

"I hope you get there, sir. There're Yankees and bummers and robbers all around. They all want the big reward for capturing President Davis. Some of them have already stolen my horse—Lance's horse. I believe the people trying to capture the president are in a bigger hurry than those who guard him. If I were you with your people, I'd just keep going without stopping to rest or eat till I got deep in Florida."

Captain John smiled and nodded. "Exactly."

"I'm just one person and I only had a horse but, as I traveled through the countryside, it was very hard to stay hidden. Daylight, I made my way through the brush off the main roads, but someone was always after my horse. They finally got it. I found it doesn't matter how hard you try, if you have something someone wants, they'll come after it. It's not just the Yankees who'll give chase. Everybody in this camp ought to be on the road right now, moving fast as they can. There are probably scouts in these woods watching, at this very moment. "

Captain John nodded. "President Davis had a big head start. He should have been in Florida by now. He left the escape party because he thought his wife and children were in danger. He chose to stay with his family. Said he's put his fate in God's hands. I'm sure he knows what the consequences of that decision may be."

Besides President Davis and his wife and children, there are other people in his party—soldiers, servants and friends and relatives. There are about fifteen horses and several mules, a dozen wagons and a cow, so the children will have milk. I haven't seen everyone all at once, but I think there must be around forty or fifty in the president's company. Since Captain John is the president's nephew, I guess he didn't really have a choice. He's where he thinks he should be.

I talked so much today and thought again of things that hurt to remember. For a long time, the captain and I wrote in our journals.

I had planned to be on my way, but the day was too long and I was drowsy. I moved my blanket over by the children's tent. Through heavy eyes, I saw Captain John had tethered his saddled horse to a tree and he slept on a grassy mound nearby. I worried about Night. Lord, I hoped those scum don't torture him. I hoped they gave him enough food and water.

Not far away, there was a settlement. I heard dogs barking, a rooster crowing, and an occasional shout or call and, nearby, the pad of footsteps of the soldiers guarding us. I wondered what else was out there. I heard the soothing sounds of sleep: strong even breathing, snoring, a quiet gasp, a whimper from the children's tent. Soon, I too felt myself sink into the deep soft pillows of sleep.

May 10, 1865

A GREAT CONFUSION OF VOICES, THUNDERING OF HOOFS, and a blast of musketry woke me the next morning. I heard Old Jim's voice, frantic, "Sir, oh sir! They're are gonna kill us. They ever'where."

Through the half-dark of early dawn, I made out Captain John springing to his horse. Uniformed men were swarming around us. They were rounding up the livestock, plundering supplies, taking over the guns. One of the cavalrymen approached the captain's side and struggled to get his horse. I saw the steel of the soldier's bayonet flash against his chest as Captain John slid from the saddle. I edged closer and stayed by his side, moving among the raiders towards the president's tent. Repeating rifles echoed in the woods.

Miss Varina stood at the flap of the tent. Captain John took her by the arm. "Hurry Varina," he urged. "To the swamp. Get the children. I'll get Uncle Jefferson. Hurry! You can escape." He pointed at a gap in the brush. "Through the brush."

"Yes, yes," she agreed.

A slush lamp burned in the president's tent. I squinted, not sure of what I was seeing. He seemed to be dressed as a woman, then I realized he was wearing one of his long nightshirts just as I had last evening. Miss Varina rushed back inside and put her own light overcoat around his shoulders and hung a pail over his arm, telling a servant to take the other arm. She ruffled his hair as she threw a shawl over his head.

Captain John paused in his tracks, "What's this?"

Varina answered, "Oh, John, this way, they won't notice him. It's still dark. I'll tell them we're just going to the stream to wash and get some water. I haven't slept all night. I kept hearing dogs barking and noises in the woods. I've been so frightened. He was exhausted and finally fell asleep."

"Varina," Captain John scolded, "Why didn't you call me? I don't think this disguise is a good idea. Let's go. We're wasting time." The captain appeared out of patience.

With the servant on one arm and pail clanging on the other, the president looked funny—like a little old woman—with his hair mussed and shawl draped over his head and shoulders. Then I noticed shiny black boots peeking below his nightshirt.

Captain John held the tent flap open. Like a shepherd with his flock, he stood tall above our group, herding us together. I stayed close. He spoke softly, "Wait by the stream."

He scooped baby Winnie and little William into his arms. Jeff, Maggie, and Jim Linder locked arms and were quiet and big-eyed. Jim was crying.

A Yankee soldier shouted at us, "Get out of the way of live fire!" He raised his gun to his shoulder.

Miss Varina started chattering, her voice rang like a bell. "Leave us alone," she cried. "We just want to bathe and get some water. We're not afraid of your guns or live fire." And then, "Don't you dare hurt the women and children or our darkies. How dare you threaten innocent children and women. See how you've frightened everyone?"

One of the soldiers nudged the president's servant with the barrel of his musket and yelled, "Hey, you dark folks. Haven't you heard? We Yankees are setting you free."

Young Jim was sobbing. At that point, the soldier pulled him away from Maggie and Jefferson. "Don't cry, fellow. You're free now." The soldier began to walk him away, nudging him along with the barrel of his gun.

The pitch of Miss Varina's voice was getting higher and then she was sobbing. I wished she'd stop. There was enough confusion. Jim Linder had been taken away, but his screams continued, piercing and desperate. The little ones cried, the servants were yelling and squalling. I felt like I was in the middle of a swarm of angry bees.

"What are you running away for? The war is over. The South got beat!" The soldier shouted after us.

"If the war is over, soldier," Miss Varina sang out, "how is it you raise your guns to fire on us? What are you doing with our little darkies?"

Captain John's raised his voice urging, "Get to the brush, everyone. You, Tench." Then, to Miss Varina, "No more. Hush."

Miss Varina paid no attention. "Where's our boy, Jim Linder? Where're you taking him? He's our boy," she persisted. "Please don't harm us. Leave us alone. You've made the children cry."

"Halt!" A strong voice shouted above the others.

Miss Varina kept on going and talking. I began to work my way through the crowd to the brush as the captain told us. As I slipped into the bushes, I heard her shout, "We're helpless innocents. You've gone through the South burning our houses and stealing us blind. We can't escape."

Again, the harsh voice shouted, "Halt. I mean you, too, lady."

Daylight spread its light around us. I parted the bushes. Swarms of soldiers and horsemen filled the camp. One stalked through the crowd, and held the muzzle of his carbine to the president's head.

Miss Varina dashed to his side, threw her arms around the president, and, putting herself between him and the soldier, cried, "No! Don't. Please." In a widening circle, the soldiers raised their carbines.

Captain John couldn't quiet her. Her voice rose and she fell to her knees in front of the soldier whose carbine rested cold against her husband's temple. "I beg you, don't shoot."

Yankee soldiers were surrounding them.

The soldier gave a deafening yell, "Look at that. Devil, if the Confederate president ain't a woman. You forgot to take off your boots, Auntie." The soldiers burst out laughing. The nightshirt had caught on the back of his high-top boots.

The men drew closer, snorting and guffawing. I saw Captain John speak to Miss Varina as he placed Winnie in her arms and William's hand in Maggie's. He dropped his haversack and kicked it beside me. Everyone's eyes were on President Jefferson Davis.

The gathering troops parted and made way for an officer on foot. As he approached, the crowd fell silent except for a few hushed sobs and cries from the children.

The officer stood straight and tall in front of the pathetic figure of the president. "Are you Jefferson Davis?" he asked.

"I am." The president's voice was clear and firm.

Again, laughter exploded all around. Some hooted and jeered.

The officer spoke loudly, identifying himself and addressing the president, "Colonel Henry Harnden, United States Army. Sir, you are under arrest and now in the custody of the First Wisconsin Cavalry. Prepare yourself and your party for immediate decampment."

The soldier who had held the carbine on the president pushed ahead to the Colonel's side and spoke with clarity, "Do I get the reward, sir? Is it mine, sir?"

Someone shouted, "You didn't do it by yourself, soldier. The First Cavalry did it. It was our duty. All of us."

Another called out, "Yes, all of us! Let's hear from the Fourth Michigan Cavalry. Gentlemen, be heard."

Scattered cheers sounded. Another officer approached on horseback and the crowd parted. He saluted Colonel Harnden and reported, "Colonel Benjamin Pritchard, Fourth Michigan Cavalry, sir."

Harnden spoke quietly as he returned the salute. "So you were the devils out there shooting at us. Our scouts told us the rebels had set camp and were sleeping. Then suddenly we were in the middle of battle. Turns out we were battling our own army."

Colonel Pritchard looked over the crowd and called, "Any casualties?"

Colonel Harnden shouted the same question. Answers echoed back from all sides as they determined none had been killed, but four had been injured.

While officers and troops noisily talked together, I saw Captain John move about through one group to another, then, speaking first to the president who now sat on the trunk of a fallen tree, the captain drew the children and Miss Varina close to my hiding place. I heard him say, "I told Uncle Jefferson I'd try to escape. He agreed I should. If I remain and they find out who I am, or if I try and don't succeed, they'll hang me. Escaping is my only answer."

I heard Varina say, "Bless you, dear John."

Then, Davis's voice as Varina clung to him, "God's will be done."

Captain John, now moving quietly about the camp, was almost ignored by the soldiers as they rounded up horses, lined up wagons, opened trunks, and threw blankets and dresses over their arms. They scattered the children's clothes and toys as they dug deeper into boxes and trunks—I supposed they were looking for greater treasures as I saw them fill their pockets with silver and trinkets, or whatever took their fancy.

When a Federal officer noticed Captain John, he pointed at him and called to one of the plunderers, "Hans, guard."

Captain John followed Hans over to the side. I recognized him as the big, husky one who had his horse and bag. He had been stuffing his haversack and pockets with loot and didn't appreciate the interruption.

I heard Captain John say, "I have something to give you."

Hans frowned. He answered in a foreign language.

"Ah ha. You German?" The captain smiled in a friendly way.

"*Ja. Jawohl,*" he answered. Captain John nodded, touched his arm, and led him to the wooded area away from the picket line. He took a coin from his pocket, showed it to him, and pointed first to himself, then the path to the stream. I followed behind the alder bushes.

Hans's face came alive. He took the coin, turned it in his fingers, put it between his teeth, and bit down hard. Satisfied it was good, he smiled broadly and followed the captain to the bushes along the bank.

Captain John pointed to Hans, and back to the campground, "Now, go. Go back."

"*Nein.*" Hans shook his head, touched the captain's pocket. Captain John gave him another coin and turned his pockets inside out, showing he had no more. The German smiled, clinked the coins in his palm, and walked back towards camp.

The captain motioned me to his side, put his hand on my shoulder, and said, "I don't know what's ahead. I'm a fugitive and can't promise anything, but I will take you along with me. I'm headed towards the St. Johns. If you want to come with me, it'll be hard, but I know you can do it."

I replied quickly, "Yes, sir, I'd like to come."

He hurried ahead down the path to the water's edge. His long legs stretched from one rock to another as he crossed the stream. He turned and, seeing me hesitate, said, "It's only water. Not very deep."

Embarrassed that I had hesitated, I jumped to the first rock and then the next. My boots slipped and slid and I sloshed the rest of the way. Once across, I followed and fell to my knees as we crept deeper into the swamp. He settled behind an uprooted tree. I watched him fold his long body, making a hollow in the long grass behind the big tree trunk. Seeing no other place to hide, I moved beside him. On our knees, we could peer through the saw grass. If we were silent and lay still, we could see but not be seen.

By the time the sun was overhead, the confusion had died away. We no longer heard the crying or wailing of the children and servants. The troops had settled to gather and pack their loot. We could see them and hear their voices. Once, there was a loud outcry and angry curses. Captain John cringed.

We saw the children and Louella washing and cleaning up. They were watched by a couple of guards with muskets. Miss Varina came, a guard behind her. She knelt and splashed her face with water. Then she stared into the water, her eyes closed, lips moving. Later, a steady file of soldiers came to fill their canteens, water their horses, and bathe.

Bugles sounded. The wagons lined up and soon lumbered out of sight. We saw the president, dressed in Confederate gray, wearing a wide-brimmed hat with a black silk kerchief at his neck. He was riding a carriage horse, back straight, head unbowed.

There was a shout. "Position! Guards to the prisoners."

Captain John muttered, "God help them."

With another command," Forward. March," we watched them move out of our sight. Shortly, the Yankee commanders and their troops followed. For a long time we lay flat against the damp earth. A mockingbird broke the new silence, its song reaching the high ceiling of tall pines. I wondered if the bird had been singing all morning. Was I only now hearing it?

Captain John rose stiffly. I followed like a shadow. We walked back to the abandoned campsite, untidy from the hastily broken camp. Food, clothing, and debris were scattered over the ground. Two large tents remained. One had collapsed, its posts sticking out in angles like broken bones jabbing through the skin of a dragon.

A battle-worn horse was caught in the brush unable to get out. Captain John immediately rescued him. In the rubbish, there were a couple of saddles and pieces of bridles. He began to patch the bridles with bits of leather. He laid a blanket over the animal's back. I held onto the mane while he outfitted him. I got our bags and haversacks from their hiding places. Hans hadn't really gotten everything.

A loud halloo sounded across the clearing. Coming towards us was a sliver of an old man. In size, he was even less than I. Wisps of silky white fringed his forehead, thickening into mutton chops on the sides.

He held out his hand to the captain, "Howdy. Fenn's the name, sir. So they caught old Jeff Davis himself? Big happenings here. I tell you I'm glad it's all over." He must have been watching from the road, or, perhaps, hiding in the brush.

The captain shook his hand while I busied myself and started gathering the food left behind.

"Boy," the old man called, "Whatcha doing with that?"

I looked at the captain who answered for me. "He's just cleaning up, Mr.Fenn. Would you like the scraps?"

"I always clean the grounds and take leftovers after folks break camp. I got a flock of hungry mouths at the house."

There were only a few pieces of hardtack left in my bag, but the captain was right in leaving the food for Mr. Fenn. The captain and I would get along.

The old man smiled, saying, "Come to the house. My wife'll fix y'all some dinner. Or you could stop at the Widow Paulk's, ten miles up the road. She's got cattle. Feds haven't found her farm yet. It's all she's got, but beef sure fills you up good."

I put scraps of potatoes and ham and pones into a piece of sacking. It wasn't easy to hand over the bundle to Mr. Fenn when I felt so hungry. I hoped that the captain might accept his invitation, or at least look up the widow. I could almost see a plate piled high with potatoes and roast beef from her. My mouth watered.

"God bless you," said the little gentleman.

"In coming days, we'll need all the blessings God can spare. Won't we, Tench?" Captain John smiled.

Mr. Fenn had a cart by the road. He brought it over and began to scoop up the leavings, all the time exclaiming, "I sure thank you. Thank you, thank you, God."

The cart filled up quickly with everything from horseshoes and cooking pots, to children's petticoats and one of the president's nightshirts.

We were ready. Captain John asked for directions to Madison and wished Mr. Fenn well. We'd just keep bearing south, following the stream to the Alapaha and we'd stay close to the river 'til the trail widened and follow it to a settlement so new it didn't have a name, then west a ways over to the main pike. It'd take us to Valdosta. Or we could take a less traveled way through the woods before we get to the pike. Everyone we asked had a different set of directions, but the main thing was that if we went south, we'd not be too far off, regardless which way we chose.

The captain went ahead leading the horse; I came up behind. My feet and legs moved from habit, but my stomach was empty and it seemed my will was weakening.

Finally he spoke, "Come alongside, Tench. I want you to tell me about your journal."

Although I thought I wasn't in the mood to talk, I moved to his side and opened my shirt to show him how I'd strapped it on.

"It's all about what happened to Lance and me since we left Avalon in April '63. It was his before it was mine. After he was killed, I knew he would want me to continue and I wanted to. When I find our folks, they'll read it and know the whole story. You can read it if you wish."

"If you want me to, I'd be glad to," he replied. "I keep a journal for the same reason. Someday, when I'm home again, I'll be able to share these times with my wife, children, and—who knows—maybe with the rest of the world."

He began to ask questions. It seemed he wanted to know everything. Soon I was telling him what I had written and how Lance and I had lived for the past two years. I forgot how hungry and tired I was. As we plodded along, I began to notice the shadows deepening and through the woods, an occasional glimmer of orange in the western sky. We crossed a thin wood bridge and kept to the edge of the thicket bordering the road.

When we heard horsemen approaching, we pushed into the brush and made our way to the stream again. All the while, I kept my story going.

He interrupted, "I think this is the Alapaha River. We can follow along for a while." He turned suddenly and looked at me. "How're you doing, Tench? You must be tired and hungry. I am."

I can't believe I hadn't complained. He had decided I would go to Florida with him and I was determined he wouldn't be sorry. I knew he wanted to get there as fast as possible. We needed to eat something without building a fire and I thought of what Mama and Miss Lottie had taught us about getting along in the woods.

"If you don't mind eating wild plants, they're all around us," I said. "Mama said we had to have them if we couldn't find vegetables and I've not had anything green for a while. This trail is full of eating weeds, lamb's quarters, wild onions, dandelions." I put my bag aside and reached down by my feet, pulled up one of the plants scattered about the trail. "We can graze like cattle. The horse might like some too."

The captain grinned. "That's sensible, Tench. My wife, Lola, would appreciate you. Her herb and green garden is a source of great pride for her." He bent over and joined me in pulling up a healthy sample of lamb's quarters.

"It's very good, cooked. But Mama and Miss Lottie serve it with a little bacon sprinkled on it, just as it is. Starting in May, I used to gather it for our table. That was one of my chores," I explained. I noticed him wrinkle up his face as he carefully sampled his bunch. I held mine up to the horse and she nibbled it daintily, then I reached into the saddlebag at my feet and pulled out some hardtack. Handing it to him, I said, "This is probably more to your liking. I've been saving it for an emergency. I'd say this is an emergency."

It was dark now. We were heading south on the west bank of the river. I was aware the river was broader here as the space of silence widened in the east and night voices came from the bank. Ahead, the throb of frogs and cicadas hushed at our step, then continued after we passed. Owls hooted in trees above us and mallards and wood ducks rustled on the shore below.

After we passed a bend in the river, the way became rougher and we began to trip over roots and driftwood and stumbled into marshy ground. Our pace slowed as our boots filled with water.

The captain was cheerful. "Abigail's doing all right."

"Sir?"

"The horse. I named her. She has slogged beside us without a whimper. All the Abigails I ever have known have been patient and long-suffering. The name is fitting."

At the next bend in the river, a fork appeared in the path ahead. The horse turned naturally into the widened trail leading away from the spongy land.

"I trust Abigail," he laughed. "With good horse sense, she leads and we'll humbly follow." Then he asked, "Tench, do you know what an enigma is?"

"I don't, sir."

"It's a mystery. A puzzle. I'm naming the settlement ahead that has no name—Enigma."

"Oh," I said. "I like the word. Enigma … Enigma … Enigma. Sounds like an Indian word."

Moving along, I became aware again of my discomfort. I admitted to myself that I was tired and weak, my stomach was empty, my boots were soggy and my feet hurt. Yet I kept my silence, remembering all the occasions in times past when I hadn't been so agreeable.

The captain stopped suddenly. A light flickered through the heavy brush. We paused and hushed. The horse moved about nervously and he patted her. I pressed against the bushes and pushed the branches back. With his head next to mine, we looked out upon a small clearing lit by a lantern hanging on a tree.

"Shh," the captain cautioned.

I saw two figures silhouetted in the light of the campfire. I leaned forward. A fat man was stuffing himself on food piled high in a metal dish. Beside him—unmistakably—was Shears, his hammer jaw working away as he forked food from a skillet over the fire into his mouth.

"Captain, sir, these are the people who stole my horse." I grasped his arm and lowered my voice.

Captain John gently pulled the branches back. I saw Night at the edge of the woods behind them. His back was towards us and he was loaded with two large packs. He was tethered to two trees with short ropes tied to each tree.

"That is Night. Lance's horse, my horse." I forgot to whisper.

"Quiet. Shush," Captain John warned and whispered, "Take Abigail down the trail. We must get her away from here. Tether her in the brush. They've put down for the night. We may have a long wait, but we'll get your horse. After I get him, you follow with Abigail. We'll need our knives."

Nervous, but glad at the chance to get Night back, I moved Abigail down into the deep shadows off the trail and took my knife from my belt. When I returned to our lookout, Captain John decided to circle the campsite to the opposite side.

"I'll go the other way. We'll meet at the trees where Night is tied. I can slash the rope on one side. You get the other," I suggested.

"Good. Tench, keep out of sight. It wouldn't be good for them to know you are with me."

Going in opposite directions through the brush, we quietly circled the camp. I caught sight of the captain a few times while the two men were always within view. I watched them polish off the food. Shears wiped his mouth on his sleeve and reached to a branch above him for a garland of moss, rolled it into a ball and wiped out the pan. The fat one wiped his fork on his pants, stuck it in his pocket, and yawned. Shears put the skillet in one of the packs strapped on Night. He adjusted the packs and picked through them. Night moved nervously, pulling from his touch.

"Hol' still, you devil!" he shouted. When Night whinnied, he struck him across the flanks. Then he tossed a couple of blankets from the pack and pulled the rope fast on both sides.

My grip tightened on the knife. I bit my lip when I saw Night try to move, lifting his hoofs in place.

"Har, Joe, blanket." Shears threw one to the other fellow and dropped one on the ground beside him.

"Gonna bank the fire?" Joe asked. "Keeps wild things away." Joe's voice was thin and whiney. Shears, coarse and loud.

"Yeah. Yeah," Shears replied. "How come yuh can't do nothing yerself? I cook and do it all an yuh set on your hunkers like a woman."

"I do nothin' cuz I can't do nothin'. I'm not very smart."

"Yuh smart as a red-tail fox." Shears fussed while he gathered an armload of wood. Joe sighed heavily as he lay down on a pile of brittle leaves and pulled the blanket around him.

"I ought to dump yuh," Shears snarled, "Yer just dead weight."

Joe's answer was muffled under the blanket. Shears poked around in the fire and added wood, then plopped down beside it. I saw him reach into his pocket, take out a quid of tobacco and, slivering off a piece, popped it into his mouth. With his eyes on the fire, he settled back and began to chew, his jaw working in hard circles. Shortly, he spit an arc of juice into the fire.

Night whinnied again. I caught my breath when I heard Abigail respond from her hiding place.

"Be damned," Shears snorted, "sounds like company."

Shears stood up and looked about. When he reached Night's side, Captain John suddenly appeared at the opening in front of Night. Shears reached for the rifle hanging over the saddle and Night began moving and jerking. I hurried through the brush towards Night, to the rope on my side, and looked out to see Shears holding the gun on the captain.

"Whatcha want?" he yelled. "Hold off. Don't want no strangahs sneaking 'round here."

The captain held his hands out and continued to approach. "I don't mean any harm, sir. I'm lost. Just trying to find my way to Valdosta."

Still covered with the blanket, Joe pushed it off and propped up on his elbow. His mouth was open and he was blinking.

"Where yuh from?" Gun steady, Shears studied the captain.

Hidden in the brush, with my hand against the tree, I drew the knife down and slashed the rope. The tether lay limp on the ground. Neither Night or Shears seemed to notice.

I heard Captain John say, "Just been paroled. I'm on my way to find my family."

"What's yer name?"

"Taylor. Kinfolk are in Valdosta. Wife, children, and my mother."

"Whole family? So how come yer lost? Yuh from here, yuh'd know yer way."

Captain John was standing at his side now. "It's not my home. Family refugeed from Virginia. Haven't seen them since the war began. Have to hunt them up after I get there."

All at once, the captain sprang forward and snatched the rifle, tossing it high into the brush. It landed an arm's length from me. I picked it up and looked back to see him mount Night and slash the other rope. Night was bucking and twisting.

I bolted through the bush onto the trail. Shears was shouting. Running through the shadows, I reached Abigail as the captain streaked by, leaving me far behind. Shots sounded. Joe or Shears was shooting into the bush. Abigail was no match for Night. I thrust the rifle through the haversack and rocked in the saddle, digging my heels into her belly. Slowly, she began to amble along with shots whizzing through the brush.

When the shouts drew closer, I stopped, jumped off, threw a bag over my shoulder, and led the horse, making better time on foot. Shears was gaining. I dropped the lead, yanked off the other haversack, and ran ahead, hoping she would follow.

A short time before, I thought I'd never been so tired or hungry. Now, my heart was racing and I was filled with excitement that lifted my body, and I moved weightlessly, my feet scarcely seeming to touch the ground.

They must have caught up with Abigail because the shouts ceased. I was sorry to have left her at their mercy, yet I knew if they depended on her, they'd never catch me.

When the trail opened onto a widened roadway, I continued south. This was still the deep backwoods, lonely and forsaken, far from civilization and the well-traveled pike.

May 10, 1865

BETWEEN SLOGGING FOOTFALLS AND BAGS JOUNCING OVER
my shoulders, I strained to hear other sounds in the night. Only the
thrum of the frog chorus or the shrill cry of some threatened animal,
and my own joggling marred the silence. I thought the captain must
have gone far ahead.

Looking upward, faraway stars pricked the black cover of night.
It seemed, as my eyes searched the darkness, the stars suddenly had
spilled from the sky as fireflies flashed their tiny lights all around me.

Later, ahead on the road, I saw a dark hulk with a thin halo of light
and I wondered if it might be the captain. Since I had left the noise
and danger of Joe and Shears behind, I stopped and put down my
bags, made a cup of my hands and blew, sounding the signal that
Night would recognize.

A horse whinnied and I rushed towards it. "Ho there," I called.

As I approached, the dark hulk took the form of a horse and buggy
in a flush of lamplight. "Ahoy there," a strong voice rang out. "Vat ees
your pleasure?"

Lamps on both sides of the buggy spread light on the scene,
revealing a plump man with a beard in a billowing black cape, a large
brimmed hat and huge travel goggles. He pulled off the big glasses
and I saw before me the strong features of a large face with dark glistening eyes.

"Vell. Vell. Vat has ve here? Are you lost, leetle black bird?" He had
a strange accent. "Vat's going on?" he asked. "First, a horseman passes
like a bat from ze bowels of ze earth and ve haf to stop our horse. Now
you come lickety-splitting along. Ver is ezrybody going by so fast?
Who you are?"

Another, a skinny, long-legged man, stepped from the shadows of the cab. I set my bags down and with my shirt sleeve, wiped sweat streaming from my forehead. We studied each other as I caught my breath. Both men were smiling.

"Vat's you running for?" he asked.

"For my life, sir. Two gunman are shooting and chasing me."

"And for vat you carry a musket? I like vat you disarm, please." He reached for the barrel sticking from my bag and threw it into the brush.

"It was their gun. It landed close to my hiding place."

"Then reason to fly, leetle bird. Do you know who vas the horseman who passed?"

"Yes, sir. I was with him."

"And who he is?"

"Mister Taylor. Mister John Taylor."

The gentlemen exchanged glances. I explained, "He's just been paroled and looking for his family who refugeed to Valdosta." Although I knew it wasn't true I repeated what I'd heard the captain say to far less friendly strangers.

As I felt and heard the sound of hoofs pounding against the earth, I spun around. At the same time, the man in the cape put his hand on my shoulder. "Out of my vay, lad!" he exclaimed, pushing me against the buggy, "Somsing's coming fast."

I cupped my hands and blew into my fist again. In a flash, the sound of hoofs ceased. There were whinnies from the approaching horse and a response from the one beside the buggy.

"Ah, leesen. He talks to horses. How did you do vat?"

The skinny one nudged his companion. "The accent's not necessary, Judah. He's not the enemy."

Here, at once, the captain and Night were moving into the circle of light. After he saw me, his gaze rested on the once-again goggled and caped stranger and his tall companion. He studied them and suddenly exploded with laughter. The captain dismounted and handed me the reins. Night bobbed his head and nuzzled me. I brushed my cheek against his forelock and latched my arms about his neck.

"And who might you be?" The captain was choking with laughter as he addressed the strangers.

"Sir, I am zee French journalist, Jacques Philipe Bonfal. My initials, JPB, you will observe are the same as the former Secretary of State, Judah P. Benjamin. And—most remarkably—the translation of my name from Cajun French is 'A Good Disguise.'"

He was grinning and said, "Thees ees my translator, Monsieur Loevy." Then, reaching over to clasp Captain John's hand, he exclaimed in unaccented speech, "Captain John Taylor Wood. I never thought I'd see you again."

Captain John grasped and embraced JPB and the colonel, as close friends would. Laying his hand on my shoulder, he turned to me and said, "This youngster is Tench Traymore, from the family of distinguished Virginia Traymores and, later, from this sovereign state of Georgia. For the past two years, he accompanied Lance Traymore Matthews into battle. Lance was killed at White Oak Road. Now Tench is on his way to Florida where he thinks his family may have resettled after General Sherman's raid through the South."

"As you can see, I know this young man," Captain John smiled. He hesitated, suddenly serious, "Judah, let me tell you about Jefferson." The merriment gone from his face and voice, he told them then of the president's capture and our escape.

As he listened, the expression on JPB's face saddened and Colonel Loevy shook his head. JPB sighed, "Poor Jefferson, beloved Varina." He took off his hat and rubbed his bearded chin before he spoke again. "So now there's more reason to move fast. They're already hard on our trail. You know, John, they'd get us both for treason."

"They'd hang me."

"Both of us."

"Who knows? I knew we'd be captured when Jefferson halted in his flight to stay with Varina. Had we continued our journey, we'd have been far from here by now. There was a chance that Varina might not be safe. We'd had word that a band of renegade soldiers planned to rob her, take her horses and household treasures, and who knows what else. His concern for her and the children has cost him his freedom. For that, he can't be faulted. I would have done the same had my wife and children been in such peril. I advised him to go on and let me stay to guard them, but he was adamant, said if it cost him his life, he would never desert her.

"Varina and the poor children," Judah sighed again. "I'm so close to them. I wonder, oh I wonder, what is to come of them?"

Captain John spoke quickly, "These are things we could not change, nor control. But now, I want to tell you of our contacts. When we reach Madison, Florida, General Joe Finegan will be waiting to help. He'll provide us with escape routes and supplies, and names of our Florida friends. He'll have plenty of good advice. He knows the country and the populace. General Breckinridge will join us there. We have many friends alerted and waiting to help us in Florida—"

JPB interrupted, "My path is more direct, John. I plan to see General Joe also, when I pass through Madison. I hope to meet with Breckinridge at the Bronson farm north of Madison. As I see it, time is primary. I'll not tarry long in one spot. I know of your concern for Breckinridge. I will not burden you with another encumbrance. I fully believe that he travels fastest who travels without Judah P. Benjamin. I'm clumsy and would slow you down. We must part, dear friend."

As they embraced in a warm farewell, the strongly built, tall captain towered above the short, round figure of JPB. Colonel Loevy backed away a few steps and stood rigidly at attention. He spoke in a clear ringing voice, "Sir, John Taylor Wood—Captain of the Navy and Colonel of the Army—greatest Sea Raider in two Armies."

The honor he showed in that salute will stay in my mind forever. All that he felt was reflected in his serious eyes and erect posture. When he clicked his heels and raised his hand, I felt his pride. There was a moment of silence before Captain John returned the salute. I heard his murmured thanks to the colonel.

As JPB and Colonel Loevy stepped back into the buggy, I told Captain John how I lost Abigail and how I had come to have the musket JPB had thrown in the brush.

"Poor Abigail," he said. "I'm afraid her future is uncertain." Night was nibbling the buttons on my shirt and butted his head gently against my chest. "You can rejoice that you have your own horse again." He reached beyond me to stroke Night's neck. "He's a splendid animal. You've served each other well, Tench. A fine combination." He turned again and included JPB and Colonel Loevy. "I must ask one last boon of all of you. Please, I need to go to Valdosta and I'd like to use your horse, Tench. Since you're going to Bronson's farm, Judah, would you take Tench with you? It'll only be a few days before I arrive, so if you must go on, you may leave Tench off for me. I will come soon as I finish my business in Valdosta." When he looked at me, I nodded, but I honestly felt disappointed that I was to be separated again, so soon, from Night.

Mister Benjamin responded quickly, smiling and nodding, "Delighted." He spoke to me, patting the seat beside him, "Here, Tench. Throw your bags on top of ours and make yourself very narrow so you can sit between us."

"Yes, sir." I did as bade, threw my bags on the floor, leaped into the buggy, and edged my way into the space offered. For a moment, I held my breath and sucked in my stomach, trying to make myself narrow and occupy as little of the seat as possible. I tried not to intrude on JPB's softness and moved closer to the thin, hard-boned colonel on my other side.

The lamps lit up the roadside making spooky shadows dance along the underbrush as the horse lunged ahead. I looked into JPB's face and saw he was smiling. Sparks of light danced in his crinkly eyes and a glow brightened his apple cheeks.

Shortly, he spoke, "Courageous man—Wood. None, braver. If everyone had fought as he, we wouldn't be fleeing now."

"Well I know," Loevy responded.

JPB leaned toward me and asked how I came to be traveling with the captain. Question followed question. He wanted to know about my life before the war. About my folks, my survival during the war and on the road. The good and the bad encounters.

I said, at last, "Lance and I recorded everything that happened. In the beginning, it was my cousin Lance Traymore Matthews' journal. After he was killed, I continued keeping the journal—in my words."

"Excellent. You've made a commitment to bring words and paper together. This is a union that outlasts time. After the dust of our bones settles, our true remains will be found in those fine trails recorded on a piece of parchment, created on the crest of some grand moment in the guise of poetry, letter, or memoir." He gave a sigh and shrugged. "For myself, somehow I fear that. I don't wish to have strangers interpreting my soul and substance when I'm not around to defend myself."

"That," said Colonel Loevy, "is precisely why it is needed. You must write while you are able so your life will be portrayed accurately later."

JPB's laughter rang through the night. "Perhaps. And, so, too, shall Tench. What story would you want to be sure was accurately told?"

"One thing I'd want to accurately tell is how, as soon as his father died, my ancestor Samuel Traymore III freed all the slaves, including my people, on Avalon. Over five hundred of them! Some neighbors and slave owners in the county burned down the mansion and stables, torched his tobacco crops, and stole his cattle. They ran him and his brother Solomon II clear out of Virginia."

Colonel Loevy shook his head and clicked his tongue, saying, "One would have hoped Virginia had a more sympathetic attitude towards freedom."

Counting on a finger as he spoke, JPB responded, "It depended on the convictions of everyone involved. Number one, your neighbors; number two, the church; and number three, the Virginia government. Those were the sources of the big debate. Many of the churches were against slavery. As I understand it, if you were able to free your slaves, it could cause an uprising among your neighbors and their slaves. There was no government that could send freed slaves back to their homeland, nor could slave owners be paid for their loss. Many reasons could have caused Samuel Traymore's neighbors to act as they did."

"Well, be that as it might, once they were burned out, he and my great grandfather Solomon ended up in Thomson, Georgia, where they built another Avalon, not as big as the first. There were only a dozen or so servants and a few field hands, but Samuel and Solomon worked together. Soon as the house was built, and the land tilled, and tobacco and cotton set out, Samuel and my great-grandfather made their first trip to Charleston. There they found their wives—Miss Harriet of the South Carolina Draytons and her maid Lucy."

Benjamin exploded into such jollity he had to struggle to control himself. He spoke at last, his voice, so full of laughter, spilled over with hiccups and giggles. "South Carolina served the Traymores well. For them, a bridal marketplace. For my family, who emigrated to Charleston and stayed there, it meant the discovery of the best of everything in the New World."

"How old are you?" Loevy asked suddenly.

"On April 24th, I was fifteen," I answered

"Judah, what were you doing at fifteen?" the colonel asked.

Benjamin chuckled and answered, "My loving parents did all they could for me, but it was rich friends who sent me a thousand miles away from my home in Charleston, up North to Yale University."

Loevy shook his head. "So young, so far away. You must have been a very smart lad."

"Too young. Too smart. I was too young to handle myself in such a rarefied atmosphere. There was nothing in the muscle of my character that could have given me strength to endure what Tench has experienced. For that reason I rather botched that great opportunity." Only then did he draw up his small mouth into a tight knot and the smile disappeared.

I don't know how he had botched up his great opportunity but I couldn't feel sorry for him. At least he'd had the chance with prospects. Not everybody did.

Did Benjamin ever think of all the advantages he had started out with as a young man, I wondered. As a bright young boy he had love and the support of his family and rich friends. When he was my age, he was able to go off to a fine university. Certainly, for dark folk, that wouldn't be possible. His success was assured by an entire family who had prepared him and backed him. Doubtless, he had been fortunate in every important step that followed.

I had to speak. "It wouldn't be easy for anyone of my skin color to start a new line or—fill a purse."

"Your color is no excuse, lad. I am a Jew, which at that time might have been a disadvantage. In respect to position and purse, I haven't done badly—though perhaps I did not fulfill my potential at Yale due to my extreme youth, not my being Jewish. As a child, my parents emphasized their pride in being Jewish. This was evidenced in their choice of Judah for my name. I learned that I had to have more ambition and had to work much harder than others. I also believed I had to be more tolerant of others while trying to ignore my own sensitive nature. Finally, after some pain, I made a great discovery. The real source of the prejudice and resentment that I thought I saw in others, began in my own mind. Once I got myself out of the way, I could see others more clearly."

In the fading glow of the lamps, I saw JPB's smile return as he reached over and touched my hand. The last I remember was the clop of hoofs and clack of wheels on the deep-rutted road and jerky motion of the wagon with the sound of their voices. JPB's was soaring and dipping like a bird in flight, while Colonel Loevy's droned like a summer locust.

When the wagon came to a stop, I wakened. My head had fallen onto Colonel Loevy's lap. He was asleep, his legs straddling the pile of saddle bags, his head propped against the buggy's steel side brace.

In the soft light just before sunrise, JPB had driven the horse deep into the shadows of a thick, piney wood. He stepped down and threw some blankets over the ground already heavily padded with pine needles.

I hopped down after him. Colonel Loevy groaned as he unfolded his long legs and straightened himself out again. "We'll rest here before we take to the road again," JPB said as he shook oats from one of the bags into a small bucket and hung it from a low branch within the horse's reach. Then he began wiping the horse down.

Both men were sleeping now. I couldn't. After my nap in the buggy, I was like water dancing on a hot skillet and I could not turn myself off. Yesterday and the night before were so full. My brain teemed with images and thoughts, and so I began filling the pages of my journal, and as I wrote, I wondered about JPB, especially when he was my age.

May 11, 1865

THE TOP OF A NEW DAY OPENED UP BEFORE ME. AFTER MAKing up many pages of missing days in this journal, I built a small wood fire, took my skillet and some meal from the knapsack, and began to prepare hoecake batter, using water from the nearby stream. I thought the gentlemen soon would be waking.

Loevy arose first and strode down the path away from the buggy. Shortly afterwards, JPB sat up, stretched, and yawned. From one of the bags, he took some maps and spread them out before him on the blanket, studying them closely. After awhile, apparently satisfied, he put them back. He took a handkerchief from his pocket, wiped his eyes, and cleared his throat.

For a while, JPB seemed to be talking to himself, as if searching through his memory, or exploring the sound of a few words. "Tears, idle tears, I know not what they mean... Tears... tears. The days that are no more..." He took a deep breath; his voice suddenly lifted, strong and clear, filling the air and ringing through the campsite:

> *Tears, idle tears, I know not what they mean*
> *Tears from the depth of some divine despair*
> *Rise in the heart, and gather to the eyes*
> *In looking on the happy autumn fields*
> *And thinking of the days that are no more*
> *Ah, sad and strange as in dark summer dawns*
> *The earliest pipe of half awakened birds*
> *To dying ears, when into dying eyes*
> *The casement slowly grows a glimmering square:*
> *So strange, the days that are no more.*

Perhaps sensing my puzzled look, JPB turned to me, "When I was a lad, I had an old schoolmaster who exercised a most effective discipline over his students. Every trouble-maker was forced to pay for his mischief by memorizing from Shakespeare, or Tennyson, or Byron, or some poet of such classic renown. I'm afraid I owe my huge literary repertoire more to my inclination towards mischief than to a youthful proclivity for literature." His laughter rang through the woods before he put his hands to his mouth and called, "Loevy!"

When the colonel finally appeared, his head was wet and his clothes clung to his body. "Took a bath in the stream yonder," he said pointing to the woods behind him.

JPB grinned. "I'm refreshed enough by sleep. After we eat Tench's meal, we best start moving towards our destination."

Loevy smiled. "Heard you spouting Tennyson again, Judah."

"Ah, so," he nodded. "I am soothed by his gentle language. In fact, I find infinite comfort in poetry. I have discovered that everything I ever experienced happened first to many of the great ones—Shakespeare, Byron, Tennyson—filtering through their remarkable minds and hearts into the most exquisite, yet relevant terms. What a rule for life—experience into poetry." He repeated, "So sad, so strange, the days that are no more."

Hungry for food, and, I suppose for some praise, I placed the food before them and watched for some sign of approval as they ate. Benjamin ate delicately with fine bites, tasting and chewing deliberately, holding his fork as a woman might. Loevy ate with great relish. Both were ravenous.

I have a secret for making good hoecake. It's all in the mixing. After greasing the pan with a piece of fatback, I pour boiling water into the cornmeal, adding just enough to hold it together. Without milk or egg, I mix lightly and cook slowly. I'm proud of what I can do with cornmeal and a little water. I hoped they'd noticed too. Although they said nothing, they kept reaching into the skillet until it was all gone. I had made a big one and had cut it into eight pieces.

"Well, what is it, lad?" JPB asked.

I had been standing before them, watching them eat, completely unaware that I was staring. I hadn't meant to be rude.

"Is it approbation you wish?" he asked. I didn't know what he meant.

"Approval. Praise." He put his fork to his mouth and ate the last small bite. Had he seen the need for praise on my face? I felt embarrassed.

"My boy, take time out for one of life's small lessons. Do not expect praise for a task well done. If it's not, you can be sure, then, you'll hear about it. Regardless of what job you have to do, there is only one way to do it—the best you can."

His words stung. I spoke almost with spite, "Excuse me, sir. I was hoping there'd be some hoecake left in the skillet. I didn't eat." Before the words had slipped out, I was sorry for what I was saying.

"Do you have some cornmeal?" He was unconcerned.

"Yes, sir."

"Use the water boiling in the pot on the coals. Make some mush. There's no time to cook more hoecake. For hoecake such as you served us, it takes careful mixing and cooking with a gentle hand. Another lesson for your book—the cook must always count himself in the pot."

He wasn't sorry for me. Too, he had respectfully described the way I had cooked. Once more, I was ashamed of my quick snappishness.

I was nudged by uneasy memory. Lance once said that sometimes I was like a pup that needed weaning, and when I got my eyeteeth, I might grow up.

JPB bent close to me and whispered, "Take heart, little black bird. When I was your age, I learned you can take nothing that doesn't belong to you—neither praise nor purse. Everything has to be earned."

While JPB fed the horse and Loevy packed things away and snuffed out the fire, I gobbled up the pan of mush and wiped out my utensils with a ball of moss.

Long scarves of moss hung from the bare limbs of a dead tree nearby. Loevy lined the buggy floor and seat with pillows of moss, with a thick layer separating me from his wet-clothed body. JPB stood by watching. "Incredible plant, this Spanish moss," he observed. "Draws its sustenance from the air and depends not on another body, dead or alive, for support. It festoons empty space with death shrouds. It's useful in housekeeping and decorating chores and it is indispensable to the toilette. It provides one of Nature's finest beddings. Alas, though, it possesses one distressing quality." Here, he quivered to an exaggerated extreme, "During a certain season, it's the nesting place for the woods' tiniest pests—redbugs." He lay his hand on Loevy's arm, halting his moss-layering progress. "Tell me, Loevy, do you know if this is that certain season?"

Loevy hesitated. "Sir, I can't be sure. I think I have experienced their greatest assaults in the heat of summer. It's not quite that yet."

"But, you aren't certain? In other words," JPB concluded, "you are making an experiment, and we, your victims, are to determine that this is not their season. If you are wrong, we all will suffer and have to bear the consequences of your mistake."

They laughed. JPB climbed to his seat and his laughter shook the buggy. I wasn't accustomed to his type of playful humor, but it now infected me so I scarcely noticed how fast we were going as JPB's whip lashed the air over the horse's back.

Both men suddenly fell silent as they watched the road ahead. I focused on the horse that JPB earlier had so thoughtfully tended and now urged on with his dancing whip. I glanced down at JPB's hands. The left lay open, the reins loose across his deeply lined palm, while the strong long fingers of his right tightly gripped the whip. The pleasant expression on his face was unchanged.

Loevy's face was less pleasant. His eyes wide, he stared ahead. A scowl ruffled his face and his mouth gaped open. His long legs were propped up on the bags. With every bump, one hand slapped against his knee while he clung to the side of the buggy with the other. JPB sat like a rock, Loevy moved about loosely, like a marionette, and I kept popping up like a jack-in-the-box.

JPB's course was set. If there was danger or discomfort in making such haste, he ignored it. He was more afraid of being captured and anxious to get along. I heard JPB say, "While we sleep and eat, refresh ourselves in a stream and recite poetry, our pursuers move on silent wings with no other thought than that of the bounty to be collected on our capture. You won't be affected, Loevy, but my name ranks high on their traitor list."

Finally, JPB stopped on a river bank. We three took part in feeding, watering, and wiping the horse down. We started again with less speed—to Loevy's (and my) great relief. His face relaxed as he settled himself and I was securely wedged between the two.

Despite the bumps, I had enjoyed the wild ride. I'd plenty of that sort of experience. Lance always had been ready for a race. With me sitting behind him, we had galloped through woods, crossed rivers, and passed troops, sometimes challenging the cavalry's gait.

But I didn't think about Lance long. It was on the last stretch of road taking us to the Bronson farm that I fell sick. I suffered such dizziness and nausea that JPB stopped to let me out of the buggy several times. Both men were patient although I knew they wanted to outrun the Feds.

At one point, Colonel Loevy set the saddlebags on the seat between them while I stretched out on the moss bed on the floor. As we pressed on, they both braced their feet against the front plate above me and JPB reined in more tightly. Through the rest of the ride, I bobbed on the surface of awareness, painfully wishing to escape into its greater depths.

A dreary dawn broke. Black and gray clouds swirled across the low-hung sky. A heavy wind lashed at the buggy, pelting us with rain and hail. JPB and Loevy's attention stayed on the road and as we rocked back and forth, I finally fell into a deep sleep.

May
(after the 10th, the dates are a jumble in my memory.)

A FIRM HAND SHOOK MY SHOULDER. "WAKE UP." IT WAS Benjamin, his head close to mine and I thought much time had passed since when I went to sleep in the buggy. "Waken, little black bird." I remember his kind voice reaching into my deep space.

Another voice. "Leave him in the barn. Don't bring the Nigra in the house."

And Benjamin, "He's with me. I pay with gold."

No more protest.

I felt myself lifted in strong arms, rain falling on my face, moving up steep steps, and then—footsteps sounding on a wooden floor. Yet, I kept rocking.

Later, I learned I had spent a day and a night on a pallet on the floor. Like pieces of a strange puzzle, that time was not of one piece. Long silences. Snatches of conversation. People coming and going. Doors opening and slamming. Dishes rattling. Laughter. Quarreling. Whispers and shouts.

Again, JPB: "So many worlds, so much to do; so little done. Such things to come." Poetry again? I couldn't ask. Then, "I must go, Tench. Captain will be coming soon. You'll be in good hands. Sing your own songs, Tench. Don't be afraid." A pause. "Godspeed, dear boy."

In my silent place, I felt the sadness of farewell. There were so many things I wanted to know about Judah Benjamin.

A whip of lightning. Thunder drumming. Voices droning beyond the large closed door. Heavy, rackety breathing filled the room. I was lying on a pallet in a large bare room, furnished only with a huge master's bed and a small washstand. The walls were bare except the one across from me where a large picture of Jefferson Davis hung. I rose up on my elbows, took out my record and pencil. I'd try to make notes.

In the bed, there was a large body, topped by a heavy thatch of dark hair, lying motionless among mussed bedding. When I pulled up, the room began to spin. I closed my eyes, let myself down onto the pallet. The door opened. Two young men entered, along with the smell of food cooking. It was a smell I ordinarily enjoyed, but now it made my stomach churn. I thought I'd vomit. I lay my face against the journal.

I noticed a chamber pot beside a pair of boots under the bed. I'd reach the pot if this urge continued. Lying on my side, I drew my knees to my chest, shut my eyes, and fought the sick feeling. I tried to refocus and watched the visitors. Each could've been any Georgia boy, but judging from their age, their erect posture, I thought they might be soldiers—probably officers.

For a while, both men stood silent beside the sleeping figure. "Father," one finally spoke in a voice too soft to waken. "Dad, it's us— Clifton and Cabell."

The taller one touched his father lightly. "He'd been coming down sick for more than a week, but he kept on going."

Cabell shook his head. "If he hadn't, he'd been captured." He pointed to me. "The boy?"

"Miss Bronson said he came in with a French journalist with his companion and translator. He told her a gentleman would pick the boy up later. She said he paid in gold for the boy to stay in the house. The man left all his fine clothes in exchange for her husband's old farm clothes. Said she sewed gold in the hems of his shirts and trousers and lined his wide belt with it, too. He told her he needed to get some important stories, but was afraid he'd be robbed and slain if he appeared too well off."

Thinking of what my knowledge would add to their conversation, I lifted my head to see better. When I did, everything began to spin again. I flattened myself and drew some deep breaths. I'd move only my eyes.

There was a flurry of movement at the door and a tall young Negro entered carrying a trunk and set it at the head of the bed. Cabell greeted him, "Thank you, Tom. Any problems?"

"Yes, suh, Mister Cabell. Nothin' too bad. Wheel come off the wagon down the road apiece. When I fine one, I'll fix it. It got real tore up. Some parolers brought me up in an army wagon. They was headin' for the St. Johns River. Like us. Said they was goin' where no one would ever fine them. They was movin' plenty fast. They had two good cav'ry horses."

"Is that you, Tom Ferguson?" The voice came from the bed.

"Yessuh. Yessuh. You feelin' better now, suh?"

"We won't be using the wagons, Tom. We're riding from now on. I'm going to get out of this bed today if it kills me. That you, Cliff?"

"And Cabell, sir." Both sons moved closer.

"Clay with you?" He swung his legs over the bedside.

"We slept in the barn last night, Dad. He's there, now. He wants to see you before we leave."

"Tom, go get him. Cabell, bring the trunk alongside here and open it."

His rich voice filled every corner. I turned slowly to my side. In the dim light of the stormy day, I could see he was a big man with a shock of dark hair and a moustache like a giant antenna that reached to his shoulders. His large blue eyes caught my interest. They were the strangest blue I'd ever seen. More unusual, because they were framed by dark shadows caused by their deep set and fringe of heavy black lashes.

Instantly, I remembered one day long ago, when I had come from the woods and brought some passion flowers to Mama Zulma. She had held them for a moment, brushed them against her cheek, then taking a piece of black velvet from her quilting basket, lay them upon it. His eyes reminded me of that.

Cabell moved the trunk to the bedside and lifted its latch. He spoke in a quiet voice, "Father, Clifton and Clay must surrender and give their paroles. They want to get it over. I want to go with you."

His father stood up. What a tall man. I noticed he was wearing underwear that was too small. The pearl buttons of the undershirt weren't buttoned and the arms scarcely reached his elbows. The large buttons of the drawers remained unfastened and the legs of the underwear reached only to his knees.

"Indeed, Cabell. You must go with them, too. Spread a blanket here." He sat down on the edge of the bed, slowly removing the trunk's contents, ticking off each item as he took it out. "I must get rid of this excess. Put them down there, Cabell. Here, these two blue checkered shirts, my Kentucky jeans and hunting jacket. Badges, insignias—throw them out." He unfolded a leather sewing kit with needles, safety pins, thread, and scissors. "Ah this, my housewife. I'll need it. And this. And this." He lay out beside him, the sewing kit, a leather personal bag, and a writing case. "And these—belt, under- wear, blanket, tobacco. Necessary and take up little space. And—" he paused and withdrew two small drawstring bags, then reached down into his boot. I watched him fill both bags halfway with gold pieces. Opening the tobacco tin, he filled the pouches to overflowing with tobacco before pulling the strings tight. He handed one to each son, saying, "Guard this. Don't smoke the tobacco."

At that moment, the door opened and a young man dragging a haversack entered. "Hello, Clay." Both sons greeted the newcomer. He had arrived half-dressed, pausing in the doorway to tuck in his shirt, buckle his belt, and attempt to smooth his hair. He settled first one foot in a shoe, then the other, and bent to tie them. Dressed, he stood quiet and erect until the general glanced up and told him to come in.

"General Breckinridge, sir." He saluted and the general rose and returned with a salute that seemed funny considering the way he was dressed.

Clay joined the circle around the trunk. The general returned to his sorting. From the bottom, he took a leather-sheathed sword and held it out to his son. "I leave this in your care, Clifton."

"Father?" Surprised, Clifton took it in his hand, withdrew the sword from its sheath and read the engraving, "A Mark of Esteem and Admiration for our Much Loved Commander." He gazed at his father. "'From Finley and Bate.' That was after Missionary Ridge., right, Father?" Even in the ashy light of the dark day, the sword flashed as Clifton passed it over to Clay to examine. He reached to his father and embraced him.

A hush filled the room. Cabell walked to the window and looked outside. I discovered, in my concentration on the scene before me, my balance was returning. I pushed onto my elbows to see better, groped for my pencil and pad, and began writing.

I saw their faces now, father and son. The general's hand rested on his son's shoulder, their fine features profiled as they gazed at each other. The father, tall and straight, and Clifton, smaller, yet erect, seemed his echo.

"Please, Dad, let me come with you," Clifton pled.

"Son, I must insist. I don't know what dangers will be ahead. Already both my sons and you, too, Clay, have risked too much. You must go home and catch up on your lives. Four years gone. Your boyhood. Cliff, your mother will need you more than ever."

"Father," Clifton paused, "whatever risks you face, I want to face with you. I'd rather die with you than live without you."

Cabell came back to his father's side. "Father, Clifton has said it best, but I feel the same. I would want to be with you, whatever might happen."

"My sons, I know." For a moment he covered his face with his hands, then he took out a handkerchief and wiped his eyes. He seemed to struggle to get a hold of himself before he continued to empty the trunk. The pile on the blanket grew while the collection beside him would fit neatly in a haversack.

I was deeply touched now that I understood what was happening. The eyes of the father and his sons were glistening, as well as Clay's. I lay my head flat against the pallet. Their pain had kindled my own and I thought again of my return down the cedar-lined road that led to the ashes of Avalon.

The general removed the trunk tray, leaned over and, reaching inside, brought out a stack of leather-bound books. He put one aside, thumbed through the others. "Ah, how much these books have meant to me—my Shakespeare. For all life's moments, he found the most fitting words. Whether speaking of a full-hot house of anger, or tongues of dying men, or traitor doubts and lover's perjuries, or of men molded out of faults, or some soul of goodness in things evil.

Words, words, words. Indeed, he suits the action to the word, the word to the action."

Cabell turned to Clay, laughing. "As others worship God and the Bible, our father worships Shakespeare."

Their father chuckled and sat down, picked up the volume he had set aside. "Then—here is Plutarch—*The Rise and Fall of Athens*. How many times I have read this to learn anew with each reading? What a reward to learn from him that what was great in that distant age can serve as a model for now. All that is now, was before."

He turned the book over in his hands. "Parting with these volumes won't be easy, but I carry Shakespeare in my head and heart. I'll take only the Plutarch. In these piles—the detritus of an anguished life— take what you wish."

I wished I were one of the lucky ones sharing in his offer. There had been a large mahogany bookcase at Avalon. Miss Lottie kept its key in her apron pocket and when it rained, or on some other rare occasion, she would unlock the lead glass doors and let Lance and me take a book down. I was excited just to handle the books and smell that certain rich fragrance coming from the old wood mingling with the leather covers of old books. Often, the leather crumbled or smudged between our fingers. Miss Lottie taught us not to mark or tear the brittle pages.

In his room, Lance had five volumes by James Fennimore Cooper. We read the books, both together and alone, and I thought of them as our books. Whatever I read by myself, was mine and mine alone for that moment. When we read together, it was ours, the whole world of Leatherstocking Tales and Natty Bumpo. Our forests surrounding Avalon became the wilderness of Indians and pioneers created by Cooper. We became all his shining heroes, triumphing over great odds, always on the side of right and the free life. How I thrived under the spell of Cooper's magic. I realized that Shakespeare had cast the same kind of spell over General Breckinridge.

Clifton paused beside his father's belongings before moving to the stack of volumes on the bed. He picked up several and turned them over in his hand before stashing them into a pack on the floor. It was plain to see that his father's clothes would not fit him. Cabell and Clay chose a few items from the clothes piles, although they might have been large and airy on Cabell. Clay, of a larger frame, took some jeans, shirts, and a hunting jacket and stuffed them in his haversack. Cabell, not as tall as his father, took a shirt and jeans, and I know the arms and legs would have to be rolled up in order to fit.

"Tom, take only what you can comfortably carry," the general warned as Tom looked longingly at the stacks of clothes.

The door flew open and a short, bearded man stood in the doorway, beaming. "Well, suh," he said. "You weren't feeling so good last night. You look better today, except for the fit of your clothes." He laughed as he held his hand out to the general. "I'm Lore Bronson." He nodded towards the tall, heavy woman following him, "This is my wife, Hattie. She's been drying your clothes and ponchos in the kitchen." Behind them, I saw clotheslines crisscrossing the big steamy room with some heavy clothes dragging on the floor. There were several women moving quietly about, trying to raise the lines to higher hooks.

I've seen lots of folks like the Bronsons. Not at all like Lottie and Carson Matthews, but more like most of their farm neighbors and friends. They were people who had done well living off the land. Among their people, they were known as good folks. I might look at them differently. My opinions were reached by different circumstances—from my close association with Lottie and Carson. They were the ideal by which I measured all others.

Carson was a true gentleman. His manner and voice were soft. Mama Zulma said he always had possessed a courtly demeanor and educated speech. His skin was fair, his silver hair, fine as silk, and his light blue eyes were like faded porcelain. There were no scars or calluses on his slender hands and no stains or soil etched into his long fingers and nails.

But this Lore Bronson, he had a different look. The sun had bronzed his skin a deep iodine and streaked his white hair with gold. His hands were coarse with calluses and his nails rimmed in black. His manner and voice were rough, his language careless.

Now in his house, I was very aware of this man's smiling good nature, with ready hospitality for any white stranger who'd cross his threshold. Yet, through others like him that I had known, I felt I knew his other side.

In all likelihood, he farmed his own acreage without much help. There were always good neighbors, poor relations, and a few Negro families who hadn't run back north who'd give a hand when needed. The Negro folks weren't slaves anymore. No one treated them so, nor did they treat them as being part of their world either—they were just the "other kind"—a fact some white folks didn't let them forget.

I carry in my mind a picture of one of Lore's "kind" who had been known to mount his horse to chase a runaway slave back to the plantation from which he'd escaped. I remember the owner had aimed a pistol at his feet, with the ground erupting under him in a storm of dust every twenty feet or so.

He might be the same kind who'd poke mean fun when he saw a Negro mother with a brood of children all dressed up for church, one who'd say, "Now wouldn't one of them little pickaninnies make a fine mouthful for a hungry ol' alligator?" Then he'd hoot and the mother would laugh because she was scared, and maybe she really didn't understand his funniness and maybe she understood he expected her to look at the ground and laugh. The children would laugh too at the man who'd made their mama laugh. They'd clap their hands and dance around him. Then, holding up their hands to his pocket, they'd ask for pennies. Because he was such a funny man, they knew he'd dig up pennies to go around.

I wondered if Lore Bronson was that same kind.

Regardless of what sort of man he might prove to be, his wife seemed nice enough—though clearly tired. Mrs. Bronson's face was flushed and damp. Lights twinkled in her eyes even though they crinkled as she smiled and greeted everyone. "We have chicken frying and corn pones and sweet potatoes and lima beans in the pot. Yawl look like yuh could use a good meal." She started towards the kitchen, returned, and, lowering her voice, added, "Lore makes good elderberry wine. I know yuh could use some."

The general agreed, "We could, ma'am. We certainly could." As he spoke, he tried to pull a hunting jacket over his layered underwear, attempting to draw it together to cover the dark curly mass of hair on his broad chest.

Mrs. Bronson quickly took off the large apron covering her blue-checkered gingham dress and held it up to the general. Seeing her offering, he dropped the jacket, held out his arms, and let her slip the apron over his head and around him, where she tied it.

She spoke to Tom Ferguson, "Come into the kitchen, boy. I'll give you a platter of food. You can eat it on the back porch."

Lying still, I watched through squinting eyes when I sensed I wasn't in anyone's complete view. I wasn't hungry, but I knew in a day, or even a few hours, I'd be wishing I had some of that food.

I saw the women moving quietly about the kitchen, unhooking the laundry lines and moving them to the sheltered porch beyond. When they finished, they entered my room. Their voices were hushed as they wiped their hands on their aprons, which they removed, shook out, and put on again. They retied their sashes and drew themselves together, patting their hair and lightly brushing and flicking traces of cooking from their clothes.

One spoke. "Who yuh reckon he is?"

"When Hattie ask me to help cook, she said they was keeping some high gov'ment people running away from the Feds. Didn't say who."

"Maybe Prez'dent Davis?"

"When he passed to the kitchen I didn't look him in the eye. Hattie's right proud of this picture she says is of Prez'dent Davis. Did he look like him?" She stood in front of it. The others joined her.

"I'm not sure. Let me take another look."

"Miz Hattie say stay out of the way."

"We'll be very quiet—act as if we're not looking at him." The women returned to the kitchen as the general and his party settled at the long table.

I heard the general say, "It's been a long time since I last saw ham bubbling in a pan of milk gravy."

"Fried chicken, collards, corn, dumplings," Clay sang out.

"Plain country food." Hattie Bronson laughed.

The general's deep voice—"I assure you madam, it is a banquet fit for the Queen of England. You honor us. But, sir and madam, will you not join us?"

Lore, taking a bottle of wine from a cabinet, answered, "We joined you once in making it. Now eat well with our blessing." He filled their glasses and set the bottle on the table.

The general's voice lowered and the Bronsons and the women paused in their steps, bowing their heads while he asked the blessing. "Our Father, we thank You for bringing us safely down this long road. Bless the many good friends who have helped us along the way and the bountiful table now set before us. I ask Your continuing love, care, and guidance for my sons, Clifton and Cabell, and also for Clay. Bless all as we go on our way. We ask these blessings in the name of our Lord. Amen."

As one, they lifted their glasses. I heard the soft clink of cutlery touching china as they filled their plates. Their attention centered on the food, their eyes on their plates as they ate and drank with obvious pleasure. I wondered at the general's quick recovery from sickbed to honored guest at the Bronson's banquet table. Really miraculous. Lore continued bringing bottles of fresh wine from the big cabinet, filling their glasses, and staying at the general's elbow, giving him particular attention.

The women stood again beside Jefferson Davis's portrait. For some time, they spoke in whispers. I heard only the fire crackling in the big kitchen stove and rain slapping against the tin roof. Suddenly, things livened. Their voices rose. They stood in front of the picture waving their arms and pointing from the portrait to the general in the kitchen.

One said firmly, "That man in there ain't the prez'dent."

"I say he must be."

"And I'd say that man in there is the best lookin' man I ever lay eyes on. The prez'dent don't look bad, but he don't look near good as this one."

"How come Lore's givin' him all his wine? He wouldn't give it to less than the prez'dent."

"Lookit that moustache. Lookit these eyes," she touched the eyes in the picture. "They're not the man's eyes at the table." She lowered her voice, "Shush. They'll hear us. We better go to the parlor."

My glance moved about the empty room, coming to rest on the pile of books. Feeling a little light-headed, I swung my legs around, slowly rising to my feet. The books had been offered, but only Clifton had selected his; Clay and Cabell hadn't. Perhaps they intended to do so later or maybe not at all. I reasoned that most folk don't miss what they've always had. I hesitated before I took two from the top of the pile, put them inside my shirt, and returned to my pallet.

Glancing over towards the kitchen, I saw everyone's attention centered on filling and emptying their plates. I breathed deeply, trying to quiet my fast-beating heart.

Finally, the general sat back in his chair, his gaze fixed on the window as the rain whipped against the panes. One by one, the guests pushed their plates away and leaned back, quietly relaxing.

Turning towards Cabell, the general broke the silence. "Son, time is running out. I repeat, it's best you return with Clifton and Clay."

Cabell protested, "Wherever you are, I want to be, Father."

Breckinridge sadly responded, "The Florida woods are wild and treacherous. Look at those bites on you. Need I remind you, you have a serious predisposition to fever and swelling from insect bites. They'd poison you. If you were to start swelling or fall into a deep faint, I wouldn't be able to help you, nor could I leave you behind. Every moment of our flight is of profound importance—meaning a moment ahead of escape or capture." Then his tone abruptly changed. "Your mother will need you. She needs you now. More than ever."

He took out his handkerchief and once more wiped away the tears. "These ready tears have been a lifetime curse. So know, dear sons, they represent only the smallest part of the pain I feel for you, your mother, and the days ahead."

Soft as a whisper, the trio of women returned to the kitchen and began to clear off the table. They moved like ghosts in and out of elbows, lingering close to the general's place, looking into his face with whisking glances.

The general stood up abruptly, saying, "This is a repast that will outlast memory." He bowed to the Bronsons and to the three ladies.

"Thank you, Mr. and Mrs. Bronson. And you, kind ladies."

From my pallet, I could see a strong red flush on the ladies' cheeks and wide grins on the faces of Lore and Hattie Bronson. I heard the young men praise the food and hospitality and saw each repeat the general's bows. Lore went to the cabinet again, took out a glass tobacco jar and a handful of pipes. He passed the pipes around and held the jar for his guests, saying, "Gentleman, you may retire to the rocking chairs on the verandah and enjoy some strong smokes from my best crop."

Their voices lifted, full of new pleasure as Lore led the way. I heard the general exclaim, "Unequaled hospitality. Food, drink, and fine tobacco. The likes we haven't seen for years. Mr. Bronson, thank you for sharing your good life."

I thought about this. It was true. The Bronsons were far enough from the beaten path to escape being greatly touched by the war. On this fine farm they hadn't suffered the food shortages common now through Virginia and Georgia and probably elsewhere in the South. Lore was not a young man and he didn't have slaves, but, perhaps, there were sons or grandsons who had gone to war and would return. Also, I wondered how long he'd be able to escape looting or robbery by some of the rough people now filling the road.

When the general and his young men retired to the verandah, Tom Ferguson entered the kitchen and gave Miss Bronson his empty plate. She nodded towards me. "Yuh can go on in with the other Nigra until they all come back from the verandah. Close the door behind you."

When Tom came in, I looked up at him and he smiled. "How you gettin' along? Feelin' better?"

I nodded. Tom was lanky and easy moving with a quick light in his eyes. In no time at all, I learned he was twenty-one years old. His folks were longtime servants of the Breckinridge family. He had been raised in the family with Cabell and Clifton, just as I had with Lance. He had been in the war with the general from the start. His time had been spent with both the general and Mrs. Breckinridge, for she followed her husband when she could, camping with other wives on the grounds of nearby plantations while their men were at battle.

"I delivered," he smiled broadly, "sometimes between two lines of fire. She cook his meals, do his laundry, fix his coffee, and get him brandy. I saw that he got it. Ain't nevah been anyone who cared for her man the way Miz Mary cared for him. I'm a tellin' you, it was a sight to see. She could've lived on Heaven's lap, but she stay close to him. She taught me to do everythin' she did too—sew and cook for times she might not be there. Good thing, too."

Tom sat on the floor beside me. He sighed. "This last week has been a trib'lation for the gen'el." He threw up his hands. "Plumb wore him out, with the Feds breathing down his back evah since we lef' Va'giny. He got the prez'dent and his gov'ment folks outta Richmond fast. They made it to Charleston and met with a slew of Yankee gen'els to talk about endin' the war. Gen'el Sherman was there and tole him he oughta run fast, cuz the Yankees afta' his blood. Gen'el Breckinridge was Vice Prez'dent of the United States and the Yankees was really mad at him for goin' to the South."

Just like me, Tom was a talker. I don't know when I fell asleep. He probably didn't either.

May 12–14

As I woke later, for a moment I did not know where I was. Then Tom spoke.

"I noticed you slippin' out on me," he said. "I jes' shut off n' closed my eyes awhile, too."

My sickness had worn me out and Tom's voice was like trancing music taking me into myself. Now I was listening again, hearing his words, not just the sound.

"Gen'el come down with fever n' cramps n' shivers, but he kept pushin' on. They're after him like bush-cats after a nestin' pigeon n' he don' know when they're comin' or what bush they'll be hidin' behine." Tom crouched like a bush-cat about to pounce.

"On May the second, he was ridin' up front guardin' the prez'dent with two thousan' soldiers marchin' behine. I got wind of a risin' r'bellion back in the end of the column. Some horse soldiers were plannin' to rob the money wagon. They said if they din't get the gold the Feds were gonna get it. I tell it to the gen'el fast as I hear it.

"The gen'el left Col'nel Wood in charge of the prez'dent in the front ranks n' I rode a mule long side him to back of the line. Already some them pirates was shoutin' n' threat'nin'. Some had their rifles drawn."

Tom's story was better than camp coffee to help me wake up more fully. "What happened?"

"He call out to them, 'genel'men, genel'men,' which they certainly weren't. He stopped his horse side them n' call again, 'genl'men.' Horsemen n' soldiers halted. Ev'ryone shushed.

"The gen'el sat straight n' tall in his saddle. He was above all of them n' his eyes moved back and forth cross the crowd. Those eyes. You seen them? Like two bright blue rays of light. Man, what a moment. You could hear only the sound of men breathing." Suddenly Tom stood, drew himself up tall. He was the general. "The gen'el called out in his deep, clear voice, 'Need I remine you, genel'men, you are Confed'rat soldiers n' southern genel'men? You are not highway robbers. You must act with honor. Confed'rat soldiers have shown how to fight n' die with honor. In this time of shadows, show you can live with honor."

Lance would have been so proud to have met the general. I felt a deep pang of sadness in my heart, but kept listening to Tom.

"An old soldier who'd been with him from the very beginnin' shouted, 'Lis'en to our commander. He march 'head of us at Shiloh. Stones River. Missionary Ridge. Always out front of us. He took hits just like we did. We can't let him down." Tom spun around in the telling of this adventure, his eyes seeming happy to be telling this story.

"Someone gave a cheer and like a primer, it set everyone off to a whistlin', cheerin', clappin' 'splosion." Tom slapped his hands together. "You can say I was proud of our gen'el, but as I watch him sit on his horse above everyone, a sad look come over his face n' I saw his head fall. I knew tears was comin'."

For a soldier, he did cry easy, I thought. "Go on, Tom. What happened next?"

"Cabell was at his side. I heard the gen'el say to him, 'I can't ask any more of these men. They mus' go on their way.' So he spen' the res' the day n' night payin' each soldier twenty-six dollahs." Tom was acting like he was passing out coins. "He was tired to death by the time he finish payin' n' dischargin' n' praisin' each for his service. The last one paid was Mr. Reagan, the Tre'shury man, n' then the gen'el paid his'sef. He divvied ev'rythin' fair, ev'ryone alike. Reagan left to catch up with Prez'dent Davis, who by then was at least two days ahead of them." Tom talked with his face and hands. If he hadn't said a word, I could understand his hands. He kept everything moving. His hands, making circles, spinning wheels, pointing skyward. His body, shrugging his shoulders and falling limp, then hunkering down low as a turtle, or pulling himself up like a giraffe. Head—shaking and nodding, frowning. Lips puckering, and eyes winking, blinking, and bugging.

He brushed his hands together spread, them in a wide arc. "The gen'el, his sons, and Mister Clay was the only ones left. The gen'el, sick in the saddle all the way from Washin'ton to Gawga. He didn't as much as whimper. Yes, he cry easy, but for his'sef, he don't. Sure, he's broke up 'bout leavin' his wife, the country, n' the boys. They tore up, too. It's hard pryin' them loose from their papa. Both them boys try to fit their feet into their papa's tracks."

Having seen the boys and the general together, I knew Tom was right.

"Couple times these last days, we most scraped skins with Yankees. Guess time they figger out we was fugitives, we was gone. In months, he ain't had no res' or good food like we have here. He needed this bad."

Maybe that was why the general came down sick. It probably wore on me, too, though I was younger—being out in the elements, scared half the time, and eating irregular and food that hadn't always been as fresh as it should have been. And the bugs, even this early in the season, were biting.

"I been lucky," Tom talked on. "I never had time to be weakly. The gen'el do get mighty peaked sometime, but he gets over it in a rabbit-hop if he can fine his'sef a libation."

"A what?" I asked.

Tom Ferguson's smile seemed to hang from his ears. "It's what he calls whiskey, wine, or brandy—anythin' that's ferment and drunk from a cup, glass, or bottle. Sometimes he call it a tonic, or spirit-raiser, or his med'cin."

Tom laughed and sat down beside me. "I done all the talkin'. It's your time."

"I'm 'most too tired to go into all the details," I said with a sigh. Told him I was looking for my folks, that I had been with Captain John who had borrowed my horse to go to Valdosta and was going to catch up with me. Be here any moment. Told him about us escaping from the Feds when they captured Jefferson Davis.

Tom's face turned serious. "John Taylor Wood. Prez'dent Davis's kin. He'll be travelin' with us, too."

"He asked if I'd want to go with him to the St. Johns," I said.

"We're meetin' him down the road not far, in Florida. At Gen'el Joe Finn'gan's in Madison, along with another big Confed'rat, Judah Benjamin."

"I met him on the road, too," I said. "But I can tell you something—he won't be there."

"Dang Bullwooly. It's taken me years, in the company of Gen'el Breckinridge, a really great gen'el man, to make the 'quaintance of such 'stinguished folks. Here you are, a mere flea-bite squit, without any such tie-up as I come by, already chummin' with the high-mightys. I declare." I was reminded of a hovering eagle as Tom crouched on the floor, hands and arms spread wide for balance, and his eyes, black and bright above his sharp nose.

The door opened with a burst of voices and laughter as the general and young men appeared. Tom rose from the floor and stood back respectfully as they entered.

Clay set his bag on the floor and spoke. "Sir, I am going. I want to thank you for all you've done for me. I hope you have a successful journey and good fortune all the way." He snapped to attention and again saluted the general.

Returning the salute, the general reached out to hold the young man in the circle of his arm and said, "I held your grandfather Henry in the highest esteem and your father James was my dearest friend. Tell him I regard his son, James B. Clay the second, as my own son. Give him my warmest regards. And tell him, I will see him again—" he hesitated, "—someday."

"Yes, sir." Clay walked to Tom, put an arm on his shoulder, shook his hand, then picked up his bag. Leaning towards Clifton, he said, "I'll wait in the barn." Then, he called out, "Coming, Cabe?"

Cabell was putting on his poncho as he headed for the door, saying, "Coming, Clay." To his father and Cliff, "I'm going to ride to the main road with them. Back shortly."

All day I'd been hearing voices on the wind, coming from the folks camping in the barn. Sometimes, I was certain, their rising laughter and boisterous shouts signaled their boredom and restlessness with the weather and being held back from their journey. Now, soon after Cabell and Clay left the house, I heard a chorus of shouts sounding, clearly farewelling Clay.

Remembering the general's tears, I faced the wall, feeling I shouldn't watch, but the general's voice was unwavering and clear, so

I turned back. The mood had been set on the verandah. Pleasant conversation mingled with Lore's best tobacco, on top of food fit for the Queen of England, and some of Lore's wine had eased the parting.

The general and Clifton seemed most unnoticing of me and I pushed up on my elbows as the general was saying, "Best thing is to throw your muskets away. Do nothing to appear hostile. Head north on the pike. When you're stopped, cooperate. Give your parole in good spirit. You shouldn't have any difficulties." He sighed, "This is, I hope. I wish it were that easy for me."

Weariness rolled over me. I lay down again, but could still see a little of what was going on.

I saw Clifton embrace his father and bid Tom a warm goodbye, telling him to take good care of the general. He threw two bags over his shoulders and moved quickly from the room. The general went to the window and watched. He returned to sit on the bed and continued to look through his things. He seemed to linger over these ties to the life he was about to leave. He took five more leather-bound volumes from the trunk.

"Get rid of these things, Tom. Better, ask the Bronsons to dispose of them." His glance rested on me. "How you doing, young fellow? Been sick, too, I hear."

"Yes, sir," I replied, propping up on my elbows again.

"The Bronsons told me you arrived with Mr. Benjamin, that Colonel Wood will pick you up. Both were traveling with us. Benjamin set off on his own. We'll meet Wood, further along."

"I'm going to look for my people in Florida. I think they've settled somewhere along the St. Johns." My story followed briefer than usual. He listened politely, but paced about, halting to look out the window from time to time. When he sat on the bed, I noticed he was going through the books again.

"Since you are returning to your home, I wonder if there's anything among these belongings you would like. Perhaps there's someone in your family who could use something here. Take whatever you want."

Tired as I was, I scrambled to my feet—my uncertain feet. For a moment, I wobbled, grasping the edge of the footboard on the general's bed. To my great shame, I had forgotten the Shakespeare I already had taken off the bed and hidden away. From underneath my loosened shirt, the two volumes tumbled to the floor.

He moved quickly, picking them up. I looked into his steady, blue eyes. "Amazing, you rescued them." He held the books before us. "Interesting you chose these. I was disappointed when my young men didn't find room in their packs to save my books from banishment to some dark corner of the Bronson's barn."

"I should've asked first," I mumbled. "I heard you say you wanted to get rid of them."

"I'm glad you have them. I hoped someone would want them," he reassured me. He held up two of the volumes. "These two, which I have read, were given to me by a reporter on an English newspaper. They are the work of a great French writer, Victor Hugo, and only recently were published in London. Perhaps they are the first copies in this part of the world. I regret leaving them behind, but my bag will hold no more."

I set mine aside and eagerly took one of the books from his hands, only to frown when I tried to read, *Les Misérables*.

Seeing my confusion, the general explained, "Only the title is in French, but it is also means the same in English. It means *The Miserable Ones*, or the poor or wretched ones. If you care for books enough to have wanted the Shakespeare volumes, you must . . ." he paused.

"I can read, sir," I said, sensing his awkwardness.

"Ah, so you do enjoy reading."

"I heard you say how much you loved Shakespeare, sir. I feel the same about James Fennimore Cooper. My people had a big cabinet in the parlor filled with books, but these were locked up and Lance and I could read them only when his mother unlocked the doors. Lance had a set of Cooper's novels in his room and I read them all, over and over."

"There's so much in these works of Hugo's," he said, looking at books. "There are splendid characters as well as exciting adventures. If you are fond of Cooper, you'll feel the same way about Hugo. It pleases me to see you are taking these books, that you are interested in reading."

I had forgotten Tom. He had gathered up the small pile of choices the general had made and was packing them in his already bulging travel bag.

"Tell Mrs. Bronson I would like to have her come by and look these over, Tom." The general suddenly was restless. "We must get on our way. We probably won't be able to get to Madison today. As long as it's raining, we'll leave no tracks. It's not raining hard enough at this moment to be intolerable."

All at once the room was full of people. Lore and Hattie and the three ladies peered in at the door. Tom was bustling about and the general was watching impatiently. He said he'd have to change clothes. Hattie sent the women to press his shirt and pants. I could see them in the kitchen setting up a board and heating flat irons on the stove. I heard the kitchen door slam as Lore went outside.

The general protested, claiming it wasn't necessary to go to the trouble of ironing his clothes, but Hattie had her way. She leaned over the trunk and blanket to examine the general's things and looked very pleased. "Oh yes, sir. I can put all these to good use. I thank you. Yes, sir. The books will look fine on the mantle in the company room. They sure are pretty books." She picked one up in her hands. "My, don't they feel good, so smooth and soft. Oh my. The pages are edged in gold. I can't read them none but I do like pretty books and I can show them off real good."

While I wished I was going with the general too, I had returned to my pallet, aware of Miss Hattie's pleasure over the new decorations for her mantle. I became protective of my pile and was hovering over my books when the general glanced at me. He saw my concern and spoke to Mrs. Bronson, "I have given the boy some books also."

Miss Hattie turned and looked at me with surprise. "Now what do you think you'd ever do with a book?"

"Read it, ma'am," I answered, and saw her eyes squint into an angry scowl. She might have made something of me being uppity, but noise from outside took her attention away from me.

We heard Cabell before we saw him. Heard his heavy boots slamming against the steep steps of the verandah. Heard him yell, "We gotta get out of here. The main roads are full of Feds. We gotta ride."

The general rushed to the door. Tom and Cabell grabbed the haversacks on the floor. Lore dashed in from outside.

"They didn't see me. They came upon Clay and Cliff, not a hundred yards where we'd said goodbye. I hid in the brush. I saw Cliff and Clay give them their paroles, but the soldiers took their horses, bags and—the sword."

Lore broke in, "There's a road through the backwoods no one will ever find. Sir, you gotta get away. I'll take you."

The women brought the general's clothes and dashed away. I never saw anyone dress so quickly as the general did. Tom shrugged his shoulders and smiled faintly.

I was standing by the bed as the general was leaving and noticed he'd left his book. I scurried to his side and handed it to him. "Sir, *The Rise and Fall of Athens*."

Thanking me, he took the book and put it inside his shirt. Suddenly, he called to Lore, "Will my boys be all right, Mister Bronson?"

"We have someone lookin' after them, Gen'ral."

Moving quickly out the back door, Lore shouted, "It's muddy in front. Come the back way to the barn. It's closer. Hurry."

After a flurry of movement, the general hastened through the kitchen to the back entrance and tramped down another flight of steps into the silence of the wet ground.

Outside, the voices that had sounded all day now ceased. Shortly, I heard the sound of hoofs treading lightly and moving away, then, were no more.

Overwhelmed, and still sickly, I lay again on the pallet, feeling weak, but no longer lightheaded, strangely sad, yet greatly rewarded. With my fingers, I traced the designs on the leather and flipped the pages of my books, amazed at the fine print and thin paper. I wondered at the magic that could create so many worlds and store them forever on such fragile leaves.

I knew the value of such a gift. A shame Hattie Bronson wouldn't know the real gold inside the general's books.

Suddenly, I thought of Lily—and Rose and Daisy. I hoped they would learn to read and get some book-learning. I wished I could have taught them. Lily's small face filled my mind. I felt an uneasiness thinking about her—something hopeless.

While I lay there thinking about Lily, Mrs. Bronson and the women were moving in and out, taking all the general's things, including the books on the bed. She told them, "Put these clothes in the cabinet in the Company room," and, "These pretty books go on the mantle."

Noticing me watching, she asked, "You hungry or something?" I guess she forgot, or forgave my being uppity to her a moment before.

Truth was, I felt a little hungry, but replied, "No, ma'am." I felt more kindly towards her and Lore, now that I had seen how good they were to the general. Other than wanting to lodge the "Nigra" in the barn and that one look across her face, they hadn't treated me badly. I guess they felt they'd made a big sacrifice in allowing me to sleep on a pallet in the house. Yet I couldn't be too grateful when I remembered that Mr. Benjamin had paid in gold for that sacrifice.

When they moved the trunk to the end of the bed, Mrs. Bronson said, "I'll use this to store blankets and bed covers." Again, she spoke to me, "Sure you don't want nothin'?"

"I don't like to bother, ma'am, but if you have a piece of cornbread, I would like some. I feel better now and I think cornbread will help settle me and give me some strength."

"Yes, boy. I'll fetch you a plate of food. My. You do talk nice. I can see you were done real good by your folks."

"Thank you, ma'am. They're good people. Do you want me to go out on the porch?"

"Yes, boy. If you're well enough to get up, you can eat out there."

Already she was in the kitchen with me close behind. She filled my plate with vegetables, a huge chunk of cornbread, and a piece of ham. I took it to the back porch. Tomorrow, I'd probably be able to eat it. I'd stow it in my haversack somehow. I didn't want Miss Hattie to see that I wasn't able to eat it and think I was ungrateful. I turned my chair so I could see when she left the kitchen.

Finally, I saw the women move from the kitchen down the hallway onto the porch. Quietly, I opened the door and went back to the pallet. My bag was nearby. First, I packed my books away, then rooted around until I found my tin cup and stored as much of the food as I could into it, wrapped up most of the cornbread in a cloth and took my empty plate back to the kitchen.

A big commotion sounded on the front verandah. I went down the hall and peeked around the corner. Mrs. Bronson and the neighbor women had been sitting in the chairs, now empty but still rocking. They stood at the head of the steep, wide steps speaking in shrill voices in answer to some harsh voices below.

"There ain't no Confed'rats here!" I heard Miss Hattie shout.

"Ain't none," another cried out.

"We heard tell yuh got some visitors," a big man said. "We'd like to meet 'em. Heard tell yuh got food a-plenty an' some hosses. We need food and we need hosses. We're Feds and yuh better treat us good."

"Where're yer menfolks? Back from the fight'n?" he shouted at them.

"They done gone to market," Mrs. Hattie lowering her voice, answered. "I expec' them back any moment."

Another voice, "Well, we hep yuh clean out yer kich'en so's they have room to put in yer new supplies."

A familiar ring in their voices and the men's rough manner of speaking filled me with alarm. I leaned over and edged closer. Through the lattice under the porch railing, I saw the blue of ill-fitting Yankee uniforms and—the dreaded features of Shears, his jaw grinding away, and fat Joe, rain streaming off his oily face and hair. My heart skipped when I saw a gleaming sword swinging from Shears' belt. As they came up the steps, I darted to the back room wishing I could tell Mrs. Bronson about the imposters.

When I heard their raucous shouts and heavy tramping in the hall only a few strides away, I grasped my bag and reached inside for some useful weapon, then I dived into the trunk and peeked out. They immediately began to go through the supplies, rooting through barrels and bins and shelves in the kitchen. Their rough voices rose in a cheer when they found Lore's wine. Shears picked up a bottle and gleefully waved it in the air. "Be damned, Joe, if there ain't a wagonload of this stuff."

"Leave my husband's wine alone. I done warn'd you, don't you dare steal our things. My husband'll shoot y'all's heads off."

The women followed them into the kitchen. Shears sneered, "He ain't gonna shoot us. We'll git him fust. Outta my way. Fine me sumpin' to put this stuff in, women."

"Ain't got nothin' that'd do," Hattie protested. "Don't you go ordering us 'round. And don't call us women. We're ladies."

Ducking down, I heard heavy steps coming through the doorway. "Yawl bring that ol' trunk in here. It's jes' fine."

The women were trying to move the trunk and I heard Miss Hattie exclaim, "Somethin's weighing this down. Wasn't this heavy when we moved it before." She lowered her voice. "Where's the boy?" Then I saw the lid raise and a row of eyes peering in at me and she, speaking low again, "Could've hidden better than this. How come he get in here?"

"Carry the trunk in heah. Whatcha dallyin' fer?" It was Joe. Then, "Gimme a han', Shears. Women are jes' good fer nothin'."

Shears shouted back, "Carry it yerself, yuh bubblin' cabbagehead." I heard them scuffle, then they started swinging the trunk around. I rolled about inside and knew I was about to get caught by foes who'd show no mercy. I was scared.

"Be damned," said Shears. "Whatcha got in heah? A big hog?" To illustrate his point, he shook the trunk and me back and forth and up and down. He dropped it then with a big thud and lifted the lid. I saw his long jaw drop and fall still. He hissed, "Damned if it ain't the li'l black piss-ant with the green eyes. Gonna smash yuh good this time."

Filled with fear and anger, I was numb and dumb.

"Best not hurt him none," said Hattie. "He has im'po'tant fightin' friends. Could get'cha in big trouble."

With Shears' hand squeezing my arm, I climbed out. At the same time, I shoved the bowie knife through my pocket until I felt its steel against my leg. His fingers tightened. I felt a pull and twist, a pitiless hold on me—a hint of what was coming.

"Git some rope, Joe. Hurry. I wanna tie 'im up good. Git shed of 'im once n' fer all. He's jes' a li'l ol' black stingin' ant, n' I aims t'take the sting outta 'im."

If they were going to take me prisoner, Mrs. Bronson needed to know who they were, so I spoke up. "These men are snakes. They're not Yankee soldiers. They probably killed the Yankees whose uniforms they're wearing and now are riding their horses. They kill, steal, loot, and plunder." Their uniforms clearly didn't fit. My eyes fell on the sheath-less sword hanging at Shears' belt. I wasn't mistaken. It was the general's gift to Clifton.

I kept talking because I was sure the women would tell all that had happened to Captain Wood when he came. I didn't know what was to happen to me. I stood in front of Shears and spoke to him.

"A little while ago, you took that sword from two Confederates who were looking for Union soldiers to surrender to, so they could give their paroles. What happened to them? What else did you steal from them?"

Like a rattlesnake striking, Shears slapped his dirty hand over my mouth. I tried to bite his hand, then his fingers, and he pulled at my lips and yanked on my mouth. I remembered what he said the first time I saw him in the meadow—he didn't want any of my old nigger things. So the thought of my teeth sinking into his flesh must have seemed as unhealthy to him as it was to me. With his free hand he boxed my ear and the side of my face. I twisted in his grip and struck and kicked him.

Just then Joe returned with a long circle of rope and tossed it to him. Shears continued to yell, "Heah, start bindin' his legs. We'll dump 'im in the first river we come to."

They started passing the rope back and forth under me. I wondered if Shears had figured out that I had been with the captain when he got my horse.

Now, again I was saying Mama Zulma's prayer. There wasn't much time. Now or never. Not knowing if I could do it, I slipped my hand into my pocket and held the knife between my fingers. I thought I might be able to get him.

He was leaning over me, his breath fouling the air, his elastic jaw strangely silent as tobacco drool trickled from the corners of his mouth. Then his scrawny neck stretched out in front of me, ready as a doomed turkey. I could have killed a turkey, but now, my fingers relaxed around the knife. As wicked and ruthless as I knew Shears to be, I closed my eyes and my will went limp. Without stopping, he continued to bind me in a cocoon of rope.

The loop of rope dropped on my chest. Everything suddenly exploded. I opened my eyes to see Miss Bronson hitting Shears over the head with a huge iron skillet. Her three neighbors waved an axe, a flat iron, and a poker. All beat unceasingly on the two men. The one using the axe hit with the blunt side—if she hadn't, there'd been blood on the ceiling. With each blow, the women screamed, "Get out!" and, "We'll kill you!" and, "Devils, to hell, to hell with you!"

I squirmed free, reached again into my pocket for the knife, and raised it to attack. Miss Hattie snatched it from my hand. It was she who sank it into Shears' chest. She drew it out and thrust it in again and again. He crumpled and slid to the floor.

Joe fell to the floor, rose to his knees, folded his hands, and whimpered, "Mercy. Mercy. I beg yuh. Don' hurt me no mo.'"

Miss Hattie was very still. Her neighbors drew close. She spoke quietly, "Ain't no reason to spare this man. They're two of the same cut."

"Please, lady, I'm sorry fer what I done. I ain't gonna do a thin' t'hurt no one. I promise." His voice faded.

Shears lay on the floor in a flood of red that soaked the blue uniform, outlining the space where his body fell. His jaw shut like a sprung trap, his teeth clamped together in an eerie, brown-smeared grin, tobacco juice oozing from his mouth, staining his chin, circling his neck, and spreading a fine network of brown through the stream of blood covering him. His eyes, almost concealed before by the distortions of his jaw, looked like two colorless stones.

Miss Hattie stood over Joe. "I'll tell you what you can do, you hear? Take your friend and throw him over your saddle. Carry him to the river and pitch him in. Leave his horse here. He won't be needing it no more. You head North. Don't ever show your face in these parts again. If you do, you'll get the tar shot out of you."

Already Joe was carrying out her orders. He moved fast. The women began cleaning the kitchen. The pump began hiccoughing and belching as they filled pails and started to mop up. He was gone before they had finished.

Miss Hattie had done my work—at least that's how I felt. What had I thought about her before? That she and Lore weren't the same kind of people as Lottie and Carson Matthews? That they were common folks? Well, I guess I've learned something. If I'd known Hattie and Lore Bronson a few days ago as well as I know them today, I would've said they are the best uncommon folks. Just as uncommon as Lottie and Carson. I'd hope that maybe they changed their opinion of me, too, but not for the worse.

May 14, 1865

LAST NIGHT, AS I WAS RECORDING THE HAPPENINGS OF THE day, the sound of footfalls on the front steps and verandah interrupted my thoughts and I hurried to the hallway corner. In the dusky lamplight, a large man's form suddenly eclipsed by several ghostly figures seemed to float into the company room. I tiptoed down the hall and, standing in the shadow of the door, I watched the phantoms come to life in the light of the large lamp centering the wide mantle over the hearth. Hattie and her neighbors, dressed in tent-like nightgowns, surrounded Captain Wood. I stood spellbound as they gave an account of my sickness, the general's illness, the big feast, the farewell to Clifton and Clay, the fatal visit of those scoundrels, Shears and Joe.

Hattie's voice rose when she spoke, drowning the others as she became more and more excited in the telling. Finally, only she spoke, while her neighbors nodded or sang out in support. Captain John remained silent during the recital of happenings.

When she finished, I stepped from the shadows into the room and exclaimed, "Oh, sir. I'm so glad you're here. Feds are all around. To escape them, Mr. Bronson is escorting the general through the backwoods to Madison. You'd better be on your way, too."

"I heard you've been sick. Are you able to go now?"

"Yes, sir. I am well. I can go."

Hattie spoke, "A horse's ready in the barn. You can leave it at General Finnegan's. Get a fresh one there. They've made all the 'rangements. People work together on this Getaway Trail. You'll find help all along the way. Everyone wants to protect our own people."

"I wasn't stopped," Captain John said. "You'll be glad to have your horse, Tench. A remarkable animal! Mrs. Bronson, we appreciate your work, your care, and all the arrangements you have made. It won't be forgotten." He suddenly asked, "What's this?"

Mrs. Bronson had taken a sword from the hearth and handed it to Captain John. It was the sword the general had given Clifton, and Shears had stolen from Clifton and hung from his own belt.

"You will be seeing the fine general. His oldest son Cabell is with him. He should have his father's sword."

"We must send a scout to find what happened to Clifton and young Clay. I must have news of their well-being to take to the general."

"We should have news soon. The husbands of these neighbor-women are out on the road now. It's their business to see and know what's happening—who's who and who's going where, and who needs help. We must help and protect our own."

"I should say you do, Mrs. Bronson," Captain John agreed.

"You certainly helped and protected me." I quickly added, "When I couldn't fight for myself, you fought for me."

"Tench, by fighting those beasts, we were fighting for our own selves and all good people," she said.

One of the women broke in, "He would've kilt all of us if'n we hadn't put up a fight."

"He came close to killing me," I said weakly.

"You ain't lived long enough to know sometimes you have to fight for your life." Mrs. Bronson was ready with an excuse for me. I didn't deserve it. I knew how bad Shears was, but when it came to fighting back, I had been a coward.

"Get your things, Tench. I'll take Night to the barn, feed and water him, wipe him down, and get a horse for myself."

"Ashby's out there waiting his turn. He'll take you to meet up with the general by way of the backwoods," Miss Hattie said as she picked up the lamp and held it high, apparently to better look at the captain. "I can see why you weren't stopped, Captain Wood. You do 'pear to be a backwoodsman out of touch with civil'zation. You've a scruffy beard and your hair's matted and you're mighty mussed up and dirty. But it's your talk that gives you away. You don't sound backwoods."

"Ah can talk that-ar way too." The captain was drawling. "This-ars my woods-tolk. I use it if'n I haf to."

"Very good, sir." Hattie Bronson laughed, "Thataway, I reckon you could fool 'most anyone."

I rushed to my pallet, strapped on my journal, and gathered my things, stuffing them into my bags. My steps were still uncertain.

The captain and Miss Hattie and her neighbors watched from the doorway. "Well, Tench, I reckon you learned a thing or two while you was here," she said.

I felt my brow wrinkle as I looked up at her and wondered what she thought I had learned. She must've known what I was thinking and spoke, "When you know someone's comin' after you, you won't wait for them to get you first." I remembered my hand against the cold steel of the knife in my pocket and my inability to use it.

"But, but—" I started to protest.

"I know," she said, "you're jes' a young'un and always had someone to do the big stuff for you. It ain't likely it'll ever be thataway again. Remember, next time, strike before you get struck."

Sink my knife into another's body? Could I do it? I had killed animals—harmless animals—without a concern. Shears was like a dangerous viper. A rattlesnake. I had killed those too without concern. I should have thought of him same as a rattlesnake. Yet I don't think I could take anyone's life. Ever.

Mrs. Bronson was leaning over me. "Next time?" she asked.

I answered, "I reckon I know now what could've happened."

Mrs. Bronson faced the others. "Killing ain't something to teach a young'un, but everyone should know what to do to stay safe and—alive."

Not wanting to talk about it, I thanked them and followed the captain to the barn. I hurried to Night's side. Did I only imagine the light brightening his eyes and the restless step in place when I threw my arms about his neck? With him at my side, I felt suddenly stronger. I wanted to mount, lean against, and rest on him. I felt a burst of new strength and the comfort of being with an old friend. He was my strongest connection to the past.

We spent a few quick moments preparing for our ride. Just as we filled a sack with a supply of grain, Mrs. Bronson came to the barn with a package of food and the blanket I had left on my pallet. When

I reached out for them, she did a very strange thing. She threw the blanket over Night's back, then reached to me, her arm falling across my shoulder. She looked at me steadily and placed the package in my hand. At this moment, I felt a warmth from her that I hadn't before. "You're a good boy, Tench. You ain't got nothing to be ashamed of. You just got a bit of growing to do. You haven't got too far to go. God bless you."

As I saddled Night and readied myself for our journey, her blessing rang in my head. We plodded through the miserable night with Ashby leading, followed by me, then Captain John. With the wind and rain thrashing us, it took all our attention to stay on the darkened trail. I was easy with the reins, trusting Night more than myself to keep us on our path.

For several days, this fierce spring storm has prowled around, its flashes of blue-white light and heavy rumbling a fitting background for my own misery. Now, as lightning leaps through the woods, cracking and torching tops of tall pines, I want it to stop. It loosens its wild fire over the countryside like fangs of angry dragons. I've had enough.

In some long-ago time, every day I'd waken eager and happy as one day stretched into another. Clear or stormy, it was all the same.

Ever since I left Thomson, I've faced each day's unfolding mystery with dread or fear and sometimes, with excitement. Rain or shine, it's not the same.

When I could, I read what Lance wrote in his journal and it was like I could hear his voice rise up from those pages. He said things I really didn't understand when I first read them. I was beginning to understand. He spoke of true selfhood and how to find it. At first, I really didn't know what he meant. Now I think he was saying, if you can get through disappointments and hard times and still keep trying, you become strong. Everything that happens to you makes you stronger.

I don't think I'd ever want to go back to those childhood days, when life was all the same. When things aren't easy and I keep trying—at least I know I am heading towards becoming a stronger person. I wish Lance could know how I feel now.

We're not too far from our night's destination, but Ashby said it wasn't safe to continue because of flash-floods. We've stopped at a deserted farmhouse. There're others here, hard asleep. Some of Lore's fugitives, I guess. Wet and a bit chilly, we're trying to dry out by the fireplace. Hope I can sleep. I'm dog-tired.

May 15, 1865

SILENCE WOKE ME UP. THE RAINS AND THUNDER AND LIGHT-
ning had ceased. I heard only the dribbling of water from off the roof
outside the paneless window and the muted songs of frogs mating
in nearby waters. I smiled as I pictured them—the small male frog
whistling and singing as he attempts to reach around the larger female
whose belly is swollen with an entire frog population waiting in the
eggs inside her, to be fertilized and brought into being. With nothing
more than a frog hug, as she lays hundreds of tiny eggs, he'll scat-
ter his special spray over them. Then the eggs, floating at the water's
edge, look like long strings of black pearls.

When I was little, I used to collect baby polliwogs. How many polliwogs lost their lives because I would catch them to play with? Later,
I learned I could help the frog parents by throwing wood chips and
sticks for the mother frog to cling to during the mating. Then—how
many more lost their lives at the end of my gigging pole?

Day was breaking, bringing soft light and the sound of low voices
and quiet motion in the dusky room. As they drew themselves
together, I watched the dim forms and heard someone say, "Stopped
raining. Going to be a clear day. Be able to get on our way." Their
movement was like whispers, not wanting to disturb.

"Awake, Captain?" Ashby's voice.

"Yes, sir. And ready, Tench?"

"Ready, sir."

The scene came into focus as daylight absorbed the shadows. The
large room was bare and empty except for the huge stone fireplace
full of ashes. The others had gone. I heard their voices ringing over
the clear air as they moved off. I gathered my things and went outside
to tend Night and observed the endless blue sky washed fresh and

clear of even the tiniest froth of a cloud. Heavy rains had cleansed the heavens and earth and left a fragrance on the breath of morning.

Outside, Ashby had some coffee and pones waiting. He was so quiet and efficient, we'd no idea he'd been up in the dark and already had planned the day's course.

"Breckinridge and his party spent the night in the stopover with us," he said, filling our cups.

"I didn't realize who was there," John exclaimed, clearly disappointed. "Wish I'd known. We'll catch up with them at the Crossing. They're not moving too fast."

They should be—hurrying, I mean. We should be, too. But the ground was soggy from the heavy rains on top of the many layers of decayed leaves. The horses' hoofs were slowed down by its spongy grip. So we had no choice. We had to move slowly.

It seemed as if the whole world had just wakened after a long sleep. Among the throb of the doves and cardinal-calls whipping the air, and mockingbirds tossing notes to heaven's high, only great numbers of grackles, their voices like squeaky hinges, scarred the harmony celebrating the week's first clear day.

Sometimes as we spoke, our voices were drowned out by the birds' songs and calls, and we continued, amused, in silence. This was truly the backwoods, unknown and untrampled by passersby, among ancient oak, sweet gum, and tall pines and blossoming trees. I recognized some of them, the dogwood and redbud, the magnolia, thanks to Lance and Miss Lottie, who was always trying to teach us. "After all," she would say, "if you love the woods, you'll love every stick and tree in it. Everything is a thing apart, yet a part of the whole, this, her constant lesson. If you know one tree, you'll know the whole forest."

About noon the trail widened into a broad clearing through the heavy growth. Beyond, I saw a river so bright under the dazzling sun, I had to look away. On the bank, as we drew closer, I recognized General Breckinridge sitting against a tree. His son, Cabell, stood at the water's edge and several others, with their horses, were boarding a small ferry.

Captain John and Ashby dismounted, but stayed in the background and didn't disturb the general, whom I could now see. He held in his hands the book he'd had the day before, *The Rise and Fall of Athens*. He was completely absorbed.

Ashby gave us another pone, which I gobbled up. Another long wait began. When the ferry returned about an hour later, the general made no move to leave. Captain John held back. I was getting anxious and hungry besides. Ashby said we'd eat on the other side of the river, but finally I reached into my bag and pulled out my food as well as the package Mrs. Bronson had given me. I asked Captain John if he'd like something, and he smiled and reached over, taking a pone and a piece of ham. It was just the beginning. We ate until everything was gone.

The ferry captain and our group along with Cabell had waited patiently when a strange thing happened. Cabell called to him, "Father. We'd better be on our way."

Breckinridge's eyes were unseeing. He seemed not to hear. Again, Cabell called and again, several times more.

At last, the general nodded to his son, told him to wait. Suddenly, he stood and closing his eyes, began to sing out in his strong voice, the verses of a poem I had heard for a long time in our home:

> *Oh, here would thy beauty most brilliantly beam*
> *and life pass away like some delicate dream;*
> *each wish of thy heart should realized be,*
> *and this beautiful land seem an Eden to thee.*

We all were affected by the sound of his rich voice and the emotion of the moment. No one spoke as we moved silently onto the ferry and crossed over. I learned from Tom Ferguson, who was waiting on the other side, that they had heard his voice clear as a bell, over there.

As soon as we reached shore, the general leaped onto his horse and called, "Mount up and away."

Tom rolled his eyes heavenward and said to me, "The gen'el's gone on ahead to have him a good cry. That's way he do. He's gotta say bye to Cabell nex' n' he's hurtin' a-plenty. He has to leave him behine." I noticed Tom's eyes were watering, too.

Evening time, we arrived at Madison. Hardly waiting long enough to hear our thanks, Lore Bronson rounded up some horses and was on his way back to the important work that he and Hattie were doing at their farm.

There was a big reunion at General Finnegan's house with a passel of important Confederate folks. Other than General Finnegan, Captain John, General Breckinridge, and Cabell, I didn't find out who they all were. I stayed in the barn with Tom and a bunch of servants who were tending the fugitives in the big house. Later, when we could see that we wouldn't be needed, Tom and I went down to the town square to see what Madison was like. It was full of Yankees and paroled soldiers with many town-folks standing on the corners and against the town buildings watching.

"Well, looka there," Tom suddenly exclaimed. Two strollers had just passed us whom I scarcely had noticed. Then I saw it was Captain John and General B. The general had shaved off his swooping mustache. They looked like just two, tall country men, both dressed in ordinary farmer's homespun and worn straw hats.

Two Yankee soldiers, coming towards them on the board walk fronting the stores, studied them with a certain curiosity. When they passed, one turned and looked back at them. We heard him say, "These hayseeds grow tall down here."

Before we spread our blankets under one of the great oaks in Finnegan's yard, Captain John came to talk to us. "We're getting our instructions," he said, "finding the best routes through the state to both coasts. We have a list of contacts. There's a man, name of Wes Vickers, who's going a ways with us. He knows the river. His brother is a purser for a steamship that runs the St. Johns. What he doesn't know, he can find out."

I was filled with excitement at the thought I might soon be with my family again. The happenings of the past weeks had eclipsed the old longings, but the need had always been there and suddenly bubbled up again.

May 16, 1865

THE FINNEGAN'S GROUNDS WERE TEEMING. ASHBY HAD brought fresh horses and was getting ready to exchange them for ours. "Not mine!" I yelled. "This one's my horse and he goes with me."

"All right, all right," Ashby answered and hastened to finish exchanging and saddling the new horses.

Tom quickly reported that two of the Bronson neighbors had arrived in the night and probably brought important news. We saw them as they strode together up the broad steps of the mansion. I followed Tom as he raced over towards the shrubbery edging the big verandah where the guests had gathered, eating breakfast.

We saw General Finnegan speak to Breckinridge, then both rose and hastened to greet the newcomers. "News of my boys?" General Breckinridge asked, extending his hand.

The gentlemen were smiling. The older responded, "They were only temporarily delayed, sir. They're now well on their way. We got horses, clothes, maps, and addresses to carry them through to Kentucky. It's not probable they'd ever meet with the likes of those two hoodlums again. The Fed soldiers have been told to treat our people good and—mostly—that's what they've been doing."

Tom leaned towards me and whispered, "This'll set off his tears again. Ain't gonna be a good day for the Gen'el with Cabell leavin' and everythin'. Lookit, Cabell's got his Pa's sword now. Yankees may be treatin' our soldiers good, but they see somethin' they want, they gonna take it."

"You can't argue with good news, General." Captain John was beside him. "Your boys are in good hands. Cabell will have the same good advantages provided Clifton and Clay."

At the mention of his name, Cabell appeared. I heard him say under his breath, "My greatest advantage has been having you as a father." Haversack in hand, he was ready to travel.

The two neighbors shook hands all around and the younger said to Cabell, "We'll go with you to Tallahassee to give your parole, then we'll accompany you back to the Bronson's. After that, you'll be on your own, but we don't think there'll be trouble. Least, that's what everybody's saying coming down the pike."

Tom was right about it being a bad day for the general. After Cabell left, Captain John, Ashby, and Tom and I spent the rest of the morning getting things together and stashing supplies on the horses.

Overnight, another member of the general's party, a Colonel Jim Wilson, had caught up after a stopover in Valdosta. Tom said the general and Colonel Jim were holding council in his room at the Finnegans. When they finally came out, carrying their bags, Tom said that it was clear to see, for sure, the general had had a libation or two. I wondered how he knew, then I noticed his watering eyes and tousled hair, and Tom explained that they always have libations when they "hold council." Before Ashby joined Cabell and the Bronson neighbors and had said his goodbyes to us, he introduced Wes Vickers, who'd take us to the St. Johns. "Wes knows Florida like God," Ashby said. "He'll take good care of you."

Captain John held out his hand to Wes and said, "We've heard good things about you, Wes."

Not wanting to get in the way, I stayed in the background. But all at once, I got bold and moved forward and said, "I hope you can help me find my folks, sir. I think they're somewhere on the St. Johns."

Wes leaned over to look at me and smiled. "That's a long river. If that's where they are, I can promise you, we'll find them."

Immediately, I was ready to be on our way. I wanted to shout with joy, but I felt so sorry for the general, I dared not show my happiness while he felt so sad.

The general, Wood, Colonel Jim, and Wes huddled in deep discussion. Tom and I both hung around, waiting to hear their mind. Finally, Wes spoke to us, "All right, Tench and Tom, y'all go with the gen'el and Col'nel Jim. Cap'n Wood and I will go on to Moseley's Ferry."

I guess my disappointment showed. Tom said, "We do what he say. We'll take good care of the gen'el and Col'nel Jim."

Tom and I waited on our horses, all set to go, while the general and Wes walked off along the boardwalk fronting Madison's stores. They went through the doorway of the store with the big General Merchandise sign. We rode our horses and took theirs down to the hitching rail in front of the store.

As we waited in saddle, I read from the long advertisement posters hanging on either side of the door: "Gents' Clothes, Shirts, Undershirts, Drawers, Finest Lot of Saddles in Florida, Fertilizer, Blood, Bone, Potash, Dry Goods, Hats and Caps, Ladies' Hats, Trimmings, Codfish, Crockery, Groceries, Glass, Spirits."

Tom interrupted, "Spirits. That's what he's afta'. Needs a supply for the trip. Don' know what he'll do when his supply runs out. Col'nel Wilson needs his, too. Keeps his humor up. He's one funny man with or without it."

"You know him, too?" I asked.

"Long time. He's been one of the gen'els right hand men. Gone through it all. Got cap'sured 'long with Cabell, during the big battle at Chat'nooga. He and Cabell was hauled off to one of them Yankee prisons up nawth. He's like family. The gen'el din't rest 'til he got both o' them back in a prisoner 'change with the Feds."

A group of Federal officers were coming along the boardwalk. Tom stopped talking and we both looked away. In a muffled voice, he said, "Go on in the store and let the gen'el know who's out here."

I quickly dismounted, entered the store, and looked about. It was filled with rows of cluttered tables, arranged, I guessed, with thought of the gender of the customers. On one side, shirt and boots, belts, hats, undershirts, drawers. On the other, ribbons, buttons, hats, shoes, and women's clothing, along with children's shoes and hats and clothes. Down the middle were merchandise for the house, including fabrics, sheeting, toweling, tablecloths, napkins, lamps, candles and table china, pots and pans. In the back, groceries, provisions, canned goods. A large wood-burning stove, not in use, was centered in the back wall. A counter and wall-shelves, full of glasses and bottles with many types of spirits, and a big table, occupied a corner of the back.

It was circled by stools, and a big sign, hung on the wall, identified the corner as The Dram Shop.

Out the back door in a lean-to, I could see large bins, which I imagined were full of bone or blood meal and stacks of feed and fertilizer. Beyond, outside, I could see a back lot with wagons and horses.

Some men were sitting and drinking on the stools in The Dram Shop and others stood talking in lively groups. There were people out back, loading supplies into wagons. Women and children were moving about from table to table, feeling fabrics and holding up clothes, trying on shoes and hats. I was fascinated. I hadn't ever been inside a store like this before; I wondered if I'd be asked to leave.

The general already was moving towards the door and Colonel Jim had gathered up their selections and was at the cash box, paying a tall, slender man wearing glasses, a visored hat, and an apron. I hurried to the general's side. I was glad for his protection in such unaccustomed surroundings. "There're Yankees all over town," I whispered.

"It's all right, Tench. I've got to face them sooner or later. I must not be fearful." I was surprised to hear him talk like this.

It was then I recognized the man who had passed him on the boardwalk the night before. As the general was exiting the store, the soldier started to enter. They both halted. The Yankee had a look of curiosity and seemed about to say something.

General B. gazed at him steadily, gave him a bold, hard look, holding himself tall and erect. Without a word, the stranger turned away and disappeared down the walk.

"We'll take the horses around back and pick up our purchases." He untied their leads and mounted quickly, keeping Colonel Jim's in hand. We followed around in back where the colonel was waiting with a couple of feedbags filled with supplies.

"Fine store," Colonel Jim declared as he put the contents of the bags into their haversacks—except for the spirits which he kept stashed in his bags. As we rode out onto the road, he said, "This is a touch of civilization we will miss in days to come."

We saw that the road already was filled with life. Beside us, an entire family filed along, pushing their belongings in a small cart, plodding barefoot along the muddy ruts. There were three towheaded young'uns, four or five scraggly boys in tattered clothes with a scrawny woman I felt sure was the mother. Behind her was a feeble old man and toothless woman who had to be the grandparents. My thoughts went immediately to Lottie and Carson with their younger ones and my Mama Zulma. What picture did they make as they refugeed south? Did people wonder about them as they passed? These people looked ill-fed and quite forlorn. I couldn't see my family in such a picture. Yet I should realize that anything could have happened to change their lives as I had known them, just as it had happened to Lance and me.

There were many parolees, quite different from those young soldiers who had joined the Army with Lance, and had been so full of life and enthusiasm. These were more like middle-aged men in tired, bent bodies, long-faced and sad-eyed. They didn't even seem joyful to be going home. Home? What was home?

There were rugged men on outspent horses, frustration and impatience clearly seen in their scowling brows and hostile eyes. There was a bunch of Negro boys, not any older than I, banded together in a knot, moving as one, heads high, haughty and indifferent, each carrying a bundle on a stick and waving the stick in the air. And a dark woman, arms swinging, hips rolling in easy rhythm to the spiritual she was singing, "I'se gonna meet my maker when the trumpets start to play and the angels b'gin to sing. You'll hear my voice a'risin' above that angel chorus. Hallelujah, Hallelujah."

Very shortly we turned off the main road and started down a country trail, once rutted, now overgrown. The general reached into his bag and took out a couple of broad-brimmed hats, the kind that he and Colonel Jim were wearing. He turned back to ride beside us and handed one to each of us.

"From now on," he said, "you'll want to keep yourself covered, head to toe. The sun can be cruel. Bugs—mosquitoes and horse flies—will be scouting for a piece of bare flesh. When you get off your horse, look about on the ground. Keep watch for yellow jackets and snakes—there're many large, harmless kinds, but in this country, there're rattlesnakes and moccasins. If you're bitten by one of them, there's not much we could do about it. Snakes'll spook horses. Remember, anything could happen. Be ready."

Tom began to button up his shirt and roll down his sleeves. "Hear tell, it best to tuck your pants legs into your boots or stockings to keep the bugs out. Specially them little redbugs you can't even see. Hear tell, they itch you for months after they bite into you. Florida living ain't like anythin' you've ever knowed."

I thought again of Mama Zulma and Lottie Matthews. How hard it must have been for them—traveling so far with Carson and two children. Great, tall pine trees suddenly had risen around us, and heavy growth had narrowed our passage.

"This corridor leads to the Old Bellamy Road, built by slaves to connect Pensacola on the west coast with St. Augustine on the east," the general told us. "It goes through the capital in Tallahassee. We want to get off it, soon as we can. I imagine the Feds will soon be beating the bushes down this road."

Colonel Wilson in the lead began to ride at a faster pace. "We'll meet John and Wes at Moseley's Ferry on the Suwannee and spend the night with the Moseleys. There's good camping, good water and—they'll put out a good spread."

"The Moseley's daughter is married to Colonel Ed Mashburn of our staff. I've no news of his whereabouts. Have you, James?"

"Nothing, sir. I last saw him in Carolina."

"Sorry I have nothing more reassuring to tell them." All afternoon I listened to the gentlemen's conversation. The colonel was doing all he could to keep the general occupied. He never allowed him to fall silent very long before he began to prattle. "I've always wanted to kill a rattlesnake and cure its skin," he was saying, "To make a beautiful reticule or a choker for a lovely lady I know in Henderson, Kentucky. It's the type of thing she'd like. Then—the fangs—I know an old witch who could mix them in with tea leaves for a most satisfying brew."

The general chuckled and Tom and I exchanged glances. Tom spoke under his breath. "He's tryin' to keep the general's mine off his troubles. He's always talkin' 'bout a byoot'fool lady in Kentucky, but she ain't got a name, least he say he forget her name. He always say he gonna marry her soon as he 'member her name. He's a fooler, he is."

We arrived at Moseley's Ferry just about sunset. The four of us, with our horses, crowded together on the small ferry and we had our first view of the Suwannee River.

"See those limestone banks, white as death," the general commented as he turned, looking all about, "and the waters, so dark and silent. Looks like the River Styx."

"Sticks?" Tom questioned. "I don't see no sticks. Where're the sticks?"

"S-t-y-x, Tom," the general answered. "In the old stories—the myths—it was the river that souls were ferried across to reach the land of the dead."

"Oh," Tom said. "Well, it bes' not be that fer us."

As the sun began to fall, gold streaked the blue above, emblazoned its pale banks, and brushed the surface of the water and heavy growth arching the river.

"My God, what a sunset!" Colonel Wilson exclaimed. "See how it lights up the world."

Color and brightness glossed our faces and our horses and blazed in the windows of some small houses on the far bank. There was mystery in this strange beauty. I knew I would keep this view of the Suwannee at sunset stashed away in my mind's eye.

When we arrived, Vickers and Captain Wood were waiting on the dock with the Moseleys and their daughter, Mrs. Mashburn. Tom and I stood back as they exchanged friendly greetings.

Almost immediately, Mrs. Mashburn asked, "General Breckinridge, sir, do you bring any news of my husband, Ed Mashburn?"

Without waiting for Breckinridge to reply, Colonel Wilson spoke up, "Good news. Good news, Mrs. Mashburn. He'll be coming almost any time. You'll be greeting him soon on this dock."

Caught by this lie, I looked around. Tom glanced at me, then away, and for a moment, he put his hands over his ears. Mrs. Mashburn's face livened with joy and her eyes glistened. I saw something more than surprise in the general's wide eyes.

Colonel Wilson continued, "My dear Mrs. Mashburn, he'll be one happy man when he reaches the Suwannee and is reunited with his charming wife and distinguished family. He is a man of great wisdom, sterling character, strong of heart and spirit. Outstanding."

Mrs. Mashburn's attention fixed on Colonel Wilson. Now her eyes were brimming with pride. Tom leaned over and whispered to me, "How he know Mashburn's comin' home? If what he say is true, how come he din't say nothin' 'bout it to the gen'el when they talkin' 'bout him this aft'noon?"

Like Tom, I was puzzled. And by the expression on the general's face, he was, too. Both gentlemen removed their bags and handed Tom and me their horses' leads. We took them to the barn behind the house where we rubbed them down, watered and fed them.

Later, Captain Wood came out to see me and told me the plans for tomorrow. I had hoped to travel with him, but it won't be so. He said Wes will go ahead of the party. Besides trying to help me locate my folks, he'll contact some of the friends who will help them. He didn't say, but I think he doesn't want to leave Breckinridge in Colonel Wilson's hands.

"Cap'n Wood, suh," Tom said. "How come Col'nel Wilson say Col'nel Mashburn's comin' when he don' know that's so?"

Captain Wood looked serious, didn't answer right away, but finally replied, "I suppose he wanted to tell Mrs. Mashburn and the Moseleys what he figured they wanted to hear. He didn't want them disappointed. I had already told them that I had no information about Colonel Mashburn. When they heard that they would be seeing him soon, it lit a lantern behind all their hopes—at least for a while. I pray his prediction comes true. Colonel Wilson will be far away when they find out—one way or the other."

Wes told me that Night and I could rest for a few hours. He and I would leave in the morning's wee hours. Suddenly, I felt like I was about to be cut off from these people whom I had come to know and hoped to know better. Every farewell is a small death.

Just as I finished the above, Captain Wood came again, sat down in the circle of light beside me. Already some folks had unrolled their blankets on the ground and were bedded down for the night. It's most too warm to be so close to the fire, but I need light. Others find safety in the firelight from creatures on the prowl. I lay my journal in my lap.

"Maybe I won't see you again," I said, "and I'm sorry."

"Tench," he said, "that's what I wanted to talk to you about. We're not at all sure you'll find your folks. Have you thought of that possibility?"

"No, sir," I answered. "I've been planning so long and with such hope, for me there is no other possibility."

"I understand. I'll try to meet you and Wes at Orange Lake. In the meanwhile, I hope to talk to Captain Dickinson who is the most knowledgeable seaman in Florida. He'll give us the safest routes. He may also have some news about your family."

"Yes, sir," I said. I was privileged to have Captain John speak to me so confidentially. I set my journal aside and moved close so I would hear what he was saying in his lowered voice.

"Tench, I want you to understand you're welcome to rejoin us, whatever develops in your search for your family." He hesitated before adding, "You know, you may not find them. Of course, by coming with us, you also face the caprice of chance. If all goes reasonably well, we all hope to make a new life on other shores. I realize whatever happens, such uncertain prospects are flimsy material to build a future on."

We both were silent. There it was, like a mine exploding in the very center. Not find my family? My reason for not giving up, or giving in, or giving out. My very reason for being.

I suddenly felt as weak and helpless as when I lay sick on the pallet at the Bronson's. Even then, I never lost sight of what I'd find when I reached my destination. The inconveniences would pass. I'd get over them, be on my way, and find my family. I never had doubted it for a minute.

"Tench, you are young and you've had some hard realities to face. The hardest reality of all is the discovery that your most cherished ideas are not always right." He watched me closely. Perhaps he saw my despair and quickly attempted to lift my spirits and said, "Again, chances are, you will find them just as you hope. But, do you understand?"

Not wanting to admit I might not find them, while at the same time, recognizing that the captain wanted me to be prepared for the worse, I understood. Of course, he was right. Many things might have kept the family from completing the journey to Florida, not to mention the Saint Johns River. I had placed all of my hopes only on what a few others thought might be so.

His gaze was steady on me. "Yes sir. I understand—"

Before I'd a chance to ask another question, I saw General Breckinridge approaching from the house with Wes. Captain Wood rose to meet them down the pathway. I heard their voices rise then lower as they drew closer. I returned to my journal and started to write again. They had halted nearby, continuing to talk. Quite unintentionally, I found myself listening as they lost themselves in conversation.

It was Captain Wood: "Tench is just a youngster, brighter than most of the same age, of either race. He has both a cultivated and natural intelligence."

"True," the general agreed. "His background has given him an appreciation of the best things, at the same time, providing him with an unusual complement of the practical."

And Captain Wood: "He doesn't grovel. He is not obsequious and he doesn't impose. He speaks and acts when bid, and shares his experience and ideas when needed. His presence is of value. The boy was raised in a fine home with deep roots in a good family."

Wes said, "Guess that's where he got those green eyes."

"And knowledge," the general said. "He's been taught well. He wasn't neglected in any manner of thinking or doing."

"Should he decide to come with us," Captain John said, "and you and Colonel Wilson support my decision, I'll be responsible for him."

"I will, John, and I can speak for Jim as well. Tench is a unique young person. Not only would we benefit from his skills, but I believe he would benefit greatly."

Colonel John nodded and spoke, "Uncle Jefferson adopted a Negro boy, Jim Linder was his name. I wonder what happened to him after the Feds captured our camp. When they took him, he was squalling his heart out. Varina and the president loved that child as their very own."

"You fixin' to adopt this boy?" Wes asked.

"If he doesn't find his family, I would." They were standing here beside me, speaking quite openly.

The thought, again, of not finding my family brought a sudden pang. Yet, the thought that Captain John would take me if I couldn't find them pleased me. Also, it was good to know that the general felt the same way as Captain John. I believed I had a special angel watching over me.

There was a big commotion during the night. Some hoodlums raided the pasture where campers had left their horses to graze and stole at least seven of them. There was yelling and screaming and a storm of hooves pounding the ground. Some of those who were robbed howled their anger into the night. I was glad Night was here beside me and the others were in the barn.

The air was finally clear of the confusion. I'd been writing fast so I could get some sleep before we left in the morning. I saw there was a light still burning at Moseley's. I wondered if Captain John knew what had been going on out here. Or was he lost in the pages of his journal?

May 17, 1865

WES VICKERS DIDN'T HAVE TO WAKE ME THE NEXT MORN-
ing. The sand fleas and mosquitoes kept me moving and scratching
all night. Wes laughed and said bugs had to live, too, that I'd get used
to them in time. Says he scarcely notices them. How could that be?
I guessed I would have to cover myself better and watch where I
made my bed at night. Wes slept in a hammock. Guess that's a better
idea. Just get off the ground. A mass of redbugs burrowed in around
my ankles. Wes brought a little cloth bag full of sulfur powder to dust
on my ankles before I tucked my pant legs into my boots. He said
redbugs and ticks were as bad as mosquitoes at this time of the year.
One moment in the night, I had thought I'd go plumb crazy with the
itching. I had just sat up and scratched.

It was hard to keep up with Wes. I think he forgot that I was with
him and he moved on his horse like lightning. I found myself almost
rocked to sleep in the saddle and several times fell across Night's
shoulders. Night sensed the lack of control in his rider and slowed to
a comfortable amble. Without much sleep the night before, and with
the heat beating down and rising up from the sand, I soon became
powerless. When he discovered I wasn't behind him, Wes back-
tracked and after a lash of his whip across Night's flank, I was wide
awake and clinging to Night for dear life.

Wes rode up to my side, broken up with laughter. He shook his
head as he passed me and yelled, "You better not sleep your way to
the St John's, boy. You could wind up dead. Folks hiding out in these
woods are as likely to kill you to git your horse as they'd be to shoot
a squirrel for supper."

While I knew I deserved his shaft, I didn't feel like laughing or pro-
testing. But still, I had to try hard to keep awake. I was worn out and

the steady sound of hooves falling on the sand and the swish of soft winds high in the tall pines surrounding us soothed and lulled me. This was a wilderness, far away from human life. The voices I heard were calls and cries of wild creatures. I looked around.

I saw whole flocks of red-cockaded woodpeckers celebrating the death of a pine as they bored and rattled, greedily feasting on the infestation that had brought it down. Becoming aware of us, they fluttered and rose as one, wheeling off through the pines out of sight.

Quail with coveys of babies moved with tiny, quick steps into heavier brush. With feathers the color of earth and pine needles, they were almost invisible to my searching eye.

Just ahead, I followed the call — *Hoo, hoo. Hoo, hoo.* — of a great barred owl to his perch on one of a pine's lower branches. Curious, but unconcerned, he watched our passing. This was his forest. We were trespassing. His call sent the little creatures scurrying for a mama's wing.

Becoming increasingly aware of the woodland's inhabitants as we moved along, I noticed that our path was crisscrossed by pairs of birds—courting, building nests, feeding babies. I wondered about all the surrounding life in their teeming, thriving communities speaking a language humans don't understand, although I thought Wes understood. He had a long-time knowledge of nature and Florida and I was certain to learn a lot from him.

A razor-back hog snorted and grunted as it rooted among the palmettos. When Night stumbled on a gopher hole, I watched more closely—holes were everywhere. Buzzards were flying overhead, reminding us that death was part of this wild country. They were the bone-pickers who helped keep the woods clean and the air sweet.

Deer flies began circling. Slapping at them, I halted long enough to cut a palmetto fan. Mounting again, Night and I tried to get away from their stings, I by fanning the air and Night by swishing his tail and jerking his head from side to side. The flies were vicious. If they could, they'd attach themselves to a body and suck blood.

Night and I were falling behind again. Seeing that Wes was nowhere in sight, I switched my mount's flanks and we outran our tormentors. After a while, I wondered if we'd outrun Wes, wondered if we'd stayed on the right path, if he'd stopped off somewhere to rest, if he'd gotten tired waiting for us, or had given up and gone ahead without us. I wondered, was he teaching me another lesson? Damned deer flies.

There was no slowing or the flies would catch us again. Leaning forward, I was cooled by air stirred by Night's speed—a speed fueled by anger at the pesky deer flies. I kept him at a fast pace while trying to avoid gopher holes and attempting to stay alert to Wes's whereabouts; I often turned about to look behind, or to see both sides of the path. My gaze raked the woods and palmetto brush, straining and threshing the scene. For a long while, I wasn't concerned until a thought flashed, bright as a silver fish through my mind. What if I were lost?

I pulled back on the reins. Back, deep in the heavy woods, I glimpsed an extraordinary sight. As far as I could see, a colony of deer—does and fawns—moved like ghosts through the trees, some resting, some grazing, others with heads together communicating in some mute harmony. Standing proudly above the others was a grand stag wearing his eight point antlers like a crown. Beyond, I saw five or six doe, agile and swift, leap high in the air, one after another. Moving off-trail into the woods, I could see they had hurdled a wide stream. Wes had insisted we take several canteens of water because there wasn't a good water supply through this wild land. Had he not known of this?

Never had I seen such a gathering of deer. Or had I ever seen more than three at a time. Here was an entire deer population. They must have heard our noise, yet they showed no alarm. Very much like the owl who seemed to own this forest, they owned it, too. I often had wondered where deer gathered during the day. Come to think of it, I only had seen them at dawn, or at dusk, or—in the moonlight.

Slowing our pace, I noticed with relief, we had lost the deer flies. Now I had to find Wes. I studied the ground below, discovered that it was covered with deer tracks. If Wes had passed this way, his horse's tracks were lost among these. The reins lay limp in my hand. Depending solely on animal instinct, I let Night choose our course.

We continued for some while, until I finally halted to consider my situation. I hadn't noticed the sun had drifted to my left side and I was

moving in a northerly direction. I dug in my bag and got the compass. I was going due north and was way off course. We had started
out heading into the sun. As the day wore on, the ceiling of green
branches blocked the sun and I had lost all sense of direction. It was
well into the afternoon and I was heading north towards Georgia. I
had let everybody down—the general, Colonel Wood, and Wes. I
had wasted Wes's time. So much depended on Wes reaching Captain Dickison at Orange Lake to complete the arrangements for the
escape journey. Besides, Wes was going out of his way to help me. I
was ashamed.

I turned around, would try to retrace my tracks, set my course due
south, until I found a trail that would take me out of here. I would
ignore the birds, animals—all wild life that not only had caused me
to get off track, but also proved this wasn't a wilderness. It belonged
to them. It was their home.

I'll never forget the sight of that great colony of deer. If I were to
judge by the thin thread of land I saw today, I'd guess that much life
is seething within its boundaries and, perhaps, humans were the the
only exception to what prospered in that dense and green territory.

Today brought me a new way of thinking—that of not wishing
to disturb the rightful inhabitants in their own territory. Night and I
went cautiously on our way.

We'd gone about two hours south when the light began to fade.
No place to put down. Tedious going. Mosquitoes singing. I was frus-
trated like a little boy, wishing someone could fix everything for me.
Tired, hungry, I had to stop.

I fed Night, wiped him down, gave him water—in the hat the general gave me. Ate some pones and a handful of hominy brought from
the Moseley's camp. Threw a blanket on the ground and wrapped
myself up in my saddle blanket. Bugs were on the hunt. I thought
about snakes. Comforted to remember that rattlesnakes won't
bother you, if you don't bother them—or accidentally step on them.
I moved very gently.

As I settled in for the night, I would write more in this journal, but
the light was gone too quickly to finish these pages.

May 18, 1865

THOUGH LOST AND WORRIED, I SLEPT MUCH BETTER THAN I expected, but then, I was really exhausted. When the sounds and first light of dawn nudged me awake, I wrote in the journal to catch up on the events of the last few days, but even as I put pen to paper, I hoped to do some real traveling before the day was over. As it ended up, I didn't. Yet, that things worked out for me at all is a miracle. The sun started out bright and strong. It looked like it was going to be a good day.

As I strapped on my journal this morning, a little bird, like a precious gem, flashed in the shrub beside me. As it streaked through the trees, I watched, breathless and unbelieving, shaken by memory. It was an indigo bunting. Miss Lottie had called this bird her talisman. I hoped it'll be mine.

Miss Lottie would ride twenty miles before breakfast for a glimpse of one. She took Mama Zulma with her one morning to Meadowsong, her cousin's plantation in Augusta, for that very reason. Mama had complained to me the night before, that she had a pile of sewing she needed to finish and wondered why on earth she had to waste all that time just to see a little bitty bird. Yet for all that, she had been ready to go before sunrise.

When they returned in the afternoon, you'd never guess Mama had ever protested going to Meadowsong. "You boys got to see that bird. It's a live sapphire."

"Same as my ring," Miss Lottie said, referring to the gem in the ring her great-great grandfather had brought from England, which she wore on special occasions.

Lance and I went to see the buntings the next morning. Mama and Miss Lottie came, too. Miss Lottie's meeting with the Committee of

Farm Reformers and Mama's sewing was postponed. We went to the far end of the meadow bordering the edge of the woodland behind the plantation. There, among tulip trees and the Balm of Gilead and Judas trees, was the small shrub that held Miss Lottie's and Mama's attention. They walked almost on tiptoes, hiding behind the screen of green of the larger trees close by.

We followed their lead, moving with their shadows, until little by little, we finally peered into the nest. The cup-shaped nest was woven into a mosaic of grasses, leaves, and petals on a branch a few feet from the ground. Standing at the edge of the nest, stretching first her wing, then a tiny leg, was a small coffee-colored bird about the size of a sparrow. I had looked at Lance, stuck my tongue in my cheek. He raised an eyebrow.

Miss Lottie had seen our response and whispered, "This little bird is the female. Not particularly spectacular. But wait."

Four tiny eggs, like light blue jewels, lay on a fluffy cushion of the mother bird's softest feathers. It reminded me—I used to collect birds' eggs. Imagine. Remembering, I felt guilty.

In the bright sunlight, in a flash, her mate appeared—just as Miss Lottie had said—the brightest blue I'd ever seen. He burst into song with rich, loud tones. His song was an excited, fast warble with little phrases of notes sung quickly, repeated, then started anew. He leaned over, looked at his mate, and studied the nest. Now, he sang again, almost whispering his melodies. Then with a flutter, he shot away in an explosion of indigo.

This morning, I watched with the same wonder. The air was still bright with his color. The memory brought both joy and pain, but above all, hope. This was my talisman. I would find my family.

After watching the bird and taking care of Night, I dusted my ankles with sulfur and put away the blankets. I ate and gave Night a good feed. We had a lot of territory to cover and both of us had to be strong.

I found it impossible to get beyond the underbrush where I had spent the night. It was so tangled and thick and I had nothing with which I could hack a way, so I went about retracing my tracks. I finally came upon a trail and set out, heading east again.

It was uncommonly quiet. A hush had fallen over the pinewoods. The woods darkened. Through the dome of the highest branches, I saw a patch of sky, the strange color of a grackle's wing. The bright day was done, and a storm headed toward me. I had to get ready.

Bad weather was nothing new to Night and me. I took the poncho from my bag, lay it in front of me. Big, heavy raindrops began to fall as we plodded along. Then thunder began to roll and the forest came alive with blinding flashes. Shortly, torrents of rain slapped my face, and struck Night across his eyes and ears and long nose. I pulled my hat down, but as if to bear no more, Night closed his eyes. We had to halt.

Like the crack of a bull whip, lightning struck in the highest limbs, wrenching and splitting trees apart. It hit again and again, all around us, trees exploded into fire that fed on the rich sap and rosin. I got off, put on my poncho, and started leading Night as carefully as I could. The dragon was loose again, just as it had been when I had gone through the woods with Ashby and Captain John. This morning was worse. Trees falling everywhere. A ceiling of flames blazed above. When we really needed the rain, it suddenly let up. The fire that lightning had ignited was spreading.

Knowing I must not panic, I continued leading Night along the trail. Ashby had told Captain John and me about the fury of these tropical summer storms. And bafflingly, he said we must always take cover but not under trees.

When pieces and bits of flaming trees dropped from above, I covered Night with a blanket and wrapped one around myself. The fire raced through the trees as fast as thought, scattering its wild seed to the lower branches and pine needles and growth on the forest's floor. Its breath was deadly. I choked and gagged. Night shook his head back and forth, gave out a long neigh. I knew we both could die and the wonder was, how did it happen so fast? I realized I could not go on leading Night through this withering heat. Only by getting control of him with the reins and whip would we move fast enough to get out alive. He had been spooked beyond any ability to use his good horse sense.

In the saddle again, I kicked my heels into his sides, tugged the bit, let the reins loose, and shouted, "Go, Night, go!" He hesitated only a moment before setting off. Under ordinary circumstance, this trail would be difficult but now it was deadly. We concentrated on the path ahead. It was like a battlefield. I tried not to think of the merciless flames and fiery volleys coming at us. I was bound to him with all my might, forcing my will into his. We moved as one.

The speed of the wind increased and the air was almost too hot to inhale. I took short, quick breaths, but my nose and throat felt scalded and dry. I commanded Night, leaned against his shoulders, stroked his head, urged him to hurry. He obeyed, not sparing his power. He didn't need the whip.

There was a large clearing ahead, a huge white sandy area, bare as a desert. I sat back, relieved. We had reached the end of the forest. I turned and looked back at the raging turmoil, filled with concern for its helpless victims. My heart sank, thinking about the deer colony and birdlife and all the others within its tall burning walls. Wes had told of bears, snakes, and wildcats, and leopards, raccoons, possums, and countless other critters that make the forests and hammocks their home.

As I looked back, I fully expected to see some of the wild ones rushing out of their sanctuary. They, who always had found protection within its boundaries, never had reason to seek refuge outside. Only one, like myself, who feared life within its wild borders, would seek safety on the outside.

A light drizzle filled the air. The dark clouds that had hung above the forest now were moving northward, replaced by a billowing crown of black smoke with fangs of fire. What kind of magic had so quickly transformed the forest from a peaceful haven to a dragon's lair?

I dismounted and poured water into my hat for Night and drank from my canteen. For a long time, I stood watching the destruction of the wilderness, thinking that we might have perished there. I reached up, hugged Night, and dropped to my knees and gave thanks.

When I rose, I heard a voice, weak and faraway, crying, "Help, God!" I looked all around, and turning in a circle, called out, "Where are you?"

The thin and desperate voice cried out, "Help me."

My eyes fell on a large object that looked more like a big log, on the far side of the sandy clearing. Already moving towards it, I called, "Where are you?"

"Help." The sound was faint but urgent.

Leading Night, we moved towards the figure. In the smoke-mottled daylight as I drew closer, I was shocked to find that it was a man bound with a rope, like a mummy. Only his head was free.

Like a jolt—it reminded me of Shears and Joe binding me in a cocoon of rope before Miss Hattie and her neighbors attacked them. So cruel.

Something I'd never seen or heard of before.

And, yet, here it was again.

Quietly, I approached the strange figure until I was looking into a very scratched, bruised face with watery bloodshot eyes. "Wes!" I cried. "What happened?"

He didn't answer. Bending over, I saw his head was bloody and his hair caked with blood. At once, I cut the rope off him, put my canteen to his lips. His body was limp. What to do? I poured water slowly over his face, then began to rub his arms and legs, the way Mama did when I had a charley horse, or my arms or legs were stiff or I had fallen asleep.

"We got to get your blood circulating," I said to him, just as she had to me.

As I worked over him, I wondered what had happened. He was in bad condition and needed attention—more than I thought I could give. He was weak, unable to move. If the general were here he'd give him a libation and it might help. I looked at the injury to his head, discovered there was a big gaping wound of some kind, but at least it had stopped bleeding. Sand and dirt were imbedded in the scratches and cuts on his face, in his mouth, his eyes, ears, and nose.

I tried to guess. Had he been robbed? Judging from his injuries, he had been dragged behind a horse. Someone had stolen his horse. They'd left him to die.

Furious at the sheer meanness of it, I couldn't help but wonder if I had been with him, would this have happened. Maybe—it would have been both of us dragged, beaten, and tied up. On the other hand, two of us might have fought the attackers off. More than one person might have done this. I was remembering the night I last had seen the girls—the Flower family, and had been waylaid by Jake and his gang.

Thinking of that naturally made me think of where Jake might be now. As I recalled, Jake was going to meet Sam in Florida. By himself,

Jake could pull off something like this, but Sam was kind of a nice old man. I don't think he'd let it happen. Then there was Shears' partner, Joe. Mrs. Bronson had told him to head north and never show his face around there or she'd shoot him. But how would she know where he'd go? One thing for sure, he was the kind of person who might do something like this. He'd done it before. Were there more than one of his kind?

But now it didn't matter who had done this to Wes, as helping him was the most important thing. I wondered what I should do next. I plumb didn't know what to do about Wes. I didn't know the way. I needed to do everything I possibly could to help him mend and get strong. For now, we all had to rest awhile. Wes was lying in a quiet sheltered spot, I placed the blankets under his head and continued to rub his arms and legs. This was the most I could do for the moment.

When I gave him and Night water again, I said, "I'm glad you insisted on bringing along extra water."

He smiled and closed his eyes. I would have to study the rough map that Ashby had drawn in my journal and try to figure out where to go and, when Wes could travel, I'd have to get him on Night. Maybe he knew the countryside so well he didn't need a map, but I needed some direction.

To give Night some ease, I took his saddlebags off, lay them beside me. Propping myself against them, I looked beyond the clearing at the forest. The harsh smell of burning woods filled the air, filled my clothes, filled my lungs, made my eyes smart. I welcomed the refreshing breeze coming up from the south, away from the path of fire.

While Night and Wes rested, I wrote several pages, then closed my eyes, which smarted and burned from the fire and smoke. I needed to start a new journal as I had used all but a few sheets of paper. When I finished with those sheets, I'd have to remove this tablet and put a new one in. Luckily, I had three more tablets in my haversack. I shouldn't worry about these pages when I had Wes to think about, but daily writing was as important to me as breathing. To think I used to wonder why Lance spent so much time writing, and now I couldn't go to sleep at night without entering something on these pages—even in the face of this bitter circumstance.

Afternoon, May 18, 1865

Wes, Night, and I all took a good nap. When I wakened, rabbits by the score were overrunning the open space and moving into a cluster of live oaks on the far side of the clearing. I leaned over Wes, holding my canteen to his mouth. His neck stiffened and I believe he was trying to sit up. I put my hand across his shoulders, trying to help him. He tried to rise and started to fall over, so I cradled his head in my arms and put the water to his cracked lips. He puckered his mouth and gently nursed the drops of water that dribbled from the canteen. Finally, he turned his head away.

"When you're able," I said, "I'll try to get you up on your feet. I'm going to soak a pone in water. I want you to eat. We must get some food in you."

Wes nodded. I mixed the pone in water until it was almost fluid, and using a spoon, held it to his mouth and he weakly drew it into his mouth as he had the water. I spent the afternoon giving him nourishment. I could see him getting stronger before my eyes.

Though the wilderness continued burning, the smoke and flames lessened. We would benefit from another downpour. When we were in the middle of the storm on our way to Madison, I had heard Ashby telling Colonel Wood that Florida needed rain badly. He said South Georgia had a wet spring, but just fifty miles south, in Florida, there had been a terrible drought. They already had lost all their spring planting. So the pines in the forest, the undergrowth, and forest floor made perfect kindling for a big fire. It would probably smolder for days to come. I wondered how the general and Colonel Wood would get onto a trail south. They should have left Moseley's Landing by now—just as we should have been a long way south of here. Everything changed when I lost Wes. Still, it might have been worse.

Well into the evening, I cared for Wes. By full sunset, I knew he was going to be all right. "You're better," I told him and he nodded.

"If you are able," I said, "tomorrow we'll try to get you on the horse. I used to ride with my master, Lance. I think we could do the same. You are a slight man and I'm not too big and Night is a big, strong horse. I think we could ride double."

"Could," he said.

"We'll try."

I went to the edge of the forest and found some pine cones, twigs, and branches and built a small fire, not enough in this warm weather to make us hot, but enough to provide some light. I gave Wes more water and tried to make him comfortable. Again, I gently worked his arms and legs and rubbed them. He fell into slumber and I wrote in my journal.

But I must have fallen asleep because Night roused me with a snort, a neigh, and hooves rising and stamping in place. I, comfortable, in deep, dreamless sleep, was slow to return to the world of smoldering fires and scorched air, and the stiff, pained body of Wes and—a restless horse.

I didn't move until long after I became aware of what Night had already known. I slipped my hand slowly into my pocket and felt the cold of the knife. At first, I looked about without moving my body, saw some creature's eyes reflect the firelight. There was something more than this.

Night was nervous. I rose. Turning slowly, I looked around the whole circle of the clearing. My eyes came to rest on the hammock of live oaks, three hundred feet away, on the eastern border of the clearing. Something drew my attention. Something in the silence— unseen, yet strong—spoke to me and I felt my heart beating hard. I felt like a target, profiled against the small campfire. Slowly and quietly, I filled my hat with sand, moved to the fire, snuffed it out and sat looking into the dark.

I returned to Wes's side and leaned close to see if he was sleeping. "Asleep?" I asked.

"No," he replied. "Something wrong?"

"I don't know. Night is uneasy. I have a strange feeling that something or someone's nearby. Can you tell me something, Wes?

He was alert. "I'll try," he answered.

"Who did this to you?"

"There was a bunch of them."

"But who?"

"Some white boys and a bunch of your kind."

"Negro?" I asked.

"Yes. They were mad. They wanted to kill me."

"I know. But why?"

"They said they'd do me like someone did to two of theirs. Dragged me behind my horse, 'round and 'round this field

"Left you for dead."

"If you hadn't come, would've been. Thanks to you, I'm alive."

"Do you know where they went?"

"No idea. I was blown out like a candle."

"Lightning liked to kill Night and me. It set the whole wilderness on fire. When you went off and left me, I got lost." I wanted him to know. "I think I'll go over to the hammock and look around. Someone might be in there."

"You be careful. You're just a boy and right now, I'm not even half a man. Worse—not even half a boy."

"I have a feeling. Will just go look in a few minutes, but first, let me tend to you."

He sounded so much better. I gave him another moistened pone which he held in his hand and ate. I was running out of water. We had to find a source.

"We need water. How far are we from a source?" I asked.

"Next community. Through the hammock, twenty miles east."

As I continued the treatment of bending and rubbing his limbs, he spoke, "You really saved me, Tench. I can't believe that it is you taking care of me."

After he was quiet, I sat for a long while in the dark. Night was still restless and I went to his side, rubbed his head and long nose. As quietly as I could, I set off on my mission to investigate the hammock. Behind me, in the west, the fury had ended, with only an occasional glow of embers. Something ghostly hung over the night. It drifted on the scorched air. I felt it in Night's uneasy pacing, in the dark hammock—in everything I couldn't see or explain.

There was a wide opening of darkness at the edge of the hammock. I entered, wondering if anyone was in its shadows—watching and waiting. Perhaps, if there was someone in here, they had been watching Wes and me. It was so quiet. What about the gang that had attacked Wes? Where did they go?

I pressed on, moving along on what I assumed was a path, trying to keep a sense of direction, touching trees, feeling my way in the dark. I stumbled on a big root, fell into a puddle. I scooped the water into my hand, smelled it, and threw it down. It had a putrid odor, was mud-thick. Wes's warning rang back to me. He had said that anywhere within twenty miles of the wilderness, the water wasn't fit to drink. Water was getting pretty low and he needed it. He was so dried out from his ordeal.

The hammock floor was full of debris from campers and campfires, and scarred with foot and horse tracks. The trail led from one side to the other of the small live oak hammock. As I passed through and back, I felt none of the uneasiness that I experienced out in the clearing.

I had to hurry back to Wes, comforted by the knowledge that the hammock was just another door we would pass through in the morning when we'd start off on our journey again. So far to go.

When I left the hammock, I was surprised to hear Night whinnying as he raced around the clearing. I had not left him tethered, which I now realized was a mistake, remembering how restless he had been.

I was cautious, not whistling for him as I would ordinarily, to get him under control. Then I heard Wes, "My God, Tench."

Without answering, I ran towards him. Within about fifteen feet from him, I came to a quick stop and crouched to the ground. Someone was beating on Wes, pummeling his head with a series of blows, smothering his cries with each fall of his hand. Lying flat against the ground, I reached into my pocket, drew out the knife and slithered along the ground towards the attacker.

In the falling darkness, I couldn't make out the other figure. I determined that he was rather small and slight, and very persistent, which gave him a great advantage over Wes's lack of strength. He was bent over Wes, his full attention on him, providing me with an advantage.

I was behind him and sprang on him, strangle-holding him with my left arm. Squirming and fighting, his arms thrashing wildly, I had distracted him away from Wes, but now he twisted until he was face to face and hand on hand with me and began to lash at me with some kind of hard weapon. I threw my legs about him, straddled him. In one awful instant, I lifted my knife over his body and ripped across his neck and into his chest. Like a beheaded chicken, he continued to writhe and flop and for seconds, I held my straddling grip. His blood, moist and warm, soaked through to my clothes.

A terrible knowledge rose inside me. I leaned over Wes. "It's all right, Wes, we're rid of him."

There was no answer. I put my face close to his, to hear a sound from him and feel his breath.

There was neither.

I had killed a man whose name and face I didn't know, but I was sure he had killed Wes and would have killed me. I was face to face with the awfulness of what I had done and what had been done to Wes. I wondered—how many times had Lance felt like this?

A moon now drifted over some ragged clouds. I felt so confused. I didn't know what time it was.

What next? I didn't know. My mind was too full to think. Full of storm and fire, of Wes and his pain. The deer in the wilderness. A flash of an indigo bunting. The blood of Shear. The blood of this one without a name, a face. This knife. I still held it in my hand. I reached down and whisked it back and forth in the sand, wiped it on my pants, put it in my pocket. I rose. My knees were weak, my steps stumbling.

Tripping over our attacker's body, I fell on a hard object at my feet. Picking it up, I realized it was a gun, and it was heavy. I knew he doubtlessly bashed Wes's head with it and attempted to do the same with mine.

I decided what to do. For a long time I worked, packing things away. I brought Night beside Wes and tied him up with the rope which had bound him when I found him in the clearing. It took all my strength to hoist him across the saddle. Night was moving restlessly, balking at the unaccustomed cargo, wanting to rear up. I held to him, speaking low and gently. I tried to soothe him.

The sun was rising. I looked now at our attacker. He was a small Negro with a bony, hard frame, his dark eyes open and lips parted and shiny. His arms were thin as pipe stems, and were outstretched, as if fighting. Blood had dried like a red bandana around his neck and left a dried hollowed well in his chest. I found no comfort in viewing my assailant in death. My only comfort was in knowing that it might have been me lying dead in this sand.

I picked up the gun, turned it in my hand. It was a very heavy unloaded pistol with the imprint of Lindsay on the barrel. Colonel John would know it. I'd never seen one like it. I stashed it away in my bag.

Already, the flies began to hum and swarm in a zipping dance over the body left on the ground. Had I a shovel, I'd have covered him with sand, but in no time, with the help of nature's scroungers, his bones would be bare.

When I mounted Night, he reared again, weighted though he was, but I got him under control. Although I laid Wes's body in front of the saddle and tied it down, it was unwieldy and rolled about, upsetting Night by throwing both of us off balance. It'd take my full attention to keep this load steady.

We started off through the hammock. We had to go carefully. Daylight dispelled the shadows. It no longer held a mystery. What seemed mysterious in the night, now was nothing more than a messy campground. There was a hole, big as a washtub, filled with thick, murky water. Someone, desperate for water had dug and found, just as Wes had said, nothing but bad water.

The charred remains of many campfires had been left under these big trees. Old rags hung from branches. Worn, holey underwear. Tins. Old filthy blanket. Scraps of garbage. People had sought the shade and shelter of these huge oaks and magnolias, had used them for their comfort, and left their trash behind. Thick with undergrowth, it was nature's hideaway.

I had no doubt this was the boy's hideaway. What was he doing by himself? Wes had said a gang had attacked him. If there were others, what happened to them and why did they leave him behind? If only I could have talked to him. Would it have made a difference?

On the trail leading out on the east side of the hammock, I saw a pile of belongings spread on a square of sacking on the ground. Beside it, a hat and a long stick were propped against a tree. I leaned over to see the contents. Two canteens, several pones, and little bits and pieces of food made up a pathetic array of property.

I dismounted, picked up the canteens, realizing that they and the pones and the hat were probably stolen from Wes. One of the canteens was empty, the other, like mine, was half full. There was a torn photograph which I examined. It was of a group of Negroes sitting and standing on the wide steps of a large mansion. They were all dressed in their best, the women with white starched aprons, the men in white shirts and dark pants. There were eight or nine children, scrubbed and brushed and dressed in white pinafores and starched shirts. Three had been circled. A bony small-faced boy of six or seven whose grin was as big as his face. He held a ball in his hand. Just above him with her hand on his shoulder, a tall woman with the same face. Her face was pleasant, and serious. Her other hand lay on the shoulder of a little girl, five or so, who looked like a flower beaming from the center of layers of white starched petals. In rough lettering in the margin were the words, "Me and my babies, Cora and Ziffa." I turned over the photograph and read: *Magnolia Hall, Commonwealth of Virginia, 1857, House Staff and Families.*

The things in this pile must have belonged to Ziffa, and I guessed that Ziffa was the name of the one I had killed in the dark last night. Now he had a face, a name, and a family. In the dark, he had been a ruthless enemy. Now I began to feel the pain that was his life.

I remembered Lance's words, written after he came face to face with one of his enemies, that it was like looking into a mirror. A moment of recognition passed between them. In that moment, he wasn't the enemy. They were the same.

For Ziffa and me, that moment never came. It came to me only after I'd seen a picture of him with his mother and sister, Cora. It was too late.

I thought of Hattie Bronson. If she knew, she'd think I really had learned a thing or two, at last. I guess she'd say that I'd lived long enough to know how to fight for my life.

May 21, 1865

DURING THIS PAST WEEK I'VE GONE FROM STANDING ON A block at the mercy of a hangman, to standing on the threshold of— I'll save that for later. I will sketch the steps of my journey now, and after I've had time to think, maybe I'll be able to sort out what has happened to me, what I feel deep down.

When I finally arrived at a little community, a group was gathered around a man who was mounted on a horse with a heavy pack, preparing to take leave. When they saw me I was at once surrounded by the entire population, several women and eight or ten men, and a whole passel of children who were standing mute and bug-eyed, hanging onto their mothers' skirts. The man on horseback quickly dismounted, drew his gun, and kept it on me, while two others yanked Wes's body, then me, off the horse. The women, with their children, stayed in the background while I was searched, but drew closer when the men uncovered my journal.

They had every reason to suspect me of being up to no good. I was covered with blood, carried both a gun and a blood-stained knife, which they examined carefully. Besides, I rode a horse and carried a dead man in front of my saddle. Naturally, from the appearance of things, they thought I'd killed the man and stolen his horse.

They wasted no time in tying me up. The women took my journal out under a tree and one began to read. When I tried to speak, I was silenced. With me in the center, the men stood around in a circle openly discussing me.

"Maybe we should get his story, see what he has to say."

"Whatever he says, it's gonna be a lie."

"He probably belongs to that band of cutthroats on the old trail."

One began to examine Wes and the others went over to watch. "It's Wes Vickers. We know him real good."

"A good man. Tracker. Guide. Hunter. No one knows the country or woods like Wes does."

"Folks everywhere know him."

"No gunshot or stab wounds. Has rough sores all over. Face is heavy blue. Bruised bad."

"What about it?" the man who'd interrupted his leave-taking asked, looking at me. He was in charge. He wasn't much larger than I. "Let's see what the boy say? What happened?"

They tied my hands behind my back with a long dragging trail of rope. He looped the rope and tightened it around my neck.

"Let me explain, please," I begged.

"Matt, we want to hear," called one of the women.

"We all do," said another. The children skulked off in the shade, the women came closer.

One of the older men waved them off with a sweep of his hand. "Miss Evelyn, this ain't woman-bidness."

"We want to hear him. I haven't had a chance to read more n' a few lines, but this here book tells all 'bout him. He don't sound like a bad type. Not the kind to kill. 'Sides, how'd somebody that little get over on Wes?"

I shivered when I heard her judgment.

Matt, backing off, rope in his hand, shouted at me, "You—covered with blood. Bloody knife. Heavy gun under your belt—"

"Sir, I had to fight Wes's killer. I was traveling with Wes. I was going with him to Orange Lake, then he was going to the St. Johns with me."

There were questions and answers. I didn't want to dip into my life and make too many explanations to strangers who were ready to kill me. But I explained what had happened to Wes and they listened.

"If I killed him, would I've brought him with me?" I asked.

Evelyn continued leafing through my journal. At last, holding it up, she spoke, "I believe this boy. Here is the whole story, just as he's told it. Let him go, Matt. Read through these papers yourself. His name's right here in front. Name's Tench and he's written down everything that's happened to him. Glance over these last pages."

Reading, she went on, "—that Ziffa was the name of the one I killed in the dark, last night. Now he has a face, a name, and a family. He had been a ruthless enemy in the dark. I began to hurt for him—"

She came up to me, put her face next to my mine. "Quickly, Tench, tell what happened, this time, everything."

Thanks to Miss Evelyn, I had a chance to speak for myself. They were listening and whenever I paused, she read from my journal. "I believe him. I know he ain't lying," Miss Evelyn exclaimed. She really believed me.

"Makes sense," Matt nodded. "He wouldn't be bringing the body with him if he'd killed him." He considered, then said, "I was just getting ready to go to Orange Lake. If you're a Negro and you're going down through middle of Florida and hope to stay alive, you'd better have a white man with you."

Matt said he'd delay leaving until morning so I'd have time to get ready and Wes could be buried properly. The ladies helped me clean up my clothes and after I'd bathed in a nearby stream, they lay out a good spread. The burial was respectful. They said prayers and sang over Wes's body. Everyone spoke of some memory they had of him. Matt said he was everyone's friend, that he'd left behind a country full of friends, yet no one there knew where he called home.

Next morning, as Matt and I set off, I was thinking how little I knew about my destination or the person who was supposed to help me after I got there. Wes had all that information. Orange Lake had been his destination. Of course, I remembered the name of Captain Dickison. He was from Waldo. And I knew that Wes had a brother who was a seaman on a steamship that traveled the St. Johns and he had hoped to find him—those were the only facts I could share with Matt.

Those long hours spent in the saddle broke down my resolve not to spill out the story of my life. Besides, he asked me lots of questions and, once I get started, I'm just a natural talker. I ended up telling Matt about Lance and Lottie and Carson and Mama Zulma and Avalon, but the story of my fellow travelers—the escaping members of the Confederacy—I didn't think was mine to tell. Miss Evelyn hadn't had time to read those pages. She'd read the first and last pages of my journal. Nothing of Jefferson Davis, or the captain. I rehashed stories of Lance and the war for Matt, told him what a coward I'd been.

"Well," he said, "you were just a boy, still no more than a boy. Yet you've lived a man's life." His words rang in my ears. It was true—I had faced an enemy and had been forced to fight my own battle. That had made the difference. Lance had insisted the war had not been mine to fight, but the happenings of the past week certainly had been.

"Sometimes, circumstances cause you to grow up in a hurry," Matt offered an explanation. "You don't know what you can do, or even if you have it in you to do it, until you're threatened in a big way. You were—and you did it. Tell the truth, you did good."

Good? I couldn't get Ziffa out of my mind. "He was no older than I am," I said, "and his name was Ziffa." Then I told him about the photograph. He shook his head. "It's important you remember that it was either him or you."

That was so.

The sun beat down on the deep, silken sand our horses were wading through. I thought of Ziffa in that large barren plot between the wilderness and the hammock. By now, the same hot sun was sparkling on the sand beside him, and the buzzards, their feathers like quivering black shrouds, probably were gathered around, cleaning his body to the bone, taking away everything that his mother or sister Cora, would recognize.

The mosquitoes and horseflies were a torment. I did as Wes instructed, covered as much of my body as possible, pulled the long sleeves of my shirt over my hands, collar high, and hat down over my ears and face.

I found that the mosquitoes weren't the worst thing that could get us. I felt my skin crawling. Rubbing, scratching didn't help. Matt, watching me squirm and twist, suggested I stop at the next lake and soak myself in the cool waters. At the next small pond, I took off my clothes and found myself covered with masses of tiny, crab-like creatures, clinging to my flesh and lodged in the creases and hollows of my body.

"Ticks," Matt exclaimed. "Do you have any liniment?"

"No, sir. I have a sulfur bag."

"Good enough. Get in the water and pull off those little devils. If you have a problem, I'll help you. When you finish, shake and dust your clothes with sulfur, then dry off and dust yourself with it real good."

Now I knew how an old yard hound feels, covered with ticks. I scrubbed and pulled the pesky vermin off my skin. I shook out my clothes and found the sulfur bag Wes had given me back at Moseley's Landing and dusted my clothes and body.

When we reached Orange Lake, I expected Matt to leave me to continue on my own. To my surprise, he had changed his mind and stopped off with his folks for only a short while. They lived in a large cabin made from split logs with a high-pitched roof, set high off the ground. I couldn't help thinking how cool it must have been in there, compared to the butchering shed, where he'd left me.

"I'll visit awhile with my folks," he said. "Shouldn't be too long. Feed the horses. Give them plenty of water. I plan to find the best way to get to the St. Johns. Haven't ever been there. Wait in the shed. Folks in these woods don't take good to dark folks."

Though I hated to be reminded of that, I knew that's the way folks are. I'm used to it. I'm not sure how long I waited. The mosquitoes stung through my clothing. Like a throbbing screen, they hovered in the shed's stagnant air. I was soon covered with another layer of bites. I can't remember having been so tortured. I was impatient. Had I been alone, I'd been on my way by now.

Brushing a path through the mosquitoes, a couple of red-faced men came into the shed. Both were short with bellies that hung out over their belts. I thought they could be Matt's brothers. When I spoke to them, they looked at me sullenly and didn't say anything.

They picked up some pails as they started outside. One of them turned around and said gruffly, "We know you're with Matt, but don'tcha dare take anything outta here. You heah?"

I looked around. What did they think I'd take? There were pails and clay pots.

Tools. Why did they think I'd take anything in the first place? Because I'm a Negro? Matt had warned me folks were like that around here. I heard one grumbling, "Darn if he don't have a horse." Their pails clanged as they sauntered into the woods.

At first, Matt had been only too ready to hang me, but he had been more than fair when he found out the truth. Was it kindness or guilt that caused his change of heart? At last, Matt came outside, followed by an elderly couple. They looked at me curiously.

"Howdy," I said.

"Well, howdy, boy," the man said.

"'Squitoes 'bout to eatcha up?" the woman asked. "Two things are good for that. Harold here uses tobaccy juice. Mysef', I favor spirits. It doesn't keep them away, but it does stop the itchin'. Most any kind will do. I'll give you a little bottle of huckleberry. Dab the sting with it." She went back to the house with Matt following. Shortly, he came back with a generous-sized bottle of spirits.

"Makes it herself," he said, handing me the bottle. "It's good for more than 'squitoes."

I'm afraid I had far too many bites to dab the treatment on one at a time. When we started up, I took off my shirt and splashed it over my body and rubbed it on. We were less apt to be stung while moving on horseback. As it cooled on my skin, I had to agree, it felt better.

It was difficult plodding through the sandy country thick with oak and scrub pine. We took an old trail through heavy growth and moved slowly. It was the most difficult going we'd encountered, every bit as bad as the wilderness. We had to cut through heavy ropes of tangled vines in the scrub. We were covered with scratches and cuts, our clothes snagged and torn.

We arrived on the shore of the Ocklawaha in the heavy dark of a clouded sky. We tethered our horses, wrapped ourselves in our blankets, and fell into a heavy sleep.

The following morning, under a tent of dark clouds and light drizzle, we wakened somewhat refreshed despite the bugs and were soon ready to go. I looked into the clear water of the Ocklawaha and noticed at the bottom, long green grass swaying with the current. The boatman, a white-bearded old man, was the owner of the low flat boat waiting to take us to the other side. He told us the horses would have no trouble swimming across, that the extra weight would help. I had a strong doubt. He said to leave the bags and gear in place, they'd make it fine. I insisted we lighten their burden, and because no one was waiting behind us, he smiled patiently, and told us to go ahead.

Although we held their leads as he poled us across, the current was strong and the horses struggled. I was truly fearful that after coming this far and going through everything I had with Night, I could lose him now. I prayed all the way.

When we reached the other side, the old man watched us gather our bags, tether the horses, and load them again. He finally said, "They'd have done better with extra weight on 'em."

Matt smiled when I said, "Yes sir, you are right."

Matt spoke to him and he told us our location and where to go next. Just ahead a few miles was the St. Johns. He told us that many settlements were clustered along its east banks from Lake George down to Mellonville on Lake Monroe. Although steamship traffic had all but stopped during the war, once a month a ship ventured down from Jacksonville and made stops at most of the settlements not only to get fat pine for fuel, but to pick up and let off passengers, and to collect and deliver cargo and supplies. Folks up Jacksonville way were just as eager to have the steamship return loaded with vegetables and fresh fruit from the farms along the St. Johns.

From what he told us, he thought some of the ship's crew might have the information we sought. They knew everyone and everybody knew them. All the land owners along the St. Johns were looking forward to the day when travel would again be normal on the river and the steamships would be making steady runs.

"How long is the river?" I asked. "It starts at the big lake down in Indian country, goes clear up to Jacksonville."

"How far is that?" Matt asked. "Quite a piece," he laughed, then explained. "Nigh on three hundred miles, it meanders through a bunch of big lakes."

"How'll I ever find my family?" I moaned.

"Don't worry. All the new settlers seem to put down 'round Lake Monroe, south to Lake Jessup. You'll find them."

I was puzzled. "How do you tell the lakes from the river?"

Our old friend laughed. "The Indians named this river Welaka which means chain of lakes. Like beads. The lakes are strung together with the river running through them. Lakes are very wide." He threw his head back, looked at me, and said, "There aren't many dark folks around here. I could count them on one hand. How many in your family?"

"Only my mother," I said no more. Another time, I might have started talking.

"I think you'll have no trouble in findin' her," he said.

"When is the next boat due?" Matt asked

"No particular day. Could be comin' most anytime. We know it's comin' when we hear that whistle soundin' across the lake. We're always ready. Was it to come one day, turn 'round and come back the next, people would come down to see it dock again. Nothin' folks like more than to see the steamship come in."

We decided to go to the settlement at Ft. Butler, which was nearest to us. We cleaned ourselves up much as possible. Matt told me as we started off that he had his own personal mission. He was looking for a place where four of the couples and their families from his settlement could move and start over again. Originally, they thought to move to Ocala or Orange Springs, but he had been giving it serious thought and wanted to look along the St. Johns before he decided. Besides lumbering, the forests offered little else. Besides, there wasn't a way to get the lumber out from the forests.

"Good place to start is the Gen'ral Store. They might've been there sometime," he said. "I'll do the talkin' and nose 'round a bit. They'd likely talk to me 'fore they'd talk to you."

The store was full of the familiar earthy smells of white and sweet potatoes and grains, vegetables, herbs, and spices. There were two country men who were busy gathering a great number of provisions, while other customers leaned over to watch them.

When asked, they said they were planning to go south. "We're usin' a large lifeboat," one was saying, "salvaged from the gunboat *Columbine* that Captain J.J. Dickison captured from the Feds." They spoke noisily, seemed to be proud of this connection, pleased that others might be listening.

They had caught my attention by mentioning Dickison and I joined the others observing them, although I was aware that Matt was talking to a man in a visored hat who seemed to be in charge.

A sun-bonneted, plump woman addressed the men. "How you happen to be usin' the *Columbine's* lifeboat? Dickison's a real hero in these parts. None equal."

"Yes, ma'am. We served under him," he said.

"We've just been paroled. I was a sergeant, name of Jerry O'Toole." He held out his hand and pointed to his companion. "Him, Corporal Richard Russell."

"We both can swear there ain't a greater soldier than Captain J.J. Dickison," Russell added.

Matt's voice sounded low and heavy below the animated voices of the sergeant and the corporal. "We're looking for a refugee family from Georgia. A couple named Matthews with a young son and daughter and a dark woman."

I didn't hear his answer. The corporal was boisterous in his pride. "The Yankee commander of the warship *Columbine* surrendered to our cavalryman from Orange Springs, Captain J.J. Dickison, hero of the river."

"We were only a small band of men, but they gave up to us when only sixty-six of their hundred forty-seven were left alive!" the sergeant boasted.

"We know, we know his story. But how do you happen to have the lifeboat? I thought the *Columbine* was burned," the woman persisted.

"It was, ma'am. We set it afire. Sank the lifeboat in a channel where we could come back and get it when we needed it."

"Wha'cha need it for now?"

"We're salvagin' on the coast."

"How're yuh gonna get over there? The river will only get'cha part way."

"Don't worry, we'll get there. Some others are comin' and we'll be doin' real treasure huntin'."

I was beginning to feel anxious. I sensed a much stronger connection between O'Toole and Russell and Captain Dickison. Colonel Wood had brought Dickison's name up before. He and the general were depending on Dickison to help them find guides and a safe escape route. But here was great need for secrecy and if they had anything to do with the general's plans, I had a feeling these paroled soldiers had been babbling too loud and freely.

Matt was at my side, his deep voice a strong monotone under the others, "We're 'bout to find your family, boy. They live downstream close to a little settlement called Holly Center. They're farmin' and settin' out an orange grove. The women do the work and some hirin'. The old man is a bit daft. He plays the piano and does needlework."

It was them! I was exploding inside. Those long days, weeks, and years that had brought me to this place and moment were crumbling and falling away. I was excited.

Matt droned on, "A lot of refugees from Georgia have located in settlements up and down the river from here. He says this is the largest supply store on the river. People from all over come to trade. Although the small settlements have their own stores, none are stocked like this one."

I wanted to shout and laugh and cry, but I held it inside and looked about, while my heart pumped joy and my thoughts leaped ahead to the reunion I'd soon be celebrating.

"Steamship should be coming most any time. Yes, you're gonna find them, boy. Mister Taylor says he's certain they live near Holly Center, a short ways down the river. It's a long ways by land so we'll leave the horses. We can get a skiff down on the shore."

I hurried to the door, looked down the bank at the river below. Matt hesitated and I said, "Let's go, Matt. If it's a short distance, there's no need to wait. Let's go."

"Hold on, Tench. Got to find a livery. Can't just leave the horses hitched, and we'll need our bags. We don't know where we're goin', how far it is—or when we'll be back."

"I'll take my bag with me," I said.

Matt continued in his role as spokesman and we were quickly accommodated at the livery and sent on our way to the waterfront. A boatman at the dock, thinking we were fishermen, told us he had nets and complete rigs. When he learned we wanted only to go to Holly Center, he loaned us one of the skiffs from his fleet of a dozen or more, said just to leave it when we finished with it and passed through again. He wouldn't charge us anything.

"But keep me in mind when you need a rig," he said as he handed us a set of oars. I threw my bag in and we climbed in the boat closest to us.

"These are real country folk, neighborly and good." Matt noticed. "I want to look around and see what's here and what kind of living can be made in these parts."

I sat in the middle, setting the oars in the locks. I commented, "We're going downstream with the current. Fast going, but harder rowing coming back."

"How long's it been since you saw your mother?" Matt, sitting in the skiff's bow, was watching me, squinting in the glare of the reappearing sun.

"Spring of '63," I replied. "More than two years ago."

"She's the lucky one. She gets her son back."

"Almost didn't a few times," I said, and, feeling feisty, I couldn't pass up the chance to get in a dig. "You know about the last time."

My energy was fueled by excitement. Suddenly, I stopped rowing. The news I brought of Lance would end any prospect of happiness I might have expected over my own safe arrival. I said as much to Matt.

"One step at a time, Tench. Indeed, you may expect them to face great sorrow, just as you have already. They must go through everything you've gone through. And you know how much you've been helped with the passin' of time. Time will bring them comfort, too."

Once more, I began to row. Matt scanned the shoreline and my glance followed. At the river's edge, a roving breeze rattled the palmetto fans and swung the long beards of moss hanging from the trees edging the water, then skipping across the river, it scalloped the surface from one side to the other.

"Lookit the view!" Matt shouted. I turned to see the scene ahead. Tropical brush on the shore was separated by a narrow channel. Beyond, there was a small cove edged with cabbage palms and cypress trees, with roots rising out of the water, like stalagmites in a cave where I once had been hidden by Lance.

The huge colony of birds—herons, egrets, and limpkins—filled the air as they soared and circled and glided about, their calls ringing and echoing through their refuge.

A long dock following the shoreline with a shorter section reaching out into the water alerted us of our arrival at another settlement. As we drew closer, we could read the lettering of a sign on the big arch straddling the dock—Holly Center.

"Pull up here," a commanding voice called. "Steamboat's coming."

I looked over my shoulder, saw the ship appear on the horizon, and heard a deep horn announcing its arrival. A group of rugged young men had gathered on the bank, sweaty and eager and ready to work soon as the boat docked.

As we were advised, we pulled up on the bank. Matt stepped out and began talking easily with them. "We're lookin' for Lottie and Carson Matthews' family from Georgia. They have two youngsters and a colored woman. Might've arrived early this year. Know them?"

"Sure do. They live up past a big oak n' cypress hammock—Sleepy Hammock. Far enough to work up a good sweat, rowing."

Another asked, "You kinfolks?"

"Yes," Matt answered. "How're they doin'?"

"Never seen a woman who can work like Miss Matthews. That little lady can do anythin'. By sweat and muscle, she built the cabin hersef'—she n' her Nigra."

"She's settin' out orange stock, now. Gonna have a big grove, one day."

"We he'ped her clear land for it."

"Put up a fancy sign. Name of their old plantation in Gawga ... was ..."

"Avalon," I said.

"Yeah, Avalon. "

I wanted to get on our way, rowing towards Avalon. Soon as the ship docked, I signaled Matt. He thanked them, turned to me, and asked, "Tench, you want me to row?" I guess he saw my grin and knew the excitement I was feeling. The bow lifted high in the water, as he sat down in the stern.

Rowing close to shore, I scanned the riverfront, hoping to catch sight of a familiar human form. There was only the dense growth of trees and plants and thick vines shielding the land beyond. "Wild country." I said, and asked, "Sleepy Hammock?"

Matt, studying the shoreline, responded, "Must be. God, lookit the cabbage palms, cypresses, oaks. And—the river. Our woods are beautiful but monotonous and—there's no water."

"You think this is what you're looking for?" I asked.

He didn't answer right away, then said, "Might be, for sure."

Matt knew much about me, yet something held me back from telling him everything. I knew nothing about him. I had seen his neighbors and met his folks, but I couldn't help but wonder why he and the people of his community lived such isolated lives.

He never mentioned the war, other than to ask me about Lance and my experiences, which he had listened to with interest. He had come this great distance with me, had been unfailingly kind to me, and I was grateful.

Without warning, we had come upon a simple log cabin standing above on a steep bank. Over the doorway, I could see the once splendid, now weathered sign with faded lettering announcing: Avalon.

My heart pounded as we reached land and dragged the boat onto the bank. Looking up, I saw Carson Matthews, sitting in the hollow of a dead oak. In faded gray shirt and pants, his hair like dandelion down, and the dusty blue of his eyes fixed in a gaze somewhere above our heads, he seemed almost unseeing.

Stumbling up the bank, and almost falling over the rooted surface, I ran to his side. "Mister Carson!" I shouted. He rose, put a limp hand in mine, and moved towards a shed in the field. There was no change in his expression. I was simply doing what was expected of me and he—what was expected of him.

I looked across the newly cleared field, rough with roots and stubble. In a far corner, I saw Miss Lottie and my mother, and Olive and young Carson, moving back and forth, carrying debris from the field to a big pile nearby.

Matt came up behind me. "Go ahead. I'll watch him."

As fast as I could, I ran towards them. They turned, still as statues at first, then they dropped their work, rushed to me. The children were screaming, "Tench! Where's Lance?" It was Mama Zulma who reached me first and hugged me close while Miss Lottie grasped my arm, saying, "Tench, he's not coming back?"

I bit my lips and struggled to find the answer. "No, ma'am." My voice broke as I held the journal before them. "But I've brought his words. I brought you his own story." Tears began to fall before I had a chance to show my family how I'd grown up.

May 23, 1865

We filed into the cabin. The children had fallen silent. Miss Lottie drew me to the plain wood table with two long benches and two heavy chairs at either end—rough and simple, handmade. She pushed me into one of the big chairs and everyone quickly took a seat at the table. She and Mama sat on either side of me. Mister Carson entered with Matt behind, and he sat at the opposite end of me. I thought Mister Carson's eyes were on me, but I soon realized his gaze was without focus; he was looking through me and beyond.

After Matt greeted everyone, he said he'd row back to Holly Center. He was going to look around. "I come from the woods up north Florida," he explained. "I'm thinking of locating on the river."

"You won't regret that, sir," Miss Lottie spoke. Her voice was soft and hesitant, her eyes were full of pain and tears at the news of Lance, yet she expressed her usual friendly warmth. "I don't know what you may be leaving behind, but if you've lost everything, this is a good place to start again. The land and the river are rich. If you don't mind working, you'll find everything again." She took a deep breath. "That's what we are doing."

Matt nodded. "I believe you are, Miss Lottie. This looks like a good place to start." He moved towards the entrance. "I'll be back tomorrow, Tench." Matt went back to the boat, returned quickly with my bag.

Mama's eyes filled and, cupping her hand over mine, asked, "Will we ever be able to catch up, my boy?"

I unstrapped my journal, put it on the table. "It's here, Mama. Lance and I saved everything that happened, for you and Miss Lottie."

Miss Lottie leaned over. "I am grateful to you, Tench."

I looked at her. Really saw her. Her hands, folded on the table before her, were large and rough. Her straight back, strong chin and firm mouth, and heavily weathered skin, bore out the promise of her hands—hard and strong; only her small frame belied its strength. Looking into the sober, green Traymore eyes, there was the softness.

After awhile, Mama trimmed the wick, poured oil in the lamp, and lit it. She served food from a pot on the wood stove. Now trying to recall, I'm not sure what it was. It was filling, possibly cornmeal mush. The cabin was small, with too few windows to cook unnecessarily, except in the cool of the day. I had noticed an open shed away from the house in the back. Besides a plow, harnesses, and garden tools stored inside, I saw the large solemn heads of two mules silhouetted in the stalls, and off a ways, a cow was tethered to a hitching stake—not too far from a vegetable garden in raging growth.

"The cow looks dry," I mentioned. If it weren't, I'd have a chore in the morning.

"She should be bred," my mother said. Shaking her head, she sighed, "We'll get everything done eventually."

I was surprised when Mama unrolled the pallets. I was remembering the old bedtime rituals: arranging the great four posters and down mattresses, the canopy curtains and netting and the stories and songs. As I was to see, they had kept an important part of the ritual.

On the wall above each mat, they had placed a hook and from the hook, mosquito netting hung. It was then spread over them and anchored under the mat, much like a canopy.

Mister Carson understood it was time. He put his hand in Mama's and dropped onto his mat. He faced the wall. "He watches the shadows until he falls asleep," Mama explained.

I saw then that with the lamp in the middle of the table, our figures turned into monstrous forms, moving and dancing on the wall. Young Carson and Olive soon took their turn to bed. Miss Lottie moved beside them and told one of the stories that Mister Carson used to tell. When she finished, she returned to the table. Mama began to sing, "Precious Lord, take my hand." I choked back a sob, thinking how often I'd longed for this moment, now empty without Lance.

Yet even without Lance, I was glad to discover that some things I had cherished hadn't changed.

Miss Lottie reached for my hands folded in front of me. I felt their roughness as she covered mine with hers. Like water behind a crumbling dam, I began to sob. The touch of her hand reminded me that her gentle kindness was Lance's source. Even further, the same kindness was borne in the Traymore veins, in a grandfather who held both families together, and back to the first Traymores, of whom I had heard endless stories revealing the good in their lives. Strange. I even considered the fact that I owed the gift of life to the great grandfather whom I hadn't known, yet long resented. Mama put her arms around my shoulders.

I looked at Carson, desolate in silence, then across at Miss Lottie, her hands clutching mine, her face bathed in tears. Despite all our sorrow and our happiness, we finally slept.

This next morning, on the front stoop, I watched the sunrise. I think the questions, and the resentments that I'd long harbored, all the hurt and frustrations I'd known, had been washed away at the table in this new Avalon when Miss Lottie's and Mama's tears flowed with mine.

May 24, 1865

LAST NIGHT, WHEN I HAD TAKEN OUT A FRESH TABLET AND started new pages in my journal, Mama and Miss Lottie had been reading the old ones. For many hours they read together, Mama, then Miss Lottie. It was good to hear their voices. I was really home again.

While the sun rose, I sat in the cool dampness of the cabin steps. Out on the river, I heard the sound of oars creaking in the oarlocks and the splash of water. I walked down the bank. To my surprise, it was Matt with a passenger. As they drew close, I saw the passenger, a heavy-bearded, scruffy vagrant. I watched the tall frame unfold as he stepped from the skiff. I found myself looking into the eyes of Captain John.

Matt grinned, "Met Mister Taylor at the General Store. He was looking for you. Said he was with you in Georgia."

I laughed. "Matt says you can find anything at the General Store."

"This proves it. Found your folks that way. Didn't you?"

Captain John was Mister Taylor. I had to remember. To Matt, I had called him that. I replied, "Yes, sir. How was your journey, sir?"

"Good. Stopped off at Silver Springs. Been there?" he asked Matt. He didn't wait for an answer. "Most amazing. You can see into the springs down hundreds of feet as distinctly as through clear air. Now, Mr. Breck and I are going over to the coast to do some salvaging. We got two men to help. They cannot go the full way." He paused and looked at me. "We wondered about you."

I thought the two men I had seen at Ft. Butler might have been those they'd hired. I also knew that Captain John had gone out of his way to find me. We always worked together well. To myself, I questioned how I could leave Avalon so soon.

Struggling for the right words, I said, "I'd like to go, Mister Taylor. But I've been looking at the work that needs to be done here."

"There are workers who can do your work here," Matt said. "I was talking to some fellows at Holly Center. They'd been helping Miss Lottie and liked working for her. They need the work."

I knew it would be next to impossible for the captain and the general to find someone for their needs, someone they could trust completely and who knew how to keep his mouth shut. Just anyone wouldn't do.

"You'd have to talk to Mama and Miss Lottie. They spent last night reading my journal. Tell them who you are and what you propose. They'll know you. My answer depends on them."

As he climbed the bank, I sat down beside Matt, who said, "Well, boy, you've proved your worth before. Doesn't surprise me. When I first saw Mister Taylor, I thought here, indeed, is a wild one."

"He's a fine person. He's not the way he looks."

"We can't know just by looking. You, for instance. All the evidence was against you—"

"And you were going to hang me for it," I snapped, a sudden flare of my old anger rose in me. Then I added, "But, yet, shortly after that, I could tell you were a good man—"

He interrupted, "Which proves you can't judge by what you think you see. You thought I was a good man, but there are plenty of folks who'd dispute that. You see," he looked at me directly, "for more than two years, I've hid in the woods from the war. Had the Rebels won, I could have been executed."

"And your neighbors?"

"My neighbors, too. We couldn't fight a war we didn't believe in. Our enemy has vanished. The war was our enemy."

Thinking of the other good people I knew who still could be executed, I said, "It was not a good war, sir."

I looked at Matt. I was grateful to him for many things. Now he had shown me what I must do. I'd go with Captain John and the general. Miss Lottie and Mama must understand. "I'll be back, Matt. I've got to tell Miss Lottie and Mama that I'm going with Captain John—"

As soon as I said it, I realized that I had given Mister Taylor away. He looked at me, flashed a smile, and said, "I don't know one captain from another, Tench, long as he doesn't know me."

Racing up to the cabin, I broke in on the conversation going on. "Miss Lottie, Mama, I must leave with Captain John."

Mama touched my arm. "I just told Captain John, if it's up to me to say whether you can go or not, I'd say you're ready. You're no longer a child when you can speak for yourself."

"Every mother recognizes when manhood bids her son." Miss Lottie sighed. "No bond, no matter how strong, would hold him. I know this well."

Captain John took my mother's hand and Miss Lottie's. "He'll be back, just as he returned to you this time—wiser and stronger. I promise you." To me, he said, "Your friend Matt will pick you up before sunrise—if the weather holds. This afternoon, one of the boys from the Center will go to the livery at Ft. Butler to bring your horse home. We're traveling in a four-oared gig from a Fed gunboat. It's heavily loaded, so travel light. We'll have tight quarters. Six of us. We'll be losing one of the guides, maybe both, later on."

Captain John started to leave, then turned back, dug into his boot, took out some gold coins, and put them on the table beside the journal and flickering lamp, now about out of oil. The children still slept. Day had not yet entered the cabin.

"Oh, no." Lottie looked at the coins. Her soft voice, not strong enough to be a protest, tried to reach Captain John before he strode out the door.

From the front stoop, he spoke," I wouldn't be able to use it myself, ma'am. It'll buy a little help, until Tench returns."

With a quick look back at Mama, I joined him outside. He reminded me, "Before sunrise, Tench."

I remembered that I also had something in the bottom of my bag that I wanted to give Mama and Miss Lottie—the surprise I had found in Jake's haversack when I'd recovered Night. Matt had left my bag beside the stoop. Now I began to root through its contents. Because the tobacco pouch was small and heavy, it had fallen to the bottom. I emptied the entire bag on the stoop. Lance's Bible, my books, tablets, underwear, pans, pones, utensils, pencils, compass, bowie knives, cloths, dirty clothes, grain, combs, brush, and the tobacco pouch. Such an assortment.

My mother watched. "Tench, I must wash these." She snatched up a pile, started towards the pump and washtub.

"Don't go yet." I reached for her hand and led her into the house again. I said to both of them, "I have something for the women of Avalon." Taking them to the table, I sat on the bench, untied the knots in the tobacco pouch, and shook the gold pieces onto the table. The children, who had been postponing the new day, jumped from their mats to see what was going on.

Funny, each wanted to touch the gold, pass it through their fingers, hold it in their hands.

"What is it?" young Carson asked.

"Real gold," Olive answered. "Mama, this will buy everything we need, won't it?"

"It will," she replied, and looked me straight in the eye. "You didn't—"

Maybe she wanted to know where and how I got it, and then could be she thought better of the question, because she didn't finish whatever she was going to ask me. Or maybe she'd already read that part in the journal.

Mama led Mister Carson to the pump at the sink and primed and pumped as it gasped and gulped and finally spewed a stream of water which she caught in a kettle and a wash pan. She put the kettle on the stove and with the wash pan, began to help Mister Carson wash and shave. She had pulled his chair over and he sat down, indifferent to her caring hands, lost in his silent world.

Miss Lottie opened the door of the big wood stove, arranged some small logs on top of lighter pine. Quickly igniting, it drew our eyes like a magnet. Even Mister Carson's gaze held to it. Our faces glowed in its lively flame. Miss Lottie pulled the bench beside it.

"Look, Mama. Tell the story. The Golden Foxes," young Carson begged. She'd never refused a plea for a story. The children settled close to her. They didn't mean to miss a word.

Vaguely, I remembered another telling—long ago, when Lance and Traymore and Edelman were with us. Sitting on another bench, at another hearth, at another Avalon.

"Do, Mama," Olive coaxed.

"Watch," she said. We all moved closer in order to see what she saw. "The flames are golden foxes leaping from the logs. See their pointed ears? Now, their long noses, bushy tails. See?" She leaned forward to better see and hear, although we knew full well what came next.

Before our eyes, the flames were transformed into a pack of golden foxes leaping from the log into the metal chimney.

"Once, not long ago in Virginia," Lottie began, "three brothers went fox hunting. They were closing in on their quarry when the old-est told his younger brothers that the woods were full of foxes like that one. He told them not to waste their powder on such poor game. 'Somewhere in the woods,' he told them, 'there is a magnificent fox, faster than quicksilver and golden as the sun, who has outwitted all the huntsmen before us.'"

Miss Lottie's gaze was fixed on the fire. She went on: "So the hunt-ers raced through the forest, passing up one fox after another, because the fox they hunted was much larger, more swift, and golden. On and on, they went, seeking and rejecting, seeking and spurning—never satisfied.

"Forever seeking. Forever empty-handed. For all we know, they're still seeking the golden fox." She fell into silence.

Olive looked at her mother, "Is that all?"

"All," she answered.

"But, Mama," Olive protested, "I feel there should be more."

Miss Lottie smiled, "Might've been."

I felt the same as Olive. I expected more. Although I'd heard it before, I still had expected more.

"Seems too short."

"But, Mama, I can't make out what the story's about—"

"Make of it what you will. Now we all have a lot of work, so let's get to it." We heard the fire roar from the pull of air when she closed the stove's steel door. She began her work, moving from supply shelves to bowls and utensils. The cabin quickly livened with the fragrance of cooking.

Still the story, fragile as a dream, haunted me, as it had Olive. Funny, I couldn't remember feeling this way when I had heard it many times before. On thinking about it, Miss Lottie's stories had a tendency to be short and puzzling. I always was left wanting more. Besides the story itself, what else did it mean? Mister Carson's stories used to be long and exciting, with marvelous heroes and heroines, great missions and journeys. Big adventures. He'd always told his before we went to sleep. Miss Lottie might tell hers anytime: at the table, as we ate; in the field, while we worked; at market; or in the buggy or wagon. We always wanted to hear more. Something always seemed to be missing.

"You'll be gone tomorrow, Tench," Miss Lottie said, "so today, Thursday, May twenty-fifth, is a holiday. I'm fixing a feast."

"After I put a wash on the line," Mama added.

The children danced about me. "Don't go away, Tench." Olive cried, "Stay with us."

"Yes, stay with us," young Carson echoed. "Don't go."

As they shouted and circled, I realized I never had been as young as they were. It came to me, that I'd always feel toward them as I'd felt toward Lance—that I must care for and help them. With brothers gone and their father afflicted, I was the only man left to help them through childhood.

Olive and young Carson had grown, especially Carson. He was big for his age, more like twelve or thirteen than nine. When I last saw Olive, I believe her size was the same, but her body had been hard and angular, like a boy's. The angles had softened, and I was aware of a new attitude. She still bustled with the joy and energy of a child; at the same time, she possessed a new seriousness. She listened and watched intently when others spoke. In the short span of my visit, I saw how ably she attended her father and young Carson. She had taken on cares equal to those of a woman. Without Olive, one could see, Mama and Lottie couldn't accomplish the goals which they had set for themselves. I was convinced they would succeed.

Already Mama and Miss Lottie were shouting our orders. We accepted one task and quickly returned for another.

"Olive and Carson, fetch some collards from the garden."

"Get a dozen sweet potatoes from the drying shed."

"Shell the peas. When you finish, cut some mint."

"Tench." Miss Lottie took the smoothbore from the pegs above the door, handed it to me with a tin of caps, some ticking, a pouch of shot, and a flask of powder. "Go to the hammock, get a mess of birds." She spoke in her strongest voice. "Shoot whatever lines up in your sights. There's plenty of quail around now, or dove—it doesn't matter. Bring what you think is enough for six of us, and enough for leftovers tomorrow. Clean them at the pump."

"And," Mama said, "take our small skiff down to Jeff Taylor's General Store and bring back a jug of milk and some butter. Hurry."

Such a pair—Mama and Miss Lottie. Such a feast. Twenty-two quail, lightly fried in butter and wild plum sauce. Baked sweet potatoes, whipped in egg whites and orange syrup. Collards, finely chopped and cooked lightly with fried onions and minted green peas and thimble biscuits. Baked guava shells with top cream, and molasses cookies. Food for the gods.

After two years of rooting for food and making do with whatever game or meat and supplies I could scavenge I couldn't help being in awe of that quickly and finely created spread. As we ate, my attention turned to Mister Carson. An extra chair was moved beside him while we ate. It would have been easy to forget about him. In fact, it might've been easier to forget him, than be reminded of that part of him that was absent. He seemed only to taste his food, sampling and pushing it about on his plate. When this happened, the family took turns moving to his side, feeding him as one would a baby, and he would really eat, spoonful after spoonful. After Olive had fed him, I moved beside him and took my turn. I was aware of an approving smile being passed around the table.

Finally, at about the same time, unable to eat any more, Mister Carson turned his head away from the spoon, just as we pushed back our plates. When little Carson reached for a big molasses cookie, Miss Lottie stopped him, put her hand over his and said, "We'll have tea later. Save the cookies, son."

"And will you read our tea leaves, Mama?" Olive asked.

"Will you tell our fortunes?" little Carson begged.

"I will," she promised, "in time."

When we finished putting the house in order, everyone went outside and sat beneath a moss-draped oak. There were swings and a
hammock and chairs of hand-hewn pine. I sat on a bed of moss on
the ground after I learned that Mama had washed the moss in lye
soap and dried it in the sun, to rid it of bugs. We all felt sleepy. Mama
and Miss Lottie had not slept the night before, and they'd worked
hard all day, and we all had stuffed ourselves into a state of drowsi-
ness. A good breeze not only cooled us, but blew most of the mosquitoes away. However, they still seemed to find me and Mister Carson,
and we both kept slapping and scratching.

All of us had put in some good napping time when voices sounded
across the clearing and wakened us. Olive and Carson were on their
feet, running to greet the visitors. Two young men on horseback
approached. One led Night. I ran to greet them.

"Tench, these boys are from Holly Center. They've been working
for Mama. This one's Prentis," Olive said, touching Prentis's horse
and, pointing to the other, "and that is Leroy."

"This's a fine horse," Leroy handed the tether to Olive. "Miz Taylor
says he was your brother's horse. The brother who got killed."

"Three of my brothers were killed in the war," Olive spoke. "Lance
was the youngest. Night was his horse." She threw her arms about
Night, rubbed her cheek against his head.

"Wish I got a sweet welcome like that," Leroy exclaimed.

Lottie had come up behind Olive. "Leroy and Prentis, I'll look for
y'all in the morning. We've things to do now. See you tomorrow on
the west field. Thanks for fetching Night."

"Yes, ma'am," they both replied, and turned to take leave.

It was clear she'd dismissed them. Her mouth was in a thin line,
her voice, now surprisingly strong, revealed displeasure.

"Tench, let me ride Night." Little Carson was tugging on my arm.
"Lance promised I could when I got older. I'm older now. He said
he'd let me sit in front of him when he rode. Please."

Springing to the saddle, I reached down, scooped him up in front
of me. I dropped the reins. Around the field, we raced, Night's hoofs
light and sure on the damp earth, and the wind, cool and soft as it
brushed our cheeks and parted our hair. Now we raced in perfect

accord: little Carson, Night, and I. Night was free of bonds, no more dusty, hidden roads—only a small boy's gentle hand to lightly hold his lead until the day when his grip became strong, and Night would follow and they'd race the wind alone.

And me? Up to this moment, I'd done as I was bid. Now I must do my own bidding.

We rode back to the lean-to. Mama had told me to let Night occupy one of the stalls, that she put the two mules together. The placid animals seemed quite content, side by side. I sensed that Night, who was accustomed to nothing more than the unreliable sky above, appeared uneasy with the low ceiling overhead and surrounding wooden slats—like a prisoner in a cell.

That thought of a prisoner brought a memory of Jefferson Davis and the last picture of him in my mind, sitting proud and erect on his horse, wearing Confederate gray, a black silk handkerchief at his neck, and a wide-brimmed hat, as he somberly followed his captors.

And Miss Varina and the children—would they always live in my mind? I thought so. They held an important moment in my time, although I was but a fleeting moment in theirs, a moment easily eclipsed by President Davis's capture.

Little Carson and I opened the cabin door on a new scene. Strange fragrances laced the warm cabin air. Within was a bright festive picture. Miss Lottie was dressed in her fine lace company gown, one that I remembered from other days. Mama looked so grand in a dress of blue cotton, it looked new, but was maybe just well patched and newly dyed with some indigo that might have been salvaged along the way. Olive's dress was of surprising beauty, especially since I recognized the source of some of its decorative touches—the lace and fine linen from Avalon's grand banquet table cloth.

From a trunk in the corner, she took out the good bone china, silver spoons, a linen tablecloth and napkins, and set the table. As my eyes fell on the trunk, I thought of its place under the large bay windows in the sewing room. It had been filled with fabrics, lace and scents of sassafras and camphor. Mama saw me looking at it, knew I was remembering, and said, "This trunk holds the only remains of the Georgia Avalon. We brought it on the wagon from Thomson.

Miss Lottie said the first thing we were going to do when we found our spot, was to have tea in our own china—"

"And so we did, and continue to do," Miss Lottie smiled as she finished Mama's explanation. From a small pitcher, she poured a little honey into each cup, then scooped a measure of leaves into each from the tea jar. Then I noticed she was wearing her sapphire ring.

Mama lifted the blackened teakettle from the stove, brought it to the table and slowly poured boiling water into each cup. "Now, stir, stir, stir," she said, and added, "Drink slowly."

We did so. We knew the ceremony. When we finished drinking, we turned our cups upside down on the saucer, turned them around three times and made a wish. Miss Lottie doesn't say much, even when she's telling fortunes. We always believe her, so she's careful of what she says.

She read Olive's tea leaves. "I see two roads." Squinting, she studied the cup. Olive jumped up to look over her shoulder. She pointed, "One goes up, the other down. The small figure is you. You're making a decision. I see you're taking the road that goes up."

Olive's eyes widened. "Think of it. Those tiny leaves grown clear over on the other side of the world can tell you that."

Mama Zulma chuckled. "This very moment started in India. Mystic leaves from mystic lands. And Miss Lottie can read them."

Miss Lottie gave Mama a sharp look and continued, "There's a key. Means opportunity. You'll find a door to open. Here's a broom. Old business to sweep away. Be good. Your wish will come true."

Olive's eyes twinkled. "You always say that, Mama."

"Maybe you're too old now for fortune-telling," Miss Lottie said.

Little Carson handed her his cup. "Mine now, Mama."

She studied the cluster of leaves, "Ah," she smiled, "building blocks. You're making bridges and roads that lead to a city far away. You're riding a dark horse, riding with the—"

"Wind!" I supplied the word. Everybody laughed. Handing her my cup, I said, "Read mine."

She tilted her head to examine the squiggles and swirls. At last, she said, "That's you in the middle of a whirlwind. But see, you are firm and straight. Around the top at the edge, see the clouds. There's a tree to climb. See the river? Alas, I see no bridge to help you across."

The children and Mama gasped. Miss Lottie bit her lip. I reassured them, "You need not worry. I've been there before. I'll come through the storm, climb the tree, and swim across the river." When my assurances met with silence, I added, "Then I'll be home to stay."

Later, I remember a choked-up silence lingering while Olive and Mama cleaned up and little Carson kept asking, "You didn't say, Mama, is my wish coming true?"

Miss Lottie stood at the back window, gazing at the newly cleared land where the orange grove would be planted. I stashed away this picture of her forever. The set of her fine features as she looked beyond the family scene, dressed in her finest salvaged from old Avalon, her strong hands resting on the sill.

"Mama, is my wish coming true?" little Carson persisted.

Miss Lottie looked down at him and answered very deliberately, "It may, son, and it may not. Depends on you. How hard are you willing to work to make it come true? Remember, nothing is as easy as a wish."

I knew I would cherish the memory of this day as long as I could remember. Beyond that, when I no longer had memory, it would be here on these pages so others will know.

Miss Lottie took out the old family journals from the big trunk that carried the treasures of old Avalon and, later, she put my journal among all the other Traymore papers. She said, "One day you'll want to read these. They belong to the family." Her gaze held mine, "They belong to you."

Then we talked a long time. There were things I needed to know to put away in memory. These things, I didn't know, I will store on future pages. I have many empty pages to fill.

May 26, 1865

MAMA AND MISS LOTTIE GOT UP WITH ME YESTERDAY morning, insisting they could not send me away hungry, that they wanted to be part of my last memory for awhile of the new Florida Avalon. I can't remember what we ate, but I still can see them as they were in the lamplight at the table. No long faces or sad eyes—at least, not that I could see.

Miss Lottie told me about her plans for the future, all about setting out the groves, a road they'd put through the hammock and into Holly Center, the railroad the local folks were striving to bring to the river. The steamships soon would be increasing their traffic on the waters. Miss Lottie was hopeful that Holly Center could become the shipping junction of both the railroad and the waterway. There was much to do in order to be ready to meet the demands of inland markets, as well as those from the port of Jacksonville.

"We must work hard to be ready when the market opens," Mama said.

Miss Lottie spread her hands open on the table. "That won't be a problem. We'll be ready."

"You're right. We will," Mama affirmed.

I didn't doubt it. I was affected by their determination, but felt the uneasiness of my differing loyalties surfacing. "Soon as Captain John and General Breckinridge are safe and out of the country, I'll be back."

Throwing a small knapsack I had packed over my shoulder, I bent to hug Mama and Miss Lottie.

"One moment, son." Mama bowed her head and she and Miss Lottie took my hands. Mama prayed, "Heavenly Father, we know You are holding our dear Lance close. We thank You for returning

Tench to us, unharmed. Now, we ask again for Your love in guiding his steps and protecting him as he leaves on this mission to help his good friends."

Miss Lottie continued. "Keep our boys and all of us in the circle of Your love. Help us accept Your will, even through pain, and to understand those things we find hard..." She hesitated and seemed almost unable to go on.

"We ask this in the name of our Lord, Jesus Christ," Mama concluded.

I hadn't heard Matt approach and was surprised to see him standing on the stoop when I turned to leave. He bolted ahead down to the bank below and into the skiff.

"Well, boy, we're both leaving today. I'll stop tonight at my folks, then head back to the woods. By the time you return, I think I too will be here again with my neighbors from the woods."

"How do you know they'll come with you?" I asked.

"I know." He was rowing and he shouted to me between strokes. "We'll find freedom here. Opportunity. Folks here are good. They're kind. We'll all get a piece of land. Don't worry. I have no fear. They're going to love it. I am going to love it."

A heavy fog hovered over the water and I felt like I could crush the air in my hands. Matt stayed close to shore. Glancing back over my shoulder, my eyes sifted the darkness. I saw the glow from the lamp on the table and knew Mama was standing in the open door waiting until all sound of us had disappeared. Funny, the smell of bacon lingered on the air. I thought of Miss Lottie down in the hammock shouldering the big smoothbore musket as she stalked and shot a wild hog. I thought of both Mama and Miss Lottie in the butchering shed, dressing and curing the spoils of her hunt. Mama never would kill an animal, but she was handy with the knife. Both women worked together, salting and hanging the meat to dry or packing it into crocks of brine. They were a good team. They stayed on my mind as we traveled.

When we reached Holly Center, I was surprised to find the scene alive with blinking lights and bustling with the first business of the morning.

An ox cart was parked at the far end of the dock. Matt explained, "That cart is full of fat pine. It's being loaded into a crib for the steamships. Local folks keep the crib full and the ship's purser pays with wood-tickets for what the ship uses. Wood-tickets are good as gold, here. Folks use them same as money. Another way to make a living."

There was much more going on besides the activity at the wood wharf. Lanterns lit the river front while workmen, pushing wheelbarrows, carried loads up the bank, then disappeared beyond our sight.

"What're they doing? It's a long time till sunrise."

"They're building an inn for travelers," he answered. "Now the war's over, they'll be coming. There'll be plenty of work."

"Yes, sir." Matt continued rowing with strong, even strokes. A wind had come up and he was quiet now, concentrating on keeping the boat on course. Usually, at this time, there were signs of coming dawn. The sky was streaked with a gray light and the fog blended with a low ceiling of clouds.

I pointed above. "Looks like a bad day."

Matt nodded. "If your boat has a sail, you'll be glad for the wind in those clouds."

As we pulled up to the landing at Ft. Butler, a group of men gathered around an open boat that was about seventeen or eighteen feet long with four oars and a place in front to set a small mast. I was struck by its size. Not very big. And all those people. The general and Tom, Colonel Jim and Captain John and—my heart sank—the two men I had seen at the General Store when we'd arrived the other day. All those men! Plus, the boat was loaded with all our supplies. I could see provisions, firearms, boxes of ammunition, camp equipment, and bags, which I guessed held other personal supplies.

I thanked Matt for everything. He was grateful that I had brought him to the St. Johns. Promising we'd meet again, he wished me luck. He shook hands with Captain John and departed.

Soon, I discovered that the other two strangers with Captain John and the general had been their guides crossing Florida. The captain and general shook hands with them, gave them their horses to take back with them. The captain handed each a small packet, which I reckoned to be tokens of their appreciation, and the strangers took their leave.

The corporal approached too close to me, squinted his eyes, and asked, "Wha'cha hangin' 'round for, boy?"

Not liking his tone, I didn't answer but looked to Captain John who responded at once. "He's going with us, his name's Tench and"— pointing to Tom—"this is Tom, the general's man. Both were in the war with their families. They know how to stay alive." Captain John nodded back at me.

The corporal grumbled, "Well, they better. We sure don't want two Nigras holding us up."

Behind the corporal, Tom made a face and I almost smiled.

Captain John ignored the remark and began to stash things away. "Tench, give me your bag." I handed him mine and didn't have to apologize for its size.

Sergeant Jerry O'Toole directed Tom and me to sit in the prow where the mast would go, a space that required us to brace ourselves steadily in place. "Don't breathe too deep," Tom quietly cautioned, "you might knock me into the river."

Captain John and Colonel Jim, along with the sergeant and corporal, started out rowing. The general sat in the stern. Tom and I balanced in the prow. It wasn't too bad.

When we got out in the middle of the river, Captain John ceased rowing. The general stood up, saying, "Before we leave, I'd like Captain John to ask for God's guidance." Everything stopped. We waited in silence, heads bowed for a few moments before the captain began.

"Heavenly Father, we ask You to lead us on this journey. Give each of us strength and patience and knowledge enough to arrive on a safe shore. We ask in Jesus' name. Amen."

"Amen," echoed from prow to stern.

"He always do the prayin'," Tom whispered to me. "Whatever we do, the gen'el always ask him to. I'm sure glad he do. Bring us together, so we all's goin' in the same direction. Lookit the gen'el. He's all teary-eyed. Thinkin' 'bout how long he gonna be sep'rated from Miss Mary and his boys and them little girls. He's thinkin' he might never see them agin."

After that, things were quiet again, except for the squeaking of the oars in their locks, the splash of the paddles, and the swish of the boat cutting through the water. We must have all been deep in our own thoughts as no one spoke for a while.

At last, the general said, "Heard you found your folks, Tench. How was everything?"

"Yes, sir. They'd moved here from Georgia more than six months ago. They're doing well. They already built a cabin, are clearing land, set out garden crops and orange trees."

"How did Mrs. Matthews take the news of her son?"

I didn't know how to answer that. Truth was, I didn't think I knew the answer. "She's a strong woman, sir. I don't think she'd want to burden others with her grief. She'd already lost her two oldest sons in the war. I believe experience has prepared her to accept things better than most folks could. She has two young children and a sick husband. She puts them above all others, yet she's thoughtful of everyone."

Captain John spoke up. "She is a grand lady. No bigger than a young girl, yet strong as steel." He glanced at me and added, "Tench's mother is made of the same stuff."

I was proud to have him speak so, and glad to have O'Toole and Russell know this about my folks. Too, I wondered if General B. and Captain John deliberately chose to speak of my family as they did, to make others aware that I just wasn't common or trashy. I wish I didn't care what folks think. Especially when they talk down to me.

The rowers began to talk among themselves. Beside me, lowering his voice just above a whisper, Tom said, "This boat might do in the river, but I think we're gonna go down fast if we take it out in the ocean."

I understood why he said that. There wasn't much space from the gunwale to the water. Later, we found out just how close it was. Tom and I took our turns, and Captain John stayed on with the general. Time on the oars was fairly divided. Tom and I had ample opportunity to show O'Toole and Russell we were capable of doing something besides getting in the way.

No sign of the sun all day long. Layers of clouds followed us. From time to time during the afternoon, the wind was strong enough to put up the mast. Evening, the wind became fierce, slapping our faces and shaking the boat when we nestled in the saw grass for the night. We couldn't sleep with the rain and wind beating against us; it soaked our clothes and supplies and covered our feet with water. By midnight we were thoroughly deluged.

During the torrents, I heard Colonel Jim say, "Beats the mosquitoes any day. I believe the rain has drowned them, or maybe the winds had blown them away."

The general said, "Anyway, it's cooled the air."

But like Tom, I kept casting worried eyes around us and thinking how small the boat and how big the waters, and we were yet just on the river, with an ocean to come.

May 27, 1865

MORNING, WE LOOKED AROUND US. SOME MALLARDS ROSE from the grass nearby and a bit of the sun peered through the clouds. It didn't take long to discover that most of the gunpowder was wet and ruined, as well as the salt, corn meal, and sugar. I picked up a pan and some cornmeal, nudged Tom to give a hand.

Captain John had started a fire and most of our clothes were drying before it. Tom and I began to look among the cattails and water grasses at the river's edge and found some freshly laid mallard's eggs. We broke them into the pan and soon were mixing up a batch of corn dodgers.

As quickly as I cooked them, Tom passed them around. Both the general and Colonel Jim spoke of them approvingly. Colonel Jim said, "But something's missing on this menu. Get your cups, gentlemen. I have the perfect complement for the boys' corn dodgers." He reached among the provisions and brought out a bottle of rum.

It turned out to be an unusual day, although we scarcely stopped except for the most pressing causes. All day long, we continued to eat corn dodgers from the great batch Tom and I had made for breakfast. Every time they were passed, Colonel Jim passed the rum. I drank water from the water jug. By day's end, Sergeant O'Toole estimated by his map that we had done thirty-five miles and even without sleep the night before, everyone remained in remarkable good humor.

"If we keep up this pace," Captain John commented, "we could arrive in the Bahamas in several days."

"Well, gentlemen." Colonel Jim laughed, then said, "Just remember our most potent fuel—corn dodgers and rum."

Too, by day's end, O'Toole and Russell had earned our respect. They taught us to be wary of alligators, which we soon discovered lay snoozing on the river banks, lifeless as hollowed logs. When we needed to go ashore, we kept big rocks handy to rouse them before we invaded their territory. Right after we stopped for the night, the soldiers caught a mess of fish and fried them before Tom or I could unpack our utensils. When they went ashore, they built two fires, one to smoke out the mosquitoes, the other to fry the fish. They were old hands at both. They made the smoker by putting damp palmetto fans over the blazing fire. For a while, their smoker worked fine, but then the wind began to blow in the wrong direction.

We had to keep moving about, slapping with one hand, and eating with the other. I must say, in spite of the pesky 'squitoes, the fish made it worthwhile. Tom and I had a lesson in efficiency we hoped to put to use. The thing about O'Toole and Russell, they worked fast; they didn't waste a moment.

O'Toole grinned as he watched us devour the fish and said, "Tomorrow's our turn to loaf. You and Tom hafta fix a feast to match ours." Both soldiers laughed, but were glad to show us up. We'd show our worth, too, I knew. There would be plenty of opportunity.

We cleaned up the site while O'Toole passed his made-by-hand map around and everyone discussed "probabilities" of this and that. This was Russell and O'Toole's territory and they knew what could be expected. They knew the nature of the land and the folks who lived here.

"Probability is," O'Toole was saying, "after tomorrow, we're going to have the devil's own time trying to stay on course. This damned old—"

"Language. Watch it," Colonel John interrupted.

"Sorry." O'Toole went on, "This old river goes wild closer we get to its headwaters. It sprawls in every direction. You think you're in the main channel and it ends nowhere."

But wilder though the river got, there was still no relief from the mosquitoes. The corporal went ashore and cut palmetto fans, and we fanned and slapped. Then Captain John said, "Let's take the boat out mid-river. We'll have a better breeze out there." He picked up a pair of oars, I took up one, and we rowed out to the middle. This would be our campsite for the night and we'd have to sleep upright.

But mid-stream, there was only a stingy breeze, giving very little of itself to our comfort. The general took out his pipe and tobacco, blazing a trail for the others to follow. Soon, I couldn't determine which was worse, the smoke of so many different origins, or the persistent, whining mosquitoes. Even Tom contributed his share to the smoke screen.

For a long time, Tom and I perched in our space. He was too busy trying to draw on his pipe to talk. For a while, Colonel Jim held our attention describing how he'd trap mosquitoes. "Now if we gave Tench a bucket and set him spinning like a weathercock, with every spin, he'd catch a bucket full of the pests."

"Or," Colonel Jim continued, "we'll keep drinking rum from our commissary until there's nothing but rum where our blood should be, and those mosquitoes will get so drunk, they won't know what end their stingers are on." The colonel had lots of company laughing at his jokes. O'Toole and Russell were ready to start passing the bottle and try out such an experiment.

"More likely," the general broke in before they got too enthusiastic, "you'd be so drunk you wouldn't know you got stung."

It was too dark to see their faces, but there was something warm in their voices. Their good humor and camaraderie seemed to rise beyond the screen of smoke and spread through the night. I didn't want to go to sleep. One by one, the voices fell silent and I realized that I was the last one awake. This was only our second night on the river.

I wondered how long the rum would last.

May 28, 1865

WE WERE REALLY GETTING TO KNOW THE RIVER AND ITS inhabitants. This was a world far removed from anything I had ever known. Here, it was wild and natural, almost empty of human life, mysterious, beautiful and—frightening. There were houses bound in vines thick as anchor rope, houses that had been deserted by their owners when Yankee gunboats first cast their shadows on the banks of the St. Johns. In the old gardens, overrun with growth, we picked a few guavas, a small yield of early, still partially green figs, and a bunch of dwarf bananas.

"What a garden this used to be." O'Toole sighed. He pointed to a huge briar patch of rose bushes covered with grape vines. "Lookit here. The grape vines lost their way among the roses. Now you can't tell one from the other. If you turn your back on anything you plant down here, in a few days, it'll become a jungle."

As we were finishing our tour of the grounds, O'Toole let out a yell. "Watch it, everyone! The granddaddy of gators is waiting for us down at the landing. He has taken up residence here."

Tom and I kept behind on the narrow path, but the general burst ahead, calling, "I have my pistol. Let me at him."

Colonel Jim made no effort to join the general; he lingered behind. Quickly, the general fired again. The alligator slid into the river, full of life. He discharged his pistol—three, four times. Russell jumped onto the boat, grabbed a coil of rope, and lassoed the gator, yanking it back towards shore. Still full of life, the animal began to roll and roll—rolling until he had completely bound himself in a cocoon of rope.

General B. stood over him and aimed between his eyes. I shivered. Tom groaned, "Oh, my God, that man is a 'gator-killer. He went through big battles n' nevah lifted a gun to his shoulder, but lookit how he's shootin' up on that po' 'gator."

Corporal Russell heard and commented, "Better we get him than he get us."

O'Toole, looking around, warned, "Probabilities are, there's another close by."

Russell and O'Toole pulled the gator up on the bank. It was a big one, about thirteen feet long. "His head's tore up," O'Toole said, "but I can sell the skin back at Ft. Butler when I return. I'll skin him, then stretch the skin and salt it down and leave it to cure in the sun, top of the shed behind the arbor out back. I'll pick it up when I return."

Russell joined the sergeant, took his bowie knife out of its sheath. "I'll give you a hand. Come, Tench and Tom, we'll get it done in no time. This section here," he pointed to the tail, "is good-eatin' meat. We can have it for supper tonight."

"I'll pass on supper," Captain John said and the general agreed at once.

"I'll try anything," Colonel Jim said, "but it doesn't mean I'll eat it if I don't like it. Gentlemen, I've heard that alligators have a bag of musk under their throats. Is that right?"

"A little bag of very strong musk," Captain John corrected.

"Ah, very good. When you find it, will you please cut it out for me? I'll put it in a smelling bottle when we reach port and send it to my very dear lady friend back in Kentucky."

The soldiers snickered but O'Toole immediately cut out the musk bag and handed it to Colonel Jim, who took it in his hands squeamishly and wrapped it in a piece of sacking.

We all squatted around the carcass, peeling the skin from the part of the body in front of us. I can't describe the odor. But if I breathe deep enough, I still can dredge up that smell from the bottom of my lungs. Several times I had to move from the butchering scene to quiet my upset stomach.

Needless to say, no one ate alligator for supper. The sergeant pushed the body into the river when we finished. "There are enough predators around to clean off these bones," he said. "By morning there'll be no meat left."

Colonel Jim decided to pick some oranges he'd found on a thorny tree, although O'Toole told him they were wild oranges, too sour to eat. The colonel insisted, "I'll fix a delicious orange drink for our supper."

By the time we'd pushed off again, buzzards were already circling. Russell advised us that we'd find a better spot to do our cooking further up. On the way, Tom, Captain John, and I started to do some fishing. I can't remember ever making such a fine catch in such a short time. Under his breath, Tom complained, "We can't cook fish better than the soldiers cooked. What can we do that they ain't already done better?"

"Get out six yellow potatoes. We're going to have potato pone-cakes. Start peeling while I clean the fish. Get a couple of Colonel Jim's oranges."

I raided the supplies and found a stick of cinnamon and a small jar of molasses. Colonel Jim used the remainder of the sugar for his orange drink. I put some white bacon in the big frying pan, began shaving potatoes and orange skin. Then I sliced circles of the oranges, so thin you could see through them. Mixing flour into the potatoes, along with shaved orange peel, molasses, a little cinnamon bark, and two mallard eggs, I added bacon fat to the batter and poured fist-size mounds into the pan. They began to cook very slowly over the lowest part of the fire.

Tom set up the frying pan with bacon fat while the pones were cooking. Just as the pones were finishing, we began to fry the fish. We dusted the pieces with cornmeal, salt, and pepper and, after cooking them on one side, I turned them over and lay the orange slices on top. It wasn't long after that till we served the men and Tom and I sat down to eat too.

After eating our offerings, and sounding their praise, everyone agreed it was time for Colonel Jim's orange punch. The colonel looked a little doubtful and said how he wished he had had more sugar. He poured a little in his cup, took a sip, and wrinkled his nose, while he sputtered wild oranges into the air. "There's one thing that might redeem this concoction," he said, lifting a jug of rum to the lip of his cup. Taking a swig, he proclaimed, "Nectar of the gods!"

For me, there was something disturbing about a man's liking for spirits. It was a deep, hurting thing, one of which I try not to remember. Once I had a father. They told me he could have been good father. He worked hard, was full of laughter and good humor. He carried me on his shoulders while he worked or gardened and I sat at his side in the cart when he worked the fields. So Mama and Miss Lottie told me. The only memory I have of him, I try to put out of my mind, for when it comes, I hear the strike of a swift hand against a body, across the face, at the neck, and I remembered seeing Mama Zulma lying on the floor, bloody and still. The memory begins and ends there. Mister Carson sent him away. Whenever I asked about him, Mama explained, "He was a drinker." She told me about the good of him and said, "But he got next to the devil—whenever he drank that stuff."

Maybe that's why I was afraid when I saw someone drinking. I didn't know how much it took to get close to the devil. People I've seen do differently. Sometimes they just fall asleep, or they got silly, or talked too much. Anyway, sometimes they were not really themselves. The Matthews used to have wine on their table, but it was used to make things good. It did, Miss Lottie said—if it was used right.

While I was thinking about drink, I heard a mallard's call and the answering soft chip of her brood. Before we anchored, we remarked at the number of birds, cranes, red and blue herons, and water turkeys feeding at the shoreline. A limpkin's screech silenced the population for a moment. Owls were out on the hunt and we heard a great roar which O'Toole said was in all probability a bull alligator. Could he have been calling a mate whose skin dried on top of a shed by the deserted house down the river?

Everyone went quiet before sleeping. Some frogs sounded constant, deep basses; others, in higher pitches and whistling tones, sang together. What did their songs mean? They were love calls and serenades. They seemed to sound the heartbeat of the night.

The general, Colonel John, and I were crowded in the boat, and we shared a lantern while the others slept. As we wrote in our journals, something told me this was a time I'd never forget.

June 3, 4, 1865

As we moved along and the scene kept changing, we became less enchanted by the southern part of the St. Johns and its surroundings. The banks changed from steep to low to flat; the landscape changed from woods to swamp to saw grass. The river narrowed from big, sprawling bellies of water, to thin, twisting, snaky branches which we tried to follow until they came to an abrupt end and we had to start over. Even with the combined experience of our crew, time and time again, we pursued a channel leading to nowhere. They all agreed it was the most bewildering stream they'd ever seen.

The numbers of wildlife increased. Hundreds of alligators. Some slept on the bank and often plunged into the water right in front of our bow, bringing the observation from the general, "That scaly back looks like a Yankee gunboat low in the water."

I shivered when they came close. Tom whispered prayers as he sat beside me and commented in a strong voice, "If this boat springs a leak, we'll all be alligator food." This possibility didn't seem too unlikely. They looked like powerful beasts. Most of them were from ten to fifteen feet long.

Sometimes we saw herds of wild cattle and deer feeding on a savannah. With O'Toole's quick eye and sharp ear, he pointed out wonders we might have missed—a panther's high pitched cry that sounded like a woman's scream, two bob-tailed wild cats, a flock of scarlet ibises, a trio of black bears.

After we reached Holden's Landing (which was no more than that—just a landing), O'Toole and the captain studied the maps, determined that they were about five miles from an inhabited spot called Saulsville. So, taking Tom with them, they hiked over and met George Saul, who with his two oxen and ox cart would meet us twenty miles upstream at Cook's Ferry.

Just waiting in the boat for the three of them to return was a nightmare. Not a breath of air. Not a tree in sight. Just straw-like grass, in which mosquitoes waited to ambush whatever living flesh they might find. To get out of their range, Russell and the general began to row back and forth and 'round and 'round. The sun bore down hot as a blacksmith's forge; we were soaking with sweat. When clouds gathered enough to block the sun, we rejoiced.

"What a waste of manpower," Colonel Jim complained as he and I took up the other set of oars just to keep moving.

At last, O'Toole and the captain sounded their calls at the landing. In a few moments, we were off again, taking turns pulling our way through the heavy grasses choking the channel.

O'Toole informed us, "George Saul's the ox-cart driver who's gonna take our boat overland to the Indian River. He'll meet us at Cook's Ferry 'bout twenty miles upstream."

Tom piped up, "Looks like a weird kine' of gypsy man. Deals like a gypsy, too. He wanted gold n' tobacco n' everythin.'"

Captain John laughed. "He's a cracker and drives a hard bargain. In these wilds, there's not much chance for him to do much business. He's got to make the most of every opportunity."

When we arrived at Cook's, it had started to storm. Saul, waiting under a shed with the ox team and cart, watched as we struggled to haul the boat on shore. He was a scrawny man of sallow coloring, with long, wide ears and heavy dark circles of flesh that hung loose around his eyes, pulling the outside corners down, causing him to resemble nothing as much as an old hunting hound. He took a big tarp off the oxen and motioned to us to get it. I ran to help.

"Spread this ovah the boat. Come on outta the rain, yawl heah?" He shouted. "That boat's biggah than I 'spected."

We were grateful to spend the night inside the house. The Cooks were happy to have company. They were O'Toole's friends and had two young women about the age of our soldiers. They helped their mother prepare a simple, delicious meal—ham and gravy with biscuits and swamp cabbage. Tom and I ate on the porch. Later, grateful for the food, we gladly cleaned the supper dishes.

Afterwards, we spread our blankets in a small room by the kitchen. The others slept on mats in the large parlor. The family, living so far from civilization, offered the same kind of fine hospitality I had known at Avalon; they gave their guests the best they had. For a long time, voices and laughter echoed through the house.

As we lay on our blankets, listening to the rain fall on the roof, I asked Tom, "Did you ever think you'd be glad you didn't have to listen to wild cries of the night? No frogs. No cicadas, limpkins, or owls. Doesn't the rain falling on the tin roof sound good?"

Tom chuckled sleepily.

Next morning, we were waked by the fragrance of bacon and biscuits cooking, a breakfast we would remember as much for the smiles and chatter of our cheerful servers as for the good food.

Saul, treated as one of our party, had taken advantage of it in every way. He was the last one out of bed and the last one to get up from the table; he cleaned out his own plate as well as all the leftovers on the table. There was one thing we all regretted he hadn't taken advantage—a good opportunity to wash up. He smelled like the beasts in his care.

When we started loading the boat onto the cart, he leaned against the fence post, watching with a lopsided grin. "Won't stay on thataway," he remarked, shaving off a slice of tobacco.

"Then give us a hand," O'Toole ordered. "Show us how."

"Jes' fixin' myself a chaw, cain't yawl see?" he answered, stuffing his cheek and throwing his arm around the post.

It must've been something he didn't want to share with us—how to keep the boat on a cart. For two days and more than twenty miles, the boat kept falling off and thumping to the ground.

Whenever it happened, Saul said he had something to do and loitered behind, or disappeared into the bushes. Everyone else struggled to get it back in place. We never learned the right way from Saul.

The road we followed was no road at all. As the worn cart bumped along, the big wheels got stuck in the muddy ruts and hung up on surfacing roots. So we all, except Saul, stayed close by ready to push or pull it out.

The sun, now bearing down from a cloud-swept sky, brought with it pesky sand fleas. Mosquitoes lurked in shade and shadows, waiting to attack. By sunset, the poor white ox, pursued by large, murderous horseflies, was bellowing in pain; his black partner, less tortured, closed his eyes and held back his agony.

Sometimes, for relief from their tormentors, they'd lie down in a stream and neither geed nor hawed without the most severe goading. With nightfall on the first day, their heads and necks were so bloody, Saul complained that the white ox would probably die. "Case he does, yawl need to pay extry."

Captain John said, "I think it'd been less labor to have tied the beasts, put them in the boat and hauled them across the portage." Everyone laughed, except Saul.

Whenever we stopped for meals, Saul suddenly came up from behind and out of the bushes. The general finally blew up, shouting, "No work, no grub, no driving the bulls, no tobacco."

Only with that, did Saul begin to drive the bulls, which we soon discovered he did very well. I wonder now if this was his way of playing a trick on us. Or did he just have a mean streak? He had lingered behind while we all prodded and pulled and pushed the animals, shouting "gee" and "haw." When Saul ordered them, he shouted "giddup" and "ho" and they started right up and stopped right away. He could've spared the bulls plenty of unnecessary prodding had he told us earlier. Yes, I think he was just plain mean.

We reached Six Mile Creek after spending a miserable night in the swamps where the mosquitoes rose up in clouds from the saw grass and palmettos and our only relief was smoke from the lightwood campfire. We were refreshed by a dinner of bacon, eggs, and roasted sweet potatoes prepared by Tom and me. Our lungs filled with smoke as we gathered about the fire, seeking refuge from the ravenous insects.

Everyone was more quiet than usual. The general broke the silence, "What a strange-looking bunch of ducks we are."

We looked about, looking at ourselves as a stranger might. Bundled in layers of clothing, heavily bearded (except me), with dirty bands of cloth wrapped about our heads, covering our necks and ears, and wearing ragtag hats over this—we are a very strange bunch. No one could possibly recognize the general or Captain John. So far, nothing to fear, the Feds had been nowhere near. We knew it could be another story when we reach the river.

That was when Saul suddenly asked, "Who're yawl's folks anyways?" No one answered.

He raised both hands and said, "Wal, ah'll tell yawl. Ah'm jes' a po' man n' if'n som'body has a job that needs doin', bidnes' is bidnes'."

The next day when we arrived at Carlisle's Landing, before Saul said goodbye, he studied the white ox and announced, "This 'uns goin' to die. Five dollars and a good chug of tobaccy will hep' pay fer another 'un."

Captain John looked at the ox, which appeared like it was going to live a very long time. As he was settling the charge, Saul took a hard look at the general and back at Captain John and said, "If any'un wants to know, I know nothin' 'bout yawl." Because Saul was crafty enough himself to figure that we were an unlikely group of travelers he chose his words carefully, I'm sure, hoping to influence the captain's payment.

We watched Saul take his leave, legs hanging over the front of the cart and hollering, giddup. The oxen waddled along slowly while Saul shaved off a piece of tobacco and soon was chewing in tempo with the oxen's rolling gait. He didn't look back.

The general shook his head as the cart lumbered out of sight. He grinned, commenting to Captain John, "He dealt pretty closely with us. Some ways, he was grossly ignorant. Yet in other ways, he was keener and more provident in all points of a contract than any Yankee I ever saw."

The captain, shaking his head, looked down the rugged overgrown road as Saul and his oxen faded into the distance, and called out, "Farewell to the bulls of Bashan. We gladly dismiss you to the wilderness."

The general leaned towards Captain John and said, "John, I think he knew me."

"I think he sensed we were fleeing from enemies," Captain John replied.

They turned and for a few moments the two men scanned the view of the river. The captain inhaled the fresh river air like he was taking a draft of wine and seemed revived. "What a welcome sight," he sighed.

"As I recall, rivers have provided the background for some of your most successful adventures," the general said. "May the coming days be among your best."

"I wish we knew about our wives and children. I wish they knew about us. Lola has borne so much alone, as I know your Mary has also. Both are the bastions of our families."

"The worst is, they don't know what's happening to us."

The general's gaze held in the distance. I glanced at Tom who whispered beside me, "Oh, Gawd. Don't let him get started. Water's gonna start fallin.'"

But it didn't. He turned away and joined the others who were launching the boat. "We wanna see how bad the boat was hurt with the bangin' it got," O'Toole explained as they shoved it into the water.

"All probabilities, it'll need caulkin.'" They leaned over, watching for signs of water. Shortly, little bubbles appeared in a few seams. Captain John said, "Let's go ahead and caulk her. We really can't tell much about it 'til she's loaded and been out in the water awhile."

We gathered around as O'Toole and Russell started preparing the pitch and oakum for caulking. Captain John took a small bag from his knapsack and shook its contents into his hat. There were five or six metal wedges; he passed them to us. He looked around asking, "Where's Wilson?"

We all saw the answer at the same time. Up on the bank, Colonel Jim was under the tarp asleep, hat covering his face—he was well protected from the mosquitoes, yet completely without air in the suffocating heat. We left him sleeping although the captain was concerned about him.

"That's Saul's tarp. He didn't know he left it," Russell said. "Had he known, it would have cost us." We laughed.

In short time, we wedged the hemp and pitch into the cracks, and loaded the boat. The general pulled back the tarp and quietly urged the colonel to waken. Colonel Jim's face was flushed, his eyes bloodshot and swollen. He blinked, breathed deeply, and rose unsteadily to his feet.

"Too much sun, no sleep," Captain John diagnosed, taking his arm to help him into the boat.

We took our positions, General Breckinridge and the captain on one set of oars, and O'Toole and Russell on the other. Tom and I were on the bow and Colonel Jim stretched out on the stern. Before we set off, Captain John asked us to bow our heads and he gave thanks for the Lord's guidance in bringing us here safely. Then he asked us to join him in saying the Twenty-third Psalm. With it, came the memory of the last time I had recited it—at Lance's grave.

"My shepherd, I shall not want ... green pastures ... still waters ... restoreth my soul ... leadeth me ... the valley of the shadow ... fear no evil ... Thou art with me ... preparest a table in the presence of mine enemies ... cup runneth over ... goodness and mercy shall follow me ... I will dwell in the house of the Lord forever."

I looked up before we had finished and saw tears in the general's eyes; his hands were clasped before him. A single tear was falling down Colonel Jim's cheek. Sergeant O'Toole and Corporal Russell's eyes were wide-open and their faces were quiet as stone. Tom's hands were folded, his eyes shut tight.

Everyone chorused, "Amen."

"Thank you, John," the general said.

Before we had loaded the boat, Tom and I had checked our food supply. We'd started out with plenty of sweet potatoes and bacon. We still had enough for a few days. Cornmeal, ruined by the rains. No sugar. Sitting there, after the prayer, I thought we would have to hunt and fish while we're on the river; this food source was always open. For that, I said another silent word of prayer. Then we were off again, and moving on the water.

The even rhythm of rowing filled the silence after our prayer, as we each moved alone through our own thoughts. I had made the choice to be here. I would have done anything in my power to help the general and Captain John escape execution. Although my contributions might have been slight and I might have served only in the smallest ways, I liked to think that my efforts might have helped save them from the awful consequences of capture.

Last night, O'Toole and Russell told us what we might expect to find after reaching the Indian River. No more white settlers or inhabitants remained. In their place, thugs and pirates, deserters, Federal patrols, former slaves, and sparsely populated Indian camps.

We'd have to stay alert for possible food supplies—deserted houses and gardens, campsites, old groves, shipwrecks. Before the war, this had been a territory flourishing with pioneer settlements, where settlers brought their families seeking a plot to stake out their dreams and harvest happy endings. I wondered what had happened to them.

We often got stuck in the shallows and we'd have to get out to haul the boat to deeper waters. O'Toole and Russell soon taught us to stir the waters with our oars before stepping in. Stingrays could lie concealed under the sand and had a deadly sword that might stab when roused. He knew a man who'd lost a leg after a stab and gangrene had set in. Shellfish, crabs, and horseshoe crabs also make rough wading. We all were learning.

For a while we had stomach problems, cramps and diarrhea, making it difficult for a party of our size to cover much distance. Colonel Jim says it's caused by the lack of cornmeal or flour. "Binds everything together," he said.

Occasionally, we've had a nice breeze, so after our stomach woes cleared, we made good time. The blame for our biggest and most constant worry went to the mosquitoes, or as Colonel Jim calls them, the "blood bandits." They were so bloodthirsty when we set up camp one night, I started covering myself with sand, then covered my head with my hat. My remedy was discovered when someone called out, "Where's Tench?"

Soon everyone was hollowing beds in the sand and covering themselves from neck to toe. Because Captain John had a pair of buckskin gauntlets, his hands were protected and he was elected to cover everyone else's hands with sand and their heads with their hats. It was the first sound night's sleep we'd had since the night at Cook's.

The following morning I was the last one up. The general was sitting on the bank reading *The Rise and Fall of Athens*. Tom and the soldiers were frying bacon and sweet potatoes (they'd cut them in round slices and fried them a golden brown). Captain John had gone out to scout the surroundings. He had dug a hole in the sand and it'd filled with some rather murky water. Every time we stopped, he did that. Russell calls it "watermining." Our supply is slight and of a bad quality.

I noticed that Colonel Jim was in great distress; he had bedded down with ants and was splashing rum from our diminishing stores over his red-welted body. I saw that where the colonel had slept, hundreds of ants that had joined in the attack, and now moved about aimlessly looking for their victim.

Tom nudged me, "Po Co'nel Jim, he do ketch Hell, don' he? Wha'cha reckon he gonna do when the spirits is all gone? One thin' though, he don' groan none. When thin's go bad fo' him, he keeps right on jokin' n' carryin' on, jes' like nothin's happen. Fer hepin' out, he ain't worth much. Cain't hold a candle to Sa'gent O'Toole. Jes' same, he's a good man."

Funny how my first opinion of the soldiers has changed. The thing I'd come to notice about everyone was how their personalities changed under different circumstances. Tom, for instance. I don't think anyone here knows Tom the way I do. I think he's more himself with me. He looked at people and really saw them, but most the time people didn't even know he was there. He didn't seem to mind, but sometimes I wondered about him.

Sergeant O'Toole? He was happy to be here with people who respected him because he could do things and knew things that they don't know. When I first saw him at the General Store at Ft. Butler, no one knew him, so he seemed boastful and loud. He wanted to let them know who he was and get their attention. I guess he needed their respect. He gave himself a history they could appreciate.

Corporal Russell was his echo; he wanted to be as admired and respected as O'Toole.

I guessed nothing was wrong with that. Where did I stand? A lot taller than I stood last year. I guess I had more pride in myself. I thought I was a lot like O'Toole; I judged myself by other's appreciation of me. Once I had their appreciation, I didn't want to let them down. I had learned much from General B, Captain John and JPB. I was grateful for all the experience I had gotten with them. I had learned lots from the soldiers, too. And Tom.

While I was studying on such matters, Captain John came back with a sack full of surprises. Coconuts, green limes, and watermelons. South on the river, a short hike away, there was a plot of land and a burned down cabin, now completely hidden by a jungle of wild growth. O'Toole taught us how to undress a coconut and we sliced the watermelon, which gave us delicious variety and made our breakfast a feast.

Afterwards, we packed up and started again. As we moved slowly into the river, O'Toole and Captain John were deep in conversation. They stopped rowing and Captain John said, "We'll go slow and stick close to the shore. We're about twenty miles from Indian River Inlet where the Feds have a camp to keep watch on the river."

"From now on," O'Toole stood, turning to see everyone as he spoke, "I don't mind telling you, everyone is responsible. Not just for yourself, but for everyone else, as well. There may not be food enough, we can't eat as much. Must ration carefully. If you have one job, you also have another. You must always be a lookout. When you see something needs doing, do it. No sleeping late." His eyes came to rest on me, "Hear me, boy? We need every hand, every eye, and every muscle—every minute."

I looked away, felt myself smarting, until I heard Colonel Wilson say, "That's not going to be easy for anyone like me who can do only one thing at a time."

Because I'd been scolded, I felt he was trying to put me at ease. I looked back at O'Toole and managed to say, "Yes, sir."

"Now on," he continued, "we have one goal—to escape being captured."

The general and Captain John exclaimed at once, "Hear, hear!" and the harmony of their voices was immediately followed by Colonel Wilson calling out in agreement. After that, we all were alert and did what we could, and the day and the river moved on.

About four in the afternoon, the bottom dropped out of the sky. Hard rain rattled and fell like a curtain of steel. We couldn't see in front or behind. We moved shoreward and for an hour, huddled together in the heat and din under the tarp.

Captain John suggested our next strategy. "We'll wait till dark and keep to the middle of the river."

And that's what we did, traveled at night. When we saw a fire on the bank, we moved like thieves to midstream. Muffling the sound of our oars as much as possible, we slipped past campers without rousing attention.

Captain John decided we must make time in the dark, to escape detection. We rowed a good distance below the inlet until first streak of dawn. There, we stashed our boat above the bank, again choosing a sandy campsite to bury ourselves away from the insects. O'Toole said he would do guard, that I would help him scout. Others would have those duties at the next stop.

Colonel Wilson bent over his sand bed, stirring and exploring its depths with a stick. Everyone else did the same, so the colonel's misfortune of the day before wouldn't be repeated.

"No meal this mornin'," O'Toole announced. "Our supply must be rationed and we'll have to hunt or fish. Now with nothin' on hand, better save our potatoes and fruit for a meal later."

Captain John dug the usual hole, leaving the water to accumulate. Everyone quickly bedded down. The sergeant began collecting long sticks, not explaining the purpose. He sent me to explore the land around us. "Here, Nigra," he said, "a walkin' stick. Might need it."

Sometimes I can't control my tongue. I wish I could see it coming. I never know when something's going to set me off. I'd heard O'Toole's kind of talk all my life, but suddenly something exploded. I tried to be polite, "Please, Sergeant O'Toole, I don't mean to be uppity, but my name is Tench. I don't like either the word Nigra or nigger. If you call me Negro, I'd not mind because it's the name of a race, like White is a race."

The sergeant was squatting on his haunches, whittling on the end of one of the sticks. He didn't look up, just kept whittling.

It was useless to wait for an answer. Swinging the stick ahead of me, I started through the tangled underbrush. It has always been hard for me to bear when someone talks down to me—or for that matter, to anyone. I was proud. I existed within my dark skin, experiencing every feeling that my white cousins experienced. My skin wasn't a dark stone cover that words could not penetrate. Why was it when some people were around me, they often spoke as if no one lived inside my skin?

The jungle was a tangled maze and I wished I'd had the sergeant's machete. I found I had to suck in my stomach to slip in and out of the mesh of growth. The thought occurred to me that coming back wouldn't be any easier. Perhaps I'd return by the river. This thicket went all the way down to the shore. I kept stirring the ground with the stick; when I did, I could see creatures rippling through layers of leaf and decay ahead of me.

Grackles fussed, beating the air with their rustling wings and grating sounds. I felt as if trapped in a great birdcage. Brazen colonies occupied the tops of cabbage palmettos, declaring their ownership; mockingbirds on tip-top branches of sweet gum and cypress disputed them in explosive song. I didn't belong in their private territory. Blue jays, cardinals, all told me so with *jay jay jay* and *tsk tsk tsk*.

I made a big circle of the land up to a small rivulet, which I leaned over, dampened my lips, and tasted; it had the taste of sulfur. I decided to follow the stream to see if it went out to the river. If so, we could come back later and fill our jugs. I'd made a valuable discovery—yet it could prove worthless.

The little stream wasn't deep or wide. Its white sandy bottom, underneath layers of leaves and pink-, yellow-, and green-tinted rocks and stones, seemed like a rippling path through the woods. I pulled off my boots, tied their laces, and threw them across my shoulder. I trod gingerly, because I felt that the rainbow colors, the result of sediments of sulfur on moss and mold, might be slippery. I paused from time to time, to stir the water, to listen and look about. The water was refreshing; I waded through it and splashed it over my face.

The voices, I first thought, were imagined—a combination of rustling breezes and birdsong. I thought the sound might be coming from far off, perhaps from our camp. Reason told me it was too far for that to be possible. But there were the smells of wood burning and food cooking. Hiding behind trees, I moved from the stream towards the sound and fragrance of good food.

All at once, ahead of me, I saw a camp. I threw my boots under a bush, quickly moved to the refuge of an old magnolia, skittered up its wide trunk, and reached up, hand over hand, from one branch above the other, into a thick upper growth where I clung to its strong limbs. Carefully, I leaned against the tree's center and looked below.

For a moment, I thought I was in a familiar dream. Looking at the scene below, I was shaken. It seemed I'd been there before. A pot bubbled over the fire. A familiar smell wafted in the air. Shaggy, dirty-bearded folks lazed around the fire, slurping from their tin cups. And me—up a tree—just as before.

Jake. Old Samuel. The gang of ruffians.

Like a bad dream, the strident voice again, snarling, "Sure ain't no good pickins 'round here. Yuh boys better do some huntin'. Plenty birds and squirrels." From my perch, I noticed he wore a patch over the empty eye socket and I saw a glint from the golden eye as it circled the band of six men. "Keep on the lookout for a good boat. Soon as yuh see one, we'll flag 'em down. Tell 'em we got some sick 'uns n' see if they'll hep us."

"Then what?"

"Then we wrap 'em up good, n' git their supplies."

Someone guffawed and asked, "What if their boat's bettah than ours?"

"Let the supplies stay put, n'trade boats." They all roared.

"We can get us a fleet of 'em, if we're smart."

"Yeah, yeah."

Fear rose up in me. I had to get back to camp. My life wouldn't be worth anything if Jake saw me. He would have a bone to pick with me. From my lookout, I could see where the shore began. If I could get down to the river, that would be the quickest way. It wouldn't be easy to go back through the jungle again. Although I could reach the river easily from here, I would have to pass the campers, first. That couldn't be.

The sun was directly overhead. It had taken me all morning to get this far. It was my hope that the gang would take off on their mission. But when? I had little choice but to wait, hidden in my perch in the tree. But what would Sergeant O'Toole think when I didn't return? Would he come looking for me? Our party needed to know who these people were. For a while, they lazed about below, talking, chewing and spitting.

Samuel was gathering up the utensils and snuffing out the campfire. The others were rolling their things in blankets and swatting and cursing mosquitoes. Up in the midst of air currents, I was spared their misery. I had my own. Besides being stuck in the tree, my face and hands were covered with bloody scratches, and my clothes snagged and ripped by thorny vines in the rough thicket.

Then I heard Samuel, his voice softer than the others. "I like this spot. Lotta folks've spent time here, what with the sulfur stream coming from the springs back in the woods n' all these purty ol' trees."

"'N dang mosquitoes!"

"Yeah, always them."

I flattened myself against the trunk again. Samuel had brought a few pans and tin cups and spoons to wash. Digging a hole in the middle of the stream, he placed them in it and stood back watching the gentle waters wash over them.

I held my breath as he walked over to the tree and picked up the walking stick I'd left below. He examined it, paying special attention to the sharpened end. He put it under his arm and bent to pick up the utensils from the water. Then he rinsed his bare feet off in the stream. I'd noticed that except for him, everyone had on shoes or boots of some kind.

So now he had a good walking stick. I was surprised he had failed to notice that the sharp end had been wet or that he hadn't looked up in the tree. I wondered if they were breaking camp. The big pot hadn't been packed away yet.

I heard one of the men say, "Take off that patch, Jake. Yuh look like a damn pirate." Jake pulled it off and stuck it in his pocket.

Only Jake and Samuel remained after the others went off towards the river. "Someone fixed an egg stick." Samuel held it up.

Jake turned his head and nodded, saying, "I hope it don' come to that fo' us. Hate 'em."

"What if yuh ain't got better?" Samuel asked.

"Long as I got this up har," Jake said, tapping his forehead, "I don' inten' to eat no turtle eggs." He waved towards the river. "We're gonna git us some good supplies this afta'noon. Jes' yuh watch n' see. I ain't never dis'point yawl men. Now, have I? Samuel, as long as yuh gonna hang 'round heah, yuh can keep an eye on our stuff."

Samuel didn't answer. They headed together towards the river. I didn't move. It was plain to see that Jake was the leader. He was the law. What he had said in the past must have paid off for his band of hoodlums. Somehow, I excluded Samuel from all my ill-will. I remembered he was the one who had covered me with a blanket and left some hardtack beneath it, when I had been their unexpected guest.

For a long while, I waited. As I watched from my tree, Samuel wandered off. I thought I heard the plop of a boat, and oars dipping in the water, then shouts sounding over the water. Only then did I come down, pick up my boots, and follow the path that both the stream and the campers took to the waterfront.

When I reached the high bank, I saw the stream stopped at a small basin full of green-blue water that trickled down to the river in a small waterfall. On the river below, there were four old worn sloops and, a good half a mile to the south, I saw Jake's sloop. From the distance, I judged it to be about the same size as ours. Beyond them, a larger vessel was circling as if in pursuit of them, but they made no effort to escape.

All at once, I was aware of movement on the shore below. There, on a jut of land reaching out into the river, Samuel was sitting alone, his back towards me, and just like me, he was watching Jake's sloop. He yawned and stretched and lay back, resting his head against a stone boulder. I immediately squatted to be out of his view, should he turn around. To the north, the jungle touched the river as far as I could see. I couldn't determine how far north our camp might be. By river, it would be a direct course, barring something unusual—a deep hole or heavy current. After all, the current here, unlike the St. Johns, runs south. Too, I couldn't tell if Samuel was going to sleep or just watching for the return of the gang.

I chose the heavy thicket beside the river, but decided first to go back to the ruffians' campsite to look around. I went to the blanket that I had seen Samuel roll up. I carefully unrolled it, noticing his meager belongings. There was a small drawstring bag, and inside, a faded photograph of a young man squatting with his arms around a young boy. Nothing written on the back. A bowie knife and some eating utensils. There was nothing here that told me anything about Samuel.

Reaching into my pants pocket, I took out two gold coins that Miss Lottie had said I might need, and put them inside the bag. Beside the big pot and the ashes of the campfire, I discovered a large supply basket. Among an assortment of guns and knives, I found what I wanted. I chose a knife with a large blade, much like the sergeant's. I entered the thicket to the north and worked my way through thirty or forty feet without using the knife. Then I pulled on my boots and continued for another twenty feet or so until I believed I was out of sight or sound of the campground. At last, I began to slash my way through the tangled growth.

I smiled as I thought of the surprise awaiting Samuel. I even had considered leaving him my boots. If I had brought along another pair like Mama had suggested, I could have. I hoped my gift for him would be like his had been for me. A private, bright discovery. I'd never know the answer. I couldn't help wondering why he stayed on with Jake.

When I got back to our camp, everyone was awake, trying to decide how they'd search for me. I'd been gone almost the entire day and they were worried. Captain John planned that he and O'Toole would take the same route I'd taken in the morning. The general, along with Colonel Jim, thought they'd follow the shoreline, taking the sloop south a short distance. Russell and Tom would wait here.

If anyone found me, they were to give a dozen sharp whistles in a series of three. That was after they realized we needed signal and rescue plans. There had been no way I could have signaled them. They gathered about me as I told what had happened, that I had been a captive without captors.

"Jake and his gang, except for Samuel, have set out this evening to find supplies and provisions. They'll even take over a boat, if they find one," I told them.

Captain John smiled, saying, "Sound like real sea-looters—"

"Pirates," the general corrected. Then amused, asked, "You know that art, John?"

Colonel Jim answered for him, "Captain Wood is a master of the art."

Everyone laughed. Tom knelt beside me, speaking low, "You know 'bout the cap'n?"

"I don't know all about him," I replied.

"Git Col'nel Jim to tell you. I heard 'bout him, but I don' know firs' hand. Col'nel Jim knows it all. Captain John was the 'Fed'racy's bigges' pirate. Cap'chured more n' forty ships." Tom held his arms far apart and lifted his hands upward.

Exhausted and hungry, I collapsed on the ground. O'Toole brought me a pan of leftover fish—boiled, because there was no fat or meal. Nevertheless, it was food and answered my need; I gladly picked through it. Captain John gave me a slice of watermelon and a piece of coconut. I was satisfied.

Exhausted, I wrote in my journal and decided to take a nap once I finished. I could not help but think of Jake and his gang of pirates and wondered if we would run into them again.

June 5, 1865

WITH THE NEED FOR SECRECY AND SPEED EVER PRESENT, we decided to continue downriver after passing the Indian River inlet. Moving under O'Toole's direction, we traveled as quickly as possible on a straight course, staying close to the shoreline, moving into the bordering thickets whenever we saw a boat or any sign of life. We knew of one strong possibility of attack—that coming from Jake and his bandits. We intended to avoid a meeting with them, but if we should, it was under the tarp for me.

Of course, the threat of running into the Feds was always present. We lay low more than a few times when a Fed patrol boat passed. Once, while we were hiding, they turned back and passed our spot several times. Captain John thought they had seen us and had decided we weren't worth a plunder.

The general said, "O'Toole, if Jake and his gang come upon us, Captain John and I have a plan. Thanks to you, Tench, we have the advantage of knowing what they might do—if they see us first. Remember, if such should happen, stay out of sight."

Certain I didn't want another meeting with Jake, I assured the general I would gladly follow his wishes. Memories of Jake, as well as those of Shears and Joe, and Ziffa, still haunted me, bobbing in and out of my mind, waiting just below the surface. I never knew when they'd come up; I wondered if I'd ever be free of them.

After following the wide river on a continuous straight course for about twenty-five or thirty miles, we passed through Old Inlet to the Juniper Narrows, where the channel narrowed and twisted through a jungle of junipers, saw grass and mangroves. Captain John said, "Only a water snake could get through this labyrinth."

Quite a few times, just like it was on the headwaters of the St. Johns, we lost our bearings and had to back up and start over. O'Toole said these everglades go clear across the southern part of the Florida peninsula. At last, when we came upon a path leading over the sand dunes, we quickly set off for the ocean. We had to carry the boat overland a half mile in order to get there, but it was a great advantage to get out of that water maze and away from the mosquitoes.

Once across, the soldiers, followed by the general, then Captain John and Colonel Jim, shed their clothes. Tom and I followed suit and began to frolic and shout as we splashed in the waves. For a short while, our frustrations dropped away and we felt stimulated and renewed by the cool, rolling salty ocean.

After our refreshing bath, we gathered on the beach and Captain John read prayers. Such a mood of seriousness came over us. Considering the small craft on which the six of us hoped to reach another land, and looking out upon the vast expanse of water, I was filled with a great uneasiness.

"Over there is where we're going," said Captain John, pointing towards the eastern horizon. "The Bahamas. Eighty miles east."

Tom rubbed his eyes and blinked, "Don' see nothin'. We's goin' somewhere you can't even see. Eighty mile's a long ways."

Colonel Jim assured us, "If anybody can get us there, Captain John will."

"Don' see how we can all go in this little ol' boat when I think of how high the water comes on the sides when all of us's in it, an' I cain't swim none. We're gonna git drownded going eighty miles out into the sea without nothin' to hang onto, to a place we cain't even see."

General Breckinridge considered Tom's concerns a moment. "Tom, we have no choice. You understand that, don't you? But the good Lord will travel with us."

Tom nodded, but he did not look any less worried. I confess, I was uneasy, too.

We had left the sloop upright on the sand, so the warm summer sun would dry it inside. The general, leaning against the bow, spoke quietly. "I'd like to set off when the winds are gentler and the sea calmer."

Sergeant O'Toole replied, "Sir, we can't wait for a perfect time. As you said, we don't have choices."

"We can try her out in the sea, gentlemen," Captain John said. "But before we set sail, we need water and more provisions. For now, we're not prepared."

The corporal was frowning. "Given a friendly wind, we could be there with no more foolin' 'round. Don't worry, we'll be finding water and food enough very shortly." Neither Russell or O'Toole wanted to delay. The soldiers were always ready to go. The possibility of failure never occurred to either of them, it would seem, and they were impatient with the general and Captain John who wanted to be sure of everything. I have a feeling they wanted to get gone so they could get back sooner.

"We'll see how the boat sets in the ocean," O'Toole said, grasping an edge of the stern.

With no more ado, we were lifting the boat into the surf and piling into it, taking our usual positions. Until now, we had been in calmer, more protected waters, unlike the white foaming waves heaving around us.

Tom's teeth were chattering. I wasn't certain if it was caused by the winds after our cool dip in the sea, or if he was shivering with fear.

As we headed into the sea, I heard Captain John say to the general, "With these winds blowing directly against us, we're not going anywhere, sir."

He was right. We were buffeted by the wind and water and couldn't get beyond fifteen feet of shore. Also, except for Russell and O'Toole, none of us gave full muscle to the effort. Reluctantly, the general ordered us back to land.

After returning to shore and beaching the boat, O'Toole passed out the sharpened sticks and took us on our first turtle egg hunt. "We'll start right now to stock our supplies," he announced. "It's nesting time for the green turtle. They come out of the sea and lay hundreds of eggs in the sand. See, when I sink this stick in the sand, it enters easily, here." He started digging gently with his hands, soon filling a pail with a great number of eggs that looked like small balls, no larger than walnuts. "Look at the shell. See, you can tear it, but you can't break it." He punctured the shell with his knife and ripped it open. "Another thing, although the yolks get hard the longer it cooks, the whites get softer. Remember, don't dig if your stick doesn't go in easy, you'll be wasting your time." We soon found that the opposite was just as true.

Corporal Russell named our new sport as he called out, "We're mining for turtle gold."

The laughter sounded good again, after the frustration of our circumstances. We immediately began our search, but in no time, fell silent. O'Toole's first quick discovery was just a stroke of good luck. We discovered that most the nests yielded nothing. Something or someone had already mined the gold out of them. After some hours, we finally found an undisturbed nest.

Captain John rejoiced. "I don't think any prospector was ever more cheered by the sight of a gold vein than we are at this find."

We continued for a long time and had lots of turtle gold on our supper menu. The eggs aren't unpleasant, yet, I can see where a diet of them might become tiresome. We can give it a little variety by adding shellfish and snails. We've lots of serious scavenging to do before we attempt crossing to the islands.

The coast from Cape Canaveral to Cape Florida, I learned, followed a straight line. From the beach, we could see ships coming or going at a great distance. South of Jupiter Inlet, we saw a steamer moving close to shore. Captain John explained that the ships stay close to avoid the three- and four-knot current of the Gulf Stream that encircles the state. We carried our boat up and hid it above the dunes and palmettos and prayed the men on the steamer hadn't seen us. There was so much litter on the beach, we hoped that's what they'd think they had seen.

They were a half a mile away or so when we noticed a group of men on deck watching the shore. When we saw them continue on south, we gave a great sigh and moved back to the boat. But we had stirred too soon. The steamer turned sharply and came back towards us, this time about three hundred yards away. They were lowering a boatload of men armed with cutlasses and pistols. There was a quick parley among us.

"Let's take to the bush, leave the boat, and hope they don't disturb it," General Breckinridge suggested.

"Let's go," Colonel Wilson agreed, already taking steps on the path leading away from the beach.

"No." Colonel John stopped them. "If we leave our boat, they might either take it or destroy it. Without it, we'd be helpless. We could starve and never get out of this country." Then with a chortle, he added, "Besides, in no time, the mosquitoes would suck us dry as Egyptian mummies."

"We wouldn't have a chance, would we?" Colonel Jim asked.

Captain John, shaking his head, spoke quickly. "Russell and O'Toole, come with me. We'll meet them halfway. Bring your papers and a pail of turtle eggs." He looked at me, "You come too, Tench."

O'Toole and the captain rowed, Russell sat in the stern, and I sat in the bow beside the pail of turtle eggs.

We could see now that the steamer had sent a ten-oared cutter with a fresh, smartly dressed crew. Captain John ignored the usual hail greeting, but stopped rowing. A young officer stood waving a revolver.

The captain began to speak; he sounded every bit as gruff as Shears or Jake and looked as grubby as they. He called out in his harsh voice, "Cap'n, please have your men put away them weapons. 'Spechally that thar pistol of yourn. I don't like the looks of it. I'll tell you all about us. We're rebs and there ain't no use sayin' we aren't, but it's all up now. We got home too late to put in a crop, so we just made up our minds to come down shore and see if we couldn't fine somethin' to salvage. It's all right, cap'n. We got our papers. All signed. Want to see 'em? Got 'em up at Jacksonville—"

O'Toole and Russell reached over and handed their paroles to the man standing at the helm. He nodded and said they were all right, but asked for Captain John's. The captain turned his pockets out, felt around his shirt pockets, looked in his hat, and said, "I muster left mine up thar in camp, but it's just same as their'n."

When asked who else was ashore, Captain John answered, "There's more of us, fixin' suppah. They're boilin' turtle eggs and swamp cabbage. Cap'n, I'd like to swap yawl some eggs for tobaccy or bread."

The crew immediately took out pieces of plugs from their clothes, which they passed to us in exchange for the eggs.

"Wal, now, that's right nice of you folks," our captain babbled noisily. Then he offered the rest of our turtle eggs. "If'n yawl come back with we'uns to the camp, we'll giv yawl all the eggs yawl can eat." I winced at his generosity.

Thankfully, they didn't accept his offer. I'm sure he convinced the seamen he was "jes' a good-hearted ol' cracker feller" who wanted to share his crumbs and get some of theirs. Their captain called out a few questions before they turned back to their cruiser. "Have you seen any unusual wreck parties? We believe the one we're looking for would be well-equipped, well-dressed, fine looking folks who're probably escaping members of the Confederate government."

"No, suh. Hain't seen likes of sich folks in these parts. Only seen people of our sort, out salvagin' jes' like we'uns."

"Have you run across any batteries on shore?"

"Batteries?"

Captain John looked puzzled and scratched his head. "Yuh mean them big guns? No, suh. Ain't even seen a pistol in these parts."

The cutter captain shouted to his crew, "Up oars—let go forward—let fall—give way."

As they shoved off, we heard the coxswain say to his skipper, "That looks like a man-of-war gig they got, sir," but the captain paid no attention.

Captain John watched them move swiftly through the water to the waiting steamer. He spoke just for our ears, "Up oars—let go forward—let fall—give way. Those familiar orders never sounded so good. Like sweet music!"

June 6, 1865

LULLED BY THE ROAR AND RHYTHM OF THE SURF, COOLED by the breezes, we slept well and wakened late after a good night's sleep. Surprised by the bright sunlight for a few dazed moments, it was as if overnight, our cares had vanished. Only then did I realize how tired I had been. The others must have felt the same.

Clustered together with our boat lying next to us on its side, a buffer against the winds, we had camped above the tide line. The winds still continued from the south and east, blowing the mosquitoes away. It still would be difficult to make any progress against the headwinds. The night before, after much talk, we had decided to scuttle our plans to go to the Bahamas and instead, make our way down the Florida coast, then south across the short neck of sea to Cuba. So far, the currents and winds had worked against us; there was nothing we could do about it.

Tom and I have been awfully hungry and we tortured ourselves by planning dream menus. The others didn't mention food and they didn't complain when we cooked fish, boiling it in salt water. It's really not very tasty cooked that way, but we ate it anyway. Now the only point of food was to eat enough to keep up our strength.

When we had set up camp in the dark, we thought that we were on good ground. Now, we could see, the tide had come up quite close in the night.

For a long while we lay on our blankets talking—first one, then the other. The general spoke of when Colonel Jim had killed and cooked a beautiful bird. It had tasted so awful that after the general had taken a bite, he had to rush into the bushes. When he came back, he'd advised Colonel Jim to give it a quick burial.

The captain said, shaking his head, "It was an American egret. I've heard that women so greatly admire the beautiful long, white plumes that appear on the birds' backs from their shoulders to their tails during mating season, they gladly pay a pretty penny for them to decorate their hats and fans. There are hunters who come down here and slaughter the poor birds just for their fine delicate plumes and the money they bring."

"I should have saved the feathers to send to my lady friend back in Kentucky," Colonel Jim said.

"Along with the alligator musk, sir?" the sergeant teased. "By the way, sir, whatever happened to that musk bag?"

Colonel Jim didn't reply at once. "Disappeared, Sergeant. Plumb disappeared."

Everyone pretended to be surprised at this news and chorused their sympathy, "Aw. Aw."

About eight o'clock in the morning, the captain pointed out several wigwams a little south of us on the dunes. "Indians," he exclaimed. "We might be able to do some trading. Alas. What do we have to trade?"

General B. replied, "Turtle eggs and two sweet potatoes."

There was snickering among us. Captain John said, "Don't worry, I'll think of something." The general leaned towards him, speaking low, "Just don't tell them your grandfather's name.

"Dear God, no!" The captain threw his hands over his head. "They would scalp me. Oh, the shame I've suffered for my grandfather's sins."

I was perplexed and looked to Tom for an explanation. Tom shrugged, "It's a big com'pa'cation which I cain't say I fully unner-stan." He spoke loud enough to be heard by the others. "Ask Col'nel Jim. He know the whole story."

Captain John heard my question and Tom's answer. He turned and looked at me, "My grandfather was a fighter—"

"Because of this, he became president of the United States," Colonel Jim finished for him, then smiled big.

"He was fascinating man," the general broke in, "an ugly, rough man with a huge head that would have well-matched the body of a giant instead of his own short, stumpy, God-given body."

Captain John went on, "During his time in the United States Army, he fought many Indian tribes in the Northwest. Chief Black Hawk was one of those who surrendered to him. And I am ashamed to reveal that in Florida, he killed off the greater part of the Seminole Indian nation at the Battle of Okeechobee."

"And do you think we'll soon be engaged in petty barter with remnants of that great tribe?" the general asked.

The captain held forth, "Because of his reputation as an Indian-conqueror, he was sent to fight against Mexico where he won fame at Buena Vista, defeated Santa Anna, and took over Mexican land in the name of the United States!"

Despite this interesting tale, I was too aware of the wigwams and kept looking at them. I thought I saw a flash of movement.

Captain John's story continued and I listened while I studied on the wigwams. "So my grandfather, Old Rough and Ready Zachary Taylor, was elected president of the United States because he was daring and brave and had fought and conquered the poor, beleaguered people." Shaking his head, he sighed. "My grandfather. So you see, Tench, we all are visited upon, one way or another, by the sins of our fathers. I abhor those sins, just as my children's children will abhor the sins of their fathers—and you and every new generation will condemn the sins of their fathers."

We were watching as a group of Indians came from the wigwams and moved slowly down the dunes. "Look," the general said, "they stand like statues carved in sand."

The Indians waited, solemn and still. There were five or so of them, standing at different levels, dressed in colorful calico shirts, turbans, and loin-cloths. Captain John moved quietly along until he stood directly in front of them.

"We are friends," he said pronouncing each word slowly and loud. "We come in peace. We come to trade."

One lifted his hand in greeting. He said, "I am Chief." Judging by the silver accenting his oily hair, he was the oldest. He studied the captain, walked around him, then came down and looked at us. He gave all of us and the boat a thorough scrutiny. His sober brown eyes met mine and his gaze rested upon me an uncomfortably long while. He spoke to the Indians and pointed to my eyes.

He returned to Captain John's side and said, "We have kountee. We trade kountee for powder for our guns."

Sergeant O'Toole called out, "Sir, kountee is Indian flour for makin' bread. He wants to trade it for gun powder."

Captain John shook his head, "Trade turtle eggs."

"We want powder. No eggs. We got."

"Can we spare the powder?" the general asked.

O'Toole answered by taking out a handful of fish hooks from his bag and handing them to the captain. "We trade fish hooks."

"Powder." The chief was firm.

The general dug into his bag and found a military cloak which Russell took over to our barterer. The captain held it up for inspection.

The old Indian insisted, "Powder!"

It was Colonel Jim's turn to find an appropriate trade. He removed a cavalry saber from his bag.

Our trader laid it out before the chief. It sparked no interest and he repeated again, "Powder."

Captain John returned to the boat and with everyone's consent, divided our powder, giving the Indian half of our slight supply.

The chief nodded, accepted the box of powder and started up the bank, waving us to follow. They gave us the remains of their morning meal—fish and our first bite of kountee, which, in spite of its unusual taste, we quickly devoured. We learned that kountee was made from a root which they hammered into a fine powder and cooked in the ashes of their campfire. It made a tough kind of bread. The general said we all ate like starved wolves. We ate everything in sight, including a generous portion of turtle eggs. The chief explained to us why the eggs had been in scant supply "This season of turtle, Okeechobee bears come rob nests. Never before."

Now we understood the empty nests. We had been competing with both the bears and the Indians. They didn't have anything else to offer us. We had to be content with the kountee, although Captain John had fully hoped for more provisions in exchange for our precious powder.

The chief signaled us to follow him into the largest wigwam where he showed us, with great pride, three long, heavy small-bore rifles with flintlocks. Captain John said they were the kind that Davy Crockett used. We watched as he filled his powder horn.

Before we parted, the chief sounded a long call. He seemed to sing out many names. From the woods, from wigwams, to his side, a dozen or more tribesmen of different ages appeared. To my amazement, they stood in front of me. He explained, "Men of tribe wish to touch dark man with green eyes. Bring good luck." One after the other, they came forward and solemnly touched my brow.

The Indians had treated us kindly and before we returned to our sloop, they passed the peace pipe to each of us. We finally had made good friends on our journey down Florida waters—an encounter that has left me feeling strangely overwhelmed.

The day was one of unusual beauty. The sky stretched its eternal blue above and the breeze, for a change, was light as a whisper. After we left the Indians, we had packed away our bags and launched the sloop. As long as we could see them, the Indians stood on the dunes watching. I was filled with such a feeling of well-being that I decided it had been rooted in the moment the old chief had spoken to me, and the ritual of his tribesmen touching my brow for good luck.

The chief's words sounded again in my mind: Men of tribe wish to touch dark man with green eyes. Good luck? To whom would it bring good luck? My green eyes. The same green eyes that others, as long as I could remember, claimed brought bad luck. Maybe the Indians knew this, and believed their touch would bring me good luck. I laughed aloud, not realizing I had, until I saw everyone's attention turned to me.

"What is it, Tench?" Sergeant O'Toole asked.

Tench? The sergeant had called me by name. Had anyone noticed? Had anyone noticed how he had spoken to me before?

"I was wondering, sir, what the chief meant when he said if the men of the tribe touched me, it would bring good luck. Now I wonder, who did he think it would bring good luck to? To them? Or to me?"

There was just a moment of silence before an explosion of laughter rocked the boat. I really hadn't meant to be funny.

As we sailed just offshore, we were fascinated by the pelicans patrolling the coastline, flying in a big V. We had been observing them ever since we had crossed to the ocean. They are such big birds, curious and comical. Finding us in their territory, they fly by, quite indifferent to our presence, but curious enough to fly over, again and again. After a few strong strokes of their broad wings, they seem suspended on air currents, coasting and gliding as lightly as dandelion down.

O'Toole called our attention. "Notice the pouch under the bird's beak. He can catch anything that floats. By swooping over the water, with a twist of one of those tremendous wings, he'll come to a dead stop and pick up the catch in his bill without getting a feather wet."

He turned to Captain John. "Sir, he's called Man-of-War. He's like a pirate and pesters and bullies all the birds until they drop their prey and he scoops it up. The pouch is a feeding trough for pelican babies and a storage trunk for jellyfish and various fish and small sea creatures."

Everybody had a good laugh and General B. remarked, "You have to admire a bird that puts to good use what might be considered a handicap among other forms of life."

Colonel Jim gave a whoop. "A lesson to all of us lower forms. Observe how the pelican derives extraordinary benefits from his misshapen anatomy."

I liked it when we all started sharing views. Sometimes it was funny. It had been sad as well. Tom and I hadn't lived long enough to contribute much, yet they included us and asked us questions—even questions about the war, about General Pickett and some other generals I had known, and about hunting, cooking, and birds and many points of nature. In answering their questions, I discovered a lot about how I really think about things.

We talked about death and each wanted to know the others' thoughts. I said I was sure Lance was in Heaven. I told what I thought Paradise was like. Tom's ideas were much like mine.

General B. and Captain John seemed to agree with us. But Colonel Jim just shook his head and said, "That's not how I believe. I think when you're dead, you're just as dead as that old shipwreck up on the beach. When it's over, it's all over."

Russell agreed, but O'Toole shook his head. "Tench, like you said, the part about Heaven and what it's like, is right. But you can't just die and go there—although a few pure souls might. Others may go straight to hell. I was told there is a first judgment, and most folks end up in purgatory, which is like a blast furnace for sins. Although it's only temporary, you could stay there hundreds of years before your sins burn off. On the final judgment day, some will go to Heaven, others to hell."

Colonel Jim interrupted, "Tench, that's what the sergeant believes. All of us look at it in our own particular way."

O'Toole went on, "If we take our sufferin' now, without carrying on 'bout it, we won't have to suffer as much later on."

As I've always been so satisfied with what I believed, I never wondered about what others thought. But now I liked discovering our differences. Things seemed so much better since O'Toole looked me in the eye and called me by my name and told us what he believed.

Soon after we finished talking about Heaven, off New River inlet, we saw a sail heading north towards us. "Looks like a sturdy, seaworthy sloop. Might be a Federal guard boat," Captain John said, concern in his voice, straining his eye in its direction. "Maybe we should go shoreward and hide beyond the dunes."

All at once, the boat turned seaward. Captain John stood, studying the boat and its occupants. "They're trying to avoid us," he said. "It looks to be a better boat than we have, and it looks like there's only three men on board."

He sat down and picked up the oars. "They act like they're afraid of us. Must be they don't have weapons, or not too many. Also, they know we outnumber them. Come, men, after them! They're probably deserters either from the Union Navy or Confederates and are afraid of getting caught. Or, they could be escaped convicts from the prison at Dry Tortugas off Key West."

General B. smiled broadly. "Looks like we're going to have a little action."

General B. and Captain John exchanged glances. The captain lowered the sail, sat beside him. They began rowing briskly. O'Toole and

Russell took up the other oars and we began to give chase, sliding smoothly through the water. "Tench, take a hard look. It's not Jake or his gang, is it?" the captain asked as we started to overtake them.

"There were many more with Jake, sir. I don't see any more boats around here. They look too clean and civilized. So does the boat. Their boats were old and weather-worn. No, it's not Jake, sir."

"Just like I thought before, men. From what I can determine, I'd say that boat's better than ours. What do you say, men, could we use a better boat?"

Our eager crew needed no urging. The general sang out, "Aye, aye, sir!" And we all called out "Aye!" in agreement.

They tried to escape, but we lowered our sail and rowed, pressing hard, finally overtaking them. The captain fired a shot across the bow of their boat and the mainsail quickly dropped. My heart leapt like a flying fish. We were pulling up near them, I could see the occupants were thoroughly frightened. After all, we must've looked like a boat-load of outlaws.

Captain John said, "By their clothes, I'd say they're a man-of-war's crew. Deserters. Arm yourselves, men. Draw your pistols." Holding his pistol on them, he addressed the three-man crew. "Who are you? What is your business?"

One finally answered, "We're seamen, searching for some of our men." He held himself erect, looked the captain squarely in the eyes, and asked, "And who are you? By what authority have you over-hauled us?"

"As far as we're concerned, the war is not over." The captain spoke loud and emphatically, "You're our prisoners, your boat's our prize. The three of you are deserters and pirates, for which the punish-ment is death. Under the circumstances, we'll take your paroles and exchange boats."

"No. No. You can't take our boat," the seaman shouted back.

With that, guns drawn, the general and captain stepped into their boat. The captain ordered the speaker to go forward. When he hesi-tated, the captain's and Colonel Jim's revolvers stared him in the face and he grimly obeyed.

The general shouted, "Wilson, disarm that man!"

Colonel Jim jumped aboard and shouted, "Hands over your heads." The seamen obeyed, while the colonel took a pistol and sheath knife from his belt.

With no further protest, the others handed over their arms and the three boarded our sloop. Tom and the soldiers and I started to transfer our things to the new boat while the captain and general looked over the booty. Their supply was small, a beaker of fresh water, some sea biscuits and hard tack.

Voices low, our men talked over the situation. Feeling sorry for them, they decided not to take all their provisions and gave them some of our kountee and turtle eggs.

In my silent core, I was amused. The general and the captain had overcome these sailors with a bold and threatening manner. Of such stuff were battles won. Yet they didn't leave their enemy without hope. The general might have been influenced by the fact that they were the age of his sons, but by nature, both were good men who strongly believed in the Christian way. This had much to do with how they treated others.

General B. said, "They are no less victims than we. They face the same odds we face." He reached inside a leather bag strapped under his shirt, took out a twenty dollar gold piece, and explained to us, "This will make up the difference for the trade." So it ended—like an honorable business transaction.

Our prisoners' attitudes quickly changed with their change of fortune. At once, they made themselves comfortable on the new boat. They were in such good humor, they asked us for directions to reach Jacksonville or Savannah.

Before we left, the captain handed them their revolvers and knife. They were unbelieving. Laughing, the general remarked, "Now they've seen how it's done, perhaps they can exchange their boat for another."

The captain was pleased with his trade. "I wouldn't be afraid to cross the Atlantic in this," he said, patting the gunwale. "It's not much longer than ours, but there's more beam and plenty of freeboard decked over to the mast and there are good sails and riggings."

Tom was exceptionally happy about the trade. He said, "What I like is that we be settin' up high 'bove the water. In our boat I kep' thinkin', if a good wave came, we'd all get drownded."

"We're about to make a decision," said the captain as he raised the mainsail. "The distance and winds will work to our advantage if we head for Cuba. And—if need be—there are many islands where we can seek refuge. You all know the chance we're taking. You can see many wrecked ships washed up on the beach that didn't reach their destination."

Captain John now was at the helm. We were making progress in spite of the light wind. He became very serious and spoke of the boat exchange. "We needed a seafaring sloop more than they did. After all, they're deserters. They'll pay for their crime with prison. We'd have to pay with our lives."

"Not all of us," Sergeant O'Toole quickly corrected. "We're not all guilty of the same crime."

There was an uncomfortable silence. O'Toole and Russell were muttering together. Then all at once, O'Toole spoke, "Sir, Russell and I really don't want to leave Florida. We wanted to help you down the coastal waters, maybe even to the Bahamas, but we didn't want to go to Cuba."

A dark shadow seemed to fall across the general's face. Since I first met him, I had seen a change gradually coming over him. I couldn't help but remember my first impression of him—his splendid appearance, the unbelievable blue of his eyes, and his erect military posture. Now, looking at him, I was saddened. Bronzed to iodine by the sun, with an untamed, gray-streaked beard, he was aging before our eyes. The blue eyes seemed faded and lost in his hollow cheeks. His face was gaunt, his body haggard and stooped. Although I knew him to be over six feet, at this moment he appeared much less.

But it was the same vibrant voice speaking to the soldiers. "We have been blessed by your guidance, my good men. Wherever you are, wherever we may be, we'll always be indebted to you for steering us on our course and bringing us safely to this moment."

Colonel Jim broke in, "We couldn't have survived the St. Johns River or gotten this far without you—through the wild, twisting channels, or the alligators and mosquitoes."

General Breckinridge rose and stood before the two men. "Now we need you more than ever. Your guidance is our talisman. Be assured, you cannot now be charged with helping the enemy of the United States because the South is no longer a foe."

I was convinced by the sense of his argument, but most of all, I saw the necessity of O'Toole's and Russell's presence. I prayed they would feel as I did. I wanted nothing as much as a passage to safety for the general and Captain John. I hoped the soldiers' reason for staying until the end would be as strong as mine—the lives of these three people must not be risked further. Nothing more was said.

Coming upon Green Turtle Key, we went ashore to get some ballast for our new craft and picked up some heavy rocks which we felt would do the job. We spent several hours again hunting for turtle gold, all trying our best to replenish our egg supply—to no avail. We recognized bear tracks; they had made a thorough raid and left nothing behind.

We screened the beach and beyond for anything that might relieve our hunger and had succeeded in finding only a few wild onions growing in a patch of weeds near the beach and we had divided and eaten them on the spot. We needed enough supplies for a few days to get us to Cuba. We decided to stop off at Fort Dallas at the mouth of the Miami River although we knew it would be a risk. We didn't know who or what we'd find after we got there. The fort had been built during the war with the Seminoles and had been abandoned after it was over. O'Toole said that ever since, it had been a notorious hideaway for pirates and outlaws of every type. Captain John said we must use caution.

As we sailed toward the fort, I saw that the entrance was quite picturesque. The Miami River was an outlet for water coming from the everglades. Along its banks, the tropical growth, the flowering plants, and the coconut trees were reflected in its crystal waters. It was unlike any of the wilds we had seen anywhere in Florida, and by far, the most beautiful.

We could see the old barracks as we moved against the current. In the clearing, the white buildings, surrounded by the jungle growth, made a striking picture.

"Undercover, Tench." Before the captain spoke, a streak of movement had alerted me. I fell to the deck, pulled the tarp over me. The captain had good reason to feel that something threatened. Peeking from under the tarp, I caught sight of a small fleet of canoes and sloops, and my face fell against the floor.

Tom lifted a corner of the tarp and reported to me. "There's twenty or thirty of the toughest lookin' men I ever seen! They's white men, red men and some Congo men. Look like they's a mighty mixed-up, wild bunch!"

Tom was silent for a moment, then continued. "Here comes a big one, taller than Cap'n John. He's carryin' a long-barrel pistol. Lis'sen."

"Who are you?" A deep, accented voice asked.

"Wreckers," Captain John answered. "Left our ship out yondah n' come in for water n' supplies."

"*Where* did you leave your ship?"

"North'rd, up the river. A gunboat spoken us a few hours ago n' inspected our papers. Said, all in order." He hadn't told the name of the ship.

Tom reported to me again. "Now, the wild-lookin' ones're confabin'."

"Come ashore here. We want to look at your papers," the stranger ordered.

"No!" the captain shouted. "Send a canoe over. I'll let one of our men go ashore and buy what we want." The captain lowered his voice, speaking to us. "I don't want our boat closer than a hundred feet from shore."

Tom spoke to me. "Two big ol' Congo Nigras are comin' up in a canoe."

A new voice, one unaccustomed to using our language, said, "Chief say, only cap'n come."

O'Toole volunteered to go, but the boatman repeated, "Only cap'n come. Chief say."

Captain John offered his terms. "Tell your chief we want to pay with gold. If he says no, we go somewhere else for supplies."

"We gettin' ready to leave," Tom told me. "We're takin' out the oars a'gin. Nice little breeze hepin' us go easy down the river. All these ruff'ins got long-nose pistols. Them two mess'gers gone back to the chief." He was excited. "Oh, dear God, looka that. Twenty'r thirty pilin' into four or five them canoes and they're headin' for us. We all's got arms ready to shoot. I'm gonna put a fresh cap in my carbine."

Captain John warned, "Give them a warm reception. Russell, Tom, try shooting at that canoe ahead of the others. That's it." A volley of shots sounded and the captain said, "Good work. You've broken two paddles on one side and hit a man on the other."

I lifted up the tarp to see. Besides, I was covered with sweat and needed air. Our enemy was shooting wild because of the motion of their canoes. The general's shot was wild, too. He called out, "Save your powder until they come within sure shooting range."

After a short wait, he and Russell started shooting again and the leader in the first canoe rolled over, almost upsetting the canoe. The boatmen paddled in together and held another pow-wow.

Shortly, three men waving a white flag came towards us. We stopped and waited for them.

Within hailing distance, Captain John called, "Well? What you want?"

"Why'd you fire at us? We're friends," one of the white men shouted to us. He was standing while two Negroes paddled.

The general answered, "Friends don't greet you with guns drawn. Friends don't give chase to friends."

"We wanted to find out who you are," the man called.

Captain John was disgusted. "I told you who we are. If you mean to be friendly, you'd be selling us some provisions."

"Come on shore and you can get what you want."

We knew it wouldn't be safe to get too close to them again. Our boat was better than any vessel of theirs that we could see. Captain John told them they could bring the supplies to the boat and they'd be paid in gold. Finally, the gang agreed that one man could go to shore in their canoe and be allowed to purchase what he needed and pay in gold. After some grumbling and discussion, O'Toole agreed he would go, but only if the general insisted the pirates must bring him back within two hours and that the general added a threat to back that up.

"Two hours? That's no time," the buccaneer protested, "not even enough time to have a drink with friends."

"Two hours," the captain warned. "If he's not back in two hours, we'll speed out of here and speak to the first federal gunboat we meet and return and have your nest of pirates and deserters broken up."

"Hard words from friends," the buccaneer shouted. But he agreed to the terms, whether because he was afraid the general would bring the feds or because he had something else up his sleeve, we didn't yet know.

The general gave O'Toole about a hundred dollars in gold to trade and warned, "Be as dumb as an oyster, but keep your eyes open wide as to what that band of thieves may have in mind."

When they left, the captain told us what he suspected of this gang. "After we started moving down the river, I noticed a column of black smoke rising from near the fort. It may have been a signal to some of their craft to return. We would be foolish to believe that they didn't have anything but canoes to do their kind of work."

"They're the dregs of humanity." The general was lowering the anchor. "From what I've seen of this motley crew, I'd judge them capable of the most villainous acts."

"What do you think others think when they look at us? We could be judged just as severely," the captain said as he leaned back and looked us all over. "General, your straw hat flaps over your head like elephant ears, while, in your old cavalry hat without a visor, Colonel Wilson, you look like a Moroccan sheepherder. Darned if your turban, Tom, made out of number four duck canvas, doesn't make you look like a Hindu beggar. And poor Tench. Your hat droops over your face like a sheep dog." Then he hooted, "And Russell looks like a he-coon in his hat of coon tails. We're all in shirts without sleeves with colors as mixed as Joseph's coat. No doubt, they're mulling us over right now and saying what a murderous band of thugs we are. But that can only work to our advantage—and for the safe return of brave O'Toole."

For the moment, Captain John had made us laugh at the thought that the pirates might be as afraid of us as we were wary of them, but after two hours, we became fearful. Our gaze swept the surrounding waters like lighthouse beams. We didn't wonder if danger was coming, we wondered only from where and how it would come.

The general asked John for devotions, and he quickly obliged, leading us all in a prayer for O'Toole's safe return. He then asked us to pray individually after he finished. So each of us gave voice to our own concern.

Tom said, "God, take care of Mister Sergeant Joseph O'Toole. Don't let them hurt him none n' let him and Co'p'ral Russell 'cide to stay with us to hep us 'scape." Tom always prayed first and put in a good order. He said Miss Breckinridge taught him.

Although I was embarrassed to pray aloud, I was so worried now about the sergeant, I prayed, "Father in Heaven, keep Sergeant O'Toole safe. Take his hand."

"I just want him to come back safely." Corporal Russell's words were few and to the point.

The general took out his timepiece and announced, "The sergeant has been gone two hours and forty five minutes."

The captain had weighed anchor and with the light breeze we were being drawn to the mouth of the river. Our view of the fort was now blocked as we had drifted a few miles from the wharf.

That was when we had a sudden view of a canoe astern. We turned and rowed vigorously towards it. It was O'Toole with two Congo men who now were smiling and chattering in contrast to our first view of them. In no time, O'Toole climbed back aboard our boat.

What a feast he had with him. Two hams and crusty salt pork. A bag of hard bread, sweet potatoes, fruit, water and—rum. Starved as we were, we tore into the food, while Sergeant O'Toole sliced some ham, saying, "Soon as I got there they took me to the quarters of Major Valdez who said he was a Federal officer. He asked me dozens of questions, like I was on trial."

"What did you tell him?" the general asked.

"Told them about the end of the Confederacy and capture of the president. Told him of the unfriendly greetin' his men had given us. He said they had a hunch we weren't wreckers. I'd say they had fairly good hunches. He told me they thought we might be escaping

Confederates with a boatload of gold, or pirates or looters. I stayed to my story in spite of all his probing. He finally came around to believin' me, I think. I told him we were all glad the war was over and we had wanted to catch up with the years we lost, but there wasn't any crops and no way to make a penny, so we were doin' whatever we could."

As O'Toole talked, we enjoyed our first sweet oranges and big, full-length bananas in years. After Colonel Jim had poured out some rum and water for the general and himself, he passed the rum around.

Sergeant O'Toole confirmed what Captain John had suspected. Valdez and his gang were looking for a schooner to return. That was one of the reasons he had tried to detain O'Toole so long. It was only when Valdez thought we were leaving that he allowed him to make his purchases and return. He didn't want to miss the opportunity to get some gold—and he didn't want us bringing the wrath of a federal gunboat on them.

To my questions about Jake, the sergeant said he didn't think he saw anyone of his description. Captain John said, "From what you've told about him, I don't think Jake would be there taking orders from anyone. Valdez is the Big Chief here."

Colonel Jim added, "I think Jake must've gone in the opposite direction. Not many people would come this far south. They just don't know what they might find."

"I hope you're right, "I said. "I've had nightmares about him ever since I took my horse from him in Georgia and saw him again up the river." They knew the story.

The captain said, "The meal we are enjoying is finer than any ever served at Cafe Riche or Delmonico's. I noticed all of us are tasting everything thoroughly and savoring every bite. Lately, we've only been eating to live, not subjecting our poor fare to any type of judgment—only grateful for what crumbs we could scrape together."

Although we quickly had moved away from the fort and out of the Miami River, we now realized Captain John had been right in guessing that Major Valdez had a more powerful vessel with which he did his business. For a few hours, a schooner pursued us, but our captain skillfully out-distanced them. We wondered about Valdez, a Federal officer who seemed to be the leader of such a strange assortment of lawless ruffians.

By nightfall, we found ourselves inside Key Biscayne, one of the first keys in the chain that ended with Key West. General B. and the captain showed us the map and we could see that the keys started here and stretched to the Tortugas, nearly two hundred miles east and west at the tip end of the Florida peninsula.

The keys, the captain was soon telling us, came about from coral formations. They are made up of tiny sea creatures that cluster together and then calcify and build up over great periods of time. Sea birds land on them, dropping seeds, and hard mangroves wash on them. Their roots spread in every direction and in time, bind the coral into rock-strong islands and reefs.

We, in our band, are like the coral formations, I thought. Though we are individually small, by banding together we contributed so much and made a whole bigger than any one of us—again, each, an important part of the entire picture, just like the tiny sea creatures building up the reefs.

June 7, 1865

IN THE COVER OF THE MANGROVES, WE SPENT A MISERABLE night suffering the heat and fighting off mosquitoes, both forever with us. Though the mangroves provided a refuge for us, it was not without the burden of the many insects that live among them. Captain John read this entry from his journal: "They almost darken the air. Their buzzing is like the roaring of the wind."

To my own journal, I added: "They riddle our bodies with their poison. We can escape bandits and pursuers, but they're like a plague; we are helpless before them."

After our restless night, we rose at sunrise and soon saw that a schooner of thirty or forty tons was heading at us from the east. The general said, "I believe it's those renegades from the fort. They probably decided they should have heeded their first impression of us— that we were escaping Confederates with a boatload of gold."

"That's possible." Captain John responded by quickly sounding orders, "Up anchor, up sail, out sweeps, down bay."

Before everyone set to work, Russell and O'Toole announced they were going with us all the way to Cuba. Our spirits quickly rose with that information.

They began lifting anchor and raising sail, then they took out a pair of oars and handed another pair to General B. and Colonel Jim. Tom and I were the take-over-and-supply crew—ready to take over and supply whenever and whatever the others needed. One of our chief functions was sharp-eyeing, keeping our eyes on all points as watch-outs. Our jobs as cooks and food-fetchers had petered out along with the food supplies and sources. If we were lucky enough to come upon ham or sea biscuits, as yesterday, the person nearest slices and passes.

Everyone began sharp-eyeing. The bay was a sheet of silver over shallow shoals separating the reefs and the mainland. We saw that the schooner was overtaking us. It was standing windward; the winds rose with the sun, so it had the advantage. Our advantage was that the water was shoaling and our draft was quite a few feet less than our pursuer's.

"We'll draw them into shoal waters," the captain said, "and try to stay afloat ourselves. By the color and break of the water, it looks as if the shoals extend nearly across the bay."

"But there're narrow channels between them like furrows in a plowed field," the general observed. "I see an occasional opening from one channel to another. Some of the shoals are just awash, others bare. There's a reef ahead with very little water, but there's no opening into the channel beyond."

Squinting into the sun, the captain commented, "To try to haul by the wind on either tack would bring us under the schooner's fire." He told me to relieve O'Toole and ordered Tom, "Throw the ballasts overboard. We'll force her over the reef."

It looked like we were headed for a little breakwater on our port bow. As the ballasts went overboard, our eyes were on the bottom. The water rapidly shoaled, and we heard the keel grating over the coral with a tremor, warning us of danger.

The remaining ballast went overboard; the boat rose up and surged ahead. The captain turned quickly to me and said, "Put our journals and the general's book in the transom locker." Then his glance circled our party and he shouted, "All overboard!"

When I saw the general hand his volume of Plutarch to Tom, I took it from his hand and stashed it with our journals in the locker built into the transom. For a moment, Tom looked befuddled.

Together, all of us, except Tom, jumped overboard. I sank up to my neck; the others, to their waists in the black, syrupy mud, scattered through with branches of old, brittle coral. It made the bottom difficult and dangerous to work in. Relieved of a half-ton of our weight, the boat surged ahead three or four lengths, then rose up again.

We pushed her forward some distance, but in spite of our efforts, she stopped suddenly. Looking astern, about a mile off, we saw the schooner coming up with sails extended on both sides.

Captain John was climbing on again, shouting, "Back aboard. Jettison provisions and equipment. Everything goes."

Tom started throwing things overboard before I could get back on. Without hesitation, everyone tossed our precious supplies, anything that weighed a pound or over—our anchor and chain, spare rope, everything.

"Overboard!" the captain shouted and we jumped in again, except for poor Tom, unable to swim and afraid of the waters. "Three men on each side," the captain directed. "Shoulders under the boat's bilges. Lift together. Lift. Lift. Lift."

Foot by foot, we moved her forward. Sometimes the water would deepen a little and relieve us; again, it would shoal. There would be seconds when we would slip between the coral branches under the slime and water; our feet, hands and bodies were cut and scratched by the sharp and ragged coral points.

The wind helped us; we kept all sail on. We labored for over a hundred yards, until the water deepened and we were clear of the reef. Wet, dirty, and bleeding, we climbed into the boat. All at once, the schooner opened fire, but we were at long range and their firing went wild. A favoring wind helped put distance between us.

General Breckinridge was exhausted and threw himself to the bottom of the boat. It had been an ordeal for all of us, but lately, I've felt that the general is not as strong as the others. He tires easily and falls asleep before everyone else. Usually he's the first one to give out. This trip has been hard on him. I think our poor, scanty rations have weakened him.

Tom came to the general's side. He was talking to him in his private way; his voice was soft, "Gen'el John, suh, would you like a little rum and water? " We all looked at each other. Tom always took care of the general.

The general rose. "Yes, indeed, Tom. I'd like it very much. But rum? I supposed it had to be sacrificed when everything was thrown overboard."

"No, suh. When we all began pitchin' our thins' out I jes' put the rum ration in the locka, cuz it's somethin' we jes' can't do wit'out."

He opened the locker in the transom and took out jugs of rum and water and passed them around. Sergeant O'Toole told me I could take a swallow since I had done a man's work, but Captain John gave me a look that told me I wasn't ready for that. I took a long draft of water and passed it back to Tom. I hoped my journal was still in that locker.

Tom said in his private voice, "Thas right. You don' have no cravin' fo spirits, no need to start it up." He shook his head violently and turned the corners of his mouth down. "No, suh, not yet." He then picked up the rum jug and took a long swallow.

Everyone revived within moments. Just in time, I should say, for the schooner was passing through an opening in the first reef. Captain John said, "The way that skipper moves around these waters, he has to be familiar with them."

Another shoal appeared ahead. This time we sailed into the wind and the captain called, "Sharp eyes for an eastward opening."

Our pursuers were fast approaching, but a reef stood in their way. When they were about half mile away, they opened fire with their small arms and boat gun. Shot from the boat gun, it grazed the mast and carried away the luff of the mainsail. Some mini balls struck on our sides but didn't penetrate. We lay low, keeping under cover. We didn't return fire.

At the break in the reef, the captain again went off before the wind. Finally, the schooner did not try to overtake us and stood to the north. The chase was over. We were free of our enemy.

Beginning to take stock, we looked about us. We had about ten pounds of hard bread, a twenty-gallon beaker of water two thirds full, and three gallons of rum. What we paid such a dear price for yesterday, today we had been forced to sacrifice. While everybody was talking, I peeked into the locker and was relieved to see my journal there with the other.

The big problem, however, was our need for ballast. The sloop isn't seaworthy without it, but we don't have ropes or tools with which to handle possible ballasts. All of the keys, the shore as well as the mainland, are swampy and low and covered with little more than mangroves. I knew Captain John and the general were worried. We all were.

We came upon Elliot's Key at nightfall. We used one of the long oars to tie to, by shoving it into the muddy bottom and securing our boat to it with strips of canvas. Again, as the mosquitoes ascended upon us, we wrapped ourselves in the sails, leaving only our noses exposed. We spent another almost sleepless night, aware of each other's wakefulness. As each of us became stiff and numb, we tried not to bother each other.

After that difficult night and, ready to move off early, we unfastened the canvas strips from the oar and began to pole our way westward through the mangroves. The fog was heavy and we strained our eyes to locate solid, dry ground and something we could use for supplies on our journey.

I spotted the trees first. "Sir, look above the shore to the west. Coconut palms." They rose above the mangroves and we saw there were bunches of coconuts under the high arch of fronds.

"Food and ballast. Coconuts and palm trees rooted in sand." The captain was joyful. We all cheered.

We plunged an oar to the bottom and again tied the sloop to it with canvas strips. Wading ashore, it was as we had hoped, but the general shook his head, "How're we goin' to get them down?"

Tom nudged me and whispered for me to follow him back to the sloop. He cut two pieces of canvas about a yard long, tied the ends of each together and, stretching the canvas between his feet, made two holes. He handed me one. "Yours," he said. "Come on. Take your boots off. We gotta show these people how to climb a tree."

I wasn't sure how I was going to do it, but I followed Tom and watched. I had never climbed a palm tree.

Machete in hand, Tom threw the canvas around the palm and put his big toes through the holes. With the canvas stretched between his feet, he moved rapidly to the top. He slashed the coconuts down and O'Toole retrieved one of them and sliced through the outer layer to the hard shell inside.

The general waited with an empty jug and poured coconut milk into it. He was grinning, "Later, we'll make a little coconut punch."

After watching Tom, I discovered my own agility in climbing a coconut tree. Russell provided another machete and I cut all the coconuts from my tree. I came down carefully as Tom worked on his second tree. I certainly wasn't in competition with Tom, but I took a little pride in the fact I wasn't doing too badly since this was my first coconut palm and none of the others had offered to do the climbing and fetching.

"Them boys sure are a wonder. Lookit 'em scramble up them trees," Russell called out.

The general laughed, "They're doing what none of us can do." Then his attention returned to the captain who was in the boat.

The captain had determined that the jib wasn't bent, then decided on our next move. "We can bring the sheet and head together, make it into a sack and fill it with sand." Immediately, he and O'Toole went to work. After filling it with sand, they slung it over an oar and hoisted it to their shoulders, carrying it on board.

Russell took a few shots at some pelicans that were peacefully fishing nearby. The birds must not have been used to being hunted and they were an easy kill. Colonel Jim groaned, "I thought we learned our lesson 'bout big old tough old birds."

"I think we have a surprise," Russell said. "These old birds' treasure chests are full of food. I watched them steal supper from a flock of wading birds who were feeding on a school of mullet that they kept dropping." With that, he fetched the birds from the water, and once he had them in hand, he took a couple dozen mullet about nine inches long from the birds' large beaks.

Tom and I were beside them at once. We built a fire and cleaned the fish, wrapping them in palmetto leaves and roasting them in the ashes. I'm sorry to think that we left the pelicans to the buzzards. I believe that everyone was also sorry about the pelicans. Russell said if we hadn't been so hungry ourselves, we wouldn't have killed the pelicans for the breakfast they hadn't a chance to digest.

We loaded the coconuts on board and held council. Captain John spoke, "We can't delay any longer. Since abandoning our plan to go to the Bahamas, the only possibility lies south. With the winds of the season, we can hope to reach Cuba in a couple to three or four days. Even with the greatest economy, our provisions will not last long, yet it seems unlikely we'll be able to get more than we have at this moment. We'll be on our way by morning."

"There'll be no more fooling around," the general said. "When we get into the Gulf Stream, there'll be no turning back."

My eagerness to go seemed shared by the others. I believed our adventures of the past month in the swamps and coast and among the mangroves had prepared us to face whatever risk that was needed to escape from these shores. We had survived the harshest conditions.

"We'll reach Caesar's Canal and Key Largo come morning." Captain John was studying the maps. "It's unlikely, but we may come across some supply source. Sharp eyes, everyone."

"Are there any stations or outposts this far south?" Colonel Jim asked.

"Used to be," O'Toole answered. "Who knows what's happened down here since the War?"

"I think we know," General Breckinridge replied. "Pirates, blockaders, Feds, thugs—all skimming what they can."

"We'll move with caution," the captain said.

"And prayers," the general reminded.

Without hesitation, the captain bowed his head and began to pray and everyone followed. I noticed that when O'Toole and Russell first came, they had backed off during prayers, with their hands in their pockets, heads held high and eyes wide open. They had changed. Now they bowed their heads with the rest of us. They seemed to take an interest in the captain's devotions.

I discovered both O'Toole and Colonel Jim were "lapsed Catholics." And although Breckinridge frequently asked Captain John for prayers, the general never led us. Prayer, for Captain John, was as natural as breathing. He seemed to express the exact need we had at the moment. I believe the others felt the same way; everyone participated so willingly. We were glad to have him speak for us.

After settling well out in the bay, we spent a fairly quiet and comfortable night. A fog-shrouded morning came with a steely gray horizon and not a glimmer of coming day, while dark cushions of clouds rolled overhead. We began to row carefully and quietly towards Caesar's Canal, the passage between Elliot's Key and Key Largo. With all our care, we couldn't overcome the swift, powerful currents of the Gulf Stream that would wash us aground among the many small mangrove islands. Constantly grounded, we had to jump overboard and push off over and over again.

Finally, exhausted, we looked for a landing, with a desire to eat some coconuts and regain our strength. We saw an inlet in the distance and began to move towards it.

Halfway there, Tom yelled, "Some'uns got there first. Lookit the sloops pull't into the mangroves."

My heart sank. I saw the same disappointment and fear reflected on the faces of the rest of our party. They were remembering, just as I, the chase down the coast. Whoever and how many they were, we were probably unfavorably matched. We wouldn't benefit—if they had two sloops about the same size as ours and more men, and more arms.

"Quiet, Tom." Captain John cautioned. "We'll steal in while we're above the landing. Chances are we'll catch a glimpse of them before they see us."

"They're probably watching us right now," O'Toole spoke in a harsh whisper. He and Russell already were rowing shoreward.

Tom nudged the captain. "If we don' get shot first, Tench and I could wade in and get the lay of the land n' see what they're up to. They might have somethin' we could use."

"We'll see. Down everyone. Quiet," Captain John ordered. "It's early enough, they could be sleeping." He was arming himself and told the others to do the same.

We reached a parting in the mangroves and Captain John said, "All right, Tench and Tom. Let's go." He lowered himself quietly into the water and we followed.

Everyone hunkered down in our sloop under a good cover of mangroves. The shoal was sharp with coral and alive with shellfish: crabs and oyster beds. I was thinking, "Good eating." We hadn't come across such trove of riches before.

Moving onto shore, we crept silently through the brush. I was reminded of the time the captain and I stole through the underbrush and came upon Shears and Joe and Night. My heart was pounding. I felt the same excitement I had then.

I trailed, while the captain and Tom edged ahead. Abruptly, the captain halted. For a long while, he bent over, peering through the mangroves. "My God! What have we here?" he finally exclaimed with no attempt to silence his words. Again, "My God!" His voice pierced like a dagger through the heavy atmosphere.

Tom joined him and as he bent over to share the view, his voice echoed the captain's, "My Gawd. Oh, my Gawd."

I groped among the branches of the mangrove, but they were unyielding, so I scurried to the captain's side. He was saying, "Back to the boat."

I leaned over long enough to see the cause for their outcries. With the first glance, I saw, in the clearing beyond, a dozen or so men sprawled, seemed to be asleep. Holding my gaze, I saw then, that each body bore a life-emptying wound in the chest or head from which his life-blood had drained and dried. I went weak and felt dizzy and was engulfed by a savage and overpowering horror. I was remembering. Shears, Joe, Wes Vickers, Ziffa, Jake, I could not cry out. I turned back towards our sloop.

When I reached the boat, our group was already in conference, deciding the next move. They would enter the main landing and explore the site. Tom and I needn't go. They had practical matters to attend. I hunched over, hugging my shoulders. In spite of the heat and humidity, I was chilled in the grey cover of fog. Tom finally left me and joined the others. I heard their somber voices echoing across the clearing and through the mangroves with Tom's continuous moan punctuating their dismal mission, "Oh my Gawd, my Gawd, my Gawd."

At last the captain appeared on the bank. "Tench," he summoned, "you better come. I want you to look at them."

I had looked at them. I had seen enough. I made no move to respond.

"You may recognize them. They look like a gang. They could be—"

"Jake?" I said. But at the same time, I thought I had looked at them, but had seen only limp bodies and white faces distorted by life-draining injuries. I hadn't been near enough to see their features. I pulled up and climbed overboard and waded inland.

Captain John took my arm. "Tell me, Tench, do any of these men look like Jake or any of his men?"

I went over towards where I saw a large cauldron hanging above the cold ashes. I saw the black eye-mask hanging from his face. It was Jake. I nodded to Captain John, remembering the first time I had seen

Jake. A fetid odor filled the air. Flies droned about the bodies and I leaned over, looking into Jake's shrunken features. I saw the deep hollow of his empty eye. Blood had dried in a path down his shirt and pants from the hole in his chest; his skeletal fingers clutched a dipper in one hand and the tin cup in the other. I glanced into the big pot, remembering the pride he took in his cooking and remembering, too, that it had been good and I had wished for more. The pot was alive with maggots, and bits of seafood bobbed about as if bubbling over the fire.

"It's Jake," I said. I looked among the others for Samuel, but saw nothing of his features. Then I thought to look for his bare feet before becoming aware that all the feet were bare.

I went back to our sloop and found O'Toole and Russell taking off all the parts that we might need from the two abandoned boats. When everyone returned, they assembled our new findings and made our boat much more comfortable and seaworthy.

The general called our attention to the edge of sunlight now showing on the clouds to the east. "I think the weather's clearing," he seemed to say to himself. Then he addressed all of us. "I believe Jake and his gang were slaughtered and robbed by pirates more deadly than themselves."

O'Toole was wading at the shoreline and filling our large buckets with shellfish. He paused and called out, "Like Major Valdez and his gang of cutthroats on the Miami River? I believe they are as bad as they come."

"N' if you got away with your life, Mister Sergeant Joseph O'Toole, you can thank us for all the prayin' we done, that brought you back safe." Tom had joined O'Toole.

Colonel Jim spoke up, "Sergeant O'Toole's own resourcefulness spared him from the most dire consequences."

I couldn't help but think the general threatening to bring down the federals had something to do with O'Toole's escape from harm. Or maybe it was just the pirate didn't want our boat to leave before their schooner could overtake us and rob us. Still O'Toole's own wits and our prayers surely helped him to return safely to us.

"I wonder what happened to Samuel," I said. My voice sounded distant, but everyone was listening. "He wasn't like Jake. I'll never know his story." I felt such uneasiness.

While I won't have to worry about Jake getting me ever again, I'd never be free of that morbid picture of Jake and his gang. I'm sorry I didn't know what happened to Samuel, but glad that he wasn't with all of them in that last scene.

"Somehow he might have gotten away from them," Colonel Jim suggested. "We'll always wonder what happened."

It was a short distance from the landing, as O'Toole and Russell began to shove off, that we found the answer. Or part of it. Samuel's body was wedged among the strangling roots of a mangrove. He was part of the sea and the coral islet, his long gray locks spreading and curling like a marine plant. That is how I'll remember Samuel.

The gold I had left him had done him no good after all. But maybe, I hoped, he got it to the boy in the photo with him.

June 8, 1865

WE ALL HAD BEEN STRUCK A SHOCKING BLOW, LEAVING US without breath, words, or strength. For a long while after our discovery of the slaughter of Jake's gang, we didn't speak. We must have all thought: "There, but for the grace of God, it could have been us."

Buffered by silence, each retreated into his own world. With Captain John at the helm and a light breeze out of the east, we continued on course. We were grounded, time after time, and by now, needed no orders. Every time we scraped bottom, we'd jump overboard, push off, and be on our way again. We spent the day maneuvering through the mangrove islets before we got clear of the Keys and outside among the reefs, three or four miles beyond them.

At last, as the sun lowered, we were beginning to feel the pulse of the ocean. I could tell that Captain John was relieved. I think we all felt a burden had been lifted. We were truly on our way now, crossing the Gulf Stream and heading towards Cuba.

A combination of the hot sun and saltwater and cuts from the coral caused everyone's feet and legs to be painfully blistered and swollen. Fortunately, we don't have to jump into the sea anymore. We all are off our feet now, and staying out of the water, so they have a chance to heal. The men suffered more than I. Their skin is burned almost as dark as mine. We've put up a make-shift awning to keep out of the sun's scorching rays.

During the day, we saw several sails and a steamer far off. We did everything in our power to keep out of their paths. For covering distance and making time, this was the best day we'd had since we started on the water.

In the quiet of my mind, I had been retracing the happenings of the past two months. Seems I had lived a lifetime in this short while. I

believed that I was a different person than the one I was when Lance
was alive. Grown up, I guess, having faced things that others used to
face for me. Yes, I had met rebuffs, frustrations, and death. With every
experience, I had discovered that a layer of my old self had dropped
away, until finally, I was reaching the self under all the layers—the person I thought I was supposed to be and I knew, at last, what I must do.

A sharp edge of disappointment wedged in my thoughts. Had
there been anything I could have done that might have helped or
changed some of the things that happened—with the Flower family? Jake and Samuel? Wes Vickers? Ziffa? Or Shears and Joe? What
could I have done to prevent some of the things that happened? Hattie Bronson said I had to learn to attack when I was attacked. I never
had before. I guess that was one thing, for sure, I'd learned. Was it the
only thing? More than anything, I wanted to know how to keep such
attacks from happening in the first place.

The general also wrote in his journal and Captain John took his
out of the locker and handed the helm over to O'Toole. Just after taking over the helm, O'Toole called our attention to clouds forming in
the eastern sky. Until now, the breeze hardly has been strong enough
to overcome the powerful current of the Gulf Stream.

I had an eerie feeling as I watched the clouds in the east build and
the winds rise. In the west, the sun had brushed the bloodshot sky
with streaks of scarlet and copper. Captain John made everything
snug and secure by tightening the mainsail and taking the bonnet off
the jib, which, he told me, would help the boat resist a rising wind.

Shortly, the captain called out, "A real squall's coming. Wilson, by
the halyards. General, the sheet. Russell and O'Toole, prepare to bail.
Stay handy, Tench and Tom."

Seconds after he finished speaking, the sun was gone. The clouds
lowered, blanketing the sea with heavy darkness. Suddenly, like the
roar of a furnace and the striking hammers of a giant forge, the storm
exploded, spewing something wet but still like wildfire and hitting us
with icy darts of rain.

I stayed beside the captain as he lowered the sails and set the stern
to the wind. He said our only chance was to run with the storm until
the rough edge abated, then we'd "heave to."

The captain called, "All hands down!" as the gale blasted with the force of a cannon, bringing with it a tower of foaming water. He clung to the tiller although he was thrown fiercely against the boom. I thought we were going to sink with the heavy torrents, but the boat rose up, half-full of water, racking with convulsions. We were helpless—blinded by lightning and deafened by thunder as the sky opened up and emptied on top of us. For a long while, the storm raged. Our heads were bowed. I know we were all saying words of the same prayer.

As each stormy blast followed another, the gale's force lessened and the waters abated. The heavy deluge had helped beat down the sea. The captain signaled to O'Toole and Russell to start bailing. So they tied themselves and the buckets to the thwarts and went to work, soon emptying our craft of its heavy load. The general had a small pocket compass and passed it to the captain. "We're running to westward," the captain said. I heard concern in his remark.

The reefs, I had been told, were several miles west of our course. If our sloop ran into them in this weather, it would splinter into kindling wood. Captain John then asked Colonel Jim to take the helm, saying, "We can't wait for the wind or the sea to calm. I'm going to heave to."

Although I am not a sailor yet, I have been learning the captain's nautical terms and most of the time I have a pretty fair idea what he means. "Heaving to" brings the ship's head to the wind and stops her motion. I watched him lash the end of the mast to the boom and loosen enough of the mainsail to make it shorter, or as he said, "I'm goose-winging it, or making a leg-of-mutton sail of it."

Then he said to Colonel Jim. "Put the helm to the right, a-starboard, and let her come to on the port tack, and head to the south." At the same time, he hoisted the altered sail.

The boat came by the wind quickly without taking in a drop of water. As the captain was tying the lines, the colonel gave her too much helm and turned the boat completely around, bringing the wind off the other bow. At that moment, the boom flew around and knocked the captain off his feet and he fell overboard into the furious sea. My heart jumped. The general dropped his assigned chore and rushed towards the spot where the captain had fallen. O'Toole gave Colonel Jim a rough shove and took the helm.

It was a good thing the boat's motion had stopped. When the captain bounded up from the raging darkness, he grabbed the lines and the general helped him struggle aboard. For more than twelve hours, the captain didn't let anyone touch the helm and steered the little boat through the remaining edges of the storm. There were still heavy gusts of wind as the storm passed from the east over the Gulf Stream to the west, causing the ocean to swell and roll. As long as we were in the trough of the waves, the boat was still, but when she rose to a twenty-foot crest, even with the shortened sail, it was as much as she could stand up under.

"Ah, the captain, what a splendid sailor," the general said to us who were huddled in the stern. "He's nursing this little craft like a baby. He's tamed her like a gull on the waters, rising and breasting every billow."

"It takes a careful hand," O'Toole said, "for any accident to sail or spar could be the end of us or—if she fell off—one wave could sink us."

"The best thing we all can do is to be quiet and still, so we won't bother the captain," Russell kindly suggested.

Tom had been alternating between lying on the bottom of the boat with his eyes shut tight and hanging his head over the side and groaning in agony. He'd never had any experience with being seasick before. Although nothing in my experience had prepared me for a battle with the sea, I was grateful I wasn't sick like Tom. I took up O'Toole's bucket and did what I could to keep the water from collecting on the bottom.

At one point, I overheard Russell and O'Toole talking in voices too low for the others to hear. "Had we lost the captain, it would've been the colonel's fault." Russell sounded angry. "If anything had happened to the captain, I'd have thrown the colonel in after him."

"I'd lend a hand in that." O'Toole laughed. "Soon as I saw the captain overboard, I looked at the colonel and he was as stiff as a stone statue. He was holding onto the rudder and the sail rope with a death grip. His hold on the rope was about to sink us. I shouted to him to let go the rope. When he did, it took the strain off and the boat righted itself."

I hadn't been aware of how great the danger was to all of us. Forgetting their words were private, I broke in and asked, "Could we've all gone down?"

O'Toole put his hand on my shoulder, "Yes, Tench, we were close to it. I don't think the captain wants—"

O'Toole stopped abruptly. The captain was speaking. "Gentlemen, in almost twenty years of experience on the sea, I've never felt in such great peril as last night. Chances were all against us. One thing is certain, we would have perished had we been in the other boat."

Then, something happened that I'm sure surprised everyone as much as it did me. Colonel Jim rose to his feet and said, "I'd like to give thanks to the Lord for watching over and bringing us through the storm." He bowed his head and continued, "Forgive me, Lord, for doubting that you were watching over us. I'd like to believe that my prayer during the thick of it tilted the scales in gaining your favor."

The storm had finally passed to the west. The sea was no longer sharp, nor did the wind growl. We all collapsed together, falling against each other in exhausted sleep. The captain remained at the helm, patient and determined.

By noon, the sea had gone down and O'Toole had taken the rudder. The captain wasn't far from his post, leaning against the side, asleep. The general was stretched out on the bottom, all six feet two inches of him. While one was asleep on the bottom, the rest had learned to sleep sitting up. There was no room for anyone else.

Under ordinary circumstance, it could be called a beautiful day. The sky, unscarred by a single fluff of cloud, was a seamless extension of the blue around us. The storm had swept the sky clean, but now the sun, unrelenting and brutal, added to the discomforts of hunger, thirst, and exhaustion that plagued us.

With Tom's illness, the general assumed the duties of the locker, and had started doling out the water and every precious drop of rum for everyone, except me. Drops—that was all that was left. Our hard tack had been soaked; I separated them and laid them out to dry in the sun. They were neither tasty nor ample, but at least provided some small relief from our hollowing hunger.

When we came upon some sails in the distance, the general and Captain John had decided we'd no longer avoid them. We were beyond the boundaries of the United States now, and would ask for food and water, regardless of the risk. When we saw a brig drifting towards us, we began waving and O'Toole and Russell took out the oars and began rowing towards them.

As we approached, their captain waved us away, shouting and ordering us, "Stay away. I warn you. Keep off."

Captain John called out, "Please, sir. We're shipwrecked men, Captain. We need some food and water and whatever provisions you can spare."

As we passed, we saw the captain was standing at the rail of the stern with a revolver trained on us. There were seven or eight men positioned at their stations, two mates were holding muskets, the cook had a large cooking fork, and the rest held iron bars.

"I tell you again, keep off or I'll let fly," their captain shouted.

"Captain, we won't come on board if you'll give us some food. We are starving." The general spoke very civilly.

The mates had us lined up in their sights. Captain John held up his right hand and asked, "Will you fire on an unarmed man? Captain, you aren't a sailor, or you'd not refuse to help a boatload of shipwrecked men."

"We've got no grub to spare. How do I know who you are?"

"Sir, we're starving. You have to trust us." The general said. "We don't want to cause any harm."

The brig's captain consulted his crew then said, "We'll give you bread and water. We have nothing more. But I warn you, don't come alongside."

They threw us a five-gallon keg of water and about a fifteen pound bag of hard-tack. We were grateful for their bounty and understood their reluctance in wanting us to get too close.

We looked like pirates. Our rough, bearded crew was a fierce-looking bunch. General Breckinridge, in particular, was a fearsome spectacle as his six-foot, two-inch frame rose and he displayed his wild, unshaved beard and long mustache under a ragged slouch hat, with the blue shirt open over his chest. He was the picture of a free-booting buccaneer aboard our pathetic little pirate sloop.

We saw the name of *Neptune of Bangor* on the brig. Captain John laughed and said, "When they get back home in Bangor, they'll tell a blood-curdling story of their encounter with a boatful of dangerous pirates off the coast of Cuba."

With our new food supply, we started to feel better—except for the general. He woke up from a nap on the floor in the boiling sun with a fever and a strange earache accompanied by an incessant ringing in his ear. Tom was feeling better and immediately began to take care of the general again, covering him with his military cloak. He started first by asking everybody if they'd sacrifice their share of rum rations to help the general and everyone gladly donated theirs to the cause.

While Tom cared for the general, Russell suddenly announced, "We're on soundings."

"What'cha mean?" Tom asked. I wondered, too.

Russell answered, "Look at the color of the water, look down. With a line and plummet, we can test the depth, here."

The captain already was letting out a line and our attention was directed below. He was explaining, "There are some rocky islets to the east of us. I had noted them on our lost charts. So we know we have crossed the Gulf Stream. We can see the world below now."

It was true: the water was crystal clear. It looked like we could reach out and touch the coral, the shells, marine flowers and fish of every size, color, and variety that were darting around in all directions beneath us. Captain John said it was from three to five fathoms deep. There are six feet in a fathom, so it wasn't very deep.

While I was fascinated by the beauty below, the sight of fish reminded me of my hunger. I was overwhelmed with frustration because we had no method or anything with which to fish.

Russell began to take off his clothes. "I see some shellfish and conch down there," he said. "I'll get some. I don't see a sign of sharks. Sharp eyes for sharks everyone."

"What is conch?" I asked.

"A large shellfish. There's a meaty body inside the beautiful shell." When he dove to the bottom, O'Toole told us Russell had been an expert swimmer and was known among the soldiers for his skill. Quickly, he surfaced with two conch shells in his hand. The shells looked as if painted by an artist's hand—tinted in soft sunset colors. Russell broke the shell and removed the animal inside. I bent close to see the creature and shuddered at the sight. It looked like a huge grub worm—not at all appetizing.

Still lying on the floor, the general looked up at Russell's trophy and said, "Try it for me, Tom."

Tom gasped, replying, "Glory, suh. I'm mighty hunk'ry. Never been so hunk'ry since we been to wah. I'd eat an ol' mule or a pole-cat or mos' anythin' but please, not that worm."

O'Toole tried to dissect it and found it tough, then he handed a piece to Captain John who tasted it, shook his head, and said, "Tom's right. It's 'bout as edible as a pickled football."

Russell mumbled something about it being good cooked in soup. He dove overboard again and came back with several large thin shells of beautiful colors, shaped like large pea pods. These were palatable and, to a great degree, satisfied our craving for food. Yet they produced a great thirst and we agreed that thirst was harder to bear than hunger.

Captain John had determined that the rocky islets we had passed were the Double-Headed-Shot Keys. About thirty miles south of them, we came upon Salt Key Bank. Shortly after, he told us we were crossing Nicholas Channel and we began straining our eyes for land formations or dark masses that might be Cuba.

"We're getting closer, but let's rest awhile. We've a distance to go," he said, giving the helm to the colonel beside him. "I'm going to take a nap."

We hoped to land in daylight and had been sailing by the North Star. I was too excited to sleep and stood watch through the night with Colonel Jim. In the early hours of June 12, we spotted the beam of the lighthouse.

The colonel was as excited as I was and he said to me, "Let's not waken anyone. We'll surprise them after we land."

Now I knew what Columbus and the American pilgrims must have felt when they first sighted land. It wasn't my nature at all, especially as excited as I was, not to waken everyone and share our joy. I needn't have worried over that point. Colonel Wilson ran the boat nearly onto the lighthouse and woke everyone for consultation. We got the boat off all right, but a few moments later, with him still at the helm, the boat hit a coral reef and thumped badly. We had a lot of trouble getting her off, but not too long after, we were steering westward along the coast.

For the rest of the night until daybreak, we made our way, staying just outside the coral reefs, searching for some sign of civilization. In the wakening sunlight, we saw in the distance an assortment of skiffs, sloops, and schooners anchored in the basin of a tranquil bay. Clustered around the waterfront and rising far above, were gleaming, white buildings with scalloped tile rooftops. The scene was etched with the shadows and the colors of coconut palms, large-leafed trees, and bright-hued flowers. My first view of Cuba brought another surge of joy.

The town seemed to be asleep, so Captain John anchored in the bay below some large, plain buildings clustered on the promontory above. I think he was waiting for someone to take notice of our arrival and hoped there might be a lookout scanning the waterfront. While we floated quietly along the shallow waters, General Breckinridge asked Captain John, once again, for prayers. For the last time, on this hard journey, we gave thanks for the miracle of our safe arrival. Magically, church bells began to ring. It was Sunday.

Probably because we were beardless and looked less grubby than the rest of the crew, Captain John took Tom and me along with him to find someone to report to. We entered the largest building. A big sign, ablaze in lights, announced in Spanish and English *Chief of Customs* and *Aduana*. The fragrance of pastries and coffee filled the room. When we entered, there were six men sitting around a table, talking and laughing and enjoying the start of a new day. They looked up as we entered, but were puzzled by the captain's greeting in English.

"Good morning, sirs. Good morning." Captain John spoke loud and pleasantly.

One responded, "No speak English. No speak."

Tom had been watching with a scowl on his face. All at once, at the top of his lungs, he began to shout, "We come all the way from Flo'da." He swung his arms and pointed outside the window to our boat in the bay below, his voice rising to make them hear. He was suddenly quiet, then, pointing to his stomach, whined very softly, "We hun'kry, we sick, we awful tired." Then, with a flourish, he collapsed in a heap on the floor.

The men had watched Tom's performance, exclaiming almost as one, "*Ai, ai, ai!*"

One of them suddenly rose and said, excitedly, "*Voy a buscar el Americano.*" He rushed from the building to the road outside. As I watched at the window, I saw him run up the hill leading towards the church where people were gathering and saw him speak to the group. Suddenly, he turned to come back. Everyone followed.

Tom had won the attention that Captain John had sought. The captain sent Tom and me back to the sloop to tell the others that, thanks to Tom, they could come ashore now. The authorities had been informed. Tom grinned and bowed as I told of his debut before the chief of customs. After being complimented and praised by our party, he beamed and pranced with delight.

The general said, "I'm not surprised. Tom could coax speech from a stone."

When we entered the Customs House, it looked as if the entire town had arrived. Some crowded inside, some gathered outside, and others still were coming from every direction.

An American gentleman named John Cahill greeted us this time. In no time, we learned Cahill was a former Kentuckian and he recognized John Breckinridge immediately. He had become a citizen of the city of Cardenas, where we had landed. He quickly took on the role of host and interpreter, and introduced Breckinridge and the entire party to the confused populace of Cardenas.

Cahill first explained that Jefferson Davis was not among us, scotching a rumor that was quickly spreading through the crowds that Davis was one of the refugees. He described his own reaction in first seeing General Breckinridge. "When I saw you step onto the wharf from that little boat in which you and your companions had made such a perilous journey, although you are quite thin now, I recognized, at once, your familiar figure in the military cape towering above the others. General Breckinridge, we welcome you to Cardenas. Welcome to Cuba. We offer you sanctuary."

The officials, who had drawn aside in private council, called Cahill to their circle. After heated discussion, the American came back and sadly told our group, "I am sorry, my dear countrymen, the council won't accept your story. They don't think it's possible you could have. made that trip in such a small craft."

Without a moment's hesitation, the general said, "We'll demonstrate our sincerity by surrendering our arms." He unbuckled his sword belt and lay his arms on the council table. One by one, our crew followed suit. Even Tom lay down his old musket and I put my bowie knife beside their arms on the table. Silence fell over the council and the assembled crowd. Then, again, they went into a noisy conference.

The officials now were convinced. The leader picked up the sword and the pistols, he gave a long speech which none of us understood, but recognized the friendly warmth of the speaker. Mister Cahill later explained. He had said, "You have fought the most heroic battles of the ages in defense of your convictions. You have won the admiration of all brave men. We recognize your nobility and understand the sad cause that brought you to these shores. We return your arms and offer you our hospitality."

Someone wired Governor-General Domingo Dulce and told him of General Breckinridge's arrival. By return telegram he promptly replied that the general and party were to be treated with all of the honor due a "person of his high position."

We were again welcomed to Cuba. The general was accorded special honors and the crew was praised for bringing him through great difficulties of storm, hunger, and hostile ships on high seas. We were given fresh clothes and lodging in the Hotel Cristobal Colon. The memory of that comfortable bed, fresh linens, the unbelievably fine foods, the kindness and generosity of our Cardenas hosts—I'll always remember. Tom and I were two of the honored guests and they didn't let us forget it either.

John Cahill introduced us to Colonel San Martin, who was the president of the Cardenas branch of the railroad to Havana, and he offered his private car for the seventy-five-mile trip. I can't help but remark that I probably never again will experience the luxury and hospitality I knew in Cuba.

There was feasting and huge crowds came to see General Breckinridge and the crew of the suddenly famous sloop, *No Name*. (Upon our arrival, after taking our names, the officials asked the name of our craft, which had none, so recorded *No Name*.)

At a big dinner in honor of the general, all the Americans in Cardenas and the surrounding countryside attended—southerners and northerners alike. A former mayor of St. Augustine presented the general and Captain Wood with new suits and gave all of the party new clothes as well. A band made up of former Confederates, the Cardenas Volunteers, briskly played, *Dixie, Yankee Doodle,* and *The Star Spangled Banner.*

"We don't take sides here," Cahill laughed.

I could tell the general was exhausted as we all were, but he graciously accepted their gifts and kindnesses, and spoke for us as well. He declined their requests for speeches, saying it didn't seem appropriate. He was more silent than usual.

"The general seems sad," I said to Captain John.

His response came out in a rush. "Yes, we both are. We don't know when we'll see our families again. Our wives face a difficult future and we can't do anything to help. Our children will be growing up without us. We are banned from the country we love." He paused, "Tench, what about you? What will you do? I made an offer at Moseley's Landing. The offer still holds, yet I can promise you only according to the uncertainty of what's ahead for myself."

"I want to thank you, sir," I said. "You honor me. Over these past days, I've been doing a lot of thinking. If there were only myself to think about, I'd go with you. But I've decided I must return to Avalon where I'm needed. I can help the family with many things, at the same time I have so much to learn."

"Your family members were good teachers. They taught you well."

"Lately, I've been thinking, when I finish my work helping my mother and Miss Lottie get their groves started, I'd like to go first to Savannah, then Richmond or maybe Washington, and maybe find a newspaper that'd hire me as a writer. Oh, I realize my goals might change a few times before I get it right."

Captain John smiled and nodded, "If only we could get everything right the first time."

"What are we getting right?" The general had just joined us.

"My thought," I replied, "of becoming a journalist."

"That's a dream I understand," the captain said. "I've always enjoyed writing. All my life I've kept journals and written letters that were more like books. I believe that I would rather write than speak." He turned to the general, "At our very first meeting, Tench and I wrote in our journals together. I think he is a very able writer. He writes clearly, uses proper syntax, and has a good vocabulary. Most important, he has imagination."

The general nodded. "In a few years, there'll be many changes in our country, with new opportunities. Tench, in another time, I might have helped you with your dream. Before the war, I had many friends in the newspaper business in the big cities in the North. Now, I doubt if they'd be willing to call me a friend." He spoke slowly, "But, here's something for you to think about, Negro journalists in the bigger cities in the North have been publishing their own newspapers for years. So when the time comes, you mustn't limit yourself to locating in the South."

A journalist on a paper up North—what a dream. I grinned. I liked the thought of working at something I fully enjoyed. At the same time, I was aware of how much I had to learn. At my present age with my lack of knowledge and experience, the thought of becoming a journalist seemed completely beyond possibility. So far, I had written only about what happened in my small world. I had a lot to learn in the years ahead and I knew I'd have to start studying and observing things beyond my own horizon.

There was a point the general had made that I needed to respond to. "Sir, I wouldn't want to limit myself to locating only in the North or the South. Nor would I want to limit myself to writing just for Negro or just for white newspapers."

The captain beamed. "Good. I applaud you."

June 12 through July 7, 1865

WHEN WE CROSSED THE BAY TO HAVANA BY FERRY, TEN thousand people were waiting to meet us—or that's what we were told later. The rumor had circulated that Jefferson Davis was with us. As the crowd pressed around the general and the rest of our party, Cahill shouted for help. Policemen and soldiers surrounded us, summoning carriages and escorting us down Calle Teniente Rey to the Hotel Cubano. The hotel was operated by a Southern lady, Mrs. Dixie Brewer. We learned that her five-story hotel was mainly occupied by Southerners, Confederates, and secessionists. Sympathy and support for General Breckinridge and his party were very strong among those folks who had also run from their homeland.

"Expatriates, what a sad bunch," the general sighed and added, "as we are now."

I watched with interest as reporters gathered around our "escape party." Colonel Wilson moved out of the circle to the far edge, leaving the general and Captain John to be interviewed. I was surprised to hear them both reveal details of our journey. They were completely open about some things, including the incident with the three seamen with whom the captain had "traded" our sloop. However, neither mentioned our meeting with Major Valdez and his band of ruffians. Nor did they tell them about that last terrible scene on the coral reef in Florida where we had found Jake and Samuel and their gang of pirates slaughtered.

Even withholding the details of those two fearful scenes, the reporter from the *New York Herald* was fascinated. He said, "The manner of your escape from the coast of Florida is a real adventure story. Who knows? It might one day form the groundwork of a thrilling drama or an exciting novel."

After hearing their story, another young man, leather-bound tablet in hand, leaned forward and addressed the *Herald* correspondent, extolling the virtues and character of the general. "Of all the statesmen from the South, Breckinridge is the most high-toned and irreproachable. How befitting the rest of the events in his extraordinary career was his risky and demanding escape."

"Sir," the *Herald* reporter spoke to the general, "we truly hope that you escape the kind of humiliation that has befallen Jefferson Davis." That was when we learned that Jefferson Davis was going before the civil court to be tried on the charge of treason. This news touched all of us deeply, but perhaps the general most of all. His health already had suffered severely. I was aware of his unusual weight loss since I first met him. It must have been a shock for those old acquaintances who remembered his former strong, robust figure to see him now. During our journey, he had weakened so much, his steps had begun to falter and his hands to tremble. Too, he had been so severely sunburned, his face and arms were covered with unsightly blotches and peeling skin.

The news of Davis added to the general's weakened condition, so that he quickly fell into a deep despondency. I had seen flashes of his melancholy nature, but he always seemed to bring himself out of the mood before despair completely took over. I noticed, for the first time, in the company of others, his thoughts appeared scattered; sometimes he seemed to lose focus and often lapsed into silence. Through it all, everyone was kind and understanding to him, as they were to all of us.

The governor-general invited him to his country palace and made generous offers of home and asylum for him and his family, as well as to all the members of our party.

But staying in Cuba, of course, was not to be. Strangely, in spite of the strong attraction of the jewel-like island and the hospitality of its kind people, we all shared a desire to get started on the next part of our lives, on our journeys home and back to our families as soon as possible. There were blockade-runners and English ships riding anchor in the harbor. Consequently, some arrangements were made with their captains, some of whom were former Confederate Navy men who were taking their ships to England or Canada, probably to be sold. The reporters would take messages back to the United States, to Captain John's wife Lola, asking her to meet him in Canada, and the general's wife Mary to meet him in England.

On June 23, Breckinridge, Wilson, O'Toole, Russell, Tom, and I went to the pier to bid our beloved friend and guide, Captain John Taylor Wood, a difficult farewell. He would accompany Skipper George E. Shryock, formerly of the Confederate Navy, aboard the *Lark*, now en route to England, via Nova Scotia (where the captain would disembark). There was so much I wished I could say to him, but I fell mute. For a long while, he and the general and Colonel Wilson stood apart from us, deep in conversation. When the general started to walk briskly from the pier, how well we knew that the tears had begun to rise.

Tom groaned, "Po' Gen'el B. When it's his turn to go, ain't gonna have no one to look after him."

We gathered close as O'Toole and Russell stood at attention and saluted Captain John. He returned their salute and reached to take their hands. Then he put an arm across my shoulder, the other on Tom's, and said, "I'll always be grateful to each of you. There never was a crew who worked against greater odds, or who was more adaptable and resourceful then the crew of the *No Name*." His voice, steady and strong, gave his last order, "Up oars. Let go forward. Let fall. Give way."

We all stood so for a few moments. Finally, I found my voice and leaned towards him. "I want to thank you, sir, for much more than you'll ever know, or more than I could ever express."

Tom said, "Cap'n John, suh, you're a really great man. Weren't for you, I don' think none of us'd be standin' on this dock right now."

Everyone nodded, with comments of, "True," and "Right," and "Well said." Tom, as he often had done on this journey, had summed up exactly how we all felt. Captain John didn't look back as he boarded the *Lark* and disappeared among the busy hands on deck. Long after the rest of our party had left, I stood alone, watching the *Lark* pull anchor and steam out of the harbor. I watched until it was just a speck on the horizon, then was no more.

Down on the pier, the following day, when Colonel Wilson boarded another blockade-runner en route to Toronto, our group gathered again. Feeling much less strong emotion, we listened to his plan for the future, which he'd often told before. "As soon as the government lets me return to Kentucky, I plan to open up a boarding house. I'll feed my guests the cheapest fare I can find, and charge them the most exorbitant prices I can get away with. I'll make a mint of greenbacks until, perhaps, one day I'm murdered by one of my infuriated victims."

Need I say more? As was his habit, he left us laughing and not at all regretting our parting.

On July 7, 1865, General Breckinridge and another former Confederate, Colonel Charles Helm, booked passage on the steamer Conway, heading first towards St. Thomas in the Danish West Indies, then on to England. Russell O'Toole, Tom Ferguson, and I went to the pier to see him for the last time.

The general seemed more cheerful than he had been since landing in Cuba. He looked rested, less tormented. Among ourselves, later, when we spoke of Colonel Helm's pleasant attitude and affection for the general, Tom became upset. "Ain't no one gonna care for him way I do." He fussed, "Gawd I don' like leavin' him, but I sho' can't go on a long ocean journey ag'in. It's gonna be bad enuff jes' to 'cross the Gulf to Al'bama."

Breckinridge divided money that Colonel San Martin had given him for the purchase of *No Name* between O'Toole and Russell and gave each extra gold pieces. Then he paid our fares to Mobile on one of the steamers anchored in the harbor. He gave both Tom and me a gold piece. And, prize of all prizes, he gave me his Plutarch. Knowing how he cherished it, I didn't want to take it. I protested, but he thrust it into my hands, and placed his hands on mine, saying, "There is a bright, big world waiting for you, Tench. Keep reading and studying and writing. Be ready."

Among the huge crowd that had come to see him off, along with Governor-General Dulce, there were reporters, Southern friends, and many Cubans. The general addressed the crowd and thanked them in the name of the crew of *No Name* for sharing the warmth and hospitality of their Cuban and Southern natures.

To all former Confederates and to the young reporters who had followed him around, faithfully recording his every word, the general gave one last message. He asked them to tell his fellow countrymen not to resist or fight any longer, to seek clemency, and ask for pardons from President Johnson. They must help rebuild the new South. He wanted no more blood shed for useless causes.

Compared to our arrival in Cuba in a small sloop over rough seas, starving and dressed in rags, how different our departure was. Dressed in fresh, clean clothes, with all the luxuries of a well-outfitted ship at our beck and call, Colonel Jilson Johnson, a former aide of General Breckinridge who was accompanying us, paved the way for all of us. He took special pains to include Tom and me. To the crew of the steamer, he said, "These young men are heroes just as much as Sergeant O'Toole and Corporal Russell. They played an important part in saving General Breckinridge and Captain Wood from capture."

Later, with pencil and tablet in hand, sitting on the deck in the bow as we moved through the peaceful swells of the Gulf towards Mobile, I almost felt myself driven by the sea's deep pulse onto an ever widening course. Never before had I been so keenly aware of the mission ahead. Many good people had been pointing the way, encouraging my first steps on another journey that doubtless will be as full of rebuffs and frustrations and constant self-renewals as any I had ever experienced.

Suddenly, looking up, I found Sergeant O'Toole sitting beside me. "I like the idea of savin' all your experiences on a tablet," he said. "I wish I'd thought of doin' something like that, a lot sooner. By now, I could've filled a big book and had something to show for the life I've been using up."

"It's not too late to start. You have lots of time. My family kept journals back several generations. My cousin, Lance, kept one until he was killed. When I continued to keep his, it was the first ever, for me. It brings us all together. Mine is part of a family story and I'll keep telling that story as long as it's mine to tell."

He studied me before saying, "I've never known a family like that, let alone a—Negro who knew—" he floundered uneasily, but quickly corrected himself, "who could read or write. I've never known any-one like you, Tench." His face was flushed.

"I understand. I had a really good family who said they wanted me to have all the tools I would need in life. Everyone has different expe-riences and you can only judge and know others by the experiences you've had. I've learned lots from you, Sergeant O'Toole. All the les-sons I've learned are right here," I tapped my forehead, then held up my journal, "and you're a part that I'll keep forever."

"Well, Tench," he said, "I've learned quite a few lessons from you."

I returned to these pages and O'Toole, stretched out beside me, was soon asleep. Russell and Tom joined us, bringing a basket of fruit to share.

"Oh, the miracle of a banana," I said, peeling away the yellow skin and taking a bite of its creamy center. "I will never take this food for granted again. To a starving man, it's food from the gods. I think I'll never forget the pain we suffered from hunger and our longings for real food like this."

It was with our happy sounds over the fragrant and colorful gifts in Russell's basket that O'Toole blinked himself awake and imme-diately selected a papaya. With his bowie knife, he scraped the tiny black seeds into the sea and cut a half-dozen slices, like small coral-colored boats, and put all, except his own, back in the basket. Now I watched as each took fruit from the basket—oranges, mango, papaya, breadfruit, banana— and each of us, like Russell, peeled, sliced, and put a portion back. Taking small bites, we thoroughly tasted and savored each mouthful. I remember when we first started out on the St. Johns, we'd take big helpings of food and gobbled them up, not at all inclined to share. I think our goal at that time was to finish as quickly as possible, so we could get to the remainders before anyone else had a chance. When we began dividing food and duties among ourselves, we discovered that the necessity of sharing had taught us concern for each other.

As we sit together on the deck, I believe that mutual experience has bound us together forever, bringing with it an understanding and respect for each other. Already, we began to sort out and talk with renewed respect for our leaders.

"If the general and captain were here, we'd be praying before we took a bite of food," Russell commented while juices of a ripe mango tracked at the corners of his mouth.

O'Toole was talking. "They are good men, by deed and example. They made me want to do my best. I confess, I'm not religious, but I came to feel that the captain's prayers were doing a lot of good. I think Col'nel Jim must've thought so, too."

"In all probability, they did," Russell admitted. "Those two worked together real well. Most the time, Breckinridge would say when to pray, but he put it on the cap'n to do the prayin'."

"Truth be known, that's how they operated—the gen'ral would say what and when and the captain would do. I also heard that when the gen'ral was a senator, no one could hold a candle to his speechifyin'. Called him the golden-throated senator."

"Right." Tom rolled his eyes. "In Kentuck', they say where evah you fine' more n' three folks, the gen'ral'd be in the middle of 'em, givin' a speech. But I never heard of him leadin' a prayer meetin'."

"Captain Dickison told us about Captain Wood," O'Toole said. "They called him the Sea Ghost 'cause he sneaked up the rivers and coastal ports in the middle of the night with his special crew. They captured more 'n forty Fed ships. Dickison told us a lot of stories about his brave, daring deeds."

Tom nudged me. "What'd I tell you? Member me tellin' you?"

"During the day he'd move his boardin' boat on a wagon by land," the sergeant continued. "Come night, he'd launch his cutter and steal alongside the Fed ship in the dark, and, takin' them by surprise, he'd capture their ship. He was never known to fail—once he chose his target. There were dangerous armed gunboats among his prizes. The Feds sent letters to all their naval commanders warnin' them of the captain's attacks, n' still he kept on capturin' them."

O'Toole became quiet for a moment. After staring off in the distance, he looked back at us.

"Strange thing," O'Toole reflected, "if they had a choice, neither of them would have fought against the North. For Wood, it was a case of geography. He'd spent so many years in the South and he and Miss Lola loved Woodland, their farm outside Annapolis where he was teachin'. During their marriage, he'd spent much time away on long cruises—on the Mediterranean, to Spain, Italy, Gibraltar, the Middle East, Greece, and Key West. So they were excited and happy when he was assigned as gunnery professor at Annapolis and they could be together."

Russell broke in. "I heard that his father, who was a general in the medical service of the Union Army, was so furious when his son refused to leave the South he told him he never wanted to see him again."

I was glad they told General B.'s and the captain's story. I often had wanted to know about them. But I couldn't help but think of the lives destroyed and the families torn apart and I couldn't help but think of Lance. There must surely have been a better way for the North and the South to have resolved their differences. But while I thought about the horrors of the war, O'Toole kept talking.

"In some ways, General Breckinridge's story goes much the same. He had been Vice President of the United States and the last thing on earth he wanted to do was to take up arms against the United States government." O'Toole shook his head sadly and went on, "Then both of his sons, Clifton and Cabel, they up and joined the Confederates."

Maybe I could only imagine how hard it must have been for General Breckinridge because I'd never been asked to make that kind of decision.

O'Toole heaved a sigh. "Hard as it was, he made a choice. He could not bear arms against the South—or his own sons."

We drifted into silence again. O'Toole was squinting into the distance while I continued writing, and Tom and Russell dozed.

Finally, O'Toole sat up and spoke again. "We know that Russell and I will have to go to prison. Yet I am proud of the part we played in helping General Breckenridge and Colonel Wood escape. I regret nothing."

"Will you give yourselves up?" I asked.

O'Toole answered, "You can be sure there'll be Feds meetin' the boat tomorrow to look over the passengers and cargo. I told Russell this mornin', there are ways to escape, but we've had enough. I'll be glad to rest awhile in the stockade, unless they have other plans for us."

"I hope I can find my way back alone," I said, remembering the other long journey home. "I'd been hoping I'd be able to travel with you and Corporal Russell to Florida."

"Don't worry, Tench. You'll find your way just fine."

WHEN I FIRST MET THEM DOWN ON THE ST. JOHNS, IF ANYone had told me I'd feel what I am feeling as it comes time to say goodbye to these two soldiers, I wouldn't have believed them.

Everything had changed, not only my country. I had changed and I was certain that Russell and O'Toole had changed also.

Nothing would ever be the way it was when Lance and I looked down the lane with our eyes full of tears back at our Georgia Avalon. Now I would help build the new Florida Avalon, and, maybe head north to be a journalist.

I had learned much, but I still had much to learn. There were many roads leading to Avalon, yet just as many leading away, and, in time, I might find a road I should follow to new challenges.

With those thoughts, I put my journal away and wrote no more of what would be a plodding, wearisome journey home. Once again, I wanted only to reach the St. Johns and my family and the peaceful haven of Avalon. There, I knew, the next pages of my life would be rich and full enough to sustain me through other uncharted roads beyond.

Acknowledgement

After an author writes and sells a manuscript, there is still much work to be done—substantive editing, style and copy editing, fact-checking, copyright issues, cover designs, and more editing and more editing. These steps are usually done in a cooperative effort between the author and the publisher. In this case, as Jill Fletcher Pelaez crossed over soon after the contract with WiDō was signed, her work in the production process was completed by what has been dubbed the Jill Team—Wendy Pelaez Morgan; Charlie Sawyer; a sweet, wise and talented woman who wishes to kept anonymous; and Claire Hamner Matturro.

The Jill Team has had the great pleasure of working with certain editors and designers at WiDo and they have invariably been patient, committed and professional in their dealings with us and with their work. The Jill Team would like to thank Nancy Cavanaugh for outstanding editing; Karen Gowen for being the point-person; Allie Maldonado for her early work on the manuscript, and Amie McCracken, the book cover designer, and Bruce Gowen for answering questions and giving encouragement and directing initial marketing plans. We would also like to thank and acknowledge the help of the wonderful people at Covenant Hospice, Jill Pelaez Baumgaetner and David Pelaez.

Jill, sweet and wise and loving, look: We made you a book.

About the Author

Jill Fletcher Pelaez was born in San Turce, Puerto Rico, grew up in Florida, studied dance in New York, and began writing as an Air Force wife with small children. She published a children's book, *Donkey Tales* (Abingdon), and several stories in children's magazines. She went on to receive the B. A. and M.A.T. from Rollins College and began a love affair with Southern history, especially the Civil War, during which her great grandfather was a foot soldier for Southern forces. *The Day is a White Tablet* is the result of many years of work and research. It was accepted for publication two months before her death at the age of eighty-eight in 2012.

CPSIA information can be obtained at www.ICGtesting.com
Printed in the USA
LVOW131052280113

317524LV00002B/123/P